CW00687595

Blackmailed by the Billionaire

A.M. Zanoria

Published by Ann Marie Sangalang, 2024.

BLACKMAILED BY THE BILLIONAIRE

First edition. May 29, 2024.

Copyright © 2024 A.M. Zanoria.

ISBN: 979-8224331345

Written by A.M. Zanoria.

BLACKMAILED BY
THE BILLIONAIRE
A.M. Zanoria

Chapter 1

"Is this the same regal gathering that you skipped by claiming that you had another headache?" Sara mocked me.

"Yes— well, it would appear that he's still a bachelor and the CEO of his own investment banking business." "My step-sister Annet wants to get a date with him, her true age mustn't be mentioned under any circumstances."

"Why was I not surprised by it?" Sarah chuckled, a sly sparkle appearing in her dark eyes as she spoke.

" You're a bad girl!" Anna cracked a grin.

Sara shrieked as she said," I only wish you would be mischievous once in a while."

"It's about time you got out there and started enjoying yourself again,"

Anna said," Well, I'm going to the party on Saturday," as she made her way across the room to the center counter and seized the order book from Sara's hand.

" And it's about time that you went to have some lunch. Gemma should be back any second now, and Gerald will not be much longer."

Gemma was a trainee, and Gerald was a good gardener; nonetheless, he spent most of his time working as their delivery motorist.

"Alright, I am leaving. But, Anna, I'm being serious. It has been two years since Allen passed away, and despite how much you loved him, it's time for you to start dating again. Or at least entertain the possibility, rather than shutting down every seductive man who so much smiles at you. Have you not been informed? Complete chastity isn't only saddening but also dangerous to one's physical health."

She had made one huge mistake, which she had pledged never to repeat, but she didn't dare tell her closest friend the truth. To Anna's eternal humiliation, she hadn't remained fully celibate in the previous two years. Instead of speaking, Anna hurled a wet sponger in her direction.

" Let's go out to lunch!" She moaned as she flipped through the order book without actually reading it and watched Sara, who was laughing and ducking out the door as she left. She had already found and married her lifelong companion, but unfortunately, they were no longer together.

Although thinking about Allen now still caused her heart to feel constricted with grief, she had at least gotten over grieving at the idea of him and was now able to move on with her life. Anna looked up as she heard a customer go through the door and noticed that the wind chimes on the door were ringing. She forced the recollections to the forefront of her mind and forced herself to smile. " How can I help you?'

It was Annet's birthday that Saturday and David Miller cast a peep down at the beautiful blonde who was adhering to his elbow. The moment, the maid led him and Bryan into the drawing room of the magnificent Georgian estate on Beverly Hills that was the Williams residence. David and Bryan were guests at the Williams home. He wished her a happy birthday and gave her a present the night before, a Prada bag.

" And my grandfather, I suppose you know," David said.

She cut him off in the middle of his sentence." Oh, I'm apprehensive of it. How awful.' she smiled in Bryan's general way before continuing.

" I was so sorry to hear that you had injured your ankle," Annet said. "But I cannot deny how happy it made me that David came to supper in your place also," lifting her gaze over to David, she gushed," It was fate that we met again."

"Is not that the truth, my sweetheart?" And as she prepared for his kiss, she leaned her head back. David whispered," Probably," as he looked down at his friend with a grin.

Annet was a clever woman who knew the score; he'd encountered her kind a thousand times, and it was no trouble for him to lower his head and encounter his lips smoothly against her scarlet mouth. Annet was a sophisticated lady who understood the game. Although it did surprise him, Bryan thought she was pretty, although he could not imagine that his grandfather would be interested in a model who was six feet tall and rake-thin like her.

Anna was the first person to hear the commotion as she down the stairway. She gave the flower arrangement that was sitting on the hallway table a critical examination before grudgingly turning her attention to the thing that was making the noise. Since Allen's death, she had only occasionally gone to events with a huge number of guests, but she couldn't skip this one.

She stepped into the packed drawing room, uncurled her shoulders, and peered about until her eyes landed on the birthday girl." Happy birthday!" she said loudly. Annet's attention was drawn overhead to a man. Her face, which was fully made up, was elevated to his in preparation for a kiss, which he dutifully gave her. Indeed, when viewed from behind, he made quite an impression due to his height(far over six feet), wide shoulders, and jet-black hair. — and he was the ideal complement to Annet's model height and smooth golden hair.

Anna found herself thinking, 'They make a striking couple,' before allowing her sight to wander away, only to find herself immediately fixated on a senior guy who was standing alone and watching the couple embrace. He was hunched over, supporting his weight with a cane with a silvered tip, and he wore a look of complete confusion on his worn face, which she recognized right down. Anna went snappily in his direction after noticing that he appeared to feel just as out of place as she did. She beamed a grin at the man who had saved her from the board meeting.

"Mr. Miller!"

She extended her hand to him, and he reluctantly took it, saying that "it was pleasurable to see you once more."

He said," It's my honor," and also, in an old-fashioned display of etiquette, he bowed slightly.

"Would you mind if you call me Bryan?"

Anna chuckled as she said," Bryan it is, you old charmer."

David recognized the sweet female voice at the same moment that he felt Bryan pulling hard on the sleeve of his jacket. Bryan was trying to get his attention. He moved his head sluggishly and saw the lady while she was holding his grandfather's hand. He tensed up, and every muscle in his body strained in response to the shock and fury he felt. She had been appearing in his dreams for the previous year, and indeed, though he detested her for her lack of morality, his body still longed for her.

Chapter 2

H e knew her in the deepest, most particular manner that was humanly conceivable. But before he could think of a hello that was very cutting, Annet tensed her grasp on the other arm she had him by and started talking to the other person.

"Anna, my sweetheart, allow me to introduce you to David. He's the wonderful man I was telling you about." David was able to pick up Annet's voice, but all he flashed back was her name. To Anna. So, what exactly had transpired with Hana? He had a pessimistic way of thinking. She was cheating on her spouse under a fictitious name. But indeed, though she had been deceitful to him, there was no denying the fact that she was much more beautiful than he'd recalled.

The first and only time he'd seen her before this party was a year ago. He and a group of his friends had taken a voyage around the Korean islets in his boat for a couple of weeks, something he did every summer. This party was the first and only time he'd seen her since that trip.

They had celebrated on board as it was one of the female visitors' birthdays, and they also went ashore to the Jeju island to eat there before returning to the boat. It was only after he'd snuck out of the eatery that was packed with visitors to take a walk along the harbor and get some fresh air down from the smoke that he'd seen her.

She appeared to have just surfaced from one of Leonardo Da Vinci's paintings as she sat at a table outside an original harbor bar enjoying a glass of red wine. More like the captivating Monalisa. Her appearance gave the impression that she had just done so.

She had not bothered to put on any makeup, yet she still managed to look divinely seductive. Her cheekbones were high, and she had a straight, small nose that was in perfect proportion to her finely shaped mouth. Her lips were full, and their natural color was a natural pink.

Her rich, incandescent black hair fell long and wavy down her back, accentuated by her dark brown eyes. Furthermore, her hair was put away behind her delicate ears to allow it to fall in this manner. Her fair honey skin glows under the light.

During the time that he was watching, two of the locals went out of the pub and accidentally knocked into her table, spilling her glass and a carafe of red wine that was just half full each over her. She had sprung to her feet, and David had sprung to her aid at the same moment.

She had no hesitation in agreeing to take him up on his invitation to join her on his yacht to remove the stains off the white tank top and shorts she was wearing. He left her in his room for a while to change but when he came back, he saw her in a lacy black bra and panty. He couldn't control himself and kissed her, she was so exquisite.

The sex that had followed was the finest he'd ever experienced, and when he recalled what had occurred after that, a particular part of his anatomy swelled presently on with his fury at what had taken place. She snappily hopped from the bed and said she had to use the bathroom to avoid meeting his eyes. She raced into the restroom, seized her bag and apparel, and also started the shower.

After she had finished getting dressed and came from the bathroom, she put a ring on her wedding finger. She was engaged. David climbed out of bed, unable to get himself to believe the truth that was gaping at him in the face.

"You are engaged?"

" No, I'm married."

"And this was really a big mistake."

David had slept with quite a many of the ladies he dated, but he never got involved with married women. He was angry with himself just as much as he was with her.

"Not on my part, honey." he'd said angrily.

"You were hot, but you should be moving now because it's getting late. My visitors will be then any second now, and I'd prefer it if they did not see you, especially my special someone."

She had turned her head to look at him, and her eyes had widened in shock as she realized what he'd been inferring. He was left standing naked, indignant, and shocked with them both as she turned on her heel and departed without saying a word.

Since then, he had not shared in any one-night stands. When he was young, he'd told himself that he'd date a lady a minimum of three times before getting serious with her. But on that night, he'd defied his own rule, and he'd done so with a lady who was already married.

When he looked back at her now, she had such a calm and refined appearance that it was hard to imagine that she had ever been the passionate woman who had participated in his bed. Her voluminous hair was styled in an elaborate twist on the crown of her head, which drew attention to the flawlessness of her features and the swan-like curve of her neck.

It was accentuated by the platinum chain she wore, which hung a delicately drafted locket in the center of which was a diamond. The locket was suspended from the chain. She was clad in a black dress that was uncomplicated in style but exquisitely constructed. The dress had short sleeves and a square neckline that was cut low, exposing the delicate curve of her high, firm breasts.

The fabric was fine, and it directly followed the figure of her curvaceous form and the soft bulge of her hips down to where it ended, which was about an inch or two above her knees. The high-heeled shoes that she wore, which showed off her pink toenails, drew attention to the length of her legs, which were stunning. She was flawless from head to toe, and the internal image of her raw body underneath him with her long legs wrapped around his midriff caused David to break for a moment and draw in a deep breath.

She was beautiful. He endured feelings of envy for his grandfather for the very first time in his life. He asked to be the center of attention whenever she laughed or displayed her stunning grin.

No, he did not because she already had a hubby. David was forced to remind himself of it. Anna was familiar with the name David, but she did not give it any attention. She gave Annet a kind smile and gently glanced over at the man who was standing by her side. After that, her eyes widened in shock, the blood left her face, and she snappily dropped her gaze while her heart pounded in her chest.

Annet's David stood head and shoulders above the crowd, faultlessly dressed in a black regal suit. With his good looks, he radiated an air of arrogant certainty mixed with mannish virility that was nearly impossible to ignore.

Anna could not believe it when she found out that the one mistake, she would ever make in her whole life was standing only one foot away from her. Indeed, though she was ignorant of his entire identity, she went ahead and slept with him. No, there had been no time at all spent sleeping in any of it.

Only sexual exertion that wasn't permitted had taken place between them. Because it was apparent that he'd been unfaithful to the woman who was with him on his boat at the time, she despised herself and disliked him even more. At the time, she was staying on his yacht. Anna's stomach was churning, and it took a tremendous amount of restraint for her to utter the words.

"How nice to meet you." After glancing at David, she switched her gaze back to Bryan and concentrated all of her attention on him.

Chapter 3

David Miller had never done anything like that before, and he didn't enjoy the experience in the least. Indeed, though he wasn't happy to recognize the seductive Anna with Annet hanging on his arm, he wasn't prepared to allow the promiscuous little vixen to get away with ignoring him. Brown eyes had glanced coolly in his direction and also back to Bryan, and he didn't like that at all.

"Hello. Anna, are you there?" David grunted gruelingly. She cast a quick look in his direction, her chocolate eyes hidden by the absurdly long lashes that framed her deep brown eyes.

"Yes. Hello," she said, before fleetly turning her head down again.

"Permit me to say this because we haven't been duly introduced to one another. The name is David Miller."

He was dead set on drawing her attention to himself, so he purposefully extended his hand to her in an attempt to do so. A stern look emanating from her eyes, followed by the extension of a delicate hand. After taking it in his hands and feeling the smoothness of her skin on his palm, he immediately became aware of a fluttering sensation in his loins.

Ever since the last time he'd encountered Anna — no, Hana — or whatever the hell it was that she called herself, he'd in no way been so presently aroused by a woman as he was by Hana. When he looked down at their hands that were gripped together, he was nearly startled, but also he noticed the marriage band ring and flashed back in the nick of time.

He avoided having sexual relations with wedded women, but an exception to this rule was made in the case of this attractive seductress, who didn't reveal her marital status to him until after he'd already taken her to bed. Anna was numb with amazement when she noticed the challenge in his look and the knowing hint of sensuality in his brown eyes. She also heard the enticing tone of his words. She precipitously removed her hand from his clutches as her shock began to set in.

"Anna Gonzales" she said under her breath. Annet made her entrance nearly exactly when she was supposed to.

" Anna, I have a favor to ask of you. Would you please take care of David 's grandfather for me?" She stated it with the same typical lack of empathy that has come to her trademark.

"He was in an accident many days ago, and he cannot walk very well."

"We need to circulate, and James wants to discuss business with David later." Whether Annet was insensitive or not, she had to give her a kiss for the interruption.

"There's no problem. It'll be my joy," Anna said as she held Bryan by the hand.

Annet seized David by the arm, and the pair started making their way through the mob toward the exit. Anna let out a jiggling shriek of relief, even though she was shaking on the inside. Imagine your darkest agonies coming true! David Miller enthralled a spot near or at the very peak of her priority list.

She couldn't believe that he was related to Bryan since Bryan was short and heavyset and had dark brown eyes. But David had to be at least six feet four inches tall, and his eyes were light brown, which was a striking contrast to his tan complexion. She was astounded by this fact. When they first met a year ago, the first thing she noticed about him was his eyes.

They were one of the reasons she had behaved in a manner that was so drastically different from who she typically was. That he showed up then at her father's house as the lover of her sister had to be the strangest coincidence in the history of the world. It made her feel queasy, and she wanted to get away from there. She was ready to give some kind of justification to Bryan when she looked around and noticed that he was still looking after Annet.

His face was a picture of complete and total surprise the entire time. Anna had a perfect understanding of how he felt, but she was confident that it was not for the same reason.

"Annet is very beautiful, and she does have a tendency to have an unanticipated effect on men, but I suppose your grandson can handle her," She said encouragingly.

"And they do make a nice couple," she said. After mumbling something incomprehensible, he brought his hand up to his lips and immediately started sneezing violently. It was too soon to consider leaving just yet because it was clear that the man was in some kind of trouble." Bryan, you do not look very good.

Anna put her arm around him and made the following suggestion" I believe that we ought to find nearly comfortable to sit, and I will get you a glass of brandy."

She made a delicate attempt at humor by saying," Also you can tell me all about your accident and what I suggested last Friday."

"Clearly," he said while maintaining a nervous smile.

" But first, would you be able to give me the name of the woman who's holding my grandson?" Bryan refocused his silver-topped cane in their way while making a stir.

Anna told him," That is my stepsister — Annet," as she eventually spotted an empty lounge and guided him toward the far corner of the magnificent drawing room.

Annet was the name of Anna's sister. She sensed that he was stumbling.

" Hello there, how are you doing?" She inquired cautiously as she supported him in taking a seat.

She regarded his wrinkled face with concerned eyes as she remarked," You look a little pale."

" So, your stepsister, is that right?" I had no idea you had a sister until today.

"Well, you do not indeed know me very well," Anna joked.

" I suppose I need that drink," Bryan rasped as he sat down on the lounge.

He also grunted in Korean something that Anna thought sounded suspiciously like a curse.

" I suppose I need that drink," he said again.

" If you'd be willing to stay then. I will fetch you a brandy and bring it back."

She felt compassion for the man, who was obviously still experiencing some kind of discomfort. While this was going on, David had his hand on Annet's back and was leading her through the crowd with him. He beamed, and he never stopped smiling for the entire proper spots, as Annet collected effusive birthday wishes from her friends. They made their way towards her mama and father who were seated at the other end of the room from where they had entered. Without any conscious effort, David was suitable to play the part of the ideal consort, and his mind was always concentrated on the gorgeous Anna.

He cast his eyes about the room, curious as to which of the men there was her husband. David reflected critically on the man's good fortune, wondering whether he really was so fortunate. There was no misunderstanding of the sexual tension and raging desire that existed between Anna and him. There had been no mistake. He concluded that her poor husband was someone who should be pitied rather than envied.

However, it was time for him to stop worrying about Annet and start doing what he had come to do, which was to assist his grandfather. He cast a glance across the room and noticed Bryan already comfortably situated, and for a few seconds, their eyes connected. David was confused for a while because he appeared to be seeing fear in his grandfather's eyes, but as he watched, Anna approached Bryan and offered him a brandy, and the elderly man broke out into a broad grin.

Anna extended her hand to Bryan and offered him the brandy glass.

"Are you sure that everything is okay?" She questioned as she sat down next to him and took a healthy gulp from her own glass of champagne. She wasn't much of a drinker, but she wanted something to calm her nerves and settle her stomach...

Bryan comforted her, "Much better," while taking a swig of brandy from his glass.

"It looks as though your sister Annet has a good relationship with David. Have the two of you ever spoken before?" he inquired casually.

Chapter 4

Anna clenched her teeth and lied to him, saying "No." She had no intention of telling this kind-hearted elderly guy about the incident that had taken place between her and David a year earlier.

She said, "But I believe Annet has known him for years," She replied. To make matters worse, Bryan started sneezing again.

"You seem to have come down with a cold, are you absolutely sure that you should be going out so soon after your accident?"

Bryan replied, "No, really, I'm fine," and then shifted the subject by explaining to her what she had voted for at the board meeting. It seems that she had consented to another stock float to obtain further capital.

Anna responded with a casual, "It doesn't make much of a difference to me."

"I have a mild form of dyslexia with numbers, and the knowledge I have regarding high finance isn't even enough to cover my little fingernail."

"However, I wouldn't turn down the money." After she finished drinking from her glass, she joined Bryan in setting it down on a nearby table.

Bryan quickly capitalized on the chance presented to him by saying, "Well, there's a simple answer to that."

"You could sell me your aunt's villa on Jeju Island," he said to her.

"You should know that many years ago, my family called that house home."

"You can call me nostalgic, but I really would like to get it back."

"If we can agree, I'm willing to pay you a price that is far higher than what it is now worth."

Anna said, "It's a nice thought, and I really would if I could, but I can't sell it to you." She did this because she observed Bryan's confused expression and wanted to explain what she meant.

"Aunt Martha put it in trust for me, and for my children, and my children's children, ad infinitum, so that it would be legally protected for future generations."

The wrinkled brow of the elderly man furrowed in careful consideration as he said, "I see."

"Have you ever given any thought to requesting to have the trust broken?"

"I have faith that it will be successful."

When she reached an age where she could no longer bear children, she told herself, "Maybe someday." She felt with a trace of melancholy that she owed it to her Aunt Martha to fulfill her wishes, but she saw no need to tell Bryan the entire tale.

"But it's not something that I would contemplate at the moment..." she said.

Bryan repeated it in a hushed tone, "Of course, that is entirely your prerogative," and then lifted his hands with the palms facing up as a sign of surrender.

"It doesn't matter. I have lived long enough to realize that in this world, one can never have all that one desires." Suddenly, he grinned and looked around the room.

"Not that my grandson runs into obstacles very frequently. Now, I want you to tell me in all honesty, what your opinion is of David."

Anna had the impression, although she didn't voice it, that he is a sexual predator who is also excellent in the art of seduction and who preys on the vulnerability of women. She lied through her teeth once more and said, "He seems...nice."

"And I am aware that Annet has very high regard for him,"

On the opposite side of the room, David gave the impression that he was paying close attention to the Williams while, mentally, he was going over the report that he had read earlier that morning. James Wiliams was a man who was in trouble and trying not to show it, the New York office of his company had done some checking over the last two days, and he thought cynically that James Wiliams was one of those people. However, with a kind smile directed down at the guy and his wife, he engaged in conversation with the couple.

David had a very solid understanding of Williams' expectations for him at this point. Once he realized David was the owner of Miller International Holdings, on Wednesday evening he dropped a few hints that pointed in that direction.

Williams wanted him to make an investment in Posh Naturals or at the very least promote it as a purchase to his customers to increase the share price and support Williams' much-vaunted development ambitions. Posh Naturals is a beauty product line. David had no intention of doing any of those things, but for the time being he needed to maintain an air of mystery.

Even though he had taken Annet out twice this week, he chose not to bring up the subject of her inheritance to her either time. He had maintained their connection at a casual and playful level the entire time. However, she was quite good at talking about herself and the modeling agency that she had just recently established. This fits in nicely with what Bryan had mentioned earlier about her now being the owner of her own company.

Because he was thinking about Bryan, he looked around the room and saw that he was still seated on the sofa with the unfaithful Anna Gonzales by his side. But as David observed the old man, the elderly man turned slightly, his black eyes colliding with David's, and he called David forward with a rather frenzied sweep of his cane. What had taken place at this point?

"Excuse me," David remarked tersely. "But it looks like my grandfather needs me," he said, and with a fleeting grin of apology directed at Annet and her parents, he made his way rapidly through the crowd to Bryan's side.

When Bryan sees him at his side. He was blasted with a barrage of Korean language. The crux of the matter was that David was the most foolish person in all of Christendom. Why was he clinging on the blonde beanpole like he was accomplishing something? He was dating the incorrect daughter—the stepdaughter—even though there were two girls in the family. Was he insane? Anna was the one he should have been dating, and now, barring a miracle, he had wrecked Bryan's prospects of ever having his house back in Jeju Island.

David, stunned by the news, glanced across at Anna before returning his attention to Bryan. He felt like a prize idiot. Then, his wrath got the better of him, and he responded in Korean. David had been the one to tell Bryan that the woman's name was Annet. How in the world was he meant to know that there were two daughters when Bryan himself had not even been aware that there were two?

David's eyes narrowed in anger as he focused on the woman in question, who had her head bowed. He wasn't shocked that she couldn't face him; in fact, he was expecting it. David then scowled at his grandfather. He had to be completely insane to have allowed himself to become engaged with Bryan's insane plan in the first place. Now he would have to free himself from a connection with Annet that he had never shown any interest in cultivating in the first place. And doing so would not be simple.

He started by telling Bryan this was not acceptable. Anna was able to hear the two men shouting in a Korean rant, and even though she detested the notion of confronting David, her concern for poor Bryan overwhelmed her anxiety about the situation. She got to her feet and then immediately launched into the conversation in a voice that was calm and controlled effectively.

"Excuse me, Mr. Miller, but your grandpa isn't feeling very well, and yelling at him won't do anything to improve his condition."

Anna was giving him a piece of her mind! David was completely speechless since the woman had such courage.

"In case you had forgotten, he was involved in an accident, and at this point, he ought to be resting at home." Their eyes met and David stared at her intensely for a second.

Chapter 5

"I was not shouting," David said after it took him some time to find his voice. He intentionally reminded her of the intensity they had shared by stating, "We Koreans are as passionate in conversation as we are in everything." He did not do so in a very subtle manner.

"And I am fully aware of what it is that Bryan requires." He cast a murderous glare at Bryan and saw that the other guy was smiling; he was taking pleasure in this, damn him! David was adamant that Bryan was not going to cast him in the role of the evening's antagonist.

He was not about to show any deference to a married lady who openly and frequently slept with other men, he fiercely thought to himself. Regardless of how stunningly beautiful she is.

David explained, "I tried to make him stay at home, but he insisted on coming to the party because he wanted to meet you again, Anna."

"Despite my efforts," David added, "he wanted to meet you again."

"Because he hasn't stopped talking about you since the board meeting, it appears that you had quite an effect on him there."

"He mentioned to me that you were in business, but he failed to mention that you had a partner..."

He paused and deliberately looked down at her ring finger before adding, "But then, his English is not so good." David gave his grandfather a withering look because it was obvious that the elderly man still did not realize the woman was married. Bryan wanted him to marry Anna so that The Villa on Jeju Island would return to their family.

"Is your husband in the house?" It was a sharp question that he asked her while his steely stare roamed insultingly over her.

"I would quite like to meet him," he said. His inquiry was meant to point out to Bryan that he had made a fundamental error. It was also intended to serve as a sarcastic reminder to Anna that there had been no mention of a husband when David was making love with her...

Anna was unable to stop the rapid flushing that broke out in her cheeks in response to the obvious masculine gaze he was casting her way and the subtle jab he was taking at the fact that she was married. She was not willing to sit idly by and let the conceited David demean his grandfather's command of the English language.

She looked at Bryan with compassion in her eyes. "There is nothing incorrect about the way you are using English."

She reassured him, "I can perfectly understand you," before lifting her head to look at the man who towered above her. The man was taller than she was.

"And you should know better than to demean your grandfather's abilities in front of others," Anna added tensely, her flashing chocolate eyes clashing violently with his. It was as if they were the only two people in the room, with the tension between them being a force that could be physically felt.

"And perhaps if you were better at listening to your grandfather, you wouldn't feel the need to resort to such measures."

"It just so happens that my partner is my closest friend Sara, but I never once mentioned to Bryan that I had a partner when we first met." This statement gives the impression that David is dishonest.

"And concerning my spouse, he passed away quite a while ago. Are you pleased with this?"

David was struck into silence for the second time in as many minutes as he thought about the opportunity, he may have had with her if Bryan had gotten his facts straight. It didn't matter to him when Anna's husband had passed away. It was enough for him to know that she was available now. However, there was one little problem, he was seeing Anna's stepsister. He needed to find a way to limit the amount of damage that might be done to his reputation as quickly as possible.

When he straightened his shoulders, he saw a flash of melancholy in her enormous brown eyes that she was unable to conceal completely, and he felt like a fool as a result.

"I'm very sorry to bother you, Anna. It was never my intention to hurt either you or Bryan"

"Could I give you my most sincere condolences on the passing of your husband?"

"Thank you," Anna said harshly, finally forcing her gaze away from his, and not for a second thinking he was telling the truth.

She was speechless from the shock, she couldn't continue. She was very furious because of David Miller's actions. To the point that she had announced Allen's passing in front of other people, which was something she had very seldom had the fortitude to do in the past, and it terrified her.

"I beg your pardon since my grandson has been so crude."

When Bryan chimed in and said, "I know exactly how you feel," she was relieved that the elderly guy had decided to step in. After offering her comfort with a compassionate grin, the man turned his attention back to his grandson and said, "I have also lost my wife, but let me assure you it does get easier."

"But David, Anna is correct; perhaps I was a touch hasty in coming out today." Suddenly jumping to his feet with more agility than Anna would have believed he was capable of, he grabbed David's elbow just as Annet walked in. "My sweet David, how are you doing? Everything okay?"

Anna got the strangest impression that Bryan and David had silently spoken with one another while she was looking back and forth between the two of them.

Annet exerted a possessive touch on David by placing her hand on the front of his shirt.

"No, I'm afraid my grandfather isn't in the best of health, so I'll have to take him back home right away." David stated with a pleasant tone, "I'm sorry, but we have to leave early, but it is necessary."

"Oh, do you have to? Annet glared at her grandfather and asked, "Surely you can stay, even if your grandfather has to leave?" I'll get him a taxi,'" she said.

David took Annet's hand off of his chest and said in a firm tone, "No, I couldn't possibly allow him to go home alone." Anna had the impression that Annet had just made a significant error in judgment with this man. David withdrew Annet's hand from his chest.

Annet exclaimed, "Oh, but you don't need to," and then she cast a beseeching glance in Anna's direction.

"Anna, could you kindly do David and me another favor and drive Mr. Miller back to his house? You are aware that you do not particularly enjoy going to parties, and he will have no problem with this. In addition, David has not yet had the opportunity to adequately communicate with James."

Anna was on the verge of laughing. Annet's self-centeredness never ceased to astonish her, even after all these years. When Bryan stepped in, she was in the process of providing a noncommittal response to her question.

"I'm sorry, but I have to decline, Miss Williams. It is not something I would feel comfortable doing to impose on your sister in such a way. It's time I got going," he said, grabbing David by the arm and explaining that he was sorry for pulling his grandson away.

"I am feeling rather feeble," he said.

David wasn't in the best of moods himself at the time. It was embarrassing for a man who was always in charge to acknowledge that he had no idea what was going to happen that evening since everything had caught him by surprise.

He desired to have a conversation with Anna. Who did he think he was kidding? He had a lot of other plans besides just talking to her. But this wasn't the right moment, and this wasn't the right location. He concluded that she would remain his, and the sooner he escaped from this horrible gathering, the better.

David replied, "Sorry, ladies, but unfortunately, we have to leave."

"Please accept my apology on behalf of your father, and I'll be sure to contact you later, Annet. I do not doubt that we will cross paths again, Anna."

Not if I catch sight of you first, Anna reasoned. Then, while Annet continued to command David's undivided attention, she leaned in close to the elderly guy and planted a peck on his cheek. "I want you to be careful, Bryan."

"Yes, I will. Anna, you have been so considerate of me. Even though, I am dissatisfied with not being able to buy back the property. I would like to show my appreciation for your compassion by taking you out to lunch the day after tomorrow before I go back to Seoul."

Chapter 6

Anna was relieved that her explanation seemed plausible and therefore declined, saying, "I can't tomorrow." She had already misled Bryan into believing that she had never met David before, and she would like to avoid having to deceive him once more. But it just so happened that she was in Fullerton at the time having lunch with Allen's parents, which was something she did once a month.

"Even though it's been almost two years since I lost my spouse, I'm having lunch with his parents tomorrow."

"Therefore, perhaps at another time," she replied in a low voice.

She had a lot of respect for the elderly guy, but she had zero interest in having anything to do with his grandson, and she would have preferred it if he had departed as soon as possible. As Anna saw Bryan follow Annet and David out of the room and into the hallway, she let out a trembling sigh of relief.

"Thanks so much," Annet told her in a sarcastic tone five minutes later, after she had returned leading the guys out of the mansion.

"You could have insisted on bringing the elderly gentleman home, and David could have stayed for a longer period with me." Annet scowled at her.

Anna shrugged her shoulders and offered, "Maybe—you know better than I do."

It was as close as Anna believed she could go to warning Annet about how much of a serial womanizer David Miller was by saying, "But he strikes me as a man who does what he wants, and gets what he wants—women included." Anna said this because she believed it was the only way she could adequately convey to Annet how much of a womanizer David Miller was.

"I hope you know what you're getting into." Annet was self-centered yet inoffensive, and she feared for her well-being if she were to get hurt.

Annet responded in her characteristically forthright manner, stating, "That is the problem."

"I haven't been able to get through to him yet, and the level of my irritation is over the roof. According to the tabloids, he has been seeing Amelia Smith, who is a former model and a prominent fashion designer in New York. But at this point, he is in Los Angeles, and I am here while she isn't; David must undoubtedly be experiencing the same thing. He is notoriously known for the large number of women he has slept with as well as for his skill as a lover."

It was a great deal more information than Anna needed, and as a result, she broke out laughing. Annet was completely oblivious to any hint of frenzy that may have been there in the music.

After two hours, Anna had returned to the modest Montebello terraced house that she and Alan had shared and was now resting comfortably in her bed.

David Miller was having a difficult time concentrating on his desk in the penthouse of his mansion across town. On the way back to the house, his grandfather had been completely silent. Upon their return to the flat, Bryan offered them each a nightcap and then simply stated that the villa was not available for purchase and that he was sorry.

He was no longer troubled by it. Now he was sitting on the sofa with his leg supported by a footstool like he had done previously. His dark eyes did not have the glitter that was so characteristic of them, and the expression on his face was one of resignation.

"Let me get this straight: after all the commotion you have made attempting to acquire the villa on Jeju Island, now you're telling me that you don't care anymore?"

"Let me get this right," David said.

"I am concerned," Bryan said softly while explaining, "It's just that I've finally concluded that it's impossible."

"Anna explained to me tonight that she is unable to sell it because her aunt left it in trust for her and her children, as well as her children's children,"

David observed that breaking the trust is a possibility. "There is still hope for you, I'm certain."

"Maybe," Bryan heaved a sigh.

"However, navigating the legal red tape can take years, and even if I live long enough—well, you've met Anna —can you honestly see a beautiful and compassionate woman like her remaining a widow for much longer?"

"She is still youthful even though her spouse has been gone for more than two years."

David sat down unexpectedly and came dangerously close to choking on his whiskey. That means Anna wasn't married when he had sexual relations with her!

"Two years? Are you sure?", he questioned.

He felt as though he had wasted enough of his time with Anna, and he was resolved to stop doing so. He was so far off base regarding her that he was almost able to chuckle about it, except that it wasn't humorous at all.

His grandpa had not only failed to achieve his goal of getting his old home in Jeju Island, but David had also slept with and then insulted the prettiest lady he had ever encountered.

"Yes, she told me about it tonight as we were getting ready to leave."

"Even though she may not be aware of it just yet, she has already completed her period of grief."

"She will very definitely be married and expecting a child far before the trust can be broken unless all American men are completely oblivious to the fact that there are women available for marriage. It's pointless, and I'm going to bed," he said, picking up his walking stick as he stood up and hobbling up the stairs.

"It's useless." After reaching the peak, he turned around and said that he and his best friend Kim would be returning to Korea the next morning.

He then departed after saying "Goodnight."

As David was leaving the room, he noticed Bryan's despondent shoulders slump as he walked out. He felt terrible that his grandpa had been let down, but he had to concede that the elderly man had made an accurate assessment. It did appear that there was little chance of acquiring the property at this moment.

In his mind's eye, he saw Anna again, and this time she was even more stunning than before. She was so serene and thoughtful with Bryan, but she was so chilly with him. His body became more rigid as he recalled her naked body in all of its minute details. Such as the silky smoothness of her light honey skin, the delicious taste of her rose-tipped breasts, and the almost dreamlike quality of their lovemaking, which had developed into a white-hot, all-consuming passion.

He also recalled the almost dreamlike nature of their union. He rose again, agitated, and was going to pour another glass of whiskey. But he did not continue. It wasn't a thirst he had; he needed some time to himself.

Anna was personally approached and presented with an offer of a significant sum of money in exchange for her agreement to violate the trust. He had never seen a woman before, with the sole exception of his grandmother, who did not place a high value on financial success. And even though he didn't think plan A would fail, he still wanted a backup plan in case it did. He was thirty-seven years old, which was much past the age at which most men got married.

The moment might have come to take the next step in life and get married. By marrying Anna and producing a child who would also be Bryan's great-grandchild to inherit the villa, then his grandpa would achieve his heart's desire to keep the villa in the family. And that was all the better for him, it was a win-win situation. In addition to this, David desired to have Anna sleep in his bed once again, and he was the type of man who always got what he desired.

Plan B suffered from just one major fault in its execution. In addition to the fact that he had almost thrown her off his boat a year earlier, Anna was aware that he was dating her stepsister, so she chose not to give him the time of day. After resuming his seat on the couch, his wide forehead furrowed into a scowl as he went over the activities of the previous evening and the knowledge he had gained over the previous few days.

The scowl on his face faded, and in its place was a predatory smile that curled his sensual mouth. As he got to his feet and started walking toward his bed, the spark of competition shone brightly in his eyes. His decision was already set, and he knew exactly what course of action to take. She cannot escape from him; he will make sure of it.

Chapter 7

Anna exited her car in a parking spot designated for residents just in front of her front door. She then retrieved her handbag and a shopping bag stuffed with veggies from the passenger seat before exiting the vehicle. She straightened up, stretched her shoulders, and sighed with contentment as her gaze swept over the narrow strip of the front yard, a riot of color in the June light. The trip to Fullerton was nice.

She had a fantastic day; she had helped Mark, her father-in-law, in the garden, and she had eaten a wonderful lunch that Marga, her mother-in-law, had provided. After that, the three of them went for a stroll on the beach, and on their way back, they stopped by Allen's grave. Following that, they went back to the house and had some tea there.

During the ride back to Los Angeles, Anna rationalized the terrible thoughts that had kept her up for most of the previous night. Her stomach was full, and her spirit was revived, thanks to the generosity of Allen's parents. After that, she firmly shoved them back into the deepest part of her mind, which was where they belonged.

For someone like herself, who had little tolerance for alcohol and seldom drank more than the occasional glass of wine. It was not unexpected that she had behaved in such an out-of-character manner when she had become depressed and had too much wine. Anna had made a terrible mistake that had been caused by both of these factors.—to the extent that they were almost certainly hallucinating.

Anna was overjoyed to be back at the home in Montebello that she and Allen had purchased together when they were married, but she was completely oblivious to the sleek black automobile that was parked twenty yards up the street. Instead, she searched her handbag for the door key. She strolled into the hallway after unlocking the door and entering it. A stifled shriek came out of her mouth as she set the shopping bag down on the floor before turning around to slam the door behind her.

"Am I allowed to come in?" David Miller had already entered her hallway and shut the door behind him before she could gather her breath and answer.

"Anna, we have to talk. I need to hear what you have to say. "

A sinister brow furrowed. "Or maybe I should just call you Hana?"

She was completely taken aback by the fact that he had shown up at her house, and she peered up at him with wide eyes. Then, both the surprise and the rapid buildup of her anger caused her to redden her cheeks angrily.

She exploded with rage and yelled at him, "I don't want you to call me anything; just get the hell out of my house."

"Such a fit of fury! You do surprise me, after all, when two old friends meet up again unexpectedly, what could be more natural than to have a great conversation?", he said with a mocking sense of delight.

Anna was able to force herself to think rationally by exerting a tremendous amount of self-control. She fervently wished that she had never come into contact with David Miller, and she had no desire to engage in conversation with him. The only thing that truly concerned her was getting rid of him. However, she just needed to take one glance at the grim resolve written all over his handsome face. Common sense informed her that he was much too huge and powerful and that there was no possibility of tossing him anywhere...

A white sports shirt that was open at the neck dramatically enhanced his fair, smooth complexion. He was dressed casually in a tan leather jacket that dropped smoothly from broad, muscular shoulders. The jacket was unbuttoned, and a belt made of hide supported the pleated pants that fitted the thin hips, muscular thighs, and long legs. But there was nothing casual about his position; with his knees slightly extended and his body towering over her, he was unmistakably masculine and undeniably menacing.

Anna straightened her back and shoulders, declaring that she would not allow herself to be intimidated in her own house. As she cocked her head back, her eyes clashed with his dark brown eyes, and she found herself wondering how she could have ever imagined that David's eyes were the same blue as her cherished Allen's had been. She had a little shiver and quickly pushed the uncomfortable memory from her mind. She repeatedly urged herself to maintain her composure. This man was the boyfriend of her stepsister, and she had absolutely nothing to do with him.

"I don't know how you found out where I live, and I don't appreciate you bursting into my home."

"I don't have anything to say to you, so I'd appreciate it if you could just leave."

" Annet told me—in fact, she was quite informative—and I'm sorry to disappoint you, Anna but I have no intention of leaving," David stated nonchalantly.

"I have no intention of leaving until you have answered a few questions."

Her outburst of rage demonstrated that she was not as impervious to him as she would have him believe. His eyes first focused with intense curiosity on her stunning face, and then they wandered more slowly over her voluptuous figure. Her glistening dark mane of hair had been caught by a yellow ribbon at the nape of her lovely neck, and it was now cascading down her back in the form of a long silky banner.

She had on a cropped top in a pink color that clung tenderly to her high breasts, and it was evident that she was not wearing a bra. The delicious nipples that tortured his night fantasies more frequently than he dared to acknowledge were clearly visible by the fine cotton that she wore.

As the top just barely reached the white pants that clung to her tiny hips and legs, an enticing strip of silky flesh was revealed. Her adorable pink toes were in full view once more, thanks to the flat shoes she wore on her feet. When did he go from being a man who was certainly into breasts and legs to being someone who was into feet? David pondered with a sardonic expression as he saw his entire body stiffen up in an attempt to rein in his hyperactive desire.

When he looked up, he noticed a flash of something that looked a lot like dread in the chocolate eyes of the woman who was looking at him. Because she had lied to him about both her name and the fact that she was married, Anna Gonzalez had every reason to be terrified of him.

A few hours ago, he took Annet out to lunch to delicately break the news to her that he did not consider her more than an old acquaintance. She had handled it incredibly well, especially when he offered to invest in her agency. During the conversation that followed, with some discreet probing, he learned from her that Anna's love was gardening and that for the last two years, she had reportedly lived the life of a nun. He had obtained this information from her during the talk that followed.

Therefore, either Anna was a very skilled actor, a very skilled liar, or both. David couldn't help but think this as he and Anna continued to look at each other, the tension between them growing to the point that it was almost palpable.

'Trust Annet to open her big mouth,' she thought. Anna was the one who first turned away. In that case, she muttered, as she ducked her head and picked up the bag of veggies to get away from his overly attentive look.

"In that case."

"It would be in your best interest to accompany me into the kitchen."

"You may tell me what you have to say while I put these things away," she said as she proceeded down the hallway, past the stairs, to the rear of the house, and into the kitchen.

She didn't want David anywhere in her house, let alone in her living room, but she reasoned that the kitchen was an appropriate setting because it was less intimate. She moved the luggage to the bench near the window, avoiding the breakfast table that was positioned at the room's far end.

When she turned around and saw David approaching from behind, the hair on the back of her neck sprang on end. As she removed the veggies from the paper bag, the thought occurred to her that perhaps the little kitchen had not been such a smart choice after all. She unwillingly turned around, holding a head of lettuce in her hand, and came face to face with David once more. The refrigerator had been placed on the opposite wall.

"Excuse me, I need to use the refrigerator."

David responded to her with a dry self-mockery, "You and me both," as his brown eyes shone with an invitation for her to partake in his humor.

Chapter 8

Anna, on the other hand, was not amused, and she had no intention to partake in his humor. She was at a noticeable disadvantage because his large frame towered over her. He was just inches away from her. She retreated involuntarily and braced herself against the bench as she came to a standstill there. Because she had nowhere else to go, she chose to ignore his implication and instead look up at him.

She spoke calmly but with a sarcastic expression on her face as she replied, "Then let me pass, and I'll get you a cold drink." She tilted one of her beautiful brows.

When he was too close, his dazzling deep stare was too knowing, and all of a sudden, the heady aroma of his perfume sent her back to another time and place—the close quarters of a yacht's cabin. She inhaled a slow breath that was shaky and deep. She had no intention of coming there...

David Miller declined to get a cold drink from Anna, saying, "I don't want a cold drink." He was trying to be sensible, even though his more primitive instincts were asking him to grab Anna into his arms and kiss her until she melted into his arms.

"What I want to do is talk to you about the possibility of breaking the trust on the house you own in Jeju Island so that my grandfather can buy it," he said.

"In addition to that, I need an explanation as to why you told me you were married the first time, we met on the island a year ago."

He stopped, the corners of his mouth turning up into a smile as he said this. He grinned as he removed the lettuce from her suddenly numb fingers and placed it on the seat behind her. Not only that, but he then set his hands on the bench at either side of her shapely torso, essentially trapping her.

"And I want you, of course...but not necessarily in that order."

Keep your cool and your composure. Anna said her mantra under her breath, but she wasn't having much luck with it since her fear was fueling her anger, and she was responding with rage.

"Not in any particular sequence. Because my aunt's house cannot be sold, there is no possibility that I can violate her trust, and I do not need to explain to you. I owe you neither my attention nor my time given the fact that you are dating my stepsister. But if you're worried that I might tell Annet about our fleeting and unlucky encounter, I'm here to put your mind at ease and put your worries to rest. If I were to admit to even lightly touching you, I would sooner sever my tongue than do that."

"Then it seems that asking you to marry me is not an option, does that sound about right?"

"Should we skip straight to plan B?" David questioned with a touch of humor in his voice as he moved on.

"You have that exactly correct! If you were the last man on the planet, I still wouldn't marry you since you're a womanizer and a pig with a bad attitude about women." Anna retorted angrily.

She put her palms on his chest in an attempt to push him away, but as soon as she did so, she realized she had made a significant error in judgment. His black head snapped back, and any sign of enjoyment was gone as his eyes, which had transformed into sparkling dark shards of cold rage, plunged into hers.

"Well, if that is how you feel about me, then I have nothing to lose, have I?" He growled as he wrapped two strong arms around her and hauled her firmly against his powerful frame. His black head whipped around unexpectedly, and his sensual mouth seized hers with a ferocious intensity that was driven more by a want to dominate than by desire.

She was unable to get away because her arms were pinned to her sides, and she was caught in the cradle formed by his legs. She made an effort to pull her head away from him, but with a quickness that overwhelmed her. One hand slid up her back and grabbed the thick swathe of hair at her nape, keeping her immovable beneath his ferocious attack.

She was acutely aware of the intense tension that permeated every inch of his body, as well as the pressing force of his arousal against her stomach. Then, unexpectedly, as his tongue explored the wet interior of her mouth, a retaliating rush of awareness erupted within her and caused her to lose her ability to breathe for a moment.

But she was enticed; heat gathered in her pelvis, and, despite her best efforts, she gave in to the temptation. The entire seduction of her senses was what she had been trying to erase from her consciousness for the last year...what she had been scared of.

She was powerless to control her treacherous body, and as a result, she swayed into him involuntarily. As he became aware of her submission, he became softer, using his tongue to tease and lick her in an expertly seductive manner that accelerated the rate of her already rapid heartbeat.

"Anna, my God!" He husked against her mouth while at the same time reaching up with one hand to stroke across her breasts, his fingers grazing the burgeoning nipples through the soft cotton of her top.

"Or Hana — whatever you call yourself," he said.

"I've never forgotten the last time you were in my arms, and I want you again—badly." His black head raised, and he locked her with a penetrating stare.

"Just give in."

Anna was brought crashing back from the edge of embarrassing submission by David's callous use of the nickname Hana for her. Hana was a name that only Allen ever used to refer to her. When Aunt Martha had first introduced her to Allen as my niece Anna Hana, Allen had said that it was a bit of a mouthful. He would call her Hana, and he had done so until the day that he died. Hana was the name that Aunt Martha had always called her. It sounded like the worst kind of betrayal to hear it on David's tongue at this point.

"I beg of you, do not attempt to address me as Hana!" she cried as she wriggled her way out of his grasp and gave him a desperate shove that sent him reeling backward on his heels. She whirled around in the kitchen on shaky legs and placed the distance between them equal to the width of the breakfast table. She was red in the face, fuming, and her heart was beating so fast and furiously that she had to grab the back of one of the wood chairs to calm herself.

David completed the circle with a nonchalant lean back against the back of the bench. He muttered a curse under his breath after observing her white-knuckled grasp on the chair as well as the rage and terror that were visible in her enormous eyes. He should not have attacked her with such ferocity in the first place. But with her evaluation of his character, she had managed to infuriate him, and he had completely lost control of the situation, which was most unlike him.

Anna, a straightforward "no" would have been sufficient, he drawled. He was adamant about finding out the reason she took offense to the name Hana. However, it was not the appropriate time.

"You may let go of your hold on the chair and bring that drink that you gave to me because I've never had to pressure a woman into bed and I don't intend to start with you." He said to her.

Chapter 9

"Would you want the drink I offered?" Anna repeated back in a tone of complete disbelief, as the man's audacity astounded her.

"Are you out of your mind? I demand that you leave my home at this very moment.

"Is this how you treat your visitors?" David straightened up and made his way forward casually.

"Consider what your father would say if he heard that his daughter had shown such a shocking lack of manners to the grandson of one of his major shareholders," he said.

"Think what your father would say if he heard that."

"Then there's Annet as well, as you were so nice to point out." He halted alongside her, his brown eyes focusing in on her hot face as he stared at her.

"My father and Annet?" Anna said once again. What exactly was he talking about? And what was the source of the unsettling sensation that there was a danger lurking somewhere in it?

"Since the death of your husband, Annet has been under the notion, as have the rest of the people, that you have become celibate and are on par with saints in terms of your behavior since his passing. As for you not telling her about our one-night stand — that you would sooner have your tongue cut out than tell her, I believe you said — well, I have no such qualms about telling her about it. I will gladly announce to the entire world that I had sex with you twelve months ago. Although it can make your mourning widow act a little less convincing. "

His insensitive remark greatly wounded her, and the tears she shed were genuine. Every day, Anna was reminded of how much she missed her late husband by how she missed his compassion, the comfort he offered, the talk they shared, and the feeling of complete love and safety that Allen had supplied. However, this pompous and self-centered guy, who most likely had never loved anybody in his life, had the guts to make fun of her loss.

The mockery that David directed toward her sadness morphed her distress into a stony fury that she refused to let go of. Anna gradually loosened her hold on the chair, spun around, and straightened her shoulders as she did so.

"Would you really do that? Would you intentionally cause Annet to be unhappy in this way?"

"That shouldn't come as a shock to me, does it?"

She mocked while shaking her head in disdain and delivering a sarcastic remark.

She didn't wait for his reaction before she continued, "Follow me, and I'll get you that drink." She then completely ignored him as she went out of the kitchen and opened the door to the living room, even though she was aware of what he would see when she did so.

She walked up to a little antique section that functioned as a drinks cabinet and poured a shot of whiskey into a crystal glass. She turned and came back to where David was standing, glancing around inquisitively as she went.

"I'm afraid I only have whisky," she said.

"Here." She held out the glass and made sure her fingers did not contact his as he took it from her with a quick "Thanks" and a knowing raise of one black brow. This only served to confirm her decision to get rid of him once and for all.

She proceeded by saying, "It's a very good Irish malt, I believe—not that I drink it," as she crossed the room to sit down on one of the enormous sofas that flanked the beautiful Victorian fireplace. The sofas were Victorian in style. However, Allen loved it the most, and he was known to be quite the connoisseur.

"Now, please remind me, what did you consider to be of such critical importance that you had to storm into my home to speak to me about it?" She stood still as he carried the glass with him as he walked around the room.

In the presence of David Miller, the space she had previously seen as being vast appeared to have the proportions of a doll's home suddenly. As the duration of the silence increased, she shifted uneasily and eventually said, "Please have a seat."

"I'd rather stand, thank you," David replied after taking one look around the room, which was sufficient for him to determine that the place was a virtual shrine to the late, lamented Allen Gonzales... He grimaced as he picked up a framed wedding photograph from among the dozen or more framed photographs arranged on top of a beautifully inlaid console table.

The bride's was Anna, and she was grinning ear to ear as she looked up into the face of her husband. She was completely smitten with him. The gentle yet triumphant smile that spread across the man's face conveyed everything that needed to be communicated. The fact that he was extremely lucky...

David's disposition did not improve as a result of staring at the woman who had smiling dark brown eyes and long black hair. Finally, he turned to face her and remarked, "You were a beautiful bride." He was looking at her across the room. She expressed her gratitude by quietly nodding her head but did not speak a word.

After looking over the other pictures for a moment, he placed the one he had just picked up. There was a picture of everyone who attended the wedding, so it was clear that it was a major deal. There were further images of the happy pair with a multitude of friends at a BBQ, as well as one of Anna by her husband's side beside a swimming pool, smiling and holding his hand while doing so. His temperament became even more gloomy as he pictured Anna wearing nothing more than a little bikini.

A frown appearing on his face, he suddenly turned aside and took a sip of the whiskey, there was no doubt that it was a quality malt. But the fact that he was drinking the whiskey of another man and lusting after the widow of a deceased guy gave him a sour taste in his mouth for some reason. He made his way back to the spot where Anna was sitting and observing him with cold, guarded eyes, and he settled his tall, lanky figure on the sofa directly across from her.

"Your husband was a very handsome man; how long did you date before you got married?" David questioned, not knowing why he was asking. However, Anna captivated him in a manner that no other woman had in years — or perhaps ever, as he sardonically admitted. Even if on the surface she appeared tranquil and lovely, he knew that on the inside she was a fiery volcano of desire.

"Do you want a condensed version of my life's story?" She said, rolling her eyes. How exactly do you plan to escape this situation? She helplessly asked herself.

Chapter 10

David concurred, saying, "If that is what you want...yes."
Anna started her speech on the assumption that he was telling the truth.

" Allen and I first crossed paths while he was working as a researcher for my Aunt Martha when I was twelve and he was twenty-one. When I was in college, he quickly became not just my closest friend but also my boyfriend. He supported my passion for landscaping designs, and once I graduated, he urged me to go into business with Sara. He was sweet, loving, and offered complete and utter support. When I was twenty-two years old, we were married. After another four years, he was eventually taken from us by a ski accident."

David mumbled, "He might have been the epitome of virtue, but he was also a fool to risk his life skiing with a passionate, sexy woman like you at home to warm his bed."

She did not like the characterization of herself as "passionate and sexy," as Anna was not at all like that; yet, she kept her expression neutral as she calmly stated, "You never knew him, so your opinion is irrelevant."

"Was he an ardent lover?" He asks.

She shouted at him, enraged that he dared to inquire, "That has nothing to do with you."

"And now that I've told you everything you wanted to know, will you kindly exit the building?"

"Surely I'm allowed to drink my whisky before we move on to the next round?" he toasted her with a toast from his glass, took a sip, and then reclined back on the couch, stretched his long legs out in front of him with an air of nonchalance.

When he so willingly consented to depart, Anna could have had a sneaking suspicion that the situation was too good to be true. She prayed that the whisky would be enough to suffocate the damned guy. But with a grin that was obviously fake, she responded in a beautiful voice, "If you must."

"I am grateful," David teased her while he allowed his eyes to gently glide over her, appraising her stunning body blatantly.

"I must say your husband did have great taste in whisky—among other things," David said.

She was sitting there looking so proper and collected, but he knew she was anything but... Her back was ramrod straight, her arms were wrapped across her beautiful breasts, and her knees were pulled tightly together. He knew she was hiding something.

If she had been any more prepared to defend herself, you would have seen her walking about with a shield and a sword. She wasn't a young girl; by his estimation, she had to be twenty-eight years old. He questioned why she was so adamant about rejecting the sexual chemistry that existed between them.

"Since the death of your husband, have you had sex with any other men besides me?" He asked her, and in the deep brown of her eyes, he saw a flicker of anger.

Without pausing for thought, Anna said, "Certainly not."

"I see—but then why me?" David replied, his right brow lifted.

"What is wrong with you?" David said, matching her furious glare with his own.

"I'm entitled to know, Anna; after all, it's not every day that a guy picks up a beautiful woman and makes love to her, and then afterward she puts a wedding band on her finger and says that she is married," David said sardonically.

"Decent men don't pick up women," she bit out, astonished at his audacity in asking so many intimate questions about her. Anna snapped. She gritted her teeth.

David shot back with a sarcastic remark, saying, "By the same token, decent women don't allow themselves to be picked up."

"It being the case, wouldn't you think it makes us two of a kind?" David was pressing his lips together tightly

Anna's cheeks became red as he made the rude statement.

She snapped back, "I would prefer not to say anything to you at all," but she could not contradict his rationale, so she did not say anything further.

"Unfortunately, that's not an option; I have no intention of leaving here until I discover what made you sleep with me—other than my undeniable charm, of course," he remarked with a smile as he explained the situation.

"Based on my recollection, you came voluntarily into my arms and my bed, and what followed was an encounter that was tremendously intense and mutually rewarding for both of us. I've seldom come across a lady who is more compatible with me in the bedroom; thus, I don't see why you'd lie about your identity and your marital status."

After a momentary, very physical encounter between the two of them, there was a drawn-out period of silence during which they simply gazed at one another. The atmosphere in the room was thick with the tension that resulted from this interaction. Anna was doing all in her power to remove the memory from her mind, even though the mere thought of it caused an unpleasant flush of heat to spread throughout her entire body.

As far as getting along with other things, he does it on any level. Her heart sank at the concept, and she tore her gaze away from his to focus on the window behind him, the evening sun streaming through the glass panes, temporarily blinding her. She then turned her attention back to him.

Anna blinked, realizing that she and David Miller, a billionaire and sophisticated behemoth in the world of finance, had virtually nothing in common with one another. Her childhood had been quite typical of someone from the middle class, and she had been well cared for by a little family enterprise. Only after her father had remarried had the house that she had spent her entire life calling home been exchanged for the lavish house in Beverly Hills, at the instigation of her stepmother. It was only after her father had remarried that the company expanded in leaps and bounds, and the family had become very wealthy, according to her father. Not that Anna had noticed; after all, she had to earn a livelihood for herself. So what made her a wanton woman on that day that they had a one-night stand?

Chapter 11

"I asked you a question."

He was able to see by the expression on her lovely face that her thoughts had wandered away from him, and this made him extremely uncomfortable.

"Why did you lie?" he asked her.

The demand in his low voice succeeded in drawing Anna's attention to the situation. She concluded that thinking about the past was not helping her deal with the circumstances of the present. She knew from her own experience that David was not going to let her forget or give her space until he had an explanation for what had happened.

She got to her feet slowly and cast a gaze down at him as she did so.

"All right, let's make a deal," she said.

"I'll tell you what you want to know."

Her intrinsic honesty compelled her to tell him the truth, disgrace the demon, and finally draw a line under the horrifying occurrence once and for all.

"But you have to promise to leave and never bother me again—no more excuses," She told him.

"No more excuses." She repeated while staring at him.

David nodded his head in agreement and said, "Fair enough."

She had her doubts about whether she could rely on his word, but she decided to give him the benefit of the doubt nonetheless. Primarily because she could not think of any other way to get rid of him. Anna got up from where she was sitting on the sofa, walked across the room, and then returned to her spot on the sofa after picking up her favorite photo of Allen from the console table. After staring at the photograph for a time, she eventually lifted her head and noticed that David had repositioned himself on the couch and was now observing her with eyes that were cold and analytical.

She stated it matter-of-factly, "The day I met you would have been my fourth wedding anniversary." When she saw the disgusted expression on his face, she knew she had succeeded.

"But that wasn't the only thing. It was the culmination of..." She hesitated for a time before continuing.

"...disasters, if you want to call them that. It was the first time I had ever been to Jeju Island, and in all honesty, I didn't even know that my Aunt Martha owned a property there. I had landed on the island two weeks earlier with my aunt, at her urging."

"She asked me to accompany her for several reasons, the primary one being that she had been informed about a month earlier that she only had a short amount of time left to live. It was only natural for me to feel sad, and as it turned out, she passed just a few months later from cancer."

Anna began to stray from the topic, her dark chocolate eyes becoming clouded with the pain she had previously experienced.

"However, Aunt Martha believed that she most likely became sick when working in laboratories many years ago. Stress is the main killer."

She proceeded by saying, "Anyway, it wasn't the happiest of holidays, but we did try to enjoy ourselves, and I built her the rockery she had always wanted."

"During the process, I knocked over a stone and it landed on my hand."

She stared at David with a gloomy expression on her face as she told him that "three of my fingers were severely swollen, and my wedding ring had to be cut off."

"I took it to a shop in the town to be repaired, and when I met you, I had just retrieved it from the jewelers," she said.

"I took it to a shop in the town." In the shop, I attempted to put it back on, but my finger was still slightly swollen, so it did not fit properly. Because you've never been married, you wouldn't understand why I was unhappy, but I was."

"I don't usually drink, but while I was waiting for the local bus, I ordered a glass of wine from the bar, and instead of bringing it to me, the waiter brought over a carafe."

"I had a couple of glasses, maybe more, and I was thinking about Allen and our wedding day when the accident with the wine happened and you appeared."

She stopped, and while leaning forward, she very deliberately presented the photograph to him. He grabbed it from her outstretched hand without commenting and said, "Take a look."

"When I looked up into your eyes that day—so concerned, just like Allen's—and you asked me my name, in my befuddled state I said Hana because that was what Allen always called me."

"That is my favorite photo of Allen, and when I looked up into your eyes that day—so blue and so concerned, just like Allen's,"

"Then, in a haze of melancholy and bafflement, I did nothing more than follow where you went."

"I will freely acknowledge that I acted unacceptably, and when I finally came to my senses, I was appalled by what I had done. Perhaps it was the reflection of the lake, or maybe it was something else." Her normally flawless forehead momentarily creased into a perplexed frown. She replied to him, "Because your eyes are nothing like Allen's, yours are dark brown, like chocolate."

As she cast a glance in his direction, she became aware that she was veering off-topic after observing the furious scowl on his face.

"Anyway, I made a mad run into the restroom, quickly got dressed, and struggled to get my ring back on my finger. The rest is common knowledge."

"Oh, my God!" David yelled as his anger reached a boiling point and engulfed him. It was awful enough to hear the lady with whom he had made love remark that she had been horrified after they had finished their sexual encounter, but as for the rest...

"You, you expect me to believe that the reason you slept with me was because I made you think about your husband?", he demanded in a condescending tone. And then, without looking back, he sprang to his feet, traversed the gap that stood between them, and grabbed the picture again.

He growled, "I don't even remotely resemble the man."

He could not remember a time in his life when he had been insulted to such a degree. Likewise, he swore to himself that he would never again allow Anna to get away with dealing such a severe blow to his dignity. Not only that, but he furiously scrutinized her, his eyes scraping all over her body. As she sat on the edge of the sofa, the cotton top she was wearing was drawn tightly across her high and firm breasts. Her hands were clutched into the soft fabric on either side of her, giving the impression that she was some kind of exotic bird getting ready to take flight.

Anna was taken aback by the magnitude of his rage. She noticed the dark flush that spread across his high cheekbones, as well as the cold glitter that appeared in his eyes. It was too late for her to realize that it had probably not been the finest idea in the world to tell such an egotistical guy the truth.

When David Miller found out that he had been used as a stand-in for another man, he was not going to take the news very well. David's ego was much larger than the average man's. It was ironic, in a sense, and she flashed the barest hint of a dry smile as she recalled Annet telling her how David was famous for exploiting women.

Her lips curled in a little smile as she thought about it. But since Anna believed that discretion was more important than bravery, she refrained from voicing her feelings and instead slid down the sofa and got up, moving as far away from him as she could.

"I didn't say you resembled him at all," she said.

She responded, "I said it was a trick of the light that your eyes appeared blue," to appease him.

"But that doesn't matter now because you promised to leave me alone if I told you the truth, and I've told you the truth, Anna said. She had kept her end of the bargain and that she wanted him gone.

David came closer to her and said, "Oh, I'm leaving all right."

For a split second, Anna believed that her suffering had finally ended and that he was leaving.

"But first I'm going to prove to you that you're fooling no one but yourself," he said. Before she could respond to his ridiculous assertion, he grabbed for her and drew her against his rugged body, his sensual mouth seizing hers with punishing passion.

Chapter 12

As he attempted to pry her lips apart, she was momentarily paralyzed with astonishment for a brief moment. But only for the span of a single heartbeat. Not again, Anna swore, boiling with wrath at his antics and the complete disrespect of his agreement to depart.

Not again. She clenched her palm into a fist and lunged at him while simultaneously bringing her knee up forcefully, aiming for the weakest area of the man's body. He was able to get away with lightning-fast reactions. But he was thrown off balance, and as he went backward, he carried her with him, and the two of them ended up in a tangled mess on the sofa.

Anna was out of breath, and before she knew what had happened, she was lying face down on him with the weight of her body pressing down on David, and he hugged her. She made another attempt to strike out at him, but he managed to grab both of her hands and hold them firmly over her head with one of his own. He moved until she was beneath him. He scoffed and said, "Oh, no, you don't."

"I won't put up with violence from anyone, and especially not from a wicked woman like you," he said.

"What would you name this, if that's the case?" She screamed as she struggled to free herself from beneath him. However, as a response to her movement, she felt the intensifying force of his manly erection against her thigh, and at that moment, she realized that she had made a mistake. The last thing she wanted was for David to lose control and get enraged; she tried to calm the fire that was permeating her own body by putting it down.

His stony mouth twisted into a menacing grin as he smiled. When he rasped, "A lesson in how to greet your lover," she knew that he was going to kiss her since she was expecting it. She jerked her head to the side in an attempt to get away from him, and he quickly shut his mouth over the fast-throbbing pulse in her neck. She let out a cry as his full lips moved closer and closer to her ear.

As he continued to blow softly, he said, "Because, regardless of how much you wish it wasn't true, I am your last lover."

"Not your hubby from so many years ago."

She struggled to maintain control of her emotions as she grappled with the conflicting reactions she felt in response to his statement. She wanted to refuse him, but the warmth of his breath in her ear, the familiar masculine fragrance of him, and the weight of his body on hers triggered a myriad of memories. Likewise, she had vigorously ignored them in the past. She wanted to deny him. David held her chin with his index and middle finger and moved her face to look at him.

"You know I'm right," he muttered as he bit at her lower lip with his teeth, demanding that she give him access and relinquish her resistance.

She tried to deny herself to the sensuous awareness that had been brewing between them ever since they had seen each other again the previous night. This awareness had been present but had been dormant until now. She would later realize just how devious he had been. But just now, as he brushed his tongue across her lips softly, she yearned to give in to his sexual demand and lose herself in the intoxicating pleasure of his kiss.

However, despite her efforts, she was unable to withstand the earth-shattering sexual effect of his mouth as it teased and tasted hers. She might have been successful if he had continued to be forceful, but he was too experienced of a lover to be so crude. And when his palm moved down from her chin to slide up beneath her cotton top and cup one of her firm breasts, an arrow of excitement raced down from her breast all the way to her crotch.

Her lips opened on their own without her even realizing it, and his tongue explored the tender, moist interior with an eroticism that awoke an answering passion in her that she fought to suppress... but ultimately failed to do so. Before moving on to give the second breast the same wonderful pleasure, his fingers discovered the pert pink tip of one breast and slowly plucked it, bringing it to a tight, hard nub of agonizing want. He then stroked his fingers across to give the other breast the same delicious pleasure. And the entire while, his enticing mouth slowly ate away at hers in a passionate kiss that only grew more intense.

His head raised, and she let out a quiet groan in response. David acted as though it was a sign he had been waiting for and let go of her wrists before pulling her shirt over her head. After being temporarily blinded, Anna opened her eyes to see David looking down at her body with eyes that were intense and hungry. Then, his black head descended, and he kissed her once more, before putting kisses down her throat and then lower, his tongue playing fully around a swollen nipple, gently pulling the tight tip between his teeth to suckle it. After that, he kissed her again.

Anna's back rounded in a helpless response as a frenzied excitement ripped through her body like a freight train. It had been much too long since she had been in the embrace of a man — in this man's arms — since she had experienced the wonderful sensation of being sexually aroused, and David had completely captivated and beguiled her. Her fingers combed involuntary through the silky black hair as she pulled him closer to her aching breasts. One of her little hands slid inside the open neck of his shirt and clung to his wide shoulder, while the other curled around the nape of his neck.

Anna's eyes began to droop in helpless response to his masterful touch, and she gave herself up entirely so that she might take pleasure in the beautiful feelings that were permeating every part of her body. She was confused because she could feel his hand on her tummy, but she had no clue when he had unzipped her pants. But she didn't care when his long fingers slid beneath her lace panties to caress the mountain of her sex. She was completely ecstatic about the sensation.

David lifted his head, his hot stare blazing over her almost naked body as he watched her. She was everything he remembered and so much more, and his own need threatened to erupt as he watched her lovely face flush with excitement and her glorious eyes... closed. David let out a low growl from the back of his throat and reared back.

"Open your eyes, Anna," he commanded her in a demanding tone. Her full lashes raised, and she smiled.

She looked up at him with a bright glance that was clouded with longing. He traced the contour of her pouting mouth with a single long finger. Now, please call me by my name.

She said " David " under her breath while frantically attempting to get his shirt off of his shoulders.

"And again," he said, dropping his head and then gently nibbling the peak of first one breast and then the other before going back to capture her lips once more. "And again," he repeated. "And again." He could feel her body spring up beneath him, and he had to be inside of her, hard and quick and right away... "My name Anna!" he demanded once again.

" David," she moaned out loud. " David, don't stop...," she said.

"Good. Very excellent," he grunted between suddenly tightened teeth, and with control beyond that of a human being, he pushed himself to seize her shoulders and shove her back against the sofa so that he could get up.

Anna couldn't help but raise her hand in David's direction as she gazed up at him with eyes glazed over with passion. She could feel the cool air against her breasts, but it was nothing compared to the chill that emanated from the look that passed quickly over her shape as she was reclining.

"But we have to come to a stop because, even though we have established that you say my name with such eagerness, you will never again confuse me with your husband or any other man," David said scornfully. His dark brown eyes scowled at her.

Chapter 13

A nna felt a chill down her spine as she listened to the unyielding tone in his voice. It appeared like something had gone wrong. She moved into a sitting position without thinking about it at all. His reply, which he delivered in a silky voice, was like a bucket of icy water dumped over Anna's hot senses. He reached out and stroked a few tendrils of hair off her brow before continuing.

"And, beautiful and wanton as you are," he said.

"I have no intention of making love to you in this shrine to your dead husband."

"Anna, the next time we make love, it will be at a location and at a time that I choose," he said.

She couldn't bring herself to accept the reality that her thoughts were painting for her, so she just kept staring at his expressionless face. She was able to see the glint of cynical victory in his chocolate brown eyes and the dark yearning in his enlarged pupils, and as a result, she turned her head away from him. He had purposefully made love to her for no other reason than to appease his colossal ego, and he had done it repeatedly. How could she have been so oblivious to the obvious?

Her body wrestled between two opposing emotions: want and hate. Her shattered eyes finally settled on the photo of Allen that was propped up on the sofa on the other side of the room, and it gave her the will to carry on. She inhaled deeply with a trembling sound in her chest, and then another breath. She wouldn't give David the satisfaction of knowing how easily he could reduce her to the wanton she had been labeled; she wouldn't let him know how easily he could degrade her. Instead, she would beat him in the game he was best at.

She slipped off the sofa while forcibly smiling through her puffy lips and said, "Nice thought." She reached for her top and said, "You're correct."

She pulled her top over her head and brushed it over her breasts, taking her time to recover some sort of control before looking up at him.

"This isn't the place." If only she hadn't been wracked with such intense guilt, and she could have chuckled at the look of astonishment on his face even though she was upset. He had not anticipated that she would share his viewpoint.

"Thank you for reminding me, and speaking of time, it's about time you left," she said.

She mustered up every ounce of willpower she could find and strolled towards the door. She had moved about three paces up the hall when David caught up with her. Likewise, she gathered every shred of willpower she could find. Taking her by the arm, he turned her around so that she was looking at him. His discerning eyes had a questioning light.

"All of a sudden, you are acting in a very reasonable manner."

"I mean, why not?" Anna shrugged her shoulders nonchalantly and pushed his hand off of her arm before casually unlocking the front door.

She reached the end of the little garden path and stepped out onto the street in a matter of seconds, and when she turned around, she saw that he was standing immediately behind her. She bravely stared him in the eye, even though she was shivering on the inside from embarrassment and anger.

"After all, you and I are both aware that it will never work," she said.

"Because you're not capable of lovemaking," she said in a low voice.

"Not Capable!" David echoed, completely dumbfounded.

"Whatever it was that gave you that suggestion?" He responded to his inquiry by saying, "Don't tell me you are frustrated because I did not continue?"

Why did this lady feel the need to disparage his sexual prowess when she knew fully well that she was putty in his arms any time he chose? Exasperated, he gave a frustrated shake of the head. Anna was the most frustrating woman he had ever talked to in his life. When he understood, without arrogance, that he could select from dozens of other women who were far more accommodating, he didn't need someone like her in his well-ordered life. He didn't need her at all. And the most perplexing part, How the heck did she get him out onto the sidewalk?

Anna saw him go rigid with anger, but she didn't give a damn about it. It was high time that the conceited demon was confronted with some simple realities.

She voiced her position directly, "No, it's not frustration talking; it's just the simple truth." "According to all accounts, you don't make love; rather, you have sex, and a lot of it, with numerous women.

"However, given your enormous fortune, I think such a sort of thing is to be anticipated."

"To give you your due, you do appear to know all the right buttons to press," she proclaimed with an expressionless smile, adding, "But you do lack a lot in the sensitivity stakes." In her final statement, she said, "And since I have known real love, I'm never going to settle for anything less." She did not attempt to conceal the complete disdain that was conveyed in her tone.

David needed to seize hold of her by the shoulders and shake her so hard that she would be rattling her teeth. He was enraged by the scathing analysis of his persona, even if a portion of his hatred was directed at himself for the fact that he could not completely refute what Anna had said. He was furious. Likewise, he pulled in a long, sharp breath as he struggled to keep his fury under control.

He smirked in an irritated manner as he said, "You say that now, Anna, but never is a very long time."

"And it's possible that you won't have a choice."

"One always has a choice," Anna stated, and she nearly added, 'and I would never pick you.' But as she glanced up at him, she saw the menace in his eyes, in the massive figure that was looming over her, and she stopped her tongue as a sliver of dread raced down her spine.

"One always has a choice," Anna stated.

"And I would never choose you."

"True... But sometimes the choice is not between good and bad, right and wrong." His eyes held hers, illuminating the sparkling depths with a light that was both cunning and frightening. "As you will undoubtedly discover, the choice is frequently between the lesser of two evils."

Anna watched as David removed his jacket, and with one final look of disdain in her direction, he turned on his heel and went away. Anna felt insulted. She watched as he entered a sleek black automobile that was parked only a few meters away along the sidewalk. He never once turned around to look at her.

She let out a sigh that was dragged out and drawn out. David was no longer there, thank God. She had finally gotten rid of the man, and she ought to have felt glad about the situation. Instead, when she went back into the home, the only thing she could feel was a lingering sensation of dread, and the last thing she could see was the scornful expression on his face as he departed. What exactly did he mean when he said that she might not have a choice?

After cleaning up the living room and preparing a refreshing cup of tea half an hour later, Anna sat down on the couch to enjoy the revitalizing beverage before continuing with her day. She looked around the room at all the familiar furnishings and portraits, everything that made the room her sanctuary, but for some strange reason, it did not give her the same sense of peace that it normally did. It appeared as though the fact that David Miller was an outsider who had thrown off her peace. A nagging dread came over her.

Chapter 14

She was a Haengsu wearing the red silk hanbok and cowers in the darkness of her closet. Her delicate hands clutch the folds of her vibrant garment as she tries to silence her breathing. It was nearly midnight. The room was dark.

Outside the closet, the room echoes with the deep, commanding voice of the enigmatic and persistently pursuing Prince. His presence exudes power, a stark contrast to the refined beauty of the Kisaeng house.

He was calling through the door, "Where are you hiding?"

"You cannot escape me."

"You cannot deny the inevitable." His voice was playful.

She presses herself deeper into the shadows, fear, and determination etched on her face. She knows the reputation of the notorious prince, a black sheep among the monarchy, relentless in his pursuits.

Just a moment ago, she was doing her duty. Amidst a mesmerizing performance, her captivating voice and graceful movements draw the attention of the crowd. Among them, he watches intently, his gaze fixated on her.

In the dimly lit performance chamber of the Kisaeng house, the air hums with anticipation. She, of unmatched grace and talent, steps onto the stage in a resplendent red hanbok that glimmers under the soft glow of lanterns.

Her movements are poetry in motion, each step deliberate and yet seemingly effortless. The melodic strains of traditional Korean music fill the room as she begins her dance, her body swaying like a gentle breeze, telling a story with every graceful gesture.

Her arms arc and flow, painting invisible pictures in the air. The intricate embroidery of her hanbok catches the light as she twirls, the fabric billowing around her like a whirlwind of colors. With each turn, she transports the audience to a world of ethereal beauty and emotion.

Her dance is a tapestry of emotions—joy, sorrow, longing—all conveyed through the fluidity of her movements. She weaves through the space, her feet tapping rhythmically against the wooden floor, a mesmerizing display of precision and elegance.

As the music reaches its crescendo, her final pose is a breathtaking tableau, her poise, and expression capturing the essence of the story she's told through her dance. The audience sits in stunned silence, moved by the sheer artistry and emotion conveyed by her performance.

In that fleeting moment, she embodies not just a dancer, but a storyteller, her dance an enchanting narrative that lingers in the hearts of those fortunate enough to witness it.

And now she was hiding, "I am a Haengsu, a singer, a dancer. Not a mere plaything for the likes of him." She said to herself quietly.

The door creaks open slightly, casting a sliver of light across the room. She clenches her jaw, steeling herself against the prince's relentless advances.

Without yielding, she remains hidden, refusing to succumb to the pressure, determined to protect her dignity, her art, against the intrusion of the powerful but insistent prince.

The tension hangs thick in the air, she holds her breath and covers her mouth so afraid that he might hear even her breath.

Her breaths quicken, her heart pounding against her chest, as beads of sweat trickle down her brow, a silent testament to her desperation. Her slender fingers clutch the fabric tightly, yearning for invisibility within the confining darkness of the closet.

'Please, let me disappear.' She said in an earnest whisper.

The weight of her existence presses heavily upon her, memories of a tumultuous past flooding her thoughts.

She saw herself as a young girl, innocence in her eyes, torn from familial warmth, as her PARENTS, burdened by debt, handed her over to the Kisaeng house. The doors close behind her, sealing her fate within its lavish walls.

Now a woman forged by hardship had honed her talents relentlessly, striving to become the pinnacle entertainer of the house. But the prince's unwelcome advances were a chilling reminder of the perilous path her life had taken.

I trained to be a beacon of artistry, not a pawn in their games. She thought bitterly.

Her chest rises and falls with each panicked breath, a silent prayer escaping her lips, pleading for sanctuary from the relentless demands of her existence.

Outside the closet, the prince's voice grows distant, his footsteps echoing away. Relief floods her features, but the weight of her reality remains, a constant reminder of the sacrifices made for survival in a world where the power plays of the elite overshadow her artistry.

She quietly got out of her hiding place and locked the door of her room. Then she lays on her bed grateful that the prince was gone. She had closed her eyes and all of a sudden someone had pinned her to the bed.

"You think I'm gone," he said silkily.

"You are the most beautiful woman I have ever seen,"

She heard him breathe heavily in her ear. She tried to scream underneath him, but he put her hand to her mouth. His strength overpowered her and the more she struggled, the more he tightened his grip.

"There is no need to be afraid, my princess, I will take you away from this hellhole." He soothingly whispered in her ears.

"No one can ever touch you but me" He softly said as his other hand slowly made its way under her hanbok and into the folds between her thighs.

His finger gently caresses her there. He was sending delicious sensations to her. She can't explain what she is feeling right now, but it's entirely new to her. She stopped moving and was confused at what he was doing to her, but it felt so good. He softly circles his finger to her moist center while she gasped uncontrollably.

He lingered there, teasing her sensitive flesh until every nerve in her body tautened to breaking point. The handsome prince kissed her mouth as she lay there beneath him, still processing the erotic desires, he had awakened in her. He played his tongue inside her mouth, tasting her. Then he opened her hanbok and suckled her nipple, her back arched, and she moaned out loud.

"Oh my God!" Anna wakes up from her dream. She was frowning deeply. "Even in my dreams, David Miller bothers me," she said in annoyance. "I have to stop watching Korean drama series," she said while gripping a pillow in frustration.

Chapter 15

No, she was simply being imaginative about it! It was just a dream. Taking the remote control for the television in her hand, she navigated to the History Channel and did her best to pay attention to the fascinating documentary that was playing on the screen.

She gave up after 10 minutes and began to aimlessly roam about the room, caressing her cherished keepsakes, while continuing to have apprehension. What she needed was first a soothing bath, and then sleep. At five in the morning on the next day, it was her responsibility to go to the flower market.

One hour later, she tried to sleep again on the bed that she and Allen had shared, but she was unable to do so. She became restless and eventually rolled over onto her back, where she stared blankly at the ceiling. She was lying flat. When she moved a finger to her lips, which were slightly swollen, the memory of David's kiss came to her mind, much to her embarrassment. Her mind was racing with disorganized pictures of the times they had previously interacted with one another.

Her horror at seeing David's darkly handsome face the night before at the party was overlaid by a clear mental memory of his wonderful nude body as he knelt between her legs on another bed in another country. She was in South Korea at the time. She heaved a sigh, rolled over, and buried her head in the pillow as she attempted to move her mind away from the painful recollections that were washing over her. However, it was of no use. David Miller represents the troubled history that had resurfaced to torment her in this present day.

When she thought about him now, she realized that their meeting had been the result of a strange chance of fate. David and she had been drawn together because of this accident. The loss of her husband a year earlier, the impending death of her much-loved aunt, her dissatisfaction with her wedding ring, and then the ultimate blow. When those jerks knocked over a wine bottle and spilled it all over her, all contributed to her mental breakdown.

Amid her predicament, she had turned a teary eye to the person who had come to her aid. Because she had wished so much for it to be her husband, she had thought that his blue eyes were the ones that had smiled back at her.

After some time had passed, David had led her to a lavish cabin and, after removing a silk robe from a closet, he had laid it out on the bed with the instructions, "Strip out of your soiled clothes and have a shower, use the robe."

"I will be coming later to pick up your clothes and get them cleaned for you by someone else."

Automatically, Anna's answer was "yes."

After ten minutes, she emerged from the shower room and returned to the cabin, this time wearing nothing more than a pair of black lace underwear and carrying her soiled clothing in one hand. She had just begun to reach for the robe that was hanging over the bed when she heard a tap on the door and David entered the room.

He had muttered something in Korean that she had not understood, but the mesmerizing power of his gaze had appeared to paralyze her. As he had advanced towards her, he cupped her chin in one slim hand and spoke almost reverently.

"You are very beautiful." She did not even flinch when he called her Hana.

Considering it at the moment. Anna only realized in retrospect that at the time, she had been experiencing a state of shock. Allen was the only male who had ever seen her in such a nearly exposed state and was the only man who had ever addressed her as Hana or complimented her on her beauty.

Therefore, it should not have come as a surprise that she had responded when David had kissed her with a searing sweetness and compassion. Anna moaned aloud as she tossed and turned in bed, unable to get comfortable. No matter how hard she tried to reject it, what transpired next with David was very different from what she had experienced with her husband. She did her best to deny it.

David's hands had massaged her body and sculpted her breasts, and his tongue had plunged between her opened lips, kindling a consuming heat that had sent shock waves smashing through her body. She had been standing there shaking furiously with her dark chocolate eyes wandering in helpless curiosity over his wonderful figure when he eventually broke the kiss to quickly remove his clothes from his body. Before she had a chance to gather her faculties, he had picked her up in his arms and lowered her to the bed while murmuring endearments in a low voice.

After the second brush of his mouth on hers, the passion between them had burst out. In a flurry of kisses and caresses, David had made love to her with a wildly sexual and intense desire, to which she had mindlessly responded.

This had all happened amid a frenzy. She had shut her eyes to the outside world, and for a little moment, the man whose arms had enfolded her and whose body sought hers was the only thing that existed in her universe. They had brushed up against one another and shared tastes in a frenzy of desire that had ultimately come to a glorious conclusion.

The climax left them both drenched in perspiration, completely satisfied, and unable to take a breath.

It was too much for Anna to think about that night right now, so she snuck out of bed and tiptoed downstairs to the kitchen to prepare a cup of hot milk. She had given up all the prospect of falling asleep, and she was just going to have to think about it.

She reassured herself that everything would appear more positively in the morning. After she had insulted him in that manner, David Miller had left, and it was quite unlikely that he would ever return. 'He was Annet's boyfriend, what was the worst thing that could happen?'

Chapter 16

Anna hobbled into the landscaping shop while lugging the final box of plants from the trunk of her car. When she finally set the box down inside the shop, she let out a sigh of relief. Even though she enjoyed going to the Plant market and picking out different varieties of plants, she did not mind getting up at the crack of morning.

Anna congratulated herself on a job well done before making her way to a bench equipped with two sinks, a kettle, and some much-needed coffee.

Because she had only had a few hours of sleep the night before, she had little trouble getting started this morning, but it was starting to catch up to her now. It was a blessing that she was able to sit down at the desk and take a revitalizing sip of coffee. In the bright daylight, everything had a considerably more favorable appearance.

She had her own company, her friends, her own house, and a tiny garden. After a terrible weekend, she was back to normal, and David Miller was no longer a part of her life for good.

After she had finished her drink, she stood up and immediately began unpacking the items that she had just acquired. Some of them she placed inside the shop, while others she put on shelves that were lined along one side of the room.

Anna had already altered the window display by the time Sara arrived at nine in the morning, and the shop was already open for business.

Sara remarked, "The place looks great," before crossing over to Anna, who was standing behind the counter propping it up.

"But you look terrible," she said.

Anna shouted back, "Thanks so much."

She tried to make Sara laugh in the hopes of distracting her from the inquiries that were inevitably going to follow.

"I know that I told you that it was time for you to begin to live a little bit, but you look as if you have burned the candle at both ends and eaten the center!"

"That must have been one heck of a birthday party," Sara giggled as she thought about it.

"Come on, spill the beans. It's the only way that this stressed-out mother can experience excitement these days."

Anna knew that Sara cherished her relationship with her husband, Mark, and her son, John, who was two years old. She also knew that Sara wouldn't trade her lifestyle for anything in the world, and she grinned in response.

"You're a liar, and there's nothing to be discovered about it."

"I left early, at around 10 in the morning, and it was the typical crowd that Dad and Jeanne attract." The end of the narrative.

"You're not going to get away with that by any means! At the very least, describe Annet's new boyfriend's appearance to me. Who is he, and how many women have he slept with? Or a significant possibility of marriage?" Sara asked with a sly smile.

"Is he young and fit, or elderly and chubby? Knowing Annet's situation makes the money a certainty."

Anna was well aware that Sara wouldn't be satisfied until she got the whole story, but on this particular occasion, she had no intention of providing Sara with all of the details...

"I would assume that he is in his mid to late thirties; he is tall, black, and not particularly ugly. As far as becoming a potential spouse goes, I have my doubts about that. I got the impression that he was interested in more than one lady. But Annet is undeniably head over heels in love, and he is loaded with cash."

"And what is his name...?' Sara asked.

She didn't want to look too confident, since Sara had a nose like a bloodhound when it came to searching out secrets. " David something—Miller, I think," Anna said.

"Oh, my goodness!" Sara yelled, "I can't believe it!" as she heard the news.

"You've met David Miller, right? He's the Korean international banker, right?"

"Anna, are you blind? That guy is drop-dead gorgeous with a killer body. But you are right about the womanizing."

"I've seen his pictures published in the most prestigious publications hundreds of times, and it's almost always with a beautiful woman on his arm."

"Because he is not the sort of person who would be interested in settling down, I seriously doubt that Annet will be successful in getting him to the altar."

"But, hey—" Sara grinned.

"Annet's still a very happy girl to receive a man like him in her bed for her birthday. She deserves all the luck she can get. I don't mind having him around as a present for the evening." Sara smiled mischievously.

Anna grinned on the outside, but on the inside, she was nauseous.

" Sara, you should be ashamed of yourself—especially since you're a married woman," she said.

What was the deal with Sara and seemingly the whole of the world knowing who David Miller was? She foolishly got into bed with him even though she didn't even know him. On the other hand, on the bright side, given what Sara had just told her, she did not need to be concerned about David Miller trying to find her.

Anna would never have to worry about being bothered by such a man again because he was unquestionably gorgeous, immensely wealthy, and had a world full of adoring ladies from which to choose.

"I dare to dream, don't you think?" Saying that with a malicious gleam in her black eyes.

"Dreaming will not get the dozen or so orders that we have completed," Anna uttered with a sarcastic tone, "to deliver before noon."

"Okay, okay," Sara said in agreement.

Sara scowled as she said, "It seems like you could use some assistance."

"Are you positive that everything is going to be, okay?"

"Yes, it will do." She stated while shrugging.

"But I drove down to Fullerton and back yesterday, and then with the early start this morning..."

"Stop talking about it. That clarifies everything—you went to see Allen's parents as well as his tomb," Sara said as she wrapped her arm around Anna and gave her a comforting embrace.

A week passed and today was her father's birthday. She exhaled a sigh of contentment as she did so. She had just spent the previous hour in a meeting with the buying manager of an upscale department store located on Beverly Hills and as a result, she had successfully negotiated a contract to supply the plant displays for the establishment, with the proviso that Sara examines the fine print.

She could easily see Anna and Sara Designs receiving much larger contracts, but it would require a greater focus from Gerald on the gardener side of the business, and they would need to hire a van driver on a full-time basis. The contract included their maintenance of the plants.

Anna's day at the office was going wonderfully, and she was looking forward to having lunch alone with her dad. As part of the birthday present, she had planned for him, she had reserved a table at a prestigious restaurant, and she was going to pick him up at noon.

She would be required to make an appearance at the party that Jeanne had planned for tonight, but she wasn't concerned about it because she knew that no one would notice if she left the party early.

As she pulled into the parking spot in Beverly Hills and looked up at the imposing façade of the home, she gritted her teeth and made a face. As far as she was concerned, Annet's birthday celebration that took place at this location over two months ago was a fiasco, but she had put that experience in the past at this point.

Since then, she hadn't seen Annet, but it wasn't all that unusual, and Anna made sure to stay in touch with the family by calling them often.

She pushed the memories of the past to the back of her mind and got out of the car. She brushed the fabric of the slim-fitting skirt down over her hips and adjusted the lapels of the short-sleeved cream silk jacket that fit precisely over her shoulders and nipped in at her thin waist.

The jacket had short sleeves and was made of silk. She did not dress up very frequently since she preferred wearing casual clothing, but over the years she had accumulated a collection of classic garments to wear on special occasions such as the one we are having today. She was brimming with self-assurance since she thought she looked nice, and she raced lightly up the stone stairs to the front door while holding her handbag in her hand.

She unlocked the door for herself and strolled down the corridor, her stiletto heels making a lively clicking sound on the marble-tiled floor. She met the housekeeper, who was standing at the bottom of the stairs with an empty tray in her hands.

"Good morning, Lucy," she said to the housekeeper.

"Where exactly is Dad? Is he still in his study?" She inquired, and in response, she was given the most peculiar expression.

"Yes. I mean he is waiting for you in the drawing room, which is located upstairs."

Anna caught a glimpse of the time on her wristwatch and saw that it was just eleven-thirty.

"What do you think of the fact that Dad is early for a change?"

"I find it hard to believe Lucy, do you think that the number sixty is starting to get to him?"

Lucy did not return Anna's grin when she offered it to her.

"Don't bother asking me. I am merely employed here," she said, before leaving her.

'What has gotten under her skin?' As Anna climbed the stairs and opened the door to the drawing room, she couldn't help but be curious. Lucy had a reputation for being the friendliest of women.

Her dad was drinking coffee while relaxing in his favorite high-backed chair, which was situated on one side of the elaborate fireplace. Anna beamed as she walked up to her father.

"Happy birthday!" She took a few steps in his approach.

"Thank you," He mumbled the word before offering her a feeble grin in return and then looking away from her.

Anna thought it wasn't exactly the most enthusiastic greeting she'd ever received when she suddenly halted, the hair on the back of her neck standing on edge. She cast a wary glance around the room and saw that they were not the only ones there...

The man was positioned such that he was facing her, his back against the rising dawn's silhouetted backdrop. Even though she couldn't get a good look at his face, she didn't feel the need to. It turned out to be David Miller. Her chest puffed out, and the shock widened the pupils of her dark chocolate eyes to their maximum capacity.

Chapter 17

"Good morning, Anna," someone said.

She stutteringly greeted him with "G...G... Good morning" and simply stood there staring as he approached her. His attire consisted of a charcoal-gray fitted business suit, a white shirt, and a blue tie. Even though he had grown his hair out since the last time she had seen him, he was still the same darkly attractive and haughty man she recalled. She sincerely hoped that she hadn't.

He grinned and remarked, "It's a pleasure to meet you again," which he stated in a smooth tone.

When she looked up, he met her gaze with eyes that did not exhibit the slightest sign of humor; rather, they displayed a ruthless focus that triggered an alarm in her mind. She quickly averted her gaze. Her self-assurance took a fall, and she had the distinct impression that David posed a threat to her mental well-being.

Anna sent an anxious glance in the direction of her father, but he was fixated on his coffee cup as if his existence relied on it, so he was of no use. There was a significant problem with...

She was not telling the truth; rather, she was allowing her imagination to run wild. David posed no threat to her in any way. She was quick to remind herself that he was Annet's boyfriend. She had always known that she might see him again in that position, and now that it had happened, she didn't find it particularly surprising. After regaining her self-assurance, she broke the growing stillness that had ensued. "It's great to see you once more, David. 'But I'm bringing my father out to lunch so we won't have time to stop and speak,' she replied with a cheerful tone of voice. But please do have a seat and make yourself at home; I'm sure Annet won't be here for long.' She was so pleased with the calm and collected manner in which she had dealt with the matter that she failed to see the gaze that was exchanged between the two men.

"So, you are keeping it a secret from Anna, Williams? Anna turned her head to look at David as she heard the sound of her name. He had a look of utter revulsion on his face as he continued to stare at her father. You haven't informed her, have you?'

You just told me what?" Anna questioned, completely perplexed.

It's not that I don't want to see Annet. "I am here to see you—among other things," David said by way of explanation before shifting his focus back to her father. "I am here to see you," David emphasized. "Well, Williams, have you?'

"I just didn't have it in me, David. I already told you. Anna has no idea what's going on in the company, and even if she did, she wouldn't comprehend it.

"What is it that I wouldn't comprehend?' What are you talking about?' she questioned, turning her perplexed eyes to her father in anger and disbelief at the casual manner in which he had insulted her intelligence in front of David.

"I think it would be best if you sat down, Anna," David said as he wrapped his hand around her forearm. Anna was so startled by his contact that she almost sprang out of her skin.

'No! She made an effort to get away from him, but he tightened his grasp on her, and rather than engage in an embarrassing battle in front of her father, she let him guide her to the sofa that was facing the fireplace.

"Sit down," was the instruction that he issued. He whispered into her ear, "Because believe me, Anna, you're going to need to," and he was so near that she could feel the warmth of his breath against her skin.

'Dad?' She pleaded with her father to help her. "What exactly is happening?

"Do as David say and sit down; I have something to tell you," Her father instructed her, and she obliged, falling onto the sofa with an icy sensation of dread penetrating her body. And the fact that David slid his big length down alongside her didn't help matters at all.

Her father said, "You know I love you, Anna," as he looked at his daughter. "And even if I did, I would never intentionally hurt you in any way." But over the previous few years, I have, regrettably, made a few poor decisions about my business. The firm does not generate a profit anymore, and...

She listened to what her father had to say with growing terror in her heart, and when he had finished, she gazed at him with a pale face. Not only did it appear that he had made a few poor choices, but it also appeared that he had been borrowing money from the company for many years. In addition, ever since the company was listed on the New York Stock exchange and began to acquire owners from outside the family, those same individuals have questioned the company's accounting practices. A local independent accounting company was chosen for the job. Her father had thought that he would be able to repay the debts gradually over time, but that opportunity had passed. He stated that the purpose of the most recent public float was not actually to expand in the United States but rather to fill the hole in the company's accounting.

"I have no idea why you have done such a terrible thing. What were you thinking, Dad?", she inquired while furiously scanning the area surrounding her.

And she was aware of the response. Jeanne had exceptionally refined tastes, as evidenced by the fact that she purchased this property. She was also aware that her father had provided the financial support necessary for the establishment of Annet's modeling agency the previous year. Anna didn't mind, but she had no idea that the money was stolen from the company. She thought it was just normal spending money. Her only response was a phony chuckle.

There is no need for you to feel unhappy, Anna. Her father spoke to her in a reassuring tone, " David has something to say to you, and it may be the perfect solution." David was present at the moment. Anna snarled at David, "Just a minute," while casting a venomous look in his direction. "This is completely unrelated to you in any way. You have no right to be in this place at all."

"It's lucky for you I am," he drawled sarcastically, and Anna saw in the shadows of his dark brown eyes an awful sparkle that looked strangely like a triumph. "Unless, of course, you want your father to end up in jail for fraud," He said sarcastically.

Chapter 18

'Jail!' She stared at her father in complete disbelief, fully anticipating that he would refute David's ridiculous remark. She pleaded with him to dispel the notion that it was even conceivable.

Her father mumbled an apology before rising to his feet and leaving the room. He was no longer the energetic guy with blue eyes that she adored; rather, he was a weary old man who looked every one of his sixty years plus ten more years than he was. His shoulders were sagged, his eyes were dim, and his face was pale and weathered. She was aware that David was being honest with her. Her father lowered his arm and placed a comforting hand on her shoulder, and she instinctively reached up to cover it with her own.

He was exhausted when he remarked to Anna, "I never meant for this to happen."

"If it's okay with you, I won't go to lunch with you," her father said weakly. Take David with you instead; he will be able to explain what has occurred far better than I can. If you and David can agree, there may be a way for all of us to escape this situation. Oh, I pray that it is. Because I fear telling Jeanne what has occurred if you are unable to.' Patting her on the head, he said, 'I'll see you tonight at the party.'

Suddenly, the gravity of the situation registered in her mind for the first time. There was a possibility that her father would go to jail for fraud, and he wanted her cooperation to prevent this from occurring. It was incomprehensible to me. It rankled more than a little on him that he was allowed to involve her yet he was not allowed to notify his wife about the situation. She was in desperate need of responses from her father, who was hurriedly making his way towards the exit.

She stood up to follow him, but a powerful hand wrapped around her wrist and jolted her to a halt as it did so. She was unable to continue following him. Amazingly, she had forgotten David was there for a few minutes, but as his fingertips brushed across her flesh, sending a tingling sensation up the length of her arm, she was immediately brought back to the present.

In a sardonic tone, he said that her father was "some piece of work" before getting to his feet and restraining her by putting his arm around her waist instead of continuing to hold her wrist. Anna screamed, "No one asked for your opinion," and then attempted to extricate herself from the hold. "Leave me alone! She gave him an angry look as she did so, and he responded by tightening his hold on her.

"So, you can go after your father and question him about things that he is not in a position to answer?'" He growled, a cynical crease appearing on one of his black brows. "That's not my impression at all."

You may as well ask, "What the hell does it have to do with you?" Anna let out a sob. She had had enough; she was frustrated and perplexed, and the sooner she could get away from David's authoritative presence, the better it would be for her. She had had enough.

He informed her in a sarcastic tone, with a wolfish smile that was not a smile at all, curling his hard lips, that she was also a stakeholder in Posh Naturals. Because Anna had been preoccupied with the precarious predicament her father was in, she had not given any attention to the stockholders who were involved; nevertheless, she did so now, and she shouted, "Oh, my God!" I can't believe how much money your granddad blew!'

Don't be concerned about Bryan because he hasn't lost anything. I acquired his shares from him two months ago, you should be concerned about me rather than him. You are aware that your father said, "Take me to lunch, and I will tell you everything."

As the entire significance of his words dawned on Anna's astounded mind, her eyes widened in disbelief. "You... Then everything falls on your shoulders!" she exploded in the room.

'No. David drew attention to the fact that your father had made the disgraceful decision to steal in the first place. But when he saw the worried look on her beautiful face and the worry that her wonderful eyes could not quite conceal, he had an immediate need to shield her from harm. He felt it was his responsibility. There was no way in hell that her father had. He was certain that Anna did not understand the extent to which her father had betrayed the family, but for a fleeting moment, he questioned the strategy that he meant to implement moving forward.

Anna said angrily, "My father is not a thief; the only contemptible person around here is you," as she attempted to distance herself from the accusation. Shackled by the curve of his arm, with the muscular length of his thigh hard against her and the warmth of his big body enveloping her. She discovered the light silk suit she wore suddenly seemed to take on the consistency of wool as heat surged through her and she panicked. "It would make much more sense if it were you being accused of stealing." She twisted to get away from him, but to her surprise, she didn't have to make much of an effort since David let her go and moved backward.

Any uncertainty that David had dissipated in the face of her insults. This woman has had more than enough taken from her by him. As his eyes swept over her, a glimmer of unyielding resolve could be seen in them.

Her black gorgeous hair was pulled back into a messy bun on the crown of her head, with a few wayward strands framing the features of her face. She was wearing a fitting jacket that displayed the creamy contours of her breasts and accentuated her tiny waist. She was also wearing a straight skirt that adhered to the delicate curve of her hips and ended a few inches above her knees. Oh my God! He desired her, and he intended to get his hands on her.

"In all my years, I've never been caught stealing." But I'll forget you said that, Anna, because I know this was a bit of a surprise for you.'

She was gazing at him as if he were something the cat had brought in, but he could tell that below it she was perplexed by what she was seeing. I propose that we have lunch together if you are serious about preventing disaster for both your father and his business. When I've had something to satisfy my appetite, I tend to be more giving, but right now I'm starving. But the decision is yours...'

Anna's thoughts reverberated with a hollow sound whenever the word choice was used. The parting remark that David had said to her the last time they had seen each other came back to haunt her. She had sensed the menace in his comments at the time, but she had written it off as the product of her hyperactive imagination. However, now that she was staring at him, she realized that she had been correct to be fearful of him.

When David was looking at her, he had a stern and defiant sparkle in his eyes, and this caused her heart to sink like a rock. In what way did she have a choice? Her father had instructed her to pay attention to what David had to say...

She brushed her sweaty fingers down her thighs while saying, "I'm not hungry." "And I have no intention of sitting in a public restaurant with you and discussing my family business where anyone can overhear the conversation." However, I am willing to hear what you say, and I figure this is as good a place as any other to do so.' She proceeded to sit down, unsure of how long her legs would be able to support her.

David took a step closer and wrapped his strong arm around her shoulders as he glared at her with his dark eyes. She became rigid, and every self-protective instinct she possessed told her to flee now, while she still had a chance, but the picture of her father's weary face prevented her from doing so.

"I understand your concern," he teased mockingly, his dark chocolate eyes grabbing hers and staring into her soul cruelly. "I understand," he mocked. "However, I am starving, and I am aware of a location where one can eat in complete seclusion while still enjoying delicious food." Should we get going?'

Chapter 19

Because of this, half an hour later, Anna was in David's high-end Los Angeles apartment. She was sitting on a black hide sofa with a glass of white wine in her hand and watching in disbelief as David placed a variety of cartons on the coffee table and whipped off the lids of the containers. It wasn't until they had driven away from Hollywood Boulevard that he placed the order on the food app, and it was only then that she realized she had made yet another mistake.

He spoke to her in a monotone voice, saying, "I hope you like Japanese food" as he handed her a bowl and a pair of chopsticks. She accepted the bowl, too astonished to do anything else, and when he forked some rice and salt-and-pepper prawns into it, she found herself eating a couple of them. She had taken the dish because she was too stunned to do anything else.

However, even though her nerves were on edge, she turned down all of his offers of more. Instead, she focused her attention on observing the flat through the dense veil of her eyelids while pondering how she could have let herself be misled into coming here. And what an apartment it was—completely white, black, and made of steel. There was a wall of glass that served as the window, although it had no curtains. A recessed lounge room that is furnished with black hide chairs and a table made of glass.

A cutting-edge media system was controlled by a microcomputer that was built into the armrest of one of the seats. The house was devoid of any color and any indication that it had ever been inhabited. It had a big smart TV installed on a white wall, an ebony cabinet, black lamps, and a couple of large modern sculptures made of bronze that were strategically positioned on the polished wood floor.

It was the epitome of all that a bachelor pad could be.

But Anna was not shocked because David Miller was not the sort to act as a homebody. Once she had collected herself sufficiently to think about what had occurred, she started to feel a little bit better.

She had been informed that confirmation had been granted the previous month when she had been called to her aunt Martha's solicitor. She was told that she now officially owned thirty percent of Posh Naturals as well as the property on Jeju Island. Not only that, but she had already called the man on the island who was in charge of looking after the house. She had made plans to come to the island on the third weekend of April to determine what kinds of improvements were required.

Anna's lifestyle was pretty comfortable thanks to the profits from the landscaping business, plus she had money from the life insurance policy that Allen had. She wanted to further finance her company, Anna and Sara Designs. It appeared as though she would never receive a dividend from the shares that she now owned in Posh Naturals; yet, she was a large shareholder, and that must be the reason why she was treated with such respect.

Her father had informed her that he required her approval of David's plan to save their company. Anna would have some influence in whether the firm was wound up or not, even though it was obvious that David wanted to retrieve the money he had lost by purchasing Bryan's shares from him.

"Do you want some more wine?" David dared to interrupt her train of thinking by giving her the bottle, and in her haste, she hurriedly put her hand over her glass. It was the alcohol that had initially gotten her into trouble with David, and she was determined not to make the same mistake twice.

"No, thank you. Do you agree with me that it's high time we got down to the serious matter at hand?"

She continued bravely, "Correct me if I am wrong, but it appears that, as I'm a major shareholder, you need my agreement to any plan to wind up my father's company, and you also can't decide what happens to him without my approval." After all, that is the reason why she was here.

David leaned back against the sofa and relaxed, a glimmer of a smile playing about his mouth as he did so.

"You're not exactly wrong," he said after a deliberate pause in the conversation. Anna let out a muffled sigh of relief after David told her, "You are the major shareholder, and as such, stand to lose the most, and legally nothing can be done without your agreement."

David continued, "Unfortunately for you, your father's problems go back a long way."

Anna's relief was short-lived as David said.

"According to the information that I have, your father served as the trustee of the ten percent part that your mother bequeathed to you until you reached the age of eighteen."

"Then, along with your aunt and your father, you became a partner in the business. For the subsequent four years, up until the time when you handed your mother's shares back to your father, you were personally responsible for the day-to-day operations of the firm, together with the other members of your family."

"You were spared the consequences of some of your father's worst excesses and the flotation on NYSE because you were not a stakeholder at the time."

"However, legally speaking, even though it is highly improbable, both you and your father may be held accountable for the first fraud."

'Me!" Anna shrieked out.

"Are you insane?"

"That cannot be true, I have never been involved in any way with the company!"

"When I got married, Allen and I decided to buy a house together, so I decided to sell the shares that my mother had given to me to my father to help pay for it."

"Before this summer, I had never even attended a board meeting, and the only reason I did so was at my father's insistence because I had inherited Aunt Martha's shares of the company. Whoever told you otherwise is spreading false information."

After getting off the couch, he stated directly, "Your father told me."

"There was nothing else he could do because I recognized your signature from earlier documents," you were told. Fair enough, you were a child, but when your father gave you the accounts and asked you to verify and sign them, didn't you at least look them over before you did either?"

Anna was ashen-faced, she fixed her gaze intently on David as she finally started to comprehend the gravity of the situation. "I never read them—I thought I was simply signing as a witness." "I had no idea what I was signing."

"If it makes any difference, I believe what you say. However, this does not change the reality that the only way to prevent the entire enterprise from failing and the full force of the law from descending on your father. It is for a significant amount of money to be injected into the corporation."

"How much cash are we talking about?"

She questioned in a monotone voice, and he casually offered a number that would have been difficult for her to write down, let alone locate.

She blinked to fight back the tears that were about to fall as she said, "I can sell my house, and in time the villa in Jeju Island, I suppose."

It was inconceivable to her that her father would have implicated her in a criminal act as far back as 10 years ago.

Nevertheless, she was able to recognize that David was telling the truth. More than words could describe, the defeated and guilty look on her father's face, as well as his abrupt escape, which left her at the mercy of David, spoke volumes.

He sat down on the bench next to her and cupped her chin in his palm before turning her face to look at him.

"But I do have a solution; I'm prepared to invest all of the money necessary to get your father out of this mess and make the company viable again, but I want something in return."

Anna said, "I have complete faith that my father will do whatever you ask him to do."

"In general, he is a decent human being; however, there are..."

David concluded for her with a caustic comment, saying, "he had an expensive wife and lifestyle."

"However, I am not interested in your father; rather, it is you, Anna," he said. I would like to get married to you.

Chapter 20

Her initial assumption was that the man had lost all semblance of sanity, but once she caught a glimpse of the steely resolve reflected in the depths of his eyes, she began to have second thoughts.

"We can announce our engagement at the birthday party for your father tonight."

Due to the ridiculous nature of his offer, Anna was jolted out of the cloud of sadness that had been threatening to devour her. She chuckled to herself internally as she pictured Annet's expression.

"Are you out of your mind?", she cried out in shock. "For heaven's sake, you're my sister's boyfriend," Anna said, and all of a sudden, she had the bright idea that would solve the issue entirely.

"Instead of asking me, you ought to address your inquiry to her." I do not doubt that she will seize the opportunity.

His fingers became firmer on her chin as he continued to say, " Annet is nothing more than an old acquaintance."

"I swear I have never known her in the sexual sense—as I have you," he said, his heavy-lidded eyes staring into hers, the sensuous awareness in the shining depths causing heat to rush to her cheeks."

His long fingers slid from her chin to trace up her cheek and curve a thin tendril of hair behind her ear as he added, "So there's no problem there." Internally, she shivered as he said, "Forget about Annet."

"If you want to save your father, marry me." His deep, dark voice grated across her raw nerves, and she darted out her tongue to moisten her suddenly too-dry lips. She noticed the knowing glitter in his eyes as she made a movement that betrayed him. You have a decision to make, and I need it as soon as possible.

It was that word choice once more, and this time she was certain that the threat was real. She had no doubts about it. She wrenched her head away from his grasp and jumped to her feet to escape.

"Why should it be me?" Anna said while glaring at him from below.

"I demand it!" He was lying back against the seat again, completely at rest, while she was standing on quivering legs wondering how a day that had started so beautifully had turned into such a nightmare. He was completely at peace. He was lounging back against the seat again.

"Is that a question that has to be asked?" David chuckled sarcastically as he swept his look over her, pausing for a while to take in the voluptuous curve of her breasts, before moving on to examine her face.

"You're not that naive, Anna, because you've already been married once."

"Exactly," Anna chimed in at this point.

"And I am aware of what the purpose of marriage is. Love is an essential component, but we don't feel love for one another." She didn't even like him!

Anna was unable to submit to his authority because he possessed excessive power, pride, wealth, and affluence. She did, however, keep enough of her senses about her to refrain from further insulting him by letting him know how she felt.

David remarked sarcastically, "Love does not exist; it's just another four-letter word for lust."

He was being sarcastic. "And this has not the slightest bit to do with the idea you said."

"To put it more plainly for you, I will personally pay off the debts owed by Posh Naturals, buy out the lesser owners, remove the company from NYSE, and reform it as a family business in which shares can only be traded between members of the same family. While your father will continue to hold his position at the company, one of my men will be put in charge of ensuring that he will not be able to steal from the business in the future. You are the one who fills the role of the surety because it is obvious that I require something in exchange for the cash. Because I am married to you, I am now considered to be a member of the family legally."

"Without marriage, there won't be any deal."

Anna forced down the ball of dread that had formed in the back of her throat. She mumbled to herself, "But that's the same thing as blackmail..." She gave a little shake of the head to try to clear her mind while her eyes searched his face, looking for any indication that this was all just a really horrible joke.

On the other hand, David's features were so expressionless that he may as well have been presiding over a business conference. And she believed that he probably was. Except for the fact that this time he was buying a marriage — and for a man who had made his wealth trading on any commodity, why would this be any different than what he had done before? She was having a sour notion.

She stated her opinion in a direct manner, "I still don't see what you get out of all this—other than a reluctant wife."

"Then one more. I could give in, and then file for divorce against you in six months; it would make me a great deal wealthier while leaving you in an even worse financial position."

He dared to laugh as he rose to his feet and reached for her, his hands curling possessively over her shoulders. He said, "Nice try, Anna."

"I'm sorry to be the one to break it to you, but it's not quite as easy as that—there is one more requirement."

"I want you to be the mother of my child, and to guarantee that you will comply with my request, I will invest my money in the business gradually over the next three years."

I will give birth to his child? Anna was horrified at the idea. They conjured up a lot of imagery for Anna. Her most pleasant recollections of her mother are the times when the two of them were working in the garden together when she was a child, tending to the plants and flowers under their care. Appreciation for the unbroken flow of life in all of its manifestations was a fundamental component of her character.

And for a fleeting instant, the concept of bearing David's child elicited a fundamental reaction from within her. Anna had desired a child ever since the day she married Allen, but Allen always wanted to wait, and by the time they were ready, it was too late to have a child.

"So, what are you going to do, Anna? Which one is it? "Why are you so reluctant on this?" David said as he moved one hand from her shoulder to the nape of her neck and tilted her face toward his.

"You know we're good together," he said as he bent his black head in preparation to kiss her.

Chapter 21

"**N**o." She hurriedly stepped back, creating some distance between them, while firmly pushing against his chest and saying, "No."

David was trying to coerce her into getting married, even though for a little while he had almost succeeded in seducing her with his proposition. She had a longing to feel his mouth on hers and to experience again the heat of his kiss. Was her sanity in danger?

David shrugged his large shoulders and muttered, "Pity."

"I fear that your father will be more disappointed than Bryan will be."

"What will you say to the two elderly men?"

In an instant of piercing insight, Anna was able to see everything.

"Oh my God, you're right!" She said, her chocolate eyes glaring aggressively into his face.

"I thought your grandfather was such a sweet old man, but both of you must have decided to ruin my father simply to get the house in Jeju Island—or at least make sure your child did."

She accused him angrily, "I can easily believe that you are that devious, but I would never have thought it of Bryan."

"What is wrong with you men of the Miller family? Is it your life's work to bring about the end of mine?'

David snapped her out of her reverie with a resounding "No" as he tightened his powerful grip on her shoulders.

"There is no connection between Bryan and this at all. And regardless of what transpires, he is never going to learn that we had this chat. After the party, he told me that he had decided against purchasing the property because he had seen you again and realized that you were a wonderful woman who was unlikely to remain single or childless for much longer. He said that this was the reason he had decided against buying the villa. Therefore, don't let the events that have transpired between Bryan and me color your impression of him."

Anna muttered, "You really do care for him," while feigning surprise. She had never imagined that David Miller was capable of showing affection for anyone.

"Yes, of course, I do," he said with a gloomy pout forming between his thick brows.

"Contrary to what you appear to believe, I do possess some degree of human feeling. To tell you the truth, though, getting married isn't something I've ever given much thought to. The primary reason I'm giving it some thought right now is because you told Bryan that the house in Jeju can only be inherited by your children."

"If I can make Bryan happy and offer him some measure of tranquility by granting his wish for a great-grandchild who will one day take over the stewardship of his home. Then I don't care how much money I get in return; it will be worth it to me no matter what."

Anna saw David's emotional aspect for the first time since they had met, and she was surprised to find that she had developed a reluctant respect for David as a result of their encounter.

"Is Bryan the only member of your family?"

David's hands slid from her shoulders, and he pointed with his palms up. "Yes, and as you have said no to my marriage proposal he is likely to remain so, but for how much longer I have no idea."

"He is an old man, after all."

She didn't want to acknowledge that she had anything in common with David, but she could empathize with how he was feeling. Her father was the only living family by blood that she had left.

"What will really happen to my father if I don't marry you?"

Anna chose her words with great deliberation as the germ of an idea began to take shape in her head. She had always wanted a child, and in her more difficult times following Allen's passing, she had feared that her opportunity to have one had passed.

"Once the story breaks, which it is bound to do without any assistance from me because there are other shareholders, the worst-case scenario is that he will end up in jail," he said.

"It's bound to happen."

"The best that can happen for him at this point is that he will end up with no money at all."

"And what if I agreed, but on the condition that you met a few of my own requirements...?"

Anna was well aware that she would never experience love in her life again, and even though she had contemplated using in vitro fertilization (IVF) to create a child, she was not fully content with the concept. Nevertheless, it appeared that she had another option at this point — there was that word once more!—by no means an ideal option, but there is a remote possibility that it could be successful.

"You are not really in a position to impose any conditions at this time, but I will listen to what you have to say."

Did she wish to carry out these actions? Anna wasn't quite certain about anything. She gazed at his stony countenance for a fleeting second. She could detect a simmering rage behind the surface of his expressionless face, which was otherwise characterized by the contraction of a muscle along his jaw.

She hadn't been able to comprehend why he wanted her until he brought up the house in Jeju. Before that, she had assumed that he could choose any woman he wanted. But now she suddenly had the sudden realization that he had still another purpose. Someone with David's level of ego couldn't take being rejected.

Both after the night on the yacht and again two months ago, she had turned him down, and he had not forgotten either time. She had rejected him twice. Knowing that made it easier for her to continue, since she knew he would soon have his fill of her and move on to another woman. She hoped that he would leave her with a kid to adore once he moved on to another lover. Knowing that made it easier for her to continue.

"From what I gather, your line of business requires you to travel quite a bit and you split your time between the New York and South Korea. That is not something that would work for me at all. I would want assurance that I can continue to live in Los Angeles and run my own business without interruption."

David looked down at her with a mysterious glint in his brown eyes as he studied her. "Agree to marry me and I'll accept your conditions, with a couple of provisos," he told her.

He wondered if she realized that she was offering him the best of both worlds: a wife to bear his child in one scenario, and a mother in the other scenario. Los Angeles, in addition to the liberty to lead the way of life that he preferred.

"You sell your house, and the two of us will live here in the apartment that I provide."

"There should be no other guys in your life, and I fully anticipate that you will stay with me in Seoul when I am there with Bryan. As for the rest, as you mentioned, the nature of my profession requires that I travel all over the world. I don't think you must travel with me, especially if you become pregnant with our child."

Chapter 22

Anna felt that the word our child had a certain allure that could not be ignored. She reasoned with herself that even if she married David, she would not be betraying the love that she felt for Allen because there would be no love involved in her relationship with David. She believed this to be true. Simple negotiations resulted in a deal that would spare her father's life and bring her the baby she had longed for.

" Anna, did you just give me a yes or a no?" Have we reached an agreement? David inquired, and while he was doing so, he tipped her chin with one long finger and said, 'You know that makes sense.' His voice was suddenly velvety deep and intensely black. "Marry me and have my child," He said to her.

Her abdominal muscles tensed up from the stress. She became hesitant as the sensation of his finger on her chin resembled the burning of a branding iron. David had previously explained to her that one must occasionally pick the option that is the "lesser of two evils," and after thinking about it, she realized that he was absolutely right. Which was more terrible? A daughter who chose not to marry a man she did not love, so sending her father to prison for his actions? Or a daughter marrying a man she did not love in order to rescue her father and also to have a child to love once the marriage has taken place? Although neither option was particularly commendable, the second one appeared to be the better choice when weighed against the first.

"Yes," was the response she gave in the end.

David's fingers slid away from her face as he said, "Good." He then motioned toward the table. Then let's get this sorted out, shall we? Before we can call it a night, we need to decide on an engagement ring.

'We do?' And the magnitude of what she had consented to do struck her like a blow to the stomach. She automatically looked down, put her hands together, and rotated the gold wedding band around her ring finger. Is it absolutely important to have an engagement ring?" I heard her mumble. She had no idea that she would have to take Allen's band off, and she wanted to put off doing so for as long as she could.

David remarked tersely, "Very necessary," as he tightly clasped his hands around her upper arms. The purpose of giving a woman an engagement ring is to make it public knowledge that the man is interested in her only. It's been two years since your husband passed away, and it's about time you stopped living in denial about the situation. Anna attempted to pull away, but David's fingers tightened around her wrist, preventing her from doing so. "Remove his ring before tonight; you don't need it any longer." He whispered, "Face it, Anna darling, I am your future," as he dragged her inexorably closer into the heat and might of his tall frame.

The atmosphere was rife with tension. Anna wanted to punch him when she saw the look of satisfaction in his eyes, which reminded her of wolves, and she was both angry and sad at the same time. But before she could turn her thoughts into action, his dark head swooped in and his mouth covered hers in a demanding kiss that was both harsh and intense. His tongue searched for a way into the moist depths of her mouth.

Anna had been leaning on him and struggling to breathe when he finally lifted his head.

David laughed and said, "Sealed with a kiss." 'It's a shame we don't have enough time for more,' he said as he let go of her and smiled.

However, the jeweler is waiting, and we have to clean up this mess before he arrives.

Anna, who was still reeling from the kiss, watched in a daze as David turned and proceeded to clear away his belongings quickly and efficiently. It is difficult to conceive of a fiancée who is less reminiscent of a lover; nonetheless, she had to keep reminding herself that theirs was not a love match. David, who was a stockbroker, had successfully negotiated a marriage contract for them. Nothing more than that. She knelt to assist in clearing the table, and as she picked up the chopsticks, she experienced a powerful urge to stab him in the back with one of them...

Anna had thought that Annet's birthday party was horrible, but in comparison, the nightmare that her father's birthday celebration was quickly turning into made Annet's party look like a picnic. She was a teeming mess of trembling nerves, and David's hand, which had barely left her waist the entire evening, hadn't helped calm her down at all.

Everything was David's fault in the end. When he whisked her away to the Bulgari store in Hollywood, she ought to have realized that he was serious about what he'd said to her earlier. He had driven her straight home after spending a fortune on an incredible diamond and emerald ring, and he had informed her that he had some business to attend to, but that he would be back to pick her up at seven thirty in the evening.

She had spent the rest of the afternoon acting in a confused manner while rambling aimlessly throughout her home. She went through the motions of taking a shower and getting dressed. It was only after she had painstakingly removed her wedding band that she had a complete understanding of the significance of what she was doing. Her soul was weighed down with grief and remorse, and she couldn't help but shed a few tears as a result.

However, around seven thirty in the evening, Anna opened the door to him while she was dressed in the timeless black designer dress, she had worn to Annet's party. She had seen the flicker of displeasure in his eyes, and then she froze as he gripped her hand and carefully observed the pale line where her wedding ring had been. He then released her hand and continued to look at the line. He'd smiled at her in complete contentment at that point. "You've been a good girl, Anna. But don't forget to remind me to get you some brighter-colored clothing. After all, the grieving stage has ended.' He'd taken her to a waiting limousine, where a chauffeur had held the door open, and she'd slipped into the back seat, soon followed by David.

She chose to ignore his joke about the fact that she was a widow and instead said, "Why are we traveling in such style?" as she gave him a sidelong glance while desperately trying not to think about how lovely he looked in his spotless evening suit.

"I always do when I intend to have a drink," he said as he went into the inside pocket of his jacket for the gorgeous engagement ring and slid it on her finger. He said. "I would think that this event also serves as our engagement party, as well as the celebration of your father's birthday, will feature the consumption of a great deal of champagne in addition to many toasts. Anna reached up and stroked the stunning emerald ring that was on her finger. "Is there really no way around this?

Chapter 23

"Dark chocolate eyes locked with hers, and fear crept down her spine as a feather. What was she thinking when she said yes to David's proposal of marriage? "What are other people going to think? My Step mother, Jeanne, and all of their close friends are not going to believe that we will get married in a flash, and how about Annet!'

They will, that is correct. Because I just got off the phone with your dad an hour ago. The answer is yes; one must have an engagement ring to fulfill the initial requirement of the customs that surround a marriage. As long as you follow my lead and don't say anything, everyone else, including the world at large, will think it's a normal marriage, even though you and I both know it's a business transaction.

She cast one last contemplative glance at the glistening gem and recalled the last time a guy had put a ring on her finger out of real love—his beloved Allen in the past. Now, it seemed to make fun of all that she had ever believed in, and it made her want to take it off.

David growled at her as he accurately read her mind and proceeded to kiss her until she was rendered unable to answer before telling her, "Don't even think about it."

When they arrived at the William's estate in Beverly Hills, the situation had only gotten worse from there. Her dad was quite happy for her and said something to the effect of, "Thank God you two have resolved your differences."

Anna was still trying to understand what her father meant when Jeanne, in an unexpected display of affection, hugged her and wished her happiness. Anna was still trying to figure out what her father meant. Annet was the most surprising of all; she was accompanied by a very young and extremely gorgeous male model, and she not only hugged Anna but also murmured in her ear, "Well done, kid." Annet was the biggest surprise of all.

It was plain to see that her loved ones were delighted for her. Anna took a quick glance around the gathering at that moment, and as far as she could tell, everyone was pleased except for her. She went for the diamond-studded locket hanging around her neck without even thinking about it. As she ran it between the tips of her fingers and sighed softly to herself, she began to feel more at ease.

David thought that when she relaxed beneath his palm it was because she was finally beginning to accept the circumstances that she was in. He looked down at her, and a smile began to grow on his strong lips as he did so. But then he heard her sigh, and he noticed that she was absentmindedly fiddling with the locket that was hanging around her neck, with a thoughtful expression on her lovely face. It was so clear that she was bored that she didn't even bother trying to hide it.

His eyes became increasingly angry as he pushed pressure with his hand on her waist and discreetly shifted her position in front of him. He was furious. He wasn't accustomed to the women in his life being anything other than completely absorbed with him, so the fact that Anna could drift off into a world of her own irritated him. "Darling, how are you enjoying the party?", he muttered smoothly.

Anna cast a wary gaze upward at him, but she was adamant that she would not lie. She told him in no uncertain terms, "No, I'm not a party person, especially not when I am the center of all eyes because of your ring on my finger." She was referring to the fact that she was wearing his ring on her ring finger. It had been a hell of a day, followed by a pig of a night, and she could feel a headache beginning to form in her skull. She was exhausted and decided that enough was enough.

"I'm going to locate my father so that I can discuss it with him. After all, this is meant to be his birthday celebration, but you've kind of taken over the occasion and made it about you. You can do whatever you want, but once I talk to my father, I'm going home," she stated defiantly, as she grabbed his hand and attempted to take it from around her waist.

David had a simple opportunity to exercise control over her, but instead, he chose to agree after calming his rage. "You have a valid point. The engagement is now known to the world, and we've been here for far too long." He lowered his head and planted a quick kiss on her lips, which were parted slightly, before letting her go. He was rewarded with a small blush that colored her pale skin and the instant spark of awareness in her incredible eyes.

Her eyes were incredible. He vowed, "I'll give you ten minutes and then I'll come looking for you," as he saw her turn around and make her way through the crowd to her father as if all the demons in hell were pursuing her.

He had a malicious grin on his face. She exhibited a level of naivety that was astonishing for a lady who had been married. She must have understood that the joy of having some time to herself would far exceed the possibility that David might want to remain at the party. Simply thinking about the night ahead got his blood pumping faster and faster.

As for Anna, she was powerless to change the unflattering color of her cheeks and was forced to live with the situation. However, she flashed a gleam of defiance in her eyes as she watched her father leave the room and enter the hallway. Her father was not going to get away so easily this time.

She desired to have confirmation of her suspicions directly from him. Had he been aware of precisely what David had in mind from the very start of their conversation not long ago in his study?

Chapter 24

What exactly did he have in mind when he stated in his remark that she and David had made peace with one another?

She had just enough time to observe him walk into his study before she entered the hallway, but before she could follow him, a slightly intoxicated version of Annet approached her.

"You are magnificent, Anna. You really deserve credit for that.

"That is something I never would have thought. Even when David took me out to lunch after my birthday, told me that he simply thought of me as a friend, and interrogated me about you, the idea that you knew him so well never crossed my mind. Up until..."

"He told me in great detail about what happened between you and him on his yacht!"

Anna shrieked out as the color left her face, leaving her as pale as a sheet. Her face had become ice-cold. As David had threatened, Annet must now know about their one-night affair. David must have told her. How was it even possible for him to be that cruel?

"Anna, you don't need to put on the look of a bereaved widow." Annet let out a malicious laugh.

"I would have thought that you had stolen him away from me" She continued, "I wouldn't believe that you could be that sinister, my sweet darling Anna that would never have suited you."

Annet let out a mocking laugh. To which Anna felt her cheeks flushed with heat.

"When I returned home this evening, my mother filled me in on all the details regarding you and David."

"What did Jeanne say to you?" It was growing worse by the second, and Anna didn't notice the arrival of her father until he was beside her. The situation was only becoming worse.

Her father slung an arm around her shoulder and gave her a bear hug while grinning broadly from ear to ear.

"It's okay, Anna; there's no need to feel surprised."

"You should know that David demanded that I was required to tell Jeanne the truth about the business, and at first, she was somewhat unhappy about it. But when I told her that you and David had known each other for more than a year but had broken up over a silly argument and that he now wanted to try to resolve your differences and hopefully marry you, Jeanne wanted to call you right away, but I wouldn't let her."

Anna glanced up and saw the proud expression on his face with incredulity. "I wouldn't let her." Even though he was going to be my future son-in-law and had offered to help salvage the firm, I told her "No" and that we were not allowed to intervene. And don't you see how accurate I was? It just took you two one meal to decide to put your differences behind you, and I couldn't be happier about it.

Or, she thought with a bitter smile, more relieved. David disclosed to you that we were familiar with one another?" Anna asked.

Annet's statement was direct and to the point: "Don't look so surprised Anna, you must have felt he was still hot at my party."

"And you could have told me you'd already met him in Jeju Island and spent time on his yacht. Instead of letting me make a fool of myself trying to get him into my bed," she said with a smug grin.

"However, hey! There should be no ill feelings between you and me because even if I did not get a wealthy husband, he offered to invest in my company while stating that we were simply friends, I really should have guessed what he was up to." Annet smiled naughtily.

"All thanks to you my dearest Anna." She drinks the wine in her mouth.

Anna could move her lips, but there was no sound coming out of her mouth. What exactly was there to discuss? David had won the game, the set, and the match. What a comedy that he turned out to be the loving, selfless giver in the end! However, she was not laughing at all. She had an insane moment where she was tempted to blurt out the truth, but after taking one look at their happy and relieved faces, she bit her tongue and kept it to herself.

"Is this a private party, or is it open to anyone who would like to attend?" Her stepmother Jeanne ambled over to Anna, hooked her elbow through that of her husband, and flashed a big smile in her direction.

" Anna, my sweetheart, I have always known that there was more to you than met the eye. Excellent work!"

Excellent work? She had the sensation that she had been flipped over and spit-roasted, and the wrath that she felt overtook her completely.

"Thank you." Anna turned to leave and bumped square into David as she was leaving. She didn't trust herself to stay another second without bursting into wrath at the unfairness of the situation, so she left.

To help her remain steady, one lengthy arm wrapped around her waist. When she looked up, she noticed a glint of mockery in his dark brown eyes, and it made her want to cut out his throat.

David hauled her roughly into his side, the warning clear in the strong touch that he applied to her with his fingers, knowing full well that she was in a raging rage. He gave her father a friendly grin.

"Would you please excuse us?"

"Considering that it's your party and all, James."

Then, with a glance down at Anna, he said, 'I guess we've stolen enough of your father's thunder for one night, darling."

Was she the only one who picked up on the fact that he emphasized the term stolen? Anna's stomach was in knots, but she managed to keep her cool and remain silent while David wished the other three a good night...

Anna's attention was immediately drawn to David the instant she exited the house.

"You bastard! You have no shame!"

David told Anna in a terse tone, "Save it, Anna, and get in the car." He shoved her in with his hand on her back as he slid in next to her and wrapped his long arm across her shoulders to keep her firmly planted in the seat.

Chapter 25

After David gave a quick instruction, the car began to drive forward.

She snapped, her chocolate eyes colliding violently with his brown eyes as she said, "Don't you order me around." She paused before continuing, "And how could you tell my father we were—.."

Were they not? A couple? She was unable to utter the phrase, and she detested the way he raised a sarcastic, dark brow in response to her obvious hesitation to proceed with the conversation.

He mocked her gently by saying, "Poor Anna."

"When the truth is revealed, you still can't admit the fact because you've buried your head in the sand for such a long time," he said.

She spewed out the following insult: "You wouldn't know the truth if it jumped up and bit you." She tore her gaze away from his and shook her head as she said, "You're a devious, conniving swine, and you might be able to fool my father, but you don't fool me." Her jaws tightened.

"I must have been crazy to think that this arrangement would be successful," she continued.

She was compelled to stare into his eyes because his fingers were digging into her shoulder and his free hand was tilting her head back slightly. This caused her to be shaken inside because of the expression she saw in his dazzling gaze.

"No, Anna, you are the one who deceives yourself." He hissed with a sibilant softness, his nostrils flaring and his lips tightening into a hard bitter line.

"I do not lie, and I would kill a man for insulting me as you have," he said, the realization hit her like a ton of bricks that she hadn't exactly made the best decision by provoking his wrath.

In a rage, David displayed the outstanding characteristics of a primitive guy. Anna's heart suddenly began its frantic beating for no apparent reason, and she became acutely aware of him in a way that she had never been before.

She noticed the rise and fall of his sculpted chest beneath the conventional attire, the strong tanned column of his throat, and the little pulse that raced in his cheek. As she watched him, his lovely face was instantly wiped clean of all expression. This caused her heart to leap frenetically, and she stared at him in awe.

"Therefore, you should count yourself fortunate that I am a man of self-control."

"If you say so." He didn't look very constrained to Anna, and she didn't feel it as his body bent over hers, which caused her nerves to jangle with a variety of feelings that had nothing to do with dread.

"If you say so." She no longer had any desire to dispute with him, since she was experiencing a different type of desire, which caused her cheeks to blush embarrassingly.

"If I may say so. I would propose that you begin trying to do the same thing if you want this marriage to have any chance of persuading both my grandfather and the rest of the world that it is genuine. We have to put on the same effort, which shouldn't be too difficult."

His face was only a few centimeters away from hers, and his palm had slid lower to curl around her breast. His thumb appeared to be idly stroking the rising peak through the fabric of her gown.

"And with that in mind, I told your father that we met a year ago and that you visited me on my yacht," he said, "because I thought it was relevant we got into a fight.

"You have to admit that I am telling the truth to the best of my ability," he said quietly as he directed his narrowed eyes to her mouth.

She lifted her hand to grab his wrist, wanting him to stop, yet aching for more, but somehow her hand landed feebly on his shirtfront, and she couldn't dispute that what he said was real. Heat coursed through Anna's body, "Yes," she mumbled more quietly. He managed to throw her into a complete loop, and the fact that he was caressing her breast in no way helped the situation for her.

"So, it seems that we have finally come to an understanding," he murmured, before continuing, "As for the rest of it, your father heard what he wanted to hear." And the fact that we came tonight as an engaged couple was enough to absolve him of any blame." He shifted his head ever-so-slightly, and his lips brushed across her mouth and back again before settling into a long, possessive kiss. He seemed completely relieved. When he finally raised his head, much to Anna's humiliation, she was pressed up against him, out of breath, and about to melt in his arms.

"I did you a favor, Anna," he said.

"Your family is certain that this is a love match, and they may sleep comfortably in their beds, free of any financial anxiety."

He gave her a knowing smile as his hand moved casually from her breast to her thigh after it had been resting on her breast. She made a feeble effort to dislodge his hand, but on the inside, she was a trembling bundle of electric ecstasy.

"And you are welcome to sleep soundly in my bed, Anna. Even if I want you almost as much as you want me, I don't expect you to say that you want me. But you will get there in the end. That is a guarantee on my part. In the meantime, as my fiancée-to-be and, God willing, future mother of my child, I expect you to conduct yourself in a manner befitting the intelligent and cultured lady that I know you to be. Do you understand what I mean?"

Anna didn't trust herself enough to talk, so she just nodded her head silently to indicate that she agreed. Even much it pained her to acknowledge it, she did comprehend everything completely. David's account of the events allowed everyone involved to save their dignity. Including hers among them.

Even before she had a complete understanding that the vehicle had stopped, he was assisting her in exiting it.

She objected by looking around and said, "Wait."

"I don't live on this street," she said.

"No, it's mine," he said. There is a lot that I want to talk to you about before I go to New York tomorrow. We must settle on the specifics of our wedding before I go, but I have no intention of doing so at the house that you and your late husband formerly inhabited.

She was about to decline, then she paused. Even though he had done a lot more than just gaze at her in the car, for some unknown reason, just the sight of him was enough to send her pulse racing. Financially, he held all the cards, and physically, for some unknown reason, just the sight of him was enough to send her pulse racing. Her wayward body was passionately reminding her of this.

"Okay."

He whispered the insult, "Very wise," as he wrapped his fingers around her elbow and led her into the entrance foyer of the building. He went to the security desk and presented her to the person working there who was dressed in uniform.

"Marvie, this is Anna —my fiancée, I'm leaving tomorrow, but Anna will be moving in here next week, so I'd appreciate it if you would accord her every courtesy, and inform the rest of your crew."

"Was it truly required to be done?" Anna demanded as soon as the elevator doors swung around behind them. "By that...,"

"What do you mean?" Would it be more convenient for you to wait to move in until after we have gotten married? Anna don't be a prude; you need to mature. You are not a virgin, and you are as aware of the situation as I am; therefore, there is no need for any more pretense."

Chapter 26

"We have a deal, and it will be best for both of us if you accept that we have it as quickly as possible."

She wasn't so sure about the rest of it, and when he placed a hand at her back and forced her into the spacious lounge of his apartment, she had the childish desire to turn and run away. David, however, realized she was conflicted and reached out to run his fingers up her back before settling his arms around her shoulders. One minute later, she was seated on the black sofa, watching as David strolled up to the drinks cabinet, taking off his jacket and tie as he did so, and dropping them on a seat nearby. She continued to watch as David walked away from the drinks cabinet.

He cast a quick glance behind him over his shoulder. "Would you like something to drink? "

"Only natural mineral water, thank you." She saw his frown as he moved back to the cabinet, but a moment later he reappeared with two crystal glasses and handed her one of them.

"My limit is two glasses of wine," Anna said.

He said it sarcastically, "Water, as requested," and then he nonchalantly laid his great length down next to her.

"Anna, we really do need to have this conversation. I felt that since you previously had a grand wedding with your family, we could do a simple civil ceremony two weeks from this coming Saturday instead."

"After I said goodbye to you earlier today in the afternoon, I went and notified the registrar's office."

"It is simply necessary for you to call in with your documents at this point. How does that come across to you?"

How appalling! Wasn't there meant to be a conversation here? David already had everything figured out, from what she could tell, which was a complete and utter joke. But she had other things planned, and she wasn't about to let him interfere and walk all over them without showing any respect. But because she was aware of his remark on her age and sophistication, Anna made a conscious effort to respond calmly.

"I'm afraid that won't be possible given that I won't be in attendance," she said. I will have two weeks off before that, as Sara and I have previously agreed upon it. I have a reservation for a flight that leaves on the following Saturday for a week; I'm traveling to Jeju Island to meet with the man who takes care of my aunt's house and decide what kinds of decoration and repairs need to be done. Because of my trip, we will have to postpone the wedding until after I get back."

David then made his way over to face her and said, "Rubbish."

Because the top button of his white dress shirt was undone, she saw an unsettling view of his tanned flesh and chest hair, both of which she could have done without seeing. After the ordeal in the car, she was just starting to recover her bearings and catch her breath again. She took a few deep breaths and made an effort to focus on what he was saying while she did so.

"There is no way that it could be changed because I have already made up my mind. I can simply make the necessary arrangements for us to get married in Seoul." He said firmly.

"Seoul?" Anna repeated while expressing disbelief.

"It's the best possible solution."

"We can get married the following Saturday, a week from now, in Seoul. I'll make the necessary arrangements for your family and friends to leave, and Bryan won't have to worry about the perils of traveling."

"We could spend the first week of our honeymoon on Jeju Island so that we could get the house in order, and then we could go somewhere else. Bryan can step in and take charge of supervising the modifications."

She contradicted him by saying, "No, we can't stay in the Villa in Jeju Island," she said bluntly. "And neither can Bryan; the location is not appropriate for him to reside in," I haven't visited for a while and I don't know if it is comfortable for him to sleep there."

"Okay, we can stay in a hotel, and Bryan will have to wait to visit his old home," he said with a sarcastic glitter in his brown eyes as he added, "But it is about time I saw the house that's costing me a fortune and my freedom."

"You've never been inside the house, have you?"| Anna asked the question.

"But it just occurred to me that you must have been born there."

"No," David responded.

"Bryan and my mother were both born there." As he emptied his glass and set it down on the table, he noticed that the charming smile that had been on his face had vanished, and in its place was a frown. "However, I was born in Seoul, and my mother had no other children." "Now you know that I am the bastard you have been calling me."

The memory of her earlier outburst caused her face to flush, and she quickly covered it up. If she had realized that he was an illegitimate child, she never would have called him a bastard. David momentarily covered her lips with his finger to prevent her from speaking, even though she had her mouth open to apologize.

"My American father who had visited the island had seduced my mother and left her after." He said solemnly.

"Don't bother; I don't mind, but unfortunately, my grandmother did." "As a result, she urged Bryan to sell the business, and they relocated to Seoul, where nobody knew who they were. My maternal grandmother and maternal grandfather raised me after my mother passed just a few days after I was born. Bryan brought up Jeju once or twice, but neither my grandmother nor I ever discussed the location, and I had no interest in it. In point of fact, and it brings me no little amount of embarrassment to admit it."

"I had no idea." Anna whispered.

"It wasn't until I found out that Bryan has been attempting to get the home back after my grandma passed away that I realized he was that upset about it." He spoke.

"But why didn't he give it a shot earlier?" Anna questioned.

David's gorgeous face broke into a wide grin, which gave the impression that he was playing a child's game. "I don't blame Bryan for being cowardly; he didn't dare." You would understand why if you'd ever had the chance to meet my grandma; despite her diminutive size, she was a very strong woman."

"When they finally departed the island, she issued an edict stating that they would never look back or even mention Jeju again. She was also as stubborn as a mule, and it would have required a more courageous guy than either Bryan or I to stand up to her." He let out a sigh while grinning.

David is also like his grandma, a very stubborn man indeed. Anna pondered these things as she tried to picture the petite Korean woman who had been able to strike fear into David Miller.

Anna remarked dryly, "I would have adored the opportunity to speak with her." And find out her little secret," she said, her lips drawing back slightly over her perfectly white teeth as a sly grin crossed her face.

David took a deep breath in response to her genuine smile, which was the first time she had shown it to him. He stretched out and grabbed her head in his palms, directing his eyes to the gently parted lips of the woman he was holding.

"I have a sneaking suspicion you might already know it," he husked and slowly covered her enticing mouth with his own. He sensed her small resistance, and then the warmth of her breath combined with his. Then, with the barest touch of her tongue, he forgot his self-control.

He intensified the kiss with a probing, ravenous passion, investigating the moist inner of her mouth just as he yearned to explore the tight, moist interior of her magnificent body, which he knew all too well. He was startled as he felt her arms stretch up to him, and he smothered a groan when he felt her fingertips lightly touch the nape of his neck.

Chapter 27

He raised his head to look down at her while effortlessly skimming the fabric from her shoulders to her waist with his hands. While he did this, he lowered the zipper of her dress down her back. He had Anna precisely where he wanted her, and he struggled to fight the impulse to have her then and now, on the sofa. Her amazing chocolate eyes were glazed over with lust, and her lush breasts were firm and full, with lovely rose-pink nipples that were begging to be tasted.

"Anna, are you going to make me hold out until after the wedding?" he shrieked before cursing himself for being one of a hundred different kinds of idiot. A beautiful and eager woman was in his arms, and he was forced to pause and inquire. "Are you taking the pill?" he asked. "Did you do that?" he inquired, making a feeble attempt to defend his idiotic behavior.

It was not Anna's usual character to jump off a cliff into unexplored waters, but she just couldn't resist him. She ran her tongue over her kiss-swollen lips, savoring the taste of David, while her body tingled with sexual anticipation and every nerve in her body trembled with excitement. She had no clear recollection of what had taken place, but she peered up at him as her blood raced erratically through her veins, and she was in a state of shock. She noticed the flush of color on his high cheekbones and the barely leashed desire in the depths of his eyes, and without thinking, she kissed him.

Furthermore, she gave in entirely to the pressing demands that her body was making on her. "The answer to both questions is no."

When he grabbed her in his arms, she let out a high-pitched scream and asked, "What are you doing?" as he stomped his way up the few stairs leading to the main level. He grinned as he looked down into her shocked eyes and said, "Taking you to bed." And before she had time to gather her composure, he was hoisting her up onto a massive bed,' it said. "Where you were meant to be," he said, a triumphant sparkle appearing in his gaze as his fingers worked quickly with his shirt.

She became red-faced and defensive as she crossed her arms in front of her chest as soon as she realized that her dress was already halfway down because of the coolness of the cover on her back.

She turned her head as she heard him laugh and looked up, her eyes widening in shock and interest as she observed his tanned and almost-naked figure. Not only that, but she felt her face flush just by looking at his body above her.

He had broad shoulders, a broad, muscular chest, and a dusting of black body hair that narrowed down to disappear inside the waistband of his black silk boxer shorts.

He was so beautifully male. He was wide-shouldered, and his chest was big and strong. She was visibly embarrassed by the underwear she was wearing, which featured her lush curves. Her eyes wandered down to his thigh muscles, and she took in his long, lean legs. Oh, God, what the hell was going on with her? She let out an internal groan as she tore her gaze away from his in preparation for the inconceivable act of lovemaking with him.

"There's no reason to be embarrassed, Anna. She sensed the mattress compressing beneath her as well as the warmth of his body pressing up against her side. As her body shook, she forced herself to look up and saw David propped up on one elbow with a seductive smile forming on his lips. "And no need to hide your exquisite body, either," he husked as he reached for one of her hands and placed it on his shoulder. Her fingers flexed as they ran over the satiny smoothness of his skin. She shuddered when he seized her other hand and pressed it to the bed, exposing her bare breasts to the rapt attention of the man who was watching them.

He mumbled, "You have perfect breasts," as his molten eyes met hers, and fire surged through her completely. Then, he gave each strained nipple a taste with his tongue, sending needles of desire from her breast to the apex of her thighs as he dipped his head. She did not want to raise her body towards him, but when she did so, he was able to sneak his fingers into the folds of her dress and remove it from her. He hissed, "I want to see you naked," as her lace underwear followed her dress. "With your magnificent hair loose across my pillow," he said. He followed his words with action by running his fingers through her hair, dislodging the delicately pinned chignon, and pulling the long strands down across her shoulders and breasts.

Anna was so overcome with enthusiasm that she no longer cared about the state of her hair. She sucked in a shaky breath, her chocolate eyes darting to his moving mouth as her heart growled in anticipation of his kiss. She pressed her palm more firmly on his shoulder while making an effort to draw him in. He was aware of her desires and, with a taunting smile, momentarily dropped his head and brushed his lips on hers.

He pressed up against her mouth. As he once more leaned back, she moaned her displeasure under her breath.

"Patience, Anna, I want to examine every inch of you." His fingers curled around her throat and then trailed with a physical thrill down her breast and the indentation of her waist. He said to her, "Patience, Anna." His sparkling eyes traveled down her body before returning to her face. She was so beautiful, and she will be hers for the taking.

He adjusted himself shakily as his hand moved lower toward her leg. "I want to taste every inch of you." His head dipped, and his lips, as soft as thistledown, trailed warm kisses over her brow, the fragile skin of her eyelids, and the smooth curve of her face. He kissed her in a way that was as gentle as the wind.

"Because I want there to be no question in your mind about who is possessing you this time," he said.

Chapter 28

It had been much too long since she had been naked in a man's arms and experienced the intense pleasure of sexual desire. She felt a flicker of unease tugging at her consciousness, but she wanted David very much. She stretched out for him with both hands and felt the heat of his firm, bare body on her own. Her mouth opened in eager anticipation of his kiss, and he did not let her down in this regard. While her arms wrapped around his wide back and her fingers reached up to tangle in the soft black hair of his head, his mouth was covering hers. His tongue stroked her mouth, and her tongue dueled with his.

Her body was on fire for David, and she let out a low groan as his strong hand curled gently around her breast. His teasing fingers plucked at the sensitized, aching tip, and she let out a low sigh in response. She trembled furiously as his long fingers stroked between the delicate curls at the junction of her thighs and reached the hot, liquid center of her femininity. She whimpered with pleasure as he stroked the swelling, moist center of exquisite sensitivity until she was writhing beneath him, every nerve in her body taut with intolerable strain. She dug her nails into his back as she whimpered with ecstasy. Her hands went down his back, reaching lower to dig into the flesh of his legs. She continued to move her hands down his back. She desired to experience the whole power of his ownership, but she didn't want him to stop the intense joy of his caressing fingertips. She wanted to feel the full force of his power.

David rasped, "Yes, open for me, Anna," and as he moved to settle between her legs, he planted another vicious kiss on her swollen lips as he continued his advance toward her. His arousal was a stiff, rigid length that rubbed against her inner thighs, but it did not go any further. She groaned low in her throat, yearning for his complete ownership with every fiber of her being. But he raised his head, and she stared at him with eyes as wild as she could muster. "Not yet," he said, curling his features into a smile that was utterly male and predatory. He husked at her, "I want you to remember this for the rest of your life."

His head dipped once more, and this time his mouth closed over the swollen apex of one of her breasts. She jerked uncontrollably as a result of the mild biting of his teeth, since she was caught up in a game in which only David knew the rules.

She bit at his shoulder before sliding her hand down his leg and finding the stiff shaft with her fingers. He ripped her hand away and pinned it to the mattress with his own while he examined every part of her body.

She was overwhelmed with an intimate sexuality that she had never imagined could exist between them, driving her to the verge of pleasure over and over again. Then his mouth found hers, and his tongue plunged with an enticing beat while his lengthy fingers moved between her legs, causing her to experience a wave of shock that slammed into her. Anna's threshold for ecstasy had been reached. She pleaded, "Please, David," while pressing ferocious kisses to his big chest. Her teeth discovered a little male nipple and bit it in a fury of hunger.

David lifted her hips and plunged into her extremely tight moist center with a forceful thrust that produced a shuddering moan of absolute bliss from his throat. Her plea was still echoing in his ears. He was making love for the first time in twenty years without the use of any sort of protection, and he halted, struggling to maintain control over the ferocity of the sensation that was exploding through every part of his body.

"David!" Anna screamed his name as she felt the pulsating strength of him stretch and fill her, and then he gradually removed his presence from her. She desperately pleaded with him, "No, no—don't stop."

David groaned helplessly, "I couldn't even if I tried," and then he began to thrust into her again, taking her in a strong, primitive pace that Anna met and matched until, a few seconds later, her body convulsed in a shattering climax.

Anna could feel David let out a trembling sigh of relief as he slumped on top of her. At the same time, her inner muscles contracted around him as his sperm poured into her. She clung to him, her hands moving instinctively to caress his broad shoulders, stroking over the satin-smooth shoulder blades, and her fingers tracing the indentation of his spine. She was awestruck by the force and the wonder of their joining.

She was pinned to the bed by the weight of his gorgeous physique, and the only sound in the room was the tormented sound of their breathing as they struggled against the silence.

After some time had passed, David lifted his now-familiar weight off of her and leaned on one forearm while staring attentively into her gorgeous, love-addled face.

"Anna, that was just incredible." He gushed with a wide grin. "And just in case there was any question about it, that was the very first time since I was a teenager that I skipped wearing protection. I can reassure you that I am in perfect health, so there is no need for you to be concerned about anything."

It was the arrogant, macho delight that Anna heard in his tone that enraged her, and it drove home to her more than anything else could how far apart they were in terms of the sexual stakes. One year ago, the only other person she had slept with was Allen. The only exception was David. But David was the exact opposite; he had been with so many women during his life that regular checkups for his health were a requirement for him to continue living.

She barely succeeded in hiding her sarcasm when she said, "Thank you for that." She began to move away from him as she said, "But now, if you don't mind—" and continued, "I have to get home." She put her feet over the edge of the table as she said, "Friday is a busy day at work."

She pulled herself up onto the side of the bed and stood up, very aware of the fact that she was naked, but adamant that she would not expose herself. She got up and proceeded to the foot of the bed, where she picked up her wrinkled dress.

"I have to be at the market by five in the morning, and I would like to get a couple of hours of sleep first." Before she dared to glance back at David, she wore her underpants and slipped the dress over her head.

He was lain across the bed, with his head supported by one hand, and his jet black hair was in an alluring state of disarray.

"Pity. Are you certain that I won't be able to convince you to go back to bed?", he asked drowsily. "I am free till nine o'clock in the evening before departing to New York.

The problem was that he could entice her. Anna admitted, with a wry smile, that he could tempt a saint. "No, David, don't forget about our arrangement. I can maintain my career."

"Okay," he said as he jumped from the bed, triumphantly naked and unmoved by the situation. "But remember the rest of it, Anna, you move in here before I return from New York," he said, grabbing her chin as he buried a quick, forceful kiss on her mouth.

"Give me five minutes, and I'll take you back," he said.

Anna observed that he did not say "back home," and for a split second, she pondered the possibility that David was green with envy regarding her late husband and the life they had spent together. That was not the case at all; if it were true, it would indicate that David cared for her, but she was certain that he did not feel that way. She caught a glimpse of him entering the restroom and immediately began frantically searching for her undergarments after observing his exit. She was fully dressed and attempting to give her tangled mess of hair some semblance of order when he reappeared, dressed in denim trousers and a sweater.

David said, "Leave it; you're only going to bed."

After giving her a quick but passionate kiss goodbye at her front door, he walked away. She slid into bed twenty minutes later, fatigued both physically and mentally, but her mind was in a state of turmoil. She was at a loss for words when it came to herself. Why had she allowed the idea of having a child to lead her into making a hasty choice to get married to David? Why in the world had she agreed to have sexual relations with a man that she neither liked nor trusted? She hid her face, hiding her confusion and her embarrassment. She was unfamiliar with herself. Her throbbing body served as a constant reminder to her that she had not merely allowed David to make love to her; rather, she had been an active, even enthusiastic participant in the act.

Chapter 29

"Damn!" Anna muttered an expletive as she hung up the phone and turned her angry gaze on Sara. "It was David again," she said.

"I will take tomorrow off from work because he has made arrangements for me to go shopping with Annet using his money! The audacity of the man! Does he believe that I am unable to clothe myself on my own?" She shot an exasperated scowl at the phone, which prompted Sara to burst out laughing.

"No, of course not," she replied.

"He probably believed it was a good way to reconcile the rift he may have caused between you and Annet because he dated her to get close to you and win you back. As a guy, he probably thought it was the right way. It's evident that David is head over heels in love with you, and I find it quite romantic the way that he calls you multiple times a day. If you had any sense at all, you would continue to take the rest of the week off from work so that you can relax and get ready for his return."

Anna rebelliously considered saying something, 'Romantic, my foot,' but she refrained. Last Friday, she informed Sara that she was engaged and provided her with David's account of the events. Everyone was overjoyed for her. It was already Tuesday, and David was anticipated to return from his trip to New York on Thursday.

On Friday, they were going to board the flight to Seoul with her family in preparation for the wedding on Saturday. The only reason he continued to call her was to update her on the progress of the wedding preparations, which included every last-minute detail as if she gave a crap! Anna jumped in response to the repeated ringing of the telephone. She has silenced her phone, but David opted to contact her on their office landline instead if she does this.

She yelled at Sara, "You answer it, and if that's David again, tell him I'm out," and then hung up the phone.

"Tell him I've gone to move my stuff into his apartment."

"Is that really what you are doing?" Sara asked as she attempted to reach for the phone. "Yes, I am," Anna responded.

"I'll take the rest of the week off, as you suggested. If you can handle it, though"

"Of course, I can do that."

She swung her bag over her shoulder and raced out of the shop before Sara could change her mind about attending the wedding on Saturday.

"Great—I'll see you at the wedding on Saturday." If she heard one more statement from Sara, her father, Annet, or anybody else on how fortunate she was to have landed a stunning multibillionaire, she would scream.

She made a little detour back home to wash up and change before continuing on her way to Fullerton. She wasn't looking forward to informing her in-laws that she was getting married again, but surprisingly, Mark and Marga took the news fairly well and were delighted for her. They told her that she was too young to stay alone for the rest of her life, and that Allen would have told her the same thing if he were still alive. Marga was happy for her.

Late the following day in the afternoon, Anna was feeling hot from the weather, so she went home in Montebello, unlocked the door to her house, and walked inside. She repositioned the shoestring strap of the basic blue slip dress she was wearing back on her shoulder for perhaps the tenth time. She dropped the items she was holding on the hall table, flexed her hurting hands, and looked at the emerald and diamond ring that was on her finger. The shopping trip and lunch with Annet had been stressful.

As she entered the living room, she did so with a nervous twitch, turning it over and over again. David would be back the next day, and she hadn't even begun to pack or organize the sale of her house, but time was running out. David would be returning. But was it necessary for her to? The query was presented by a petty demon with an independent streak lurking in the recesses of her psyche.

She ambled about, putting her hands on things that were familiar to her. She smiled fondly at the memory as she picked up her wedding photo, but she quickly placed it back down since she had already made up her mind.

After an hour had passed, she exited her home as she always had, locking the door behind her. She then drove across to David's place in Four Seasons Private Residence Beverly Hills, carrying three suitcases in the trunk of her car that were stuffed with clothing and the things necessary for daily life.

Marvie insisted on lugging her baggage up to the penthouse, and she thanked him by flashing a smile and handing him a sizable tip before shutting the door behind her. Anna cast her gaze around the living room and saw that it was just as bare as she recalled. She had a look around the cutting-edge kitchen, which was made entirely of stainless steel. Almost little had changed in the dining room; it was still made of glass and steel.

The bedrooms were not much better; one was blue and the other was white; both were practical but lacked soul. The only thing that took her by surprise was the study, which was quite cozy and had walls that were loaded with books, an old desk, a ton of technical equipment, of course, but also a very nice fireplace and two high-backed winged armchairs covered in the softest mint-green hide.

She grabbed a suitcase from the floor and walked inside the master bedroom. The previous time she came here, she hadn't paid much attention to the interior design, so she found herself pleasantly surprised by it. The floor was covered by a thick cream carpet with a Grecian border in indigo, and the room was furnished in tones of cream and indigo. Large glass doors that opened onto a terrace were hidden from view by long flowing drapes that were kept back with indigo ties. On one side of the patio there was a soft cushioned sofa, chair, and a modest table. The overall atmosphere was noticeably less likely than in the other parts of the property.

Anna's eyes wandered over to the enormous bed that was situated in the middle of the room, and an unanticipated flush of heat covered her entire body. Suddenly, she averted her gaze. She moved quickly across the room to go to the pair of doors that were located on the other side of the area.

She opened the first one and found a gorgeous white bathroom with a double shower and twin vanity basins, and in the corner, elevated on a dais, a large whirlpool bath. All of the fixtures in the bathroom were white. She turned around and tried the second door, which led her to a dressing room with built-in closets and the same plush carpet continuing through to the next room. She closed the first door and moved on to the next one.

Anna swiftly removed her belongings from her suitcases and put them away in the closet. There was a significant amount of unused space, David's belongings only partially filled one of the closets. As she set her makeup box on the dressing table, she thought, "It's a good thing he didn't spend much time in here," and she questioned herself: "Isn't that what I want?" She was trying to remove her jewelry box from its case when she accidentally bumped into the table, which caused the contents of the box to fall out onto the floor.

Anna was still searching for the final piece of jewelry five minutes later. It was a platinum locket in the shape of a heart. She was on her hands and knees, with her head buried under the table.

"Now that is what I like to call a warm and friendly sight!" When David saw the plump buttocks barely covered by the blue silk dress pushed out in the air, his body immediately responded with sudden manly enthusiasm, and he laughed. He was overjoyed to recognize her sexy backside, and the sense of relief he experienced upon discovering Anna already in his apartment was so overwhelming that it was nearly euphoric. He was too helpless to resist and ended up patting her bottom.

Chapter 30

Anna was only aware of the hand touching her behind for a split second before she recognized the voice. The sudden movement of her head caused her to strike the bottom of the table with it. "What the heck? "She shrieked as she rolled onto her back and rolled out from behind the table, looking her adversary in the eye with angry eyes as she glared at them. "You almost knocked me out, you fool," she said as she moved her hand to stroke her head. The horrible man was laughing uncontrollably, which added insult to injury...

David sputtered, "I'm sorry," as an apology.

Her magnificent hair was a jumble of tangles about her shoulders, and her brown eyes shone like chocolate in contrast to her flushed cheeks. The blue silk dress was twisted around her shapely contours, displaying more of her rounded breasts than she was aware of. At the same time, his body stiffened another notch.

"But you have such a delightful backside, Anna, that I couldn't help myself," he said as he extended a hand to help her to her feet.

"I couldn't resist." He smiled in amusement.

Her heartbeat increased at an alarming pace as she became flustered by his sudden arrival and well aware of the amused male scrutiny, he was giving her. Anna, however, paid no attention to his hand as she stumbled her way to standing.

She retorted angrily, "Then it's about time you tried."

She remarked in a condescending tone "You're a bit old to be smacking a woman's bottom."

"My, you have led a sheltered sex life, Anna darling," he drawled with a mocking amusement that infuriated her even more. Because she had been thinking the same treacherous notion during the past few days and nights when the memory of his lovemaking was still very fresh in her mind.

She jumped back, her eyes finding his eyes, and she saw the amusement evaporate and be replaced by a much more menacing glare.

"No one can say that of you, that's for sure," she said.

"And what exactly are you doing in this room?"

She abruptly shifted the topic of discussion.

"You weren't supposed to be back until the next day."

"I finished earlier than I expected." He moved closer, and Anna moved away, but she was prevented from doing so by the edge of the dressing table. "I couldn't wait any longer," he said as he wrapped his hands around her waist and smiled with a seductively dark twist to his lips. He then slipped one hand up her spine and grabbed the back of her head with the other.

"I couldn't wait any longer."

"To see you," he whispered, bending his dark head, and Anna's immediate reaction was to struggle. "And do this," he prompted her with a breath against her mouth as he slid his tongue in between her partially parted lips. Anna's pulse leaped in her chest as the taste of his tongue, which was warm and moist, brushed against hers. Any idea of struggling faded away as she became consumed by the ravenous pleasure of his mouth.

She melted in his arms, her hands moving across his shoulders of their own accord as they stroked him. She was intoxicated by the scent of him, the power of his embrace, and the driving passion of his mouth, and she groaned in protest when he ended the kiss they were sharing. She was drunk by all of these things.

David mumbled something incomprehensible before lifting her onto the table and placing her there. When he removed the strap of her garment from her shoulder and grabbed her breast, her nipple rose instantly into the palm of his hand. His mouth covered the pulse that beat frantically in her throat and sucked at the delicate flesh with ferocious hunger.

She let out a loud groan as his mouth wrapped itself over the hard peak of her breast after his hand had dropped to his sides. He drove her absolutely crazy by using his tongue and teeth. Then his hand found the hem of her skirt and slipped up to rub over the silk of her underwear between her thighs. The tormented sob that she let out caused him to raise his head. Their eyes met, the question was asked, and the answer was given without a word being spoken. His fingers slipped beneath her panties and caressed her damp silken flesh while his tongue moved once more to torment her other breast.

Anna's arousal was intense and immediate. He removed her lace panty with astonishing dexterity by sliding his fingers down her thigh and removing her underwear. She let out a gasp as her legs involuntarily spread apart to offer him easier access, and her thighs shook as his kisses traveled down to her navel until his head was in between her legs. His tongue gave her intense pleasure, and she couldn't control her moans. She closed her eyes and took it all in. The immense pleasure that he gave her was beyond anything she had ever encountered. He was tasting her until she convulsed with her climax.

Then all of a sudden he stopped moving and straightened up, and the only thing that kept her from collapsing onto the dressing table was her elbows.

She watched him unzip his fly with wild eyes and a yearning in her heart as she stood there transfixed. Then, in a fit of raging, exploding passion, his hands went under her to hold her buttocks, and he drove into her, forcing her back with the driving might of his possession so that reflexively, she clenched her teeth together.

She wrapped his legs around his waist. Each stroke of his stiff and pulsating flesh drove her higher and higher until their bodies climaxed together in a volcanic eruption of fire and liquid heat. His mouth crashed down on hers as he thrust to the hilt, again and again. While Anna clung to him with her arms and legs and her inner muscles continued to tremble around him, his hips came to a shuddering stop.

David muttered an expletive under his breath. Since he was an immature teenager, he had never lost control and taken a lady so rapidly, and the last thing he wanted was to terrify Anna in the days leading up to the wedding. When he noticed the surprise in her eyes, he quickly removed himself from her body and repositioned the dress straps so that they were over her shoulders again. While he kept one hand on her to keep her from moving, the other hand was rapidly used to adjust himself and zip up his pants. After that, he pulled her off the table and adjusted the garment so that it hung more gracefully over her hips.

When he called her name, " Anna," she turned her large, round eyes toward him but remained silent. He continued to speak. "Are you alright?

Anna was rendered speechless and too ashamed to maintain eye contact with him due to her state of shock. She felt as though she had been struck by a lightning bolt, although David was completely dressed, and not even the knot in his tie had moved. She felt as though she had been hit by a lightning bolt. She experienced an immediate replay of the previous five minutes in her mind, and as a result, her cheeks turned a blazing scarlet color.

She had never before experienced such primal lust in her life, but as she sat on the table with her dress wrapped around her waist, she could not help but feel it. David was keeping a wary eye on her the entire time, and when she dared to look at his face, she did it with extreme caution. She was asking herself, How was she feeling?

Chapter 31

If he wasn't trying to get her into bed, David had revealed himself to be a clever and amusing company. "Not even close," he responded as he set his drink down and placed his hand on her as it was lying on the table. "I am completely informed on the subject." He stared at her eyes and added, "You are an extremely attractive and alluring woman." She tried to pull her hand away, but his fingers intertwined with hers and kept her from doing so. He then said, "I didn't mean just sex."

"Allow me to complete. I am confident that we are compatible in that regard." He released her hand and leaned in close to her, reaching out with one finger to tilt her head while his glittering eyes held hers. "It is impossible to deny the fact that we share a potent chemistry." He looked at her hungrily.

"When I touch you, you turn to mush, and the same thing happens to me. That is a significant benefit in any marriage, and as for the rest, we have a lifetime to get to know each other." Anna's cheeks burned from the heat. She heaved an internal sigh of relief when David sat back and was silent for a time, since the sexual tension had returned in full force and she had been looking forward to it. After that, he proceeded by saying, "But I also know you and I both want the same thing—to have a child or two and be a family, and at the same time make the families we already have happy."

"You believe that to be sufficient, don't you?" He said it in a pretty cynical manner, but it sounded like he was saying. "It's a lot more than most people in this day and age aspire to."

He leaned forward once more and said, "A growing percentage of people have children with no more thought than they would give to purchasing a new coat, and they cast off their responsibilities with the same ease as shedding a coat." He said this while grinning ironically. "But let me reassure you, Anna," he said. My schedule will need to be reorganized after we have a child, even though I travel a lot. I'm not going to be a parent who is never around."

He made a comment that shocked her, which is why she remained silent. She wasn't sure if the possibility of his improved presence in her life would give her comfort. He stood up and tossed money onto the table before sitting back down. David gave her the order to "Come on, let's go," then moved around to her side, extended his hand to her, and said, "Let's go." It was taken by Anna...

Anna awoke the following morning in David's bed, complaining of painful muscles in parts of her body she had no idea she had. She jumped out of bed and dashed into the bathroom as soon as she realized there was no trace of David. She slipped on a pair of peach-colored slacks and paired them with a silk shirt of the same color, grateful that she had brought some things over yesterday, even if it had been in a fit of fury. She combed her hair and then pulled it back with a scarf that had a variety of colors before placing her feet into supple suede mules. She had to muster every ounce of her strength of will to drag herself out of the bedroom.

Anna brewed a cup of coffee for herself in the kitchen's stainless steel appliance and then made her way back into the living area, unsure of what she should do next. Leaving it the way it was seemed like a decent alternative, she pondered right before David walked in, looking incredible in a dark gray business suit, a lighter gray shirt, and a silk tie. She had a hard time taking her eyes away from his, and she had to fight back the flush that was threatening to appear.

"I was about to wake you up, but I see that you've already dressed; that's a good sign." Anna was still processing this sentence when he came across the room and grinned brilliantly down at her. "My lawyer will be here in fifteen minutes so that you can sign the prenup, and that's it." Anna was still thinking of his comment when he strolled across the room. "Honey, the wedding is tomorrow, and everything is ready."

He gently planted a kiss on the top of her head. "I have people who can help you sell your home if you haven't done so already, and I can get them to do it for you if you let me know." His inquisitive eyes looked at her.

He appeared to be very unruffled and unconcerned about anything. It was evident that a night of passionate sex had no impact on him other than to leave him with a contented smile on his face. Anna suddenly became aware that she needed to act in the same way.

"No, we won't need that," she replied. She didn't like to lie, but she didn't know what else to say because she was at a loss for words. "I have it all arranged." It was now time for her to move on with her life which was in his bed. After what happened the night before, staying in that specific bed wasn't going to be a challenge for her, but considering the rest of her life...

David's attorney was quite productive, and he insisted on reading the entire pre-nuptial agreement to both of them before signing it. In essence, they both kept everything they had, but Anna was not entitled to anything if they divorced within the first three years of their marriage. This wasn't surprising given that David would be contributing to Push Naturals throughout the next three years. After that, David went with the attorney and informed Anna that he would be back at six in the evening, allowing Anna to finally be left alone.

It was now their wedding day. For the first time in what felt like hours, Anna was no longer affected by the overpowering presence of David, and she looked around the mass of people in bewilderment. They were just a few short hours away from getting married in the

Grand Walkerhill in Seoul. It is a dream venue that is beautifully nestled on the bank of the Hangang River.

Anna remained at David's side throughout the entire spectacular feast. After what felt like an endless string of lectures, the music finally started playing. David had brought her out onto the patio and into the middle of the space, and then he and she had begun to dance. She was in his arms, and their eyes locked. Indeed, it's true that they had sexual chemistry, but is it enough for a happy and enduring marriage? She thought as they danced together in front of all their guests.

Chapter 32

If he wasn't trying to get her into bed, David had revealed himself to be a clever and amusing company. "Not even close," he responded as he set his drink down and placed his hand on her as it was lying on the table. "I am completely informed on the subject." He stared at her eyes and added, "You are an extremely attractive and alluring woman." She tried to pull her hand away, but his fingers intertwined with hers and kept her from doing so. He then said, "I didn't mean just sex."

"Allow me to complete. I am confident that we are compatible in that regard." He released her hand and leaned in close to her, reaching out with one finger to tilt her head while his glittering eyes held hers. "It is impossible to deny the fact that we share a potent chemistry." He looked at her hungrily.

"When I touch you, you turn to mush, and the same thing happens to me. That is a significant benefit in any marriage, and as for the rest, we have a lifetime to get to know each other." Anna's cheeks burned from the heat. She heaved an internal sigh of relief when David sat back and was silent for a time, since the sexual tension had returned in full force and she had been looking forward to it. After that, he proceeded by saying, "But I also know you and I both want the same thing—to have a child or two and be a family, and at the same time make the families we already have happy."

"You believe that to be sufficient, don't you?" He said it in a pretty cynical manner, but it sounded like he was saying. "It's a lot more than most people in this day and age aspire to."

He leaned forward once more and said, "A growing percentage of people have children with no more thought than they would give to purchasing a new coat, and they cast off their responsibilities with the same ease as shedding a coat." He said this while grinning ironically. "But let me reassure you, Anna," he said. My schedule will need to be reorganized after we have a child, even though I travel a lot. I'm not going to be a parent who is never around."

He made a comment that shocked her, which is why she remained silent. She wasn't sure if the possibility of his improved presence in her life would give her comfort. He stood up and tossed money onto the table before sitting back down. David gave her the order to "Come on, let's go," then moved around to her side, extended his hand to her, and said, "Let's go." It was taken by Anna...

Anna awoke the following morning in David's bed, complaining of painful muscles in parts of her body she had no idea she had. She jumped out of bed and dashed into the bathroom as soon as she realized there was no trace of David. She slipped on a pair of peach-colored slacks and paired them with a silk shirt of the same color, grateful that she had brought some things over yesterday, even if it had been in a fit of fury. She combed her hair and then pulled it back with a scarf that had a variety of colors before placing her feet into supple suede mules. She had to muster every ounce of her strength of will to drag herself out of the bedroom.

Anna brewed a cup of coffee for herself in the kitchen's stainless steel appliance and then made her way back into the living area, unsure of what she should do next. Leaving it the way it was seemed like a decent alternative, she pondered right before David walked in, looking incredible in a dark gray business suit, a lighter gray shirt, and a silk tie. She had a hard time taking her eyes away from his, and she had to fight back the flush that was threatening to appear.

"I was about to wake you up, but I see that you've already dressed; that's a good sign." Anna was still processing this sentence when he came across the room and grinned brilliantly down at her. "My lawyer will be here in fifteen minutes so that you can sign the prenup, and that's it." Anna was still thinking of his comment when he strolled across the room. "Honey, the wedding is tomorrow, and everything is ready."

He gently planted a kiss on the top of her head. "I have people who can help you sell your home if you haven't done so already, and I can get them to do it for you if you let me know." His inquisitive eyes looked at her.

He appeared to be very unruffled and unconcerned about anything. It was evident that a night of passionate sex had no impact on him other than to leave him with a contented smile on his face. Anna suddenly became aware that she needed to act in the same way.

"No, we won't need that," she replied. She didn't like to lie, but she didn't know what else to say because she was at a loss for words. "I have it all arranged." It was now time for her to move on with her life which was in his bed. After what happened the night before, staying in that specific bed wasn't going to be a challenge for her, but considering the rest of her life...

David's attorney was quite productive, and he insisted on reading the entire pre-nuptial agreement to both of them before signing it. In essence, they both kept everything they had, but Anna was not entitled to anything if they divorced within the first three years of their marriage. This wasn't surprising given that David would be contributing to Push Naturals throughout the next three years. After that, David went with the attorney and informed Anna that he would be back at six in the evening, allowing Anna to finally be left alone.

It was now their wedding day. For the first time in what felt like hours, Anna was no longer affected by the overpowering presence of David, and she looked around the mass of people in bewilderment. They were just a few short hours away from getting married in the

Grand Walkerhill in Seoul. It is a dream venue that is beautifully nestled on the bank of the Hangang River.

Anna remained at David's side throughout the entire spectacular feast. After what felt like an endless string of lectures, the music finally started playing. David had brought her out onto the patio and into the middle of the space, and then he and she had begun to dance. She was in his arms, and their eyes locked. Indeed, it's true that they had sexual chemistry, but is it enough for a happy and enduring marriage? She thought as they danced together in front of all their guests.

Chapter 33

David decided that they would have a Korean traditional wedding. To begin the ceremony her stepmother Jenna along with David's female friend Jin performed the Jum-chok Rye. It turns out that since David's mother had already passed away, Bryan's friend Kim's wife, Jin takes the role traditionally assigned to the mother in the wedding procession. They lit candles to invoke the god of heaven to be present at the ceremony by sending up candle flames. Jin lit a red candle and Jenna lit a blue candle. They ended by bowing toward each other and then toward the guests.

David entered with Bryan carrying a wooden goose. Once they got to the front David handed the goose to my father. It is said that the goose keeps the promise of love forever. The goose was placed on the table with its head facing west while David bowed to the floor twice. My father took the small table with the goose where my family was seated.

Anna walked down the aisle to take her position on the west with David on the east side of the table. They both washed their hands to symbolize the purity of mind and body before the sacred ceremony. She was wearing a magnificent red silk hanbok and David had a blue hanbok. Then moments later they moved their positions on the mat.

They have to bow to each other to pay homage to their union as a couple and pledge respect for each other throughout their lives. Anna bowed twice, followed by once from David, twice more from her, once more from him, and rounded it out with two more from her. Anna was stunned at her bowing technique. She bowed six times deeply to the floor while David only bowed two times. It seems that in Korean culture in the past, females had a more subservient role in marriage. Anna thought, would she be satisfied with that same role in their marriage? At this time, she has been subservient to him due to her family's circumstances.

The rest of the ceremony was a lot of drinking and eating. With the Seo-cheon-ji Rye, they pledge to the gods of heaven and earth that they would fulfill their obligations as husband and wife. They raised their cup of wine to the sky and then poured it out, and then filled it again to pour into the ground, and then put some of the food on the table. They filled up the cups again and this time pledged to each other and drank from the cups.

Finally, a gourd that had been split in two was filled with wine, they exchanged their halves and drank from it. This ritual declared them as becoming one body and one mind. They then bowed to their families and guests to thank them for coming and then the conclusion of their marriage was declared.

Anna allowed her gaze to linger for a brief period on the man who had recently become her husband. He was surrounded by his guests. Her mind was spinning because she was exhausted by the ceremony. In a hurry, she averted her gaze. She walked around to the corner to reach one of the enormous marble columns that supported the upper balcony. Along the way, she noticed a large potted vine and walked over to lightly touch the leaves of the plant. She supported herself on it. She was uncomfortable in her wedding hanbok, but the shade and the cool marble at her back provided some much-needed reprieve from the oppressive conditions.

She had finally accomplished her goal and was now married, which made everyone happy. That is correct regarding Bryan. Her normally rigid face suddenly broke into a fleeting smile. She felt a lot less anxious about the prospect of getting married to David thanks to the excitement David's grandfather displayed when she arrived yesterday and the gentle charm that he exuded.

In consideration of the fact that it was her wedding day and Bryan's moral standards on what was appropriate, she had been provided with a room of her very own the night before, much to David's chagrin. Having spent the previous two nights in David's bed, however, Anna was relieved to finally have some breathing room to herself. It turned out to be far more difficult than she had anticipated to match David's sex drive.

This morning, at a very early hour, Bryan had entered her bedroom while carrying a coffee tray, which had taken her completely by surprise.

After that, he had assured her that David was a nice man and that he was certain that his grandson loved her. They had enjoyed some coffee together. But he had also remarked that he knew David could be domineering in the pursuit of what he wanted and that if Anna had any questions about marrying him, she should tell so now, and Bryan would understand.

Anna had said that she had some reservations about marrying David. She had calmed the elderly man and apologized for lying to him in Los Angeles when she told him she had never seen David before. She had justified the deception by mentioning David's attachment to Annet then, so the old guy had accepted her apology.

"Pardon, but..." Anna raised an eyebrow and caught a glimpse of an elderly, incredibly handsome man with a head full of white hair standing in front of her. "I was wondering if I might have a brief conversation with you.'

"Why, yes, of course!" Is it you, Mr. Park?' She remembered his name because earlier when he was in the receiving line, he had appeared shocked when he spotted her. This helped her remember his name. Along with his wife and kids, he had a son in a wheelchair who was roughly David's age.

You are Anna Williams, or you formerly were. Yes?'

"Yes, why are you asking?" His brown eyes darkened with some deep emotion, and at that moment, Anna wondered if it was wise to talk to a man she didn't know. All of a sudden, he grinned, and his lovely face sprang to life.

You are my lovely Martha's... I don't know how to phrase it... niece, right?'

After five minutes had passed, Anna's eyes were filled with tears, and she was holding the man's hand tightly with both of hers. Her aunt had been having an affair with him for the past three decades, and the fact that Mr. Park had a son in a wheelchair was the reason he had never left his wife.

After Anna informed him about her aunt's will and the house on Jeju Island, he became overcome with emotion and began to cry. "Excuse a silly old man, but meeting you and knowing you will keep her memory alive for me, and keeping our secret, I am satisfied." And as he said this, he leaned forward and kissed her on the cheek. "I can see her in your eyes, and if you ever, ever, ever need anything at all, call on me," he said.

Where on earth could she have been? David had been walking on the premises when he suddenly stopped. His bride of a few hours was leaning back against a marble pillar, holding hands with the banker, and allowing him to kiss her cheek. Mr. Park was also holding her hand. A man she had just met, and very likely the only man in Seoul who had David's level of riches. What was Anna's fascination with older men? Bryan only needed to catch a glimpse of her before liking her, and Mr. Park, who was renowned for being a model of decorum, was visibly surprised by her allure.

Anna's head shot up at the sound of David's voice, and she watched the older man's eyes narrow as he focused on her. David had asked, "So this is where you're hiding." He uttered the statement in Korean. In response, Mr. Park mumbled something, after which he laughed and turned to face Anna.

"Anna, it has been a pleasure to meet you finally, but unfortunately, I have to go."

"But I hope that we cross paths again."

Anna broke into a happy smile. She said quietly, "So do I," as she watched him leave the place.

"It is quite moving. But do you really need to isolate yourself and flirt with every old man you come across?" David snorted angrily.

Chapter 34

"Neither was I trying to hide nor was I flirting with anyone," Anna insisted. I was trying to cool off, but seeing David with sweat beads on his forehead and his big chest did little to lower her heat. The sight of him caused her temperature to rise. But if there was one thing that she got from her time with David, she learned that it was to have a far better understanding of her aunt Martha. She thought to herself with a smile that curled her lips, and now she and her aunt had a passion for handsome Korean males in common in addition to their passion for plants.

"If you say so," he shrugged, but she could sense the rage that was brewing beneath his surface. "You can cool off in the helicopter because it's time we said goodbye to our guests and left for Jeju Island," he told her, firmly gripping her hand as he led her back into the mass of guests. After a little time had passed, Anna disembarked from the chopper and looked around. They touched down on a helipad that was located on the top of a building. "Where exactly are we?" She was asking him. David reached out and took her arm while also looking at her. "My hotel," he said to her.

Anna was startled out of a deep slumber by a tingling feeling that ran down the entirety of her spine. It was a finger running over her body, and when she opened her eyes, she saw a rough, hairy chest. She turned over onto her back with a sigh of relief and a stretch. David was gazing down at her. The thought of getting started without you had me worried. There was no mistake in his arousal level, as his entire length rubbed firmly against her thigh. 'You are insatiable,' Anna said, looking lazily up at him.

"Mmm, but morning arousal in men is a fact of life—one we poor guys have to cope with," David murmured drolly, one hand reaching out to cup her breast. "Is that so?" Anna moaned, "I didn't know that," as savory feelings began to permeate her body.

"Then you must have been exceptionally unobservant of the males in your life, which brings to mind..." He paused, his fingers moving in a figure-eight motion across both of her breasts. "I talked to Sara about how early you get up, and we both decided that it would be in everyone's best interest if the person you employ worked the overnights and early mornings.

"What did you do?" No longer relaxed, Anna tensed in anger. "It was inappropriate for you to talk about my work behind my back." David's fingers stopped stroking her chest. "I would not have intervened if I had even the slightest doubt that you and Sara were okay with the way things are, but I do know for a fact that Sara isn't upset with the situation. Because of your friendship, she exclusively trades early mornings with you." He explained.

Anna looked at him in disbelief. Did she say it to you? She has never told me about it. Anna's voice trailed off as she murmured, "But I asked her dozens of times if she minded." And "no" was usually her response. "She probably didn't want to appear to be taking advantage of the position as a married lady caring for a young child. But you must have known that the last thing she needed was to wake up at the crack of dawn to go to work when her baby was keeping her up at night." David continued.

"Oh my God!" Anna cussed. Why hadn't she demanded that Sara ignore the early mornings? Since, if she were being frank. She also doesn't want to wake up early and work. She said with embarrassment, "You're correct.

David laughed and continued to run his fingers over her breasts slowly. "I often am," he said playfully. His kisses brushed softly across her mouth as he said, "So, no more arguments." The teasing caresses lulled her back into languorous bliss. She watched the shadow of desire darken his chiseled features as he husked, "But in consolation, you were right about my being insatiable." After a long, slow, sensual kiss, he said, "And you love it, Anna." She couldn't deny the truth in his words.

After half an hour of his gentle yet scorching lovemaking, she declined his invitation to join him in the shower. She lay there for a while, her eyes wide as she tried to process what had just occurred to her. Since arriving on Saturday night, they hadn't been out of the suite until this morning, a Monday. They had hardly even gotten out of bed at that point.

She had never known there was another side to her sexuality until David showed it to her. She had adored Allen and their first night together. Not only that, but she remembers sobbing afterward, overtaken with emotion at the magic of his lovemaking. They had made love regularly, and she never worried that she wasn't being loved, even if she rarely had climaxes. The anguish she had felt over his death had nearly destroyed her, and she vowed never to feel that way again. David, on the other hand, was an expert in lovemaking, and the fact is that she doesn't love him like he loved Allen. This comparison had bothered her immensely. Her body's carnal need always wins over her feelings.

However, she felt nothing close to tears when she thought about or talked to David. Her sole reaction, if it could be called an emotion, had been a wild and reckless carnal as he led her down the various seductive avenues of sexuality with such skill and experience that she was driven senseless.

Where did it leave her, then? Anna got out of bed, wrapped herself in a towel, and strolled to the window to contemplate the beach and water outside. When she heard the water running in the bathroom, she turned to gaze at the door, her heart racing at the thought of David showering in his underwear.

As she headed for the restroom, she realized the answer to her question. She would have been a wonderful wife for David, who was a known womanizer and considered marriage a commercial transaction. They both desired something from the relationship, but love did not factor into the equation. That was fine with Anna. Opening the bathroom door, she slipped off her robe and joined David in the shower stall.

While he was turning on the faucets in the shower, he leaned in close to her. As he submerged her hand in the water and held her palm in his own, he whispered," Is that okay?" while holding her languid gaze with his own." Is that all right?" Anna replied," Just right," while purposefully inviting David to look at her mouth with her own before whispering," Just right." His eyes lit up like fire when he heard her invitation, but he decided against accepting her offer. Rather, he led her into the bathroom's shower and began washing himself with a bar of soap, while Anna stood there and watched him. She concentrated all her attention on the sensation of the water on her skin and yearned for more of the same.

She reached out her hand for the soap. When David handed it to her, she moved closer to him and began rubbing the soap on his body. This had very little to do with cleaning him and everything to do with taking pleasure in the sensation of his skin beneath her hands.

She ran her hands over him, swirling soap in intricate patterns, finding the exact moment to tease him erotically, and occasionally touching him with the tips of her breasts. She delighted in every instant of the quiet, planned seduction she utilized. She watched as his arousal sprang into life and flicked her eyes up at his eyes and the stiff set of his jaw. She felt the tension in him grow as she watched his erection develop into life.

Chapter 35

B ut just as she was about to torment him in the most personal way conceivable, he grabbed the bar of soap out of her hands. With a twisted smile, he proceeded to do to her what she had done to him. Utilized her strategies with just as much success as she had achieved.

At last, Anna's need for him had worn her down to the point that she had to rest against the shower wall. She moaned quietly as she pleaded for some kind of relief or satisfaction. " David..." she croaked his name from the back of her throat.

David turns the shower off and takes Anna to their bed. Anna gasped his name, "David," as his fingers gently stroked between her thighs, slowly and lightly. She felt electric shock-waves of sensation jolting through her body. She wanted him, and she wanted to cry out, but instead, she pressed her mouth to his throat and bit down in a fever of frustration.

David stifled a groan, and the swift kiss he pressed on her swollen lips turned into a savage duel of tongues. His long fingers parted the petals of her womanhood and found the hot, damp, velvet flesh throbbing, waiting for him..... He touched her gently, softly, fast, then slowly, until her hips arched towards him, her hands dug into his shoulders, and she was calling out his name. Please, she moaned, her head thrashing from side to side. David waited for her at the peak of her arousal until she shuddered in the ecstasy of her orgasm.

His hands slipped under her hips and lifted her slightly off the bed. She felt the velvet tip of his hard male flesh stroke, and then, with one thrust, he was there, where she wanted him to be. She moaned his name, and he moved deeper and harder, filling her, stretching her, and taking her on a wild journey of almost mystical proportion. She felt the mighty strength of his thrusting, driving her on until she cried out as her slender body convulsed in a climax, and he joined her in ecstasy.

Later that day, David glanced at Anna and then at the granite stairs. "Is there no other way to descend?" There's a jetty, and you can get to the home by boat, but other than that, this is all, she told him with a grin. She went by him and started walking down the stairs, saying, "I hope you're fit." David said, "No—wait," and he seized her arm. "Let me go first," he said, "then if you fall, I can catch you." He didn't want to lose his brand-new bride in a fatal plunge to the rocks below.

Anna joked, "My, what a gentleman," but she did what she was told. They visited Jeju Island today. Aunt Martha's home was a single-story structure about twenty feet wide and forty feet long, located in the center of a small strip of ground that was elevated slightly above the shore. It had been enlarged a decade or so ago, fairly cheaply, by adding another twenty feet to one end to create a pleasant living room with floor-to-ceiling glass doors to take full advantage of the spectacular view.

Anna allowed herself a little grin when David said, "It's not as bad as I thought" as they halted outside the initial door. He was in for a surprise when Anna said, "I've arranged for an architect to look over the place on Thursday." She opened the door and ushered David into the living room. The room was just as Anna remembered it. Two enormous cream couches with soft cushions look a little worn from years of usage. A glass-topped table propped up by two dragons and a little semicircular bar in one corner. There was a wall of book-filled shelves. Her aunt's influence was everywhere she looked, and the memories flooded back. She wandered restlessly to the window and stared out at the ocean, much troubled by the thought of whether or not her aunt would approve of what she had done.

David approached from behind and placed his arm through the opening they had made. She leaned back against him, appreciative of his support. "I just don't understand why you decided it wasn't habitable. The space is tight, but enough for weekend getaways. Bryan's desire to return here is clear, and I can understand it. The cove indeed provides a breathtaking panorama," he said.

The steep cliffs that protruded about a hundred feet on either side of the small bay protected it from the worst of the storms, and Anna nodded as she looked out over it. Her gaze went to the other side, where a landing had been carved out of the rock, and a walkway wound its way through the garden and back to the house.

"Let's go ahead and check out the bedroom. Bryan mentioned there were two, but I think they'll have expansion and another couple built to accommodate the scale of the structure," David remarked, turning her in his arms and gazing into her eyes. Cleverly adding, "I don't like to feel constrained in the bedroom," he sounded really unhappy.

Anna's cheeks were pink from a little blush. She said, "I know," her eyes growing noticeably darker, and he dipped his head to take her barely parted lips, delving directly between them with the overpowering sexiness of a pro.

The familiar sensuous pleasure lanced through her, and she locked her hands around the nape of his neck and pressed into the firm muscular wall of his chest, her breasts tingling at the touch. Anna allowed herself to indulge in the kind of sensual pleasure that only David could provide. However, temporarily. She then had a brilliant plan and put her hands between them, ripping her mouth away from his. She caught the look of bewilderment on his face and smiled devilishly.

"You wanted to see the bedroom," she reminded him, and, spinning away, she giggled as she dashed through the great room to the corridor. As he came to a halt by her side, David gave her a puzzled glance. If I had to guess, I'd say that Anna is up to no good.

She smiled as she entered the bedroom door and turned on the light, casting a soft light through the curtains. She threw her arms wide and said, "ta-da...!'

"Oh, my God!"' David exclaimed. Anna found the look of shock on his face hilarious. The house's original two bedrooms and bathroom have been combined to create a single, spacious bedroom with an attached bathroom.

The paintings spanning three walls featured sexual nude individuals in astonishing poses and intimate detail. The ceiling was covered with a mirror and wild silk laced with gold. The middle was a beaten gold canopy held up by snake-entwined gold rods, both of which were an integral part of the enormous circular bed below.

David pulled her close and murmured, "Now I understand why you didn't want Bryan to visit," his admiring eyes narrowed. "But I don't get why you deemed it inappropriate for you and me." An insatiable fire burned in her core. She murmured softly, "Perhaps because I didn't know you so well when I said that," and then, a little taken aback by her own audacity, she encircled him in her arms. The sexual tension between them was palpable.

"You now understand, so how about we hang together for a while?" David's question was heavy. "Oh, absolutely. I—" His tongue slid between her partially closed lips. That she could finish the sentence was not in question. She clung to him, shaking, as he hoisted her up and slipped off her sandals before setting her down on the enormous bed.

"Every time I look at you, I want to strip you naked," David said. He quickly stripped down to his underwear, kicked off his sandals, and joined her on the bed. A chuckle followed.

Chapter 36

"I know." She moved her fingers over his biceps and across to linger sensually on the powerful bulk of his chest as yearning surged inside her. As David reached for her, she beamed. "Your touch, as much as I like it, is not a smart idea right now. I want to take my time with you," so he took her hand and slipped her top down from her shoulders, dropping his head so he could taste the soft curves of her breasts. Her mouth dropped open in shock.

"You are very responsive," David said huskily. He laid her down gently on the bed and removed her underwear. His eyes swept over her lovely face and delicate shoulders before he leaned back and stared at her. When Anna realized how intensely aroused he was, she gasped for air.

David smirked, a wickedly amused twist of his mouth revealing an irresistibly alluring "for you" expression. However, not just yet. He reached forward and grasped her hands, spreading them out to the sides of her body. He told her to "stay like that" as his eyes swept down past her pert, rose-tipped breasts, and into the shaven part in between her legs. As he grasped her breasts and gently kneaded them, Anna's hands curled into the soft, silky sheets at her sides, but she did as he instructed. Then he bit the stiff points with his finger and thumb until she let out a squeaky squeal of ecstasy.

"I want to make the most of this incredible space," he whispered. He went in close enough to trace the edge of her mouth with his tongue before slipping it inside with a wickedness that made her blood thicken and then flow like molten lava. Attempting to embrace him, she raised her arms, but he returned them to the bed.

133

Not yet, he said, as he started playing with her breasts again, this time with his tongue. She finally called out to him as the rhythmic suction transmitted more potent sexual signals through her body.

"How about that?" he said huskily.

"Yes," she muttered as his tongue went lower to her stomach until it reached her shaven, moist center below, gliding between the velvet folds and remaining there to tease and caress with gentle precision. "Oh, yeah," Anna writhed, her body on fire with ecstasy. Then she gasped when she saw her reflection in the canopy's mirrored ceiling. She had stretched out underneath him, submitting to his torturous kisses. She saw herself so wanton as his head moved in between her legs. She noticed the perspiration on his toned physique and the effort in his arousal. His tongue tortured her with delight as he moved faster and faster at the thrust of her hips until she shuddered with ecstasy.

She opened her eyes wide as David reared up and plunged into the smooth, wet heat of her, and she felt the agonizing anguish of unfulfilled longing leave her body. As his strong shoulders locked, he drove deeply, shattering her hold. She grabbed him tightly, her fingernails cutting into his back as her abdominal muscles tightened to encompass his entire body.

He sighed, "Ah, Anna," and leaned back. Don't stop, she pleaded weakly. And with that, he leaned in and gave her a passionate kiss. "But it's my turn to view," he said as he turned her around to straddle him, fire imminent in his smoldering eyes. She was on top of him. Their bodies were engaged in a furious, primal embrace as he shook Anna to her core. In a tangle of arms and legs, he whirled her around on the sumptuous bed with a thrusting, driven desire that finally destroyed his control. A gruff grunt was wrenched from his throat, and the world shattered around Anna in wave after wave of bliss so magnificent that she thought she would die of it. Her last conscious thought was to sob out his name, and suddenly David was on top of her again, his huge body stiff and racked with enormous, shuddering spasms.

David's head was buried in the crook of her shoulder when she opened her eyes. She looked up and saw his wonderful bronzed form reflected there, his skin drenched with perspiration, his buttocks clenched, and she felt the still-throbbing length of him inside her. Again, her eyes were closed. After waiting for a while, she felt David's heavy voice rasping in her ear. He moved over onto his back and said, "I'm too heavy—I don't want to flatten you into the bed."

Anna's eyes opened, and she looked up at him in the mirror. "You're not that heavy," she said, her eyes lingering over his lovely chest. Is it the beginning of a belly pouch, I, see?" she flirted, stealing another glance at his abs. The focus of his gaze led her to the realization that she, too, was exposed. She had an uneasy feeling in her gut. Naked intimacy between partners was one thing, but a mirrored bed added awkwardness and discomfort.

David put his weight on one elbow and peered down at her, saying, "Cheeky." "I'm a man at the height of my prime," he beamed. "But your aunt must have been one heck of a woman, with a tremendously sensual imagination," he said, his face almost turning pink at the sight of a picture on the wall. "The notion may have come from her partner, though, so that's a possibility." He added.

"You might be correct about the fantasy thing." Anna remarked sarcastically, "I know it was after spending ten days sharing this room with my aunt last year that I fell into your bed on the yacht."

"Perhaps the wine wasn't to blame. Perhaps some sort of subconscious message was conveyed to me."

David laughed, and he thought that was far better than thinking that she may have substituted him for her dead spouse. Like the man who had paid for this love nest, he understood and appreciated pure passion.

"Do you know who your aunt's boyfriend was?" he asked lazily.

"No, I don't know what you're talking about." She spoke.

David stared at her in the mirror on the ceiling. A tiny blush of pink was creeping over her cheeks and coloring her wonderful face, and her magnificent hair was fanning out in a wild halo about her head, with a few strands falling over her breasts. Her beautiful, dark chocolate eyes avoided his, and he immediately sensed that she was lying. The subtle stiffness of her body against his told him just how she felt. If so, why?

"Your aunt never dropped a clue on you?" He added.

She had an opportunity to tell the truth, which he urged.

Anna sat up and pushed her tangled mane off her brow, shaking her head firmly. "Now that she's dead, it doesn't matter anyhow," she told him with a sidelong glance. "Are you aware that the two of us are lying on our backs in this bed?" she said, bringing her thighs together.

Chapter 37

"There isn't a right way on a round bed," David pointed out with a somewhat sarcastic smile, well-knowing that she had purposely sought to divert the subject and opted to let it go. Even if it had nothing to do with him, the fact that Anna had lied still bothered him. She didn't trust him with the truth. But why should he care? He was wedded to her, and he understood without arrogance the raging passion that burned within him whenever he even thought about her.

David gazed at her, and she gave the same amount of attention back to him. They had excellent chemistry in bed. Even though she couldn't hide her reaction to his touch, he couldn't help but wonder what else she was keeping from him.

Anna said with a resigned, "No, I suppose not," and she shuddered for no apparent reason. She felt an overwhelming need to leave the room as its confines began to seem oppressive. She stepped into her underwear and shorts, but had to circle the bed to reach her top. When she did, she put it on and buttoned it up with trembling fingers.

Until David noticed the darkness in her eyes and the rush with which she had put on her clothes, her smile seemed encouraging. Did she come to regret the luxurious bed they shared? Or maybe she was just thinking about her ex-husband and wished she had experienced the moment with him instead. The idea came to him out of the blue.

No way, no how. For a lady who had been married previously, David's stunning wife was surprisingly inexperienced in the bedroom, yet she was eager to please when it came to making love. When he sank his tongue into her moist center in between her legs and tipped her into a shuddering climax, he felt the nervousness in her touch, saw the shock in her eyes, and felt the small resistance.

She had revealed breathlessly that it was something she'd never done before. After one especially exciting session in the spa bath, he overheard her exclaim, "I didn't know that was possible," and just now, he overheard her claim that she had never heard of male morning arousal. Perhaps her late husband lacked a strong libido.

He saw her delicate pink-toed feet as she slipped on her sandals. He found himself daydreaming as his gaze lingered over her beautiful feet. He adored her for all of her qualities. Her black gorgeous hair ran down her back in a velvety disorder, her face was free of make-up, gleaming in the aftermath of sex, and the swelling shapes of her full lips made him want to kiss her again. Reawaken her passion for him...

Anna had turned out to be a fantastic lover—shy at first, but increasingly confident as time went on. In a flash, he was aroused once again by the memory of her laughter as she threw open the door to this room and ran into his arms. As she fumbled with her top, his eyes drifted down to her cleavage. She was as genuine as the flowers she admired, and perhaps even more beautiful. But she was familiar with another man...

It returned once again. The naive desire to learn more about her previous husband's sexual prowess. Why the hell did it even concern him? This was quite unlike him. There had never been a woman he knew of whom he was interested in learning more about their background.

David had many lovers, and he never addressed the ladies in his past. He knew he was a wonderful lover, and he knew he made Anna happy in bed; that was all that counted, wasn't it...? He noticed that she was heading for the exit. 'Leaving so soon?' he said teasingly.

Anna shot him an over-the-shoulder glance. 'Yes. You've seen the property now, and we'll be back the day after tomorrow with the architect. You were right, the house is suitable for use as a vacation residence. Without waiting for an answer, she flung open the door, sprinted down the corridor, and out into the open air, saying, "But in my opinion, it's not really suitable for Bryan to live in. The access is far too difficult."

David felt a sharp pain in his gut as Anna abruptly turned her back on him and bolted from the room, proving to him once and for all that he cared about more than just making Anna happy in bed. He wants a great deal more. He wanted to be so important to her that she couldn't bear to be without him.

Despite his skepticism about love, David Miller found himself hopelessly infatuated. Since the moment he saw her, he had been trying to convince himself that she was married and therefore off-limits. However, the reality dawned on him quickly. He had remained celibate for a year after meeting Anna, and as a man who had never gone more than a couple of months without a woman since he was a teenager, he should have noticed something was wrong.

It had been pure desperation that had pushed him into dating Amelia Smith. His single-minded goal to make Anna his had begun the moment he saw her again and realized she was available.

He took a startled look around the bedroom, which had been decorated by former loves but no longer held any significance for David. The home was Theo's dream, not his, yet he nonetheless used it and the pressure from her father to convince Anna to marry him.

Oh, for crying out loud... After everything he'd done to her, how could he expect her to fall in love with him? In fact, if this gut-wrenching fearful emotion was love, he wasn't sure he wanted it.

Anna took a long, steadying breath as she went carefully down to the water's edge.

Do I assume that the wild sex is canceled? She looked up to see David's dryly amused gaze as he suddenly materialized by her side. A witty "You've got it right" came back from her lips. "Let's go back to our nice hotel, where I can relax and have my every whim catered to." David cupped her face in his hands; her long, free hair shone in the light. Despite her witty remark, she looked at him with a hint of wariness, and he really wanted to tell her how he felt at that very moment. He wants to witness her magnificent eyes lose their wariness and light with a more profound feeling. He didn't, though. Instead, he gave her a deep, passionate kiss. Anna was finally his, and he intended to do whatever was in his power to retain her.

On Thursday, however, when Anna had stubbornly waited outside while David gave architect Jang a tour of the property, he began to have second thoughts. Jang's eyes widened in excitement as he entered the bedroom. After he drew out a rough plan, they stepped outside to find Anna lounging on a towel on the beach in a skimpy bikini, and things got a lot hotter from there.

David realized that he was far from pleased to watch other guys admire Anna's great figure, despite his own admiration for it. The architect's very subtle statement in Korean, "Are you sure you want to get rid of that bedroom?" did not go over well with him, either." David concentrated his gaze on his wife while giving him a gimlet-eyed glare that drove the grin from his lips. He said, "You've had enough sun for one day, Anna," and he reached down to lift her. He reached for the towel and slung it over her neck

Chapter 38

He looked into her chocolate eyes, saw astonishment and curiosity, and realized he had come off as harsh. But he had never experienced jealousy before, so maybe that was why. David thought, How have the mighty fallen? He wrapped his arm protectively around her and grinned cynically.

Through her voluminous lashes, she gave him a sidelong glance. That means destroying the garden and rock garden, right?'

"Yes. It all adds up perfectly. Don't you see?", he said with rising fervor. A veranda will stretch the length of the structure to provide shelter from the afternoon sun, which will be on that side. The remaining space will be a brick patio where you may have outdoor meals surrounded by beautiful vines and palms in pots. There will be minimal upkeep required.

"No,' she denied firmly, yanking out of his arm as she disregarded David and turned to Jang, saying, 'Sorry, you'll have to think of some other method, maybe adding a second story to the home, or reinstating the original two bedrooms?"

David was perplexed and perhaps irritated by her abrupt rejection of the scheme. "Think rationally, Anna because that's the only available space. And as I recall, you hurt your fingers, creating the rockery. The garden is unnecessary because of the breathtaking scenery of the bay.

She said bluntly, "It is to me,' averting his look. He did not doubt that his wife enjoyed gardening, but her antics were getting on his nerves. 'Show my wife the sketch, and I'm sure when she understands how magnificent it would be, she'll agree.' But, to his shock, Anna grabbed the sketch that Jang handed out to her, gazed at it, and then tore it into small pieces.

"My husband has unfortunately misled you, Jang. This home is mine and mine alone, and any renovations or adjustments to it shall be performed solely at my direction and with my approval." Anna was distressed.

"David, don't you think so?" She glared at him with fire in her eyes. 'As I recall, it's laid out as so in our pre-nup,' she informed him scathingly. 'You keep what's yours, and I keep what's mine. I have to go swimming now, please forgive me. "She tossed down the towel and dashed down the beach toward the water."

David wanted to strangle the architect out of frustration, but he had to walk him off the property instead. He promised to get back to her later. After taking the time to go to the top of the cliff and then back down to the beach, David was able to calm himself and think things through.

He was a bright individual who had previously made a fortune via stock market analysis, and investment. He used the same perceptiveness in his reading of Anna. She was incredibly attractive, but she was also a good person who would do anything for everyone. It showed in her interactions with everyone she came into contact with. The hotel staff adored her; he overheard her this morning inquiring about the health of the porter's newborn. She could make friends with anyone, and even though David had forced her to marry him, she hadn't put up much of a fight and had done more than her fair share of the housekeeping.

He had never had more incredible sex with a woman, and yet he still wanted more. It wasn't simply the physical proximity to Anna that scared him; his intense emotions did, too. He felt a love for her that he'd never experienced before. Because of this, he recognized that Anna's reaction to a sketch proposing an addition to the house was out of character. With a narrowing of his gray eyes, he cast his eyes away and wandered over the cove and then the lawn. The garden meant a lot to her, but why exactly did it cause her such distress?

He changed into his black Speedo trunks and headed for the water. She straightened up, bending her head to squeeze out the last water, and then, like Aphrodite emerging from the sea, she flicked her long hair over one shoulder. As soon as she saw him, tension shot through her, and he watched her move toward him with reluctance.

They connected along the shore. His usually brown eyes suddenly looked much darker. Oh my God, she was so beautiful! However, he dismissed the idea of sexual activity as a solution. He wanted to know what had made her react so out of character just now.

Jang has gone and won't be returning until you say so,' he said as he stretched out and interlaced his fingers with hers and said, "I think it's time for us to have a chat."

She said to him, "That sounds ominous," and then she started to giggle. He covered her lips. He brought her to where the towel was lying on the beach and, sitting down, dragged her down next to him, clamping her to his side with one arm over her waist. For real, David. You just admitted that I've gotten too much sun; therefore, it's time for me to cover up. She peered up into his apprehensive eyes and said, "You're not going anywhere until you tell me why you were so adamant that the garden couldn't be built on." What I don't see is why you give a hoot about what happens to the home where your aunt was having an affair with the man who gave it to her. If this is only your second trip here, then there must be some sort of family secret that your aunt is keeping from you.

Anna trembled, David was direct, and though she had shed a lot of her inhibitions in the last week—inhibitions she hadn't even known she had until David became her lover—she was having enough problem breathing, much mind attempting to come up with a good explanation for her earlier actions.

The brown eyes were searching for hers. David murmured, with a smirk twitching the edges of his lips, "Don't even bother to try to conceal what you are thinking."

"Your eyes are always a dead giveaway. What if you trusted me instead?"

The idea of trusting David was completely foreign to her.

He reassured her, "I promise your secret will be safe with me."

Chapter 39

Curiously, she accepted his word. Anna detected an incorruptible aura of inner strength about him, despite his status as a powerful billionaire who had become a multimillionaire before the age of thirty and with enough sexual appeal to attract any woman.

Perhaps that was something he'd gotten from his granddad. In her mind, maybe she was wishing that to be true. With his arm around her, she felt safe, and as his light, musky aroma filled the air, she felt an overwhelming need to open up to him. She had been her aunt's lone protector for nearly a year, and she felt the burden of that responsibility.

David bowed his head, his eyes meeting hers through his thick lashes. I am an excellent listener," he argued.

How long are you going to keep harping on this? She sighed and informed him with her hands clasped.

"Twenty years ago, my aunt was expecting a baby from her lover. As they had done numerous times before, she was five months pregnant when they sailed into Jeju Island for their escapades, but this time she fell from the boat." "Within an hour, she had a miscarriage. It happened too fast to call for aid, not that it would have made a difference. She and her boyfriend buried the unborn child at the foot of the cliff and placed a few stones over the grave as a memorial."

"According to Aunt Martha, what they did wasn't against the law. If this had occurred at a hospital back then, the infant would have been immediately abandoned. But to my aunt, the baby was genuine, and it represented her undying love for her partner." Anna's eyes welled up as she remembered her aunt's pained expression as she told her the story. "She wanted a gravestone, but that wasn't an option, so instead I built the rockery as a memorial, and I also promised to preserve the baby's resting place."

Even though David was not an emotional guy, he could see why the home had been left in trust in the manner in which it had been. The lady had been unable to give it to her child, so she had left it to Anna's children, and then to her children's children. Whether this was fair to Anna, David was not so sure. He noticed the melancholy in her eyes and, using his free hand, carefully combed through the knotted mess of her hair to turn her around to face him. When he noticed that she was crying, he took a big breath. 'Don't say any more, hon, I understand.' Brushing his kisses across her brow, he wrapped his arm around her waist and drew her close, stroking his other hand up and down her back in an age-old gesture of reassurance.

Anna felt comforted in David's embrace, and her predominant reaction was relief at having shared the load. "Do you truly comprehend, I wonder?", she whispered. David's hand dropped from her back, and she scarcely felt the abrupt tightening of his lips as she said, "You don't believe in love, and maybe that's the best way to be, it only causes pain." She continued. "My aunt had a lifetime of unfulfilled dreams, including a family with the man she loved but could never have." "Instead, she has become his mistress and only be able to see him for a few weeks out of the year. That's very tragic." Anna cast her eye out over the harbor. "This is paradise, but maybe there's a snake in the grass." To which David said, "Now you're just being unbelievable," sarcastically. The location of your aunt's death is irrelevant, since she decided to live the way she did.

The warmth of his body and the charm of his grin won her over. But Anna was well aware of David's stance on freedom of choice, after all, she was the one sitting next to him, having married him. And here she was revealing to him all her darkest secrets!

She responded in a hurry, "Believe what you like," revealing her insecurity in confiding in him. She twisted out of his grip and stood up. "But I can't shake the notion that this place is cursed. Not only did it not bode well for Bryan, but it also did not bode well for Aunt Martha."

"He had to leave it when your mother got pregnant out of wedlock, and then she died very young. There's not much of a family left now; it's just you and Bryan."

David stood up and glared at her for many tense seconds. His mouth was set in a hard line. His eyes got really dark for no apparent reason, and then he attempted to relax and grin. "Put the house on hold for the time being. Let's leave this island behind and spend the rest of our vacation on my yacht where we can chat and I can try to fix my pathetically little family." He said ironically.

Anna awoke from a deep sleep when she heard the running water in the shower. She yawned and drew the soft cotton sheet up to cover her chest as she stretched. She sighed when she saw the time, it was just six o'clock in the morning. Then she recalled it was Monday— David was catching an early-morning flight to New York. He would arrive in New York in time for a business lunch, thanks to the time difference. Her tired muscles were a constant reminder of what happened last night.

The door of the en-suite bathroom opened and Anna's attention instantly shifted to her husband of four months. He had nothing on but a towel hanging over his slim hips. A solitary drop of water from his recent shower was making its way slowly down his thick, black hair. When he walked into the room, Anna's breath abruptly stopped and she realized she'd been holding it in shock. He was six feet plus of pure male perfection.

"I recognize that glare. Her eyes met Anna's. Then, after saying, "But I have to be in New York by noon and you've delayed me once already," he went into the back room to change. Anna shifted uneasily in her sleep, hitting the pillows and propping herself up with them. She should be delighted that David was leaving—one of the reasons she had married him was because he'd agreed to her wish to stay in Los Angeles, and she had depended on his not being around much. However, things weren't quite as she'd hoped. Now, she wished to spend most of her time with him. "What have I gotten myself into?" She asked herself regretfully. "Is it harder to have a long-distance relationship with him now because I'm getting too attached?" Get yourself together, she scolded herself. I might just be too inexperienced with sex; that's why my body longed for him. She assured herself.

Chapter 40

When they got back to Los Angeles from their trip, Anna had found a new BMW car waiting for her—a wedding present from David. He claimed to have seen that her car had long past its expiration date. He had only spent 20 days in Los Angeles, but he had already become friends with Sara and Mark before taking his departure. He didn't stop at just offering Mark a position with his firm; he went above and beyond. He recommended that Sara and her husband take a more hands-off approach to running Anna and Sara's Designs, significantly reduce the number of hours they put in, and hire at least two additional assistants to handle the workload associated with the new contract they had received. David was like a juggernaut, forcing everyone in his direction, so Anna's objections were disregarded.

Her lone success had been the Villa on Jeju Island. To make her changes, David had to travel to Seoul a week later and whisk her away for a few days so that they could convince Bryan to go along with her proposal on the island of Jeju. She had been glad to discover that the sensual bedroom had been stripped before they'd arrived. A new level was added to the house, and four bedrooms with private bathrooms were planned for the second story.

She looked around the room, thinking "home" was a very emotional term. Was she starting to feel at home here? She just knew that David didn't spend nearly as much time away from home as she had been led to think.

They had fantastic sex as husband and wife, but she didn't care whether they were any closer or further apart personally than they were on their wedding day. They have become friendly with one another, she thought.

They had a great time celebrating Christmas with Bryan in Seoul and are now back in Los Angeles for three days. On Sunday night, David gave her a diamond bracelet and demanded that they go to the opera to mark their six-month anniversary, which she enjoyed but knew he didn't.

He was quite generous in his gift-giving to her. She had more jewelry and clothing than she could possibly wear. She was slowly coming to terms with the fact that he was immensely wealthy and incredibly generous. She didn't care about wealth per se so long as she had enough to eat and pay the bills, but she suspected there was a crisis on the horizon.

She hadn't informed David yet, but her period was three weeks overdue. Her optimistic expectations that she could raise their child however she pleased, without much interference, were quickly dispelled. Her usually flawless brow was slightly furrowed. She knew that if they had a child, David would try to involve himself in every part of raising that child.

"Frowning? I'm flattered." Anna's head turned as David went towards her. Is it too much to ask that you miss me while I'm gone? "He looked at her from head to toe with a drawl in his voice and a flash of anger in his eyes. She looked down and saw that the sheet was wrapped around her thighs. She took a deep breath and pulled the cover over her breasts, surprised and embarrassed by his unexpected sight. She was thrown off guard since the first thing that sprang to her in response to David's inquiry was yes, she would miss him, even though he had cured her of all her inhibitions in the bedroom.

She didn't feel confident enough to talk as he approached the bed. She was so perplexed that she stared at his physique rather than his face, but this did not help. His superbly fitted navy jacket hung perfectly from his wide shoulders, a pristine cotton shirt covered his muscular chest, and his long, delicate fingers, which had stroked every inch of her, were sliding a silk tie beneath the shirt collar. Dear God, she couldn't possibly miss him. She certainly couldn't be developing feelings for him. She wouldn't let that happen.

"With just a phone call," he casually suggested, "You could come to New York with me; I can delay leaving for the airport for half an hour to give you time to get ready." Anna raised an eyebrow in disbelief. She was certain that any airline would bump a passenger to accommodate David Miller, as he invariably traveled first class. His request to bring her along sent her into a frenzy. "No, I just couldn't; I have to get to work," she said.

"With the new personnel, your presence in the shop is barely needed," he pointed out. "Please come with me this time, ok? I think it would be fun to give you a tour of New York."

The fact that he was asking her to humor him and travel with him startled her. The difficulty was that, for a minute, she was truly tempted, and that scared her. "The inclusion of me traveling with you is not part of our agreement." She said to him.

"Of course it isn't." A shadow flickered in his eyes before disappearing. "How stupid of me to forget," he said as he bent down to give her a quick, firm kiss on the lips. He mocked her by saying, "I'll be back in two weeks, but try not to miss me too much," as he spun on his heel and went.

As she felt worse and worse, Anna sat in the workshop. She had just finished her breakfast after David had departed when her phone rang. Anna's chuckle had been hollow as she remembered that it had been Bryan who had wished David a happy 35th birthday before he departed. She had to cut the talk short because she had to get to work on time, she informed him.

"What the heck is wrong with you? Sara approached the bench and frowned anxiously at Anna as she sat down. "Is David on your mind a lot?" Anna looked up at her friend and said, "Something like that." It's his birthday today, and I failed to wish him well before he went to work this morning."

"Not good," Sara observed dryly. However, the situation is not hopeless. Have some Zoom sex with him when you call him and apologize tonight. That ought to do it because the man is really smitten with you. Anna felt compelled to crack a grin. When Anna scowled at this offhand remark, Sara chuckled and said, "I didn't think you would appreciate it until you married a hunk like David."

Why wasn't she already a member of the Club of Hot Wives just because she was married to Allen? Suddenly she recognized she had scarcely thought of Allen for a while, and when she did, it had been with regret that he had died so young. She was able to recall the happy times of their marriage with a soft smile on her face instead of tears.

She recalled David's plea that she come with him to New York and her subsequent denial. When she pictured him, he was standing by the bed, as arrogant as ever. Suddenly, Anna felt awful remorse as she recalled the quick, forceful kiss, his mocking smirk, and the stiffness in his shoulders when he turned his back on her and fled. If it was his birthday and he was too proud to notify his wife, then what sort of wife was she? She felt awful.

Chapter 41

David stood up from his desk, zipped up his briefcase, and cast a gloomy gaze around the room. He could have sat at home and done nothing and yet accomplished as much as he did today. But just where was "home"? Anywhere his lovely wife was... He had grown to actively hate the Los Angeles flat because it had slowly dawned on him that, while Anna was there, she hadn't made the least attempt to impose her personality on the property. She had not included any visuals or floral accents. The flat was as stark as Bryan had originally suggested—nothing at all like the comfortable abode Anna had enjoyed with her first husband.

David sighed. His birthday was rather disappointing compared to others. He had been in a foul mood ever since he had asked Anna to accompany him this morning, and she had refused him outright and pointed out that doing so was not part of their agreement. He had believed Anna had gotten used to the circumstances of their marriage, but apparently, she hadn't.

Crossing to the bar, he poured himself a shot of Scotch into a crystal glass and with it in his hand, he moved across to the window to look moodily out over the New York cityscape. He understood Anna's perspective and felt sorry for her. She had agreed to marry him after he proposed, and he had followed through. Seven months ago, he would have scoffed at anybody who said he would be married and then fall so deeply in love with his wife that he would put off his work.

But the joke was on him. He had tried everything he could think of to win Anna's affection. He had purchased her gold, clothes—anything she desired she could have. The difficulty was she didn't want anything from him. Except for sexual activity.

Most men would be satisfied with an ever-willing wife, and yet even in that area, he was feeling increasingly desperate. In the physical sense, she gave him everything, but slowly it had dawned on him that there was a fundamental part of herself that she was keeping concealed from him. Loving her had weakened him. He had ignored his business to a significant extent already. Ordinarily, he would not have spent more than a few of weeks in Los Angeles during the previous four months, and instead, he had spent most of his time there—with Anna ...

The sex was addicting, and he didn't want to give it up, wasn't even sure he could... But now he understood that love was much more seductive, and it was time he made a decision. To keep on as he was, but reorganize his workload to center on Los Angeles. Maybe purchased a bigger house there and was pleased with what he had—or cut and fled. Straightening his shoulders, he noticed his face reflected in the glass and frowned. God, he was becoming overemotional—and why? Because his wife had forgotten his birthday.

No, Anna hadn't forgotten, he amended. She didn't know when his birthday was since she had never cared enough to ask. But if he hadn't been so proud, he could have told her this morning. What a childish act!

He was deep in thought when someone rapped on the door. Who the heck was that? It was already evening, and everyone had already departed...

Shock, horror! Amelia Smith walked through the threshold carrying a champagne bottle. "Happy birthday, sweetheart!" She hummed.

"I appreciate it," he said. She seemed as stunning as ever, though it was difficult to look beyond the obvious signs of makeup and other artificial enhancements. However, at least she remembered his special day.

She pressed the bottle against his chest and said, "Open this," before looking up at him with a bright grin. I'd want to properly wish you a happy birthday, but first, we should get together for a celebration drink as old friends.

There was nothing slightly innocent about the invitation in the sparkling eyes she lifted to his. Despite ignoring the invitation, the gentleman in him prevented him from declining the drink. After removing the cork from the bottle, he walked over to the bar and grabbed two glasses.

His desk phone rang at that moment. "What do you think?" Amelia inquired, picking up the phone without waiting for an answer. "Office of David Miller this is Amelia. May I be of service? Who do you claim to be? Ah, wife of David?" "Anna!" The receiver was ripped from Amelia's grasp by David. Something must have happened for her to start calling him. "What happened?" He asked worriedly.

The response of "Nothing—nothing at all" left him feeling relieved and elated, and she apologized for "disturbing you, David." I'm merely calling to wish you a happy birthday, I can't reach you on your mobile phone that's why I called here". "I didn't realize it was your birthday until Bryan rang this morning to speak to you, and I feel bad I didn't get you a present. But I'll have one ready for you when you return. I was thinking maybe a shiny new briefcase. Or anything you like. A choice is up to you."

David had never heard Anna talk so much, and she still wasn't done. But merely to hear her speak was a delight, and his previous anxieties dissipated like snow on a fire.

"Would you rather I just take you by surprise? Look, I'll hang up now; you're clearly busy at the moment," she said in a hurry. "You bet I'm not. A glass of champagne was just brought to me as a surprise by my assistant, and he looked across at Amelia and waved for her to go." David sat down at his desk and mouthed the word "out" to Amelia, who shrugged and slammed the door behind her as she left. "She left, and at this point, I was going to leave." He explained. "Just as well, I don't want to bother you," she said slowly.

"Never, ever hang up," he commanded. "I appreciate your calling to find out what I would like for my birthday. He heard her gasp, and then he allowed his imagination to go wild as he told her precisely what he wanted and where he wanted it—which was, of course, "you naked in bed." He said teasingly.

Anna delayed calling David all evening out of concern, and it was nearly midnight by the time she finally did so. In spite of this, she knew it was still early evening there, because of the time difference. She was so nervous she knew she was going on and on incoherently. But now, when David whispered seductive ideas in her ear, she was taken aback.

She pleaded with a ragged breath, " David —please." "You shouldn't make sexual comments over the phone!" But that didn't stop her core temperature from climbing and her abdominal area from getting hotter. He smiled as he pushed her to "think of me," and she could hear the grin in his voice. "Yes, I believe you can reasonably say that's a foregone conclusion given your extremely colorful flights of fancy," she remarked and heard him giggle.

"Good, because I'll be taking a freezing cold shower for the rest of the night!" If I can make it back sooner than two weeks, I will. You might want to have a look at the real estate market in the interim. I've come up with a new wish. I can see you're not happy there, so I suggest you start looking for a property on the outskirts of town with a big garden instead."

Anna remained silent for a while as she processed the depth of his offer. She was overjoyed at the prospect of leaving the city behind and settling down in the country as he had planned. He called her name and asked whether she was still there, and she heard him. "Yes, David, I'll do as you say, she responded, placing a palm on her tummy. And with that, she hung up the phone for the night.

Over in New York, David beamed and popped the cork on a bottle of champagne. His birthday was made one hundred times better by the memory of Anna's voice.

In Los Angeles however, Anna was thinking. She was confused because Amelia is a familiar name. What is she doing in his office in the early evening?

Chapter 42

On Friday afternoon, Anna inserted the key into the lock of her former Montebello residence and strolled inside with a cardboard box in tow. The home smelled chilly and abandoned as if no one had lived there in a long time. As expected, given that David had been away for the holidays and she had only made a few brief visits.

She discarded her jacket and made one more circuit of the empty rooms. After tossing and turning in the king-size bed all night thinking about David, she made up her mind on Tuesday morning. Anna had taken a good, long look in the mirror, and she wasn't happy with what she saw. She had married for the promise of a child and excellent sex but had avoided deeper commitment. She'd been so determined not to become involved with David on anything other than a surface level that she hadn't even realized it was his birthday. She felt bad since she knew she should have asked him when it was.

When had she become so terrified of emotional involvement? She was able to trace its origins back to when her mother passed away. She was considerably closer to her Aunt Martha and Allen than she was to her stepmother and stepsister. When she lost Allen, she was crushed, and then the next year, when she lost her aunt, the pain intensified. She was innately kind, but she had never dated guys or had close relationships. She had avoided anyone who would let her feel her true feelings, so she pushed them aside. What about David? She had been too afraid to let him in for fear of the anguish that would come with losing him as well.

As the sun rose, Anna realized she had to stop dwelling on the bad times and stop being afraid of the future she shared with David. She might have been pregnant, and if she was, her baby deserved a healthy mother, not a fragile one. Yesterday, she had her period and therefore presumed that she was not pregnant, but that did not sway her. It was time for her to go on with optimism for the future. When David advised that she talk to an estate agent about purchasing a home in the country, she did just that. An appraiser was in the neighborhood.

She had snuck away from her job at the shop this afternoon to gather the possessions she valued most, such as photographs of her family, including those of her parents, aunt, and Allen, taken during her youth. She dreamed of having a kid someday and introducing her offspring to their extended relatives.

It was something she should have done months ago, but she finally got around to it as she set the box on the coffee table in the living room. She looked at a few things for an unusually long time, and she chuckled and groaned at others. She took a quick look around the bedroom and concluded that she had absolutely nothing left to save except for a small collection of cherished keepsakes. Then she would just need to give it a quick dusting and run the vacuum over it.

Anna didn't hear the front door open or the sound of someone ascending the stairs. She had sat down on the bed and was looking through a tattered tin box containing items from her younger years. A collection of shells she had gathered during summer holidays spent with her parents. What a stunning coincidence. It was a heart-shaped stone. As she thought back to that day, she finally found it, tears welled up in her eyes. Anna and her mother had gone to the beach for the day without her father since he was too busy working, and Anna had pulled the stone out of the sand. Before her mother passed away, this was their final trip together.

She sighed, dried her eyes on the back of her palm, and stood up from the box. There was no longer any melancholy, only happy recollections. She made a move for the exit, and then she stopped.

David was framed in the doorway, dressed casually in a dark blue cashmere sweater and navy slacks, and her heart sprang in surprise and joy. She said, "Why are you here?" She stated it cheerfully.

The subtle twist of his mouth made her feel uneasy, and the eyes were mysterious as they inspected her. When he saw that she wasn't at the apartment, he called her store, Anna and Sara Designs, and casually added, "I thought I'd surprise you, and when you weren't there, Marvie told me you'd gone to your house in Montebello."

"I had assumed you had sold this shrine to your late husband a long time ago, but of course, I should have known better."

"No, you're mistaken." She raced to correct him.

"Am I?" David inquired as he walked up to her, an arrogant look in his eyes as they swept her over. As he looked at the bed, something from the depths of his mind sprung to life. "You must have used this room every time I'm gone," he said. "I don't," Anna said hastily, in denial. His expression was calm, but she could see there was rage below.

It confused her. The estate agent is scheduled to arrive tomorrow, so I came today solely to retrieve a few sentimental items. Sarcastically, a dark brow furrowed. "It's funny, but I think you mentioned to me last year that you met with an estate agent." He hissed.

The guilty thoughts caused Anna to blush. "Okay, that was a mistake," she said. "I just never got around to doing it."

"Don't bother lying, Anna." He scoffed, "I've heard it all before," and reached out to grab her wrist in a firm grasp, dragging her towards him. It wasn't truly a lie. She tried to explain that she was enjoying the sensation of his strong, muscled thigh pressing against hers, but that he was rushing her at the moment.

"Did I rush you? To paraphrase his harsh words, I seem to recall you falling into my bed the minute you set eyes on me, and you didn't take much persuading the next time."

She got her first clear look at his wrath, sending chills down her spine.

"What the heck do you think I am? An easily duped moron? I am not second best to any man, either alive or dead." He said this to her, his eyes staring dangerously at hers. Anna just gave him the cold shoulder and looked back at him. How could he be so incensed by such a minor lie? "I never..."

"Ignore it!" he growled. "I can't stand to hear any more of your lies."

"You're like a limpet, clinging to your ex-lover. But your physical self has no such inhibitions, my dear wife." He dragged her tight against him, the powerful planes of his face strained with some dark passion.

"It would take me no time at all to get you onto that bed."

David's long fingers reached up to grasp her head so that she couldn't move an inch. "David, please," she pleaded in a weak voice.

His lips crushed down on hers before she could finish her sentence, releasing her luscious lips for him to devour. When he finally let go of her mouth, she sprang away, shivering from head to toe, but he tipped her back onto the bed, catching her off guard. She was left gasping for air and filled with rage. She didn't give a damn about whatever she had done to make him angry or whether he was jealous. She would not submit to his physical abuse. When she made an effort to sit up, he swooped down and pinned her under.

"David!" She sobbed.

His smile was unnerving. "If you're going to sleep in a bed made of happy memories, I want you to know who's transporting you there. If you lie in that bed again, you'll always remember me."

Chapter 43

She put her hands on his chest in an attempt to push him away, but her efforts were mostly in vain. His lips were once again within reach of his, and he pounced on the opportunity with ravenous desire. She could feel the strain in his massive body and hear his heart thumping with rage. As his hands tore at her clothing, she closed her eyes. Her pants and top were undone, and his hands were frantically stroking her body. Even as the usual wild excitement coursed through her veins, she gasped out demands for him to stop working his mouth over her throat, shoulders, and breasts.

He slid between her knees, his ripped thigh thrusting between them, his tongue ravaging hers again with a frantic fervor that she eagerly matched. Her head spun wildly as her mouth parted in a moan of ecstasy as she was sucked into a whirlwind of need. She grabbed at him desperately, her fingers tangled in his thick black hair, and then slid beneath his shirt to feel the pounding of his heart and the warmth of his skin. When he finally paused, she could feel the full extent of his deliberate movement against her and the intensity of the heat emanating from their bodies.

After he had lain on top of her for a few seconds, taking shallow breaths, she finally opened her eyes. He kept a wary eye on her while he watched. "What the heck am I doing?" Drunk on desire, her body excruciatingly aroused, she opened her eyes in stunned amazement as he rose and smoothed his sweater over his slacks.

He looked down at her gloomily while stuffing his hands into his pockets. It was at this point that he paused and shook his head. "God bless me; I found out just in time. You're just as bad as any other woman who's willing to sell her body for money."

"What a low and vile thing to say!" Anna screamed and sprang to a sitting position, but he looked away. She was completely perplexed and questioned, "What's wrong with you?" He couldn't stand how pitiful her voice sounded.

"What, you have no idea? I found you here crying on your dead husband's old bed. "I wasn't crying," she said, but he didn't hear her.

"Hope deferred makes the heart sick," "as the old proverb goes. And I'm sick of you," he ground out. Anna felt an inward withering. "I need some space." He gave her a cynical look, implying that she didn't belong in his apartment anymore. "To think otherwise was insane on my part. I'll send over your belongings to where you want to live. Your stipend is yours to spend as you see fit. I hope I never run into you again." His brows furrowed, and his hands curled into fists.

She stared into his ice-like gaze and saw the disdain written all over the hard, harsh line of his mouth—the mouth that had driven her mad just seconds before. She lowered her legs over the edge of the bed, turned her back on him, and buttoned her pants. She realized what she'd known since the first day she met David—that she really needed him right now.

Allen had never impacted her this deeply before. Theirs was a delicate, loving love that grew out of their long-friendly relationship. But David was all that was on her mind and in her body. She had put all her efforts into establishing a barrier between them, and now, when it was too late, it struck her like a dagger through the heart—she loved David.

The anguish started then, but Anna refused to let him know how much he had hurt her. She buttoned the last of her shirt and got to her feet. It took everything she had to look up into his eyes. "As you want," she answered, and she even managed to pull off a shrug. "As long as it doesn't hurt my dad's feelings or the business," she said.

"Not at all, I'm afraid to say." He continued, "Your father and the firm will continue to have my monetary assistance, as promised." His mouth twisted.

"And don't worry about Bryan because he is always welcome in the Jeju Villa," Anna replied.

The only person who hadn't gotten what they wanted out of the marriage was her. She thought sadly.

"I appreciate it, but I can't let him stay in your villa without paying rent. It's not like Bryan needs to know." David said it tersely. She glared at him in indignation at the suggestion of payment, but David had already turned on his heel and disappeared before she could respond.

Anna sat back down on the bed, attempting to process what had just occurred; her eyes glazed over. David had gone to New York without any warning, and when she contacted him that night, he seemed fine.

Her breathing was shallow and labored. A lady answered the phone. Davina—the word niggled in the back of her mind, and suddenly she recalled. Annet claims that the woman David dated before he wed Anna was a New Yorker by the name of Amelia Someone. Suddenly, Anna saw it all. It's safe to assume that David and Amelia are back together and that the romantic things he mumbled to her over the phone on his birthday were actually directed at the woman sitting next to him at the workplace. Were they giggling at her expense behind her back?

His idea to buy a rural house with a garden was because he understood the apartment did not fit her. She had naively imagined he'd planned for them to share the new property. Instead, it was meant as a signal for Anna to vacate the premises so that he could bring his new girlfriend to live there. She was such a naive and stupid person. David was seeing another lady. To be perfectly frank, that was exactly what she had anticipated all along. It was probably for the best that their marriage had lasted seven months at all. But she didn't think of herself as particularly fortunate. She blinked, then blinked again, but her eyes still welled up with tears.

Chest heaving, David climbed into his car and closed the door. He turned on the engine and took a shaky hold of the wheel. He had to go as far and as quickly as he could in the opposite direction. He couldn't believe he'd taken Anna without caring what she wanted, and he felt sick to his stomach about it. He'd never experienced rage like that before, and he had never forced a woman to have sex, either. His obsession with her was driving him insane. His wife is his weakness, but can he move on with his life without her?

Chapter 44

After three exhausting days in New York, it hit him last night He had given Anna everything and yearned for her affection, but he had never told her he loved her. He had hired an aircraft and flown to Los Angeles to tell her how he felt. He was hoping that she would throw herself into his arms and feel the same way.

He knew as soon as Marvie told him Anna was in Montebello, but he chose to ignore the information. He had fully lost it when he saw her sobbing over her husband's memories in the bedroom. Love had previously turned him into a raving idiot, but not anymore. Aside from his relationship with Anna, his life was a resounding success. After that, he avoided being near her at all costs. He had no choice but to end their relationship since his weakness for her was becoming too great to bear.

A week later, Anna sat in a restaurant with Sara, pretending to enjoy a meal she had no stomach for.

Anna, don't be down. Sara beamed, "David will be returning on Saturday."

Anna made a pathetic attempt at a grin. "I don't see the point."

"Didn't the truth have to come out eventually? No, Sara, he won't do that. It's finished."

"No, I can't accept the fact that David adores you," Sara said.

Anna said sarcastically, "You know his reputation. He worships women in the plural." But not just one, and I know he has someone else.

You must be mistaken, Sara said. David wouldn't hurt her like that.

"I'm not mistaken. I saw him last Thursday. He rushed to New York to tell me the project was over there. Is it clear to you that he is tired of me and no longer wishes to interact with me?'

"What a complete jerk! Sara shouted, "Oh my gosh, the sleaziness of super-rich playboys!" and went on and on about it. Anna agreed, and then stood up and asked, "Can we get out of here?"

Anna had feared informing her father, but she learned she didn't need to. The following weekend, she answered a knock on the door, intending to show a couple around the house, but her father was waiting at the doorway.

Is everything okay, Anna? She was taken aback when he unexpectedly hugged her. "I'm very sorry. I thought David would keep you, not abandon you."

He let her go of his embrace. The fact that David had informed her father that he had abandoned her was the ultimate insult. She stated this with a cynicism that was an automatic defense against the bitter feelings that threatened to swallow her: "Don't worry, Dad, your position in the company and the money from David are guaranteed."

"I know— David told me. But can't a parent care for his daughter? How heartbroken must you be?"

She said, "No, not really," denying that she was sad. David's attention span is like that of a gnat when it comes to women. If you had to guess, why do you think we split up? It wasn't only David who could embellish the reality of their connection. It was enjoyable while it lasted, but it's ultimately harmless. "I'd love to have you stay, but I have a couple coming to look at the house any second."

"What? You're putting the house up for sale?" Her father was surprised. "You have my sympathies. David can afford to pay through the nose for freedom; therefore, he should be able to afford a larger, more expensive luxury apartment." "In the meantime, you can live in my house until you are ready to move into your new home." To which she agreed. Her father departed on a cordial note. It made Anna chuckle.

But in the weeks that followed, nobody seemed to be able to laugh at anything. She blamed David for her inability to eat and sleep. She had made several attempts to prevent herself from falling in love with him, but it had occurred.

Spring had hardly begun when Anna, in disbelief, left her doctor's office. After passing out at work, Sara pressured her into making the appointment. It was a miracle—she was pregnant! Elation swelled up inside her. She had believed she was having light menstruation, but the doctor assured her that the spotting she had experienced was a sign of pregnancy and that she was, in fact, just over three months along. Anna, practically skipping to her car, believed the timing couldn't have been better. She just sold her home and relocated to her father's house as agreed in the meantime. The change has already given her good fortune.

"What did the physician say?" As Anna entered the store, Sara yelled.

Come with me behind the scenes, and I'll fill you in. "But what about David?' Sara inquired moments later, after Anna had finished gushing over the thought of being a mother. You are obligated to inform him.

'No! Anna's response was swift, and she became stubborn despite Sara's best efforts to persuade her otherwise. I mean, really, Sara. I spotted one of your trashy magazines not so long ago, although you attempted to cover it, with that photo of David with the gorgeous Amelia on his arm. "Sober up. Never again would he want to see me, he insisted. For Pete's sake, he had the apartment's contents returned to me by courier."

Sara shook her head. "I had no idea. This person is such a twerp. He deserves to know that he's going to be a dad, but I still think you should inform him."

"If it would make you feel any better, I will if I see him," Anna responded. Perhaps pigs could even fly, she reasoned. He told me he would never see me again, she thought.

An email from Bryan arrived for Anna a few weeks later. The repairs to the Jeju home were finally done, and he wanted Anna to know that he appreciated her friendship, despite his disappointment that she and his grandson had drifted apart. She wrote back and informed him she had directed the caretaker to give him a key and enable him to use the house whenever he liked. She felt guilty. But she didn't want David and Bryan to know about the pregnancy just yet, even though she knew she couldn't keep it a secret for long. Her feelings were still too fresh to be handled properly. Then something happened that changed everything.

Chapter 45

Waking up was something she drew back from. At this time, no. Because he would be by her side when she did.

They informed her that her husband had kept a near-constant watch for days after her admittance, and she found him sitting in a chair by the bed.

Three times a day, in the morning, mid-afternoon, and evening, he had limited his visits over the previous week.

While she was up, the nurses relayed the comment in an informed but slightly envious tone, which they had made while they believed she was asleep. The new information sparked interest in her. She was sent to this posh, incredibly costly private facility with its circle of consulting specialists after being taken unconscious by ambulance from the scene of the accident to a neighboring public hospital. It seemed like chaos ensued within the hour.

This is Anna.

The sound of the voice—a low, somewhat inflected drawl—triggered her heart rate to increase.

Oh no. At this point, she would be forced to admit his existence. After a brief quiver, her eyelashes gently open, and looks at him.

His physical presence was so overwhelming that she almost closed her eyes again to avoid looking at him.

An intimidatingly towering man with a broad shoulder and a massive build, even when at rest,,. He had a broad, sculptured face with sharply chiseled features that seemed to have been cut from stone. His eyes were so dark, nearly as black as his well-styled hair.

His polished exterior belied a hunter's untamed and violent nature, reminiscent of a wild forest beast.

David Miller. His name and the information passed to her were more statistical than informative.

The corporate world held him in the highest esteem as the leader of a financial empire, and he was in his mid-30s.

An incredibly rich man, as one of the nurses had disclosed, he was considered to be among the most prominent members of the country's elite due to his entrepreneurial prowess.

The underlying degree of power and brutality was somewhat terrifying to Anna, but she didn't find it surprising.

At first, she was astonished and disappointed to hear that she was his wife. Every nerve ending in her body had protested that she couldn't be tied to him in any manner.

Oh my god, she was in mute agony because she didn't feel married.

Also, she had no indication that she was expecting a child. The four-month-old baby in her womb had been unharmed, according to an ultrasound scan.

This is his baby.

She could never have imagined falling in love with him—or him with her—in a million years.

But there were wedding photos from seven months ago to confirm their legal union, and no matter how many times she looked at them, she could only see joy on her face. In the image, her delicate figure appeared frail. She had a warm smile, full lips, and finely-boned features framed by long black hair. But a stranger with pale, symmetrical features and brown eyes appeared to her in the mirror. She can't even remember what she looks like.

In her wordless agony, she compared losing one's memory, even temporarily, to being stuck at a door with no key. The other side was where the solutions lay, out of grasp.

Temporary amnesia following such an accident was typical, and it was also her case. She had been told that some people regain full recall within days, while others had intermittent flashes over weeks before everything eventually clicked into place, but there was no telling when her memory would come back.

"Hello, Anna. Did you get a good night's rest?"

Anna observed in dispassionate interest as his wide mouth curled into a kind smile; his voice was low and almost husky. Why bother asking? She wanted to question you when you could have just asked the attendant nurse before you even stepped foot in my suite. You bet. She considered her need for the monosyllabic response in silence. She offered a polite "thank you," but she was well aware of the calculated darkness in his eyes.

Deep within her mind, shouldn't there be some kind of recognition—anything that would let her know him? There must be some innate sixth sense that would make her notice him, even if her thoughts couldn't connect with him on a personal level.

She muttered an expletive in her head. The fact that David Miller had a brief but passionate courtship wasn't sufficient. Too many aspects remained unanswered when they were married a month later in Seoul, South Korea.

Looking through a thick album full of family photos had piqued my interest in the past, but I was disappointed that not a single one had sparked any sort of familiarity. Over the past week, she has perused the numerous pages adorned with glossy prints that chronicled her life from birth to childhood and praised her decision to become a landscape designer, among other things. Photos of her parents were on display, including her mother, whom she had lost when she was young, and her father, whose love for his only child was seen in numerous of the images. His father's new family as well. All of those faces she doesn't recognize. Photos she had shot on vacation with friends but couldn't place. David told her that she and her father had lived in the suburban family house together until she was married. All told, they covered her life for the last quarter of a century.

A person's hand? David asked a gentle question. "Did you feel any relief this morning?"

"A bit," she said rigidly, omitting the details of her continued shoulder and rib pain as well as the fact that her right hand, which was severely bandaged and had titanium pins inserted to realign multiple fractured bones, felt rigid in its supporting splint. The other car had smashed into her passenger side after ignoring a "Stop" sign, so the physicians had reassured her that things could have been worse.

"Do you need anything?" he asked.

After a little period of closure, Anna gently reopened her eyes. You shower me with flowers daily. She glanced over the enormous bunches of exotic flowers without asking. The roses ranged in color from pale cream to the deepest red; their velvet petals and long stems proved they were grown in an expensive hothouse. The arrangements were beautiful, made with care, and supposedly supplied by one of the nurses from one of Los Angeles's most upscale flower shops. Plus, food. Within easy reach was a bowl with a broad assortment. She obviously tried to make her voice sound friendlier. "What else could I desire?"

"Maybe to return home?" While she tried to hide her shock, David asked with playful indifference, his brown eyes watching her closely. She could feel her spine tingling at the idea of them together in their home. This man is a total stranger to her.

Chapter 46

No, my goodness. A hushed scream escaped from some dark corner of her being. She was sad to leave this safe haven that was the hospital and this room in particular. Still, she couldn't remain forever.

Felt a small lump form in her throat, which made her swallow. In an act of abstracted agitation, her fingers started to pleat the hem of the sheet. "Am I to be set free?" His features were relaxed and his mouth curled into a warm smile as she studied him intently, trying to decipher something more from his face.

"There is no reason why it should not be this afternoon," the obstetrician and neurologist have both told me.

How quickly. It ought to have been tomorrow or the day after that, right? Then she could adjust to the notion more easily.

She felt an overwhelming, unexplainable fear whenever she considered returning to the house, she had supposedly shared with him. Her hesitation was hard to pin down. This man is a stranger to her but why is it that she feels apprehensive to go with him?

After studying his countenance, she concluded that he was a formidable opponent—the kind of guy no rival would want on their side. His self-confidence shone through, and she could feel his unwavering character. As for romantically? Uneasiness snaked its way down her spine. No one could possibly coexist with a man of his kind and remain oblivious to his or her sexuality. I have no doubt that he would have shown her every sensual pleasure and intimate experience imaginable and shown her how to reciprocate in the same way.

"My husky chastisement is telling you not to look at me like that." David hissed.

Silently distressed, Anna closed her eyes and then reopened them, her expression shifting between bewilderment and curiosity. "You have no idea."

It was as if there was an electric current coursing through the room, and she appeared to be struggling to control her breathing. She just woke up and she already felt her sexual tension growing by the minute.

"You don't think so?" He stared at her.

His vocal intonation served no purpose for her.

"My wife treats me like a total stranger, and I can't imagine how tough it must be for you to be married to someone you don't recognize."

A cry escaped her voice as she watched in what seemed like slow motion as he slowly moved her palm upwards and buried his mouth in the soft hollow, clutching her unhurt hand and raising it to his lips.

She was enamored by the way his eyes pierced into her femininity and filled it with a heavy, languorous warmth, betraying the depth of his emotions.

"When I touch you, your eyes widen in fear, and you have no idea how it makes me feel. To know that you'd rather have my lips caress your cheek than your mouth?" His brows furrowed in agony.

As if frozen in time, she was unable to move or say a word as her view of the room and its furnishings dwindled to a mere outline.

The doorbell was a letdown, and he quickly released his grip on her hand when the kitchen staff member brought in a breakfast plate.

The woman turned to the man sitting beside the bed and said, "Good morning." She then slid the tray onto the bed trolley and slid it into place. "I was wondering if I could get Mr. Miller a cup of coffee?"

David's mouth creased as he smiled, and deepened the vertical lines that cut each cheek. "No, thank you."

As he rose from the chair, Anna observed him. Her lips quivered as he delicately covered her mouth with his own, leaning forward.

Two o'clock is when you are supposed to be discharged. Until next time, my dear.

He stood up straight and headed for the door after a brief, disorienting moment during which she felt curiously empty as if she needed more than that little touch.

With confusion, David watched as he walked away. His gentle kisses against hers, along with the subtle intensity of his need, had heightened her perceptions to the point that she felt as if some entity deep within was determined to demand acknowledgment.

The sweet-faced kitchen assistant proudly announced, "There you are, Mrs. Miller," as she tossed a little cereal box into the fruit bowl after opening it. "Toasted bread with which spread would you rather have it?"

The hectic schedule at the hospital left little room for brooding, as Anna wryly acknowledged. A nurse was there to help with the shower less than ten minutes after the breakfast tray was taken away. Then there was the doctor's round, physiotherapy, morning tea, and the daily visit from the hairdresser, something her husband had arranged, she was told.

Although she couldn't help but try to understand his motive, it was nonetheless a considerate gesture. That backfired since it highlighted her friendship with David and caused her to question her values once again.

It seems absurd to question David's profound concern when there was ample proof of his devotion in this hotel room with the meticulously arranged cards in the drawer of her bedside pedestal. Each one with the words 'Love' inscribed in black ink and signed 'David' with a strong cutting hand.

Did she love him, more importantly? Indeed, she had tied the knot with him, but had love been her driving force?

Oh my goodness, she certainly wasn't the type of woman who would have planned to use her feminine charms to ensnare a rich man, would she? She never would have thought in a million years that she would do such things.

After thinking about it in mute agony, Anna thought of it again.

Time and patience were words that the neurologist had emphasized with gravity. Still, the lack of clarity in such an answer was annoying.

A delicious bowl of beef stew was the main course of the lunch, which also included thin slices of roast beef with veggies and fresh fruit pieces for dessert.

Anxieties knotted up in her belly, and they only became worse when the nurse came into the room.

She then told Anna, smiling brightly, that her husband would be picking her up in thirty minutes. "All right, I'll dress you and help you pack."

Some part of me muttered an emphatic, "No way!" if I were to go. She had a flurry of confused ideas racing through her mind. Maybe she might imagine a minor problem, like a headache or her hand, to put off her departure.

Still, she thought it would be pointless, so she pushed the bedcovers aside and got to her feet, observing the nurse's extraction process with a dispassionate eye. Her garments were prepared at the top of the shelves. The outfit consists of sage-green silk pants, a cream silk top, lace-trimmed panties, and low-heeled shoes. The obvious regard with which they were handled made each item appear extremely expensive, which it most assuredly was. Oh my God, am I a high-maintenance wife? Anna thought about this.

Chapter 47

'I'll use the outermost clip,' the nurse announced as she delicately fastened the bra and then the blouse. We can remove it if it's too tight or too uncomfortable. Do you need any assistance with your makeup?

There was a case full of cosmetics, but for the last seven days, she had resorted to using only moisturizer and light lipstick. She cautiously withdrew her fingers from the curved glass bottle of Dior. Why start now when she hasn't even used it in the hospital?

Anna observed in idling curiosity as the nurse retrieved a piece of luggage and loaded it with all of her belongings.

"Please," Anna said, stepping in as the girl snatched up multiple expensive magazines. 'Keep them.' Can you assure me?

"I agree." The nurse said "Along with the flowers", Anna chimed in. "The day and night shifts should each get one. "And the chocolates, the fruits." She added.

The expression on the nurse's face showed appreciation. "Thank you so much. People will really value them." A gentle smile spread across Anna's face. "You've all taken excellent care of me."

There was, however, an exceptionally high level of commitment to this one patient. She thought.

Why? Because he was an absolute force that necessitated nothing less. On the other hand, could it have been the ethereal aura of intrigue, the eerie exposure of the beautiful girl who had stayed in this room?

"The sister will be right over to officially discharge you from the hospital system," the nurse said.

Anna looked helplessly after the nurse as she departed and mumbled a decent response.

Why was she filled with such crippling insecurity and uncertainty? An instinctive response, a voice within her assured her, using tones strikingly similar to the consultant neurologist's.

She walked up to the ward sister as the door swung open, took the appropriate appointment cards, and listened to the expert counsel, which ended with, "Don't try anything too strenuous too soon."

From the doorway, a slightly accented male voice reassured Anna, "I will personally see that she doesn't," and Anna hesitantly turned to face her husband.

Instead of the work suit he wore that morning, he was wearing dark pants and an unbuttoned polo shirt. The loose-fitting knit highlighted his broad shoulders, fitted to his taut waist, and showed off his heavily-muscled, forearms.

Anna noticed the subtle expression of gratitude on the nurse's face despite her professional demeanor, and she studied her reply with an air of detached fascination as he grinned warmly.

Was this the reaction of every woman to David Miller? While Anna pondered in silence. Her mind was far from at rest as she remained motionless as he drew near and gently kissed her temple.

"A car is waiting for us outside." He narrowed his eyes slightly to take in her pale features and the level of hesitation in her beautiful brown eyes, so it must have been clear that she was not sure.

"Careful not to be nervous," he whispered.

Is this for real? Her need to yell was strong. He's taking me to a house I don't recognize, and I feel like I don't know him. Feeling desperate, she wanted to get a memory, anything that would give her some peace of mind.

However, she was once again cursing herself for trying to control an outcome she had no say in creating.

They walked down the carpeted hall, his bulk seemingly dwarfing hers; her stomach did many unpleasant somersaults as she beheld a huge, expensive-looking car parked right next to the entrance.

Unmistakably his, it appeared as powerful as the man who had it. She cautiously settled into the passenger seat, holding her breath unconsciously as he bent down to adjust her seatbelt.

As his palm touched her breast, her heart rate spiked and then settled into an anxious rhythm. He then carefully secured the clip, leaving her to feel ensnared and unable to free herself.

Oh! My. She quietly advised herself to rein in her vivid imagination as he shut the door and slid around to get behind the wheel.

The car slid ahead, and she had the wild need to beg him to stop and let her out, which made no sense because she had nowhere else to go.

A few minutes later, the massive vehicle swung out into the constant flow of traffic, and she resolutely fixed her gaze on what was beyond the windshield.

Posh houses, well-kept lawns, and trees lined the streets, sheltering passers-by from the sun's glare; there were many electronically controlled stores.

Everything seemed so ordinary, so mundane. Nothing about it seemed familiar, though. David glanced across at her with interest, suggesting that she was showing signs of stress.

"Are you feeling uneasy?"

She looked up at his intense stare, her pupils dilating slightly. She said "no" courteously, and he looked back to the road.

Anna let out a sigh of relief as he turned on the stereo, thankful for the calming effects of the music since it eliminated the need to speak, as the midsummer heat was lowered by the car's air conditioning.

She watched, as if captivated, as the houses along the broad main road evolved in quality and style, going from modest, dark, aged brick buildings on little plots of land to bigger, more majestic ones.

A visual testament of riches, their magnificent facades reflect a mingling of old and new.

David had shown her a view of A huge, two-story home. When would they get there? She mused.

David said, "Just a little longer, we are already in Pasadena " as if he could read her mind.

David skillfully guided the enormous vehicle along a spacious driveway, which included elaborate steel gates that opened and closed at the touch of a button.

Nestled away from the road in picturesque sculptured grounds, the two-story house was a work of art in cream cement-rendered brick and floor-to-ceiling tinted glass. Its silver-white tiled roof and abundance of flowers and shrubs showcased the meticulous attention to detail of the gardener.

At the main entrance, the car came to a stop, and Anna couldn't help but gasp in astonishment at the huge lobby. Behind the massive paneled doors stood a pair of large, ornate urns.

The focal point was a marble fountain with tiers and slowly falling water; the high glass-domed ceiling provided light and space, and an elaborate crystal chandelier dangled from it. Two wings were accessible from an oval balcony via opposite corridors from a wide, double staircase that curled up to it.

The enormous atrium's exotically created stained glass panels reflected multicolored light from prisms onto the white walls, enhancing the pattern in a constantly shifting sweep dictated by the sun's beams.

"It's magnificent." Unintentionally, she spoke those words and then stepped forward to pause before the marble fountain. "Did you come up with the idea?"

He grinned once his dark, quite motionless eyes had met. Yes, to a certain extent. "In order to achieve this result, I consulted with numerous experts for the renovation."

Reaching out a hand, she traced her fingers across the water, feeling its gentle caress against her skin. With a tiny tilt towards him, she shifted her attention.

"You seem to have quite a few parties."

His gentle grin exuded comfort. "Inviting business associates to one's home can sometimes be more relaxing," he said with a relaxed tone.

"Including their spouses?" From where did that materialize? She silently reassured herself that it was a natural assumption. The most successful guys had at least one spouse. Probably some of them had more.

Was David having an affair? She was lost in thought.

Chapter 48

He walked the short distance to her side and put his hand under her elbow. We can enter the lounge now. Amy will have brewed some tea and baked treats to whet your taste buds.

Amy does the cooking and takes care of the house, he whispered, responding to the silent question reflected in her eyes. Jacob, her spouse, is a general handyman who also tends to the lawn and the cars.

Beautiful Chinese rugs spread across the marble floor served as a sophisticated backdrop to the expensive artworks scattered at regular intervals on the silk-covered walls. Large rugs, mostly in a light blue color with patterns that included a subtle combination of cream and the lightest pink, complemented the cream-upholstered furniture, rosewood accents, and an abundance of glass-topped side tables.

Just as Anna was getting into her padded chair, a middle-aged woman with a lovely figure rolled into the room, pushing a trolley that held two pots of steaming milk, sugar, and cream as well as several plates with a variety of little cakes, pastries, and delicate sandwiches.

With a friendly greeting, Amy made tea, added milk and sugar, and set the cup and saucer on a glass-topped table next to Anna's chair so they were easily accessible.

'I am grateful.' Coming face-to-face with a lady she must have dealt with every day for the six months of her marriage seemed weird. Anna doesn't remember her either. The house is unfamiliar to her.

Dinner will be ready at seven o'clock, I promise. Do you have any particular requests? Amy asked her.

Anna made her voice sound more friendly. I think chicken soup will work.

"And what comes next?" How about an omelet with mushrooms, cheese, tomatoes, and ham?

As she watched Amy pour coffee into a demitasse and give it to David, Anna said, "That sounds delicious." Amy then exited the room.

Anna took a tiny sandwich, relishing the exquisite smoked salmon and cream cheese filling, accepted another, and then declined anything further; the tea had the flavor of honey and lemon

Need more tea?

With a grateful "please," she watched his long figure emerge from the chair. As he filled her cup again and set it where she could easily reach it, his movements were precise and brief, and his hands were steady and confident.

"How long have you been a resident here?" Her fingers quivered as she raised a hand to supposedly brush back a lock of hair behind one ear, as if the urge to speak were of the utmost importance.

He cocked his head slightly at the anxious sign, and she tried her best to calm him down before his worry got the best of him.

"Just weeks after your accident, I bought our new home here and leased the apartment in Los Angeles. I'm now in the process of transferring the main office of Miller International from New York to LA. As I've already told you before at the start of our marriage, I am not going to be an absentee father to our child." David explains to Anna.

She was engrossed in the chat and couldn't seem to get off. While I've wasted the last week poring around meaningless photo albums, you've given me the information I need. Please elaborate on our first meeting and its significance.

He grinned as if he were lost in thought. "Is it necessary to answer some questions?" "And you seem to be losing your patience."

"You expect me to respond to each of your questions simultaneously?" A troubled look crept into her eyes. "I must be informed," Anna said desperately.

"We met in Jeju Island, and I invited you to my yacht, and we made love," David said teasingly with a wink.

Anna could feel her cheeks burning with shame, and her eyes widened in shock. She wished it could have been a different answer. "I don't believe you?" She said it shyly. "Are you teasing me?"

David was amused at her reaction. "No, It's the truth." He said with a firm grin, "Then one year after, we meet again during your stepsister's birthday party." He continued, "We dated, and then the rest is history." David smiled at her. He was truly amused by her reaction.

"I was so captivated by your unwavering devotion to your family that I insisted we have supper together. I was able to convince you to marry me in just twenty-four hours." His dark chocolate eyes intensely held hers.

"And set the wedding date for a month afterward." Anna was stunned. My goodness. That kind of power was catastrophic. She was lost in thought with the discovery. The fact that she had granted her approval was rather shocking to her. Is it expected of me to assume you're a decent human being, or should I face facts? Anna was grateful, David couldn't read her thoughts, but he was studying her expression.

His head arched in sarcastic cynicism. "Anna, which reality do you prefer?" She choked out the words, "You have the advantage," but she managed to get them out. Even if I don't have any. "Wait for your tea to be finished," he whispered. "Then I'll bring you upstairs so you can relax."

Even though she pretended not to be exhausted, she set her cup back on its saucer since she was looking forward to a couple of hours away from his disturbing company.

"At Manhattan Beach, I own a home with a view of the water. It's the perfect spot for you to unwind and recharge." David said softly.

"Are you saying that we should remain there together?" Just the two of us, right?" She was in excruciating pain, knowing that he had captured the ephemeral feelings that were visible on her face.

He reached up and ran his warm fingertips across her cheek. "It is obvious. I care deeply about you and your well-being."

A creeping unease crept subtly down her spine for some reason she couldn't put her finger on. Why? Quietly, she thought as they made their way to the grand staircase. But her unease grew as she continued to go.

A calm tranquility was provided by the thick-piled powder-blue carpet that covered the entire floor.

The rooms that Anna caught sight of had the most exquisitely coordinated color schemes—mauves, pinks, greens, blues, and creams—and she started to wonder if he had hired an interior decorator.

Two exquisitely made mahogany chests of drawers, complemented by matching cabinets and bedside pedestals, made up the master suite. The bed cover and draperies had a striking pattern in shades of blue, mild lilac, and cream.

She observed as he made his way to the bed to pull back the duvet, then skillfully selected multiple pillows from a nearby cupboard and arranged them into a cozy nest against the bedhead.

As she took off her shoes and leaned back against the pillows, David informed her that there was an intercom device on the pedestal.

She choked on her breath as he dipped his head, caressed her lips in a provocative kiss, then stood up straight and stepped aside.

I plan to spend at least half an hour on my studies. To get in touch with anyone, simply turn on the intercom. After a gentle "Rest well, Anna," he turned and departed from the room.

With her eyelids heavy with exhaustion, Anna leisurely perused two of the magazines from the collection that was within easy reach before tossing them.

David stood just a few feet away from her bed when she woke up after a restless night's sleep, his dark eyes somewhat gloomy as they studied her fair face.

"I'll ask Amy to fetch you a tray," he said. His outstretched fingers tucked a stray hair behind her ear. "Come," he said, removing the blanket. I will assist you in taking off your clothes. Anna unconsciously crossed her arms at the thought of him removing her clothes. Her eyes widened in shock as her cheeks instantly flushed.

Chapter 49

N o, her inner voice yelled out. She whispered in a choked voice, "I should be able to manage."

David shot out, "I doubt it," his expression turning noticeably gloomy as he took in her clear hesitation. He drawled, "Think of me as a nurse," as he narrowed his eyes to see her dogged determination as she stood up.

There is no way a male nurse could look that good or wreak such sensory havoc on her. As he gently removed one button after another, it was clear that he was thinking things over.

"The idea of a man you can't recall taking off your clothes," David continued in a smooth voice, "a man who, as your husband, has slept with you in this bed every night, tasted you thoroughly, and implanted his sperm in your womb... frightens you?" David stared intensely at her.

With a quiver in her voice, Anna corrected, "Unnerves me." The words had tormented her ever since she found out she was pregnant. "Had we intended to have a child of our own?"

As he leaned down and gently brushed his lips across the edge of her mouth, a radiant fire radiated from his gaze. "The decision regarding the choice and timing of conception was yours." After releasing the third button, he proceeded to the fourth. "You have my unequivocal approval."

She remained motionless as he undid the final button, freed the silk blouse from her left arm, took the sling off her injured right hand, and delicately pulled the garment free.

She would have given anything to not have to rely on him when he reached for the clip that fastened her bra; she couldn't control her heart rate or force herself to breathe.

He cautioned, "Close your eyes if you must," with a touch of playful indulgence. "Unfortunately, I am unable to do the same because I am afraid, I may inflict unneeded pain upon you."

He found it funny, dang it! Her resentment erupted, giving her eyes a dazzling shine as she erupted into barely controlled speech. Do you believe I take pleasure in being dependent on you? My foolish eyes started to moisten, and a tear almost fell out.

His brows sharpened when she raised an arm to conceal her breasts, and he reprimanded, "I've already seen you naked in the past," before releasing the clip and easing the straps off each shoulder.

She let out a sharp gasp as he delicately withdrew his grip from her left wrist.

Being conscious of her sprained shoulder, she shut her eyes. From a deep crimson to a purplish shade, the hue had transformed. It had changed to a strong bluish-green hue.

"Oh God." His eyes grew black with silent rage as he noticed the bruises ran the length of her right side ribcage, and a whispered swear word dissolved into the silence of the room.

Her nerves were frazzled by the length of time there was complete stillness between them. She felt as if she could melt at the way he had inspected her naked body.

"It could have been worse," she said, and she could see his face tighten into a terrifying mask.

"Yes," David responded with vicious cynicism. "You could have died because of that stupid naive young driver."

She did nothing as he delicately followed the smooth curve of her breasts, his gaze fixed on them. He gently ran his fingers over their rounded edges, shaping one at a time, before running a thumb across a delicate nipple.

An overwhelming wave of intense sensation surged through Anna, causing her to let out an audible gasp. It all began at the point where her thighs met, triggering a whirlwind of emotions she wasn't prepared to face.

Her mouth parted in a worried whimper. She pleaded with him, as he wound his way to the gentle recesses at the base of her neck. He waited a few terrifying seconds over her pounding heart before he trailed up to her mouth. With his dark, penetrating gaze, he cautiously ventured, "You look so incredibly fragile, it takes my breath away." It was as if he had permission to peer into her very soul.

Convulsively swallowing, Anna let her lashes fall to cover her eyes, but they fluttered open as he gently traced the contour of her ample bottom lip. Caressing its gentle fullness until it parted instinctively, enabling him to resume his exquisite exploration. He dropped his head gently to close his mouth over hers in a provocative, sensuous tasting so exquisitely soft it almost made her weep, and she was powerless as a little trembling shook her slim frame.

She was unable to break free for some profoundly innate desire, and she endured the gentle caress of his tongue as it probed the delicate corners of her mouth, evoking a sharp pang of loss as he gradually pulled away. He enchanted her for a few long, ethereal seconds as he gently pulled the straps of her nightgown over her injured hand and her head. He then gently gathered the silk around her waist as he undressed her, removing her underwear and pants.

Do you want assistance in the shower? She said, "No," unbearably happy that he didn't have to enter this area.

"I'll be right back in ten minutes with a tray," David said as he started to the door. As the door shut behind him, she said a prayer. What on earth was going on with her? How could she respond so hysterically to someone whose identity her rational mind had disregarded? He had begun a sensual expedition that had wreaked havoc on her delicate emotions, and she had done nothing to resist his kiss.

"Why are there two dinner plates?" Anna announced with a little scowl as David returned to the room and placed the covered bed tray on her lap. As he gave her a long, thoughtful look from under his black-fringed lashes, one of his eyebrows arched in a curious question. "Did you really think I let you fend for yourself"

She was hoping he would. He gave out a tremendous, maybe lethal, sensuous vibrancy. Just thinking about him as a romantic interest sent shockwaves through her system, triggering emotions and questions she was reluctant to face.

David ordered Anna to eat. "Before the food gets cold."

She dutifully began with the soup, then used a fork to cut the omelet into bite-sized pieces. Even though he was sitting comfortably a few feet away, she couldn't help but notice the power in his jaw and mouth as she watched his spare movements.

The memory of his lips gently brushing against hers in what had been merely an affectionate salutation brought a blush to her cheeks. She could not help but fantasize about what it would be like to be kissed by him, the genuine deal, not just a controlled brush. He appeared to be the type of man who could fill a woman to the brim with his intense, drugged-out need, demanding an all-or-nothing surrender from her. She was oblivious to the magnitude of her own feelings and personality. But not even in her most fantastical fantasies could she fathom behaving carelessly while he was holding her.

He claimed to have sampled every part of her. He probably didn't intend for... "Are you through?"

Her mouth dropped open as she stared into his incomprehensible eyes in response to his startling question.

"Yes, thank you". Quickly dismissing him, she continued, "I'll be fine now." As he took the tray away, she noticed his eyes narrow significantly. Behind the velvety sound of his speech, there was hidden hardness as he stared at her intently. "The bed is big enough to fit the two of us."

Unenviable anxieties knotted her stomach at the idea of sharing the bed with him. "I would rather have my own room," she said.

"No." David stared at her intensely.

The rejection was clear. Something that made her quite angry. 'I think—'

David said in a menacingly gentle tone, "Don't think," and her eyes gleamed with anger.

"How can I not?" she exclaimed, her voice somewhat sharp. As far as your sexuality is concerned, I am completely ignorant. Resuming physical contact is something I am not yet prepared to do. 'I can't even remember if we're—-" she screamed out in anger.

"Sexually compatible?" he said with an air of sophistication. "Yes, I can tell you that we are. Very much so, in fact, it's primal." His eyes were dark as they caressed her whole body. Anna felt that she would melt as her cheeks blushed. She instinctively crossed her arms. Oh my God, what am I going to do?

Chapter 50

A s he started unbuttoning his shirt, the retort she was going to say to him slipped out of her mouth. Despite her best efforts, she couldn't tear her eyes away from him. She watched as his fingers skillfully undid the remaining buttons on his shirt and then proceeded to release the belt around his waist. In a matter of seconds, both his pants and shirt were thrown over a chair that was nearby.

His vast shoulders, narrow waist, long, powerful thighs, thin hips, and tapering chest were all features of his magnificently muscular physique. At the sight of his chest, which was covered in whorls of dark hair that arrowed down over a muscular waist to disappear behind black silk briefs, something deep inside her stirred and then slowly unfurled. "Are you planning to jump in the shower with me?" He must have been kidding! As Anna's eyes widened and her focus moved to a spot beyond his right shoulder, a faint flush of color spread across her cheeks, and she felt unable to control her wild imagination.

She longed to slam his ruthless head or, worse, strike him. She lifted her chin in an obvious act of rebellion.

She should have been alerted by his voice tone, but she was too furious to pay attention. Holding himself firmly in check, he tensed up, his massive physique a sight to behold. Every crevice on his face betrayed his rage, and his eyes were as black as polished onyx. He spoke with a harsh tone, suggesting that perhaps you should express gratitude to God. "I would show you something you would never forget if it weren't for your wounds."

Exactly as he used to? Was he a violent man, my God? her agony was met with stunned stillness. His voice was a discord of incoherent, cruelly soft phrases, and the very idea made her face turn pale. His drawl betrayed his disgust as he threw off his underwear and entered the shower.

David stepped out of the shower moments later. Astonished by the sight of his incredibly toned physique, Anna quickly averted her gaze. She was sitting in the bed and felt that she was an animal waiting to be slaughtered. His manhood is adorned with a lush, curly mane that gracefully cascades down from his navel in a delicate line. Glistening water droplets trapped in masculine body hair, the fluid grace of well-honed muscle fiber moving beneath satiny, delicately bronzed skin—it was all very sensual.

As he dried himself with a towel, she flexed her fingers tremblingly and ran a brush through her hair, acutely aware of his every move. The degree of controlled strength in repose was a deeply unsettling entity. David gave her a long, serious look that she struggled to contain as the seconds passed, and her eyes darkened with powerless surrender.

He reached up and gently ran his fingers through her hair at the nape of her neck. In what felt like an eternity, he locked his lips on hers, claiming hers with an intensity she knew would intensify if she tried to break free. She gulped violently as pleasure overwhelmed her, a tingling sensation coursing through her body. Uncomfortably, she was terrified of herself, not of him, but of the untamed sweetness that entwined within, prompting a response she was reluctant to offer.

His tongue explored every crevice and ridge, then delicately caressed her tongue in a sensual dance that tapped into her most primal desires and sent her reeling. As he delicately pulled his lips from hers, she was obliviously melted, submerged in an ocean of pleasurable feeling. "Sleep well, my dear," David bade with conviction. As soon as her head hit the pillow, her eyes started to go heavy, and she decided to give in to sleepiness instead of fighting it.

Standing in quiet contemplation, David studied her features—finely chiseled, with a sweep of black hair, exquisite fair honey-colored skin, long, thick eyelashes, and a generous mouth that had been slightly enlarged from his kiss. His gaze was dark and brooding.

He leaned forward and turned out the light as a muscle at the corner of his mouth tensed. Then crossed to the opposite side of the bed to delicately slide his lengthy form beneath the covers. Just a few seconds after that, he turned off his own light and stared at the ceiling in gloom. Life gave him a chance to start over with Anna and he will do everything to make it right this time.

Anna relaxed on the leather-cushioned seat, the air conditioning has cooled the car to a pleasant degree despite the summer heat. She made an earnest remark about how lovely the car was as it silently cruised north on the main route.

"You have been incredibly submissive all morning," he whispered with a hint of contemplation. "If I didn't know better, I would think you are being really cautious."

"I don't have much energy today; I have woken up rather early this morning and been unable to sleep" A scowl crossed his face as he looked at her. "You should have woken me up."

"Why?" She nearly managed to muster a smile. "So, we could have stayed up all night?" What could she say to him about the range of feelings she had while watching him sleep? Before the dawn sky lit up the room, she had been captivated by the stark beauty of his face while sleeping. His deeply carved features had been scarcely discernible in the darkness. His jaw and mouth softened, and his long, glossy lashes curled ever-so-slightly. The sharpness had vanished. Intrigued, she wished she could gently touch his lips with her finger, run her fingers slowly over his hard curve, and feel his warmth as he roused consciousness, opening his eyes to see her. The second he appeared like he was going to wake up, she pretended to be asleep till she felt he finally, get up from the bed. After that, she got herself dressed, and as she was about to descend the stairs, an astonished Amy quickly escorted her out onto the terrace to have breakfast with David.

"Was the car I was driving severely damaged?" After bringing the Bentley to a stop at a set of traffic lights, David turned to give her an inquiring look.

"No car can compare to you," he said. "It's totally wrecked."

"You won't be able to get behind the wheel of a car for a few weeks after you have medical clearance," "Meanwhile, Jacob is more than willing to take you anywhere you require."

'You can't be serious,' she finally said after staring at him in disbelief for a few seconds.

"Absolutely not." He said firmly.

Another facet of his character was enhanced by Anna. Lacking flexibility. He thought she had changed him unconsciously.

"Are you typically this... domineering?" Anna exclaimed.

"Protective," he corrected himself. The baby could have been lost. Oh no, I almost lost you. David thought.

As soon as the lights changed, he focused again on the road ahead. Anna seemed engrossed in the sights as the Bentley gained speed. The coastline was adorned with several inlets and bays, as well as beautiful beaches with fine sand, tree branches swaying in the light wind, and a boundless expanse of sky-blue water that seemed to go on forever.

"When will we arrive at Manhattan Beach?" "Roughly forty minutes, give or take with traffic."

A road leading to a grand, two-story house with an ocean view was swung into view by David shortly after noon.

As he showed her around the lower level rooms, she felt a wave of disbelief wash over her since it was very different from her beach house fantasies. Its exquisite furnishings made it nearly as grand as the mansion at Pasadena. With the beach just a few steps away, the swimming pool that was attached to the terrace seemed like an unnecessary extravagance.

On the second story, there were four bedrooms with private bathrooms; when Anna accompanied David into the master suite, she couldn't help but ask how often he used the house.

"Do you come here often?" she asked, observing him as he put their luggage down. "Not very much, this is just one of my investments." As she made her way to the enormous picture window, she delicately pulled back the curtain to take in the scenery. Little children, accompanied by their mothers, play joyfully in the beach while the sun dapples the water. A handful of cruisers are anchored offshore. A tranquil scene, I must say.

She felt his presence approaching from behind her, rather than hearing him, and a wave of awareness washed over her, leaving her feeling exposed and defenseless. All the little hairs on her body sprung up in an innate attempt at self-defense as his body heat appeared to envelop her.

Chapter 51

I acquired the house for that same purpose, he informed her.

His hands gently rested on her waist, and she couldn't hide the shiver that ran down her delicate body as his fingers found their way to the nape of her neck.

"David..." She lost some of the power in her voice, but soon it was back. "I would prefer to descend the stairs," she replied with an air of urgency. His proximity was excessively near. She was puzzled as to why it irritated her. She said, "Lunch," and she felt an immense sense of relief as he released her hand and backed slightly away.

Afterward, we will have a meal. I have plenty of food in the fridge and cupboard. To meet his gaze, Anna gently pivoted. Is it going to be you in the kitchen? To gently tilt her chin, he raised a hand and traced delicate fingers across her cheek, allowing them to fall down the jawline. In hypnotic stillness, she studied his broad face in all its sharp angles and planes, from the vertical furrow that sliced across each cheek to the strong sweep of his jaw and wide mouth.

"The thought of spending time alone with me is so terrifying to you?" David said huskily. It appeared so unfair that he had the upper hand while she had none as he teased her. Her wide eyes betrayed her internal turmoil as she stared at him, a mix of uncertainty and a brief, faint dread.

As he softly hissed, "little fool," his eyes become nearly black. It seems like you're battling terror while you gaze at me. Tell me what kind of man you think I am.

She was made to admit, "I don't know," even though she knew it was completely true. Very few of the details that had been shared with her had even hinted at his character.

With a release of her chin, David motioned for her to come. "Let's grab something to eat from the kitchen." With a delicate touch like a butterfly's wing, he dipped his head and caressed her lips. "Within a few days, you'll start to expect my company." Uncertainty crept into her mind. Still, she conceded that trying was her only option.

He carried out the task of reheating the cooked chicken in the microwave by taking it out of the fridge, slicing it into pieces, and setting many pieces on a tray.

He proceeded to whip up a nutritious salad with an impressive ease that Anna was taken aback by. Things moved quickly enough that dinner was ready in no time.

With a plea, she stopped David from piling food onto her plate. "That's excessive." While using his silverware to portion her food into bite-sized pieces that she could easily eat with a fork, he casually said, "Eat what you can.".

She made a valiant effort to recognize the familiarity in his behavior, which suggested a studied intimacy, but she couldn't bring herself to remember any of the numerous meals they had shared. "Why is there a little scowl?" David asked lifting his right brow.

She timidly said, "Did we socialize much?" before swiftly making her point. "You have two very spacious houses."

As I've said before, I just recently bought the mansion in Pasadena, weeks after your accident. This beach house in Manhattan was mostly for leasing and adding to my real estate investments. I live mostly in my bachelor pads in New York and Los Angeles. We have just been married for six months and during those times, I traveled a lot for my business.

But gathering a group of friends who are always out and about is a piece of cake, he said. If you don't start picking and choosing, you could end yourself spending three out of every seven evenings at a dinner party. There was a mischievous glow in his gaze. "Since we were married, I've decided to host only when absolutely necessary, and I love nothing more than a romantic candlelit dinner for two with my lovely wife." He paused, then he said, "You don't really like socializing" Still, a guy of his kind would have a wide circle of friends and be in high demand. She looked destined to be his social hostess. Anna thought about this.

"Why don't you have something to eat?" he whispered. 'The chicken will roast in the oven.'

She felt full just by looking at it, so she grabbed a fork and speared some chicken and salad until she was satisfied.

A little fruit?

After picking out an apple, she relaxed back in her chair to enjoy the crisp, tart white flesh.

"Cold water?" In response to David's question, she silently moved her head from side to side and said "no." He kindly suggested that "you can rest and go upstairs. I will wash the dishes and then come join you after."

"Your concern is excessive," Anna remarked hastily, her unease rising at his plan.

He maintained an unusually unwavering stare and a subtle grin curved upwards from the corners of his mouth. "And you'd rather be by yourself," he murmured.

In her sincere response, "Yes," Anna caught a hint of humor in his expressionless eyes as she started for the stairs. Why? Because you frighten the living daylights out of me, she thought. I don't understand why every defense system in my body is screaming at me. She finally made it to her bedroom, where she settled down with a magazine and some cushions after a long day.

She fell asleep, and when she awoke, she found a message on the bedside table. It was signed by her spouse and written in black ink. The process of getting ready and heading downstairs took no more than a few minutes. As she entered the study, David looked up from the stack of papers he was poring over, a subtle grin forming on his lips. He said with an air of contemplation, "You look rested," and she felt her heart race for a few seconds before returning to its regular rhythm.

His sluggish grin reached all the way down to his eyes, and he got to his feet with a light grace, leisurely making his way around the desk. She felt an overwhelming urge to cry out in pain as she stood defenseless against the shaky feeling that was engulfing her body as he bent his head to gently kiss her lips. She felt a range of feelings as his lips slipped from hers, including astonishment at the overwhelming want to lean towards him. Embrace, bewilder, or lament? She smiled nervously as he took her hand, expressing her desire to avoid analyzing her emotions.

David stooped and swapped off his long pants and shoes for shorts and Reeboks. He was expecting Anna do the same, which caused her tummy to flutter with fearful butterflies.

The summer sun's rays gently brushed against her skin as they leisurely strolled along the tightly packed beach, which was just slightly damp from the previous tide. The weather was perfect for a romantic stroll. A light wind played with her long hair, teasing strands that drooped over her cheek.

After being in the hospital for the past twenty days, she had a newfound sensation of lightness and freedom, and she took a few deep breaths to enjoy the fragrance of the ocean and the fresh air. From a distance, you could make out the sounds of a few kids playing while they were running back and forth, heads bowed, in search of seashells.

Anna concluded with a small smile that it was good to be alive, but her smile quickly faded as she realized that if Fate had been cruel, she would have lost not only her life but also the life of her unborn child. She spun around to face him as his arm gently curled around her waist, her gaze wide as she studied his rugged, deeply carved features.

His grip tightened slightly, and his lips lightly touched the crown of her head, he noticed that she was experiencing some kind of internal agony. His closeness, warmth, and powerful frame provided a sense of security, and she was acutely aware of all three.

Until David stopped, they kept on walking. "In my opinion, this is enough."

Anna looked at the little distance they had covered and gave him the side eye. She said, "I feel fine," as she resisted going back to her residence at that moment. She shouted, "Look!" as a huge golden retriever loped leisurely up the shore. He's stunning, isn't he? The dog's gait was like a moving poem, with deliberate, leisurely hops, his long, golden locks cascading down his youthful frame.

David agreed, saying, "Beautiful." As she faced him, she noticed that his attention was fixed on her rather than the puppy. Her jaw tightened as she felt her eyes swell to impossible proportions, finally, a hint of humor lifted the corners of her wide mouth as she grinned. "Is it possible that I could convince you to continue walking a little further?"

He gazed down into her raised face and said, "No," with a lazy refusal that betrayed his enjoyment.

"Is this all for the day?" She pouted her lips.

"Don't come across as dissatisfied." He gently placed a stray hair behind her ear with a raised palm. "The next day is always an option." So, there is no choice but to go back to the beach house with him. Anna thought solemnly. She could feel her heart rising to a crescendo at the thought of them sharing the same bed together.

Chapter 52

S he retreated silently to the house, where she would later rejoin him. When they were inside, he showed them how to navigate the kitchen. She needed a long, cool drink because it was hot. Observing, she saw him take out two glasses, fill them with fruit juice, and then offer her one.

"Have you relished the opportunity to bask in the sunshine and open air?"

"Until the freedom to move anywhere at will is taken away, I don't think anyone truly values the choice to do so." She raised the glass and sipped the cold liquid slowly, observing his every move.

On the spacious, partially covered patio, there were several chairs and two sun loungers. Anna went outside and happily settled into one of the loungers. The sun was starting to lose some of its heat, but the house shielded us from the wind well enough that sitting outside was still a delight.

As David selected the adjacent lounger, he made the observation, "Your face has regained a little color." She endured his examination calmly.

"If I have to go through another two weeks of this, I'll look like a hedonist," she said.

"I care deeply about you and your well-being."

Her sensitive nerve endings were pricked by the softly said words, and she studied his face intently. Her words came out slowly as she hesitated to think about the expense.

A brief, unidentifiable feeling flashed across his eyes, and she managed to keep it disguised.

"I hold employees who are highly competent."

David would immediately fire from their jobs inside Miller's corporation if they were to disappoint him in any manner. She remained silent for a considerable amount of time as if the knowledge were an intuitive judgment that did not require any supporting evidence.

"It's hard to believe that I used to know all there was to know about you," Anna admitted.

"At this point, all that's left are holes?"

She said, "a deep, yawning abyss," without barely furrowing her brow. So, which role are you hoping I'll take on?

To a certain degree, you accomplished it while I was in the hospital. Facts, specifics. Nothing about the private details that she wished she knew.

With a subtle mockery, he probed her serious face and asked, "So, where would you like me to begin?"

With you, I think. The place and year of your birth. People closest to you. Interests of yours. "The shortened version?" "An extended biography?"

As he raised the glass to his lips and effortlessly swallowed its contents, she couldn't help but notice the warm humor in his eyes and how his gentle laughter softened his chiseled bone structure. For a little minute, he seemed almost human.

I'm the bastard son of a rich winery, my dad was born in California. My maternal lineage is traced back to South Korea. I was born in Seoul. My mother passed away days after giving birth to me. My Maternal grandparents raised me and I finished my business degree in Seoul but to my grandfather's dismay, I worked in a leisure cruise ship instead.

He halted to flash her a slightly mischievous grin. " I was known to exhibit defiance."

In Anna's head, she saw a towering young man whose wide bones hadn't yet grown the full complement of muscles that adults possess.

I met my financial mentor on the cruise ship and I joined his financial empire soon after.

"At the most basic level," David qualified with a scowl.

I had to work hard for several years to be on top. I was propelled to a position on the board of directors soon after. He gave her a somewhat skeptical look. What followed was a string of years that were, well, challenging. A young man running a conglomerate of international corporations or making decisions that go against the grain is not well-received by more seasoned men.

Observing his resoluteness and frightening degree of toughness, Anna gave him a serious glance.

she was aware of it and just managed to keep a small chill from creeping down her spine. You came out on top. As if anybody could ever question that.

After what seemed like an eternity, his face finally broke the monotony. "Yes," he said with a touch of dry cynicism. Had they been on equal footing? For some reason, she didn't believe it.

"I am not sure I remember much about my childhood," she said with a hint of self-reflection. You brought picture albums to the hospital, and they show things that I don't remember. Visual memories of a carefree youth are all I have. My father must have been devastated by the loss of a mother whose name escapes me. To what degree I missed her, I am utterly ignorant."

"I'm not sure if I was in a relationship or not. Or the kind of life I was living before our meeting."

"I don't think many people have lovers who are serious about their relationships," David said with a hint of humor. "You were not very experienced."

Resignation tinged her gaze with resentment. "A situation that you probably fixed quickly."

She nearly fell victim to his deep, gravelly laugh. "It is my deepest delight. Your performance as a student was commendable."

As she instinctively pulled away from his contact, he moved in for a kiss, his eyes sparkling with amusement.

"I believe it's time to make supper," she said.

They sat down to soup an hour later, then grilled steak and salad, and watched TV until David said it was time to go to bed.

Anna stood there biting her lower lips, helpless, as he unbuttoned her garments. As his warm fingertips delicately caressed her sensitive skin, he attended to the buttons on her blouse, a very sensual act in and of itself. So, he can gently press his hand against each breast once he unclips her bra.

She should have been ready for the long, intimate moment of standing partially naked before him after last night. However hard she tried, neither the shallowness of her breathing nor the subtle flushing of her cheeks could be suppressed.

She sat in the shower for as long as she felt comfortable before coming out to find David ready to dry her off. Having the privacy of the suite's bathroom was a huge relief.

For an instant, she considered claiming she could handle it, but a glance at his gloomy features made her understand that would be completely silly.

Just as her nightgown was fastened, she attempted to turn away, but her motion was interrupted when her chin was ensnared between a strong thumb and forefinger.

"Don't," David started with a warning.

She felt an uneasy knot in her throat and swallowed hard as the gentle drawl mirrored the subtle scorn in those deep brown eyes.

As she studied the rugged male features, taking note of the furrows that split his cheeks and the fine creases that flared out from the edges of his eyes, her jaw quivered and the pain of unshed tears ached.

She asked in a choked voice, "How can you say that?" as if she couldn't handle the overwhelming masculinity he possessed.

Raising a hand, he ran a finger down the bridge of her nose, across its tip to rest on her lip's curve.

With a gentle touch over the fullness of the bottom contour, David comforted her, "Easily." He then proceeded to explore the generous line above.

A delectably warm feeling gradually spread across her entire body as his touch—which was both provocative and delicate—sent warning flares to every nerve ending.

As Anna allowed herself to be swept away by her emotions, she contemplated the possibility of losing herself in her thoughts. A part of her longed for his mouth and hands, and she pleaded with him in an irrational attempt to make her erogenous fantasies come true.

His lips gently explored hers, bringing her body close to his in an instinctive movement as he tenderly intensified the kiss. A faint moan escaped her throat as he teased and tasted her.

Chapter 53

S he made the hazy decision that it was heaven, brimming with such excruciating sweetness that she felt like she was melting.

For her, it wasn't enough that they kissed. A great deal more. As his tongue delicately retreated from its exquisite stroking dance with hers, she let out a small, despondent groan, as if some hidden part of her knew something she couldn't articulate.

For several long seconds, when he raised his head, her huge, quite hypnotic eyes clung to his before the details of his face came into view.

Anna saw a glimpse of his restrained intensity, the underlying emotion that clouded his eyes, and something else that was beyond her comprehension. She questioned her ability to speak due to her swollen lips and the extremely sensitive interior of her mouth.

She had never felt so delicate or eerily exposed before. Likewise, she raised her left hand to steady herself, but her left wrist sank to her side as her heart raced, and a visible pulse pounded at the base of her throat.

"Bed, I think," David ordered, his gaze narrowing as he caught a glimpse of the struggle, she had to muster to maintain some control.

With deft precision, he grabbed her left shoulder, moved to her breast, and skillfully shaped the tumescent mound by sliding beneath the silk.

His touch caused it to grow, its peak tautening with sensitive desire, his lips twisted into a sardonic grin as he raised both hands to frame her face.

'Would you rather watch TV or read?'

She let him guide her to the bed, and it was a real struggle to muster even a small grin. 'Television,' she said with an odd accent. assuming I have the choice of which show to watch.

'You are quite courageous, my dear,' he playfully mocked. "I will have shaved and showered by the time you are probably asleep."

Her tummy fluttered with an uncontrollable flutter, and she stared thoughtfully as he undressed to his underwear and made his way to the shower.

As Anna tried to focus on the flitting images on the television, she came to the thoughtful conclusion that he was a mystery.

Almost terrifying in its dark intensity. Still, he had the potential to be kind and thoughtful. She calmly absorbed the cocktail, wondering if she had ever understood him—a tricky combination, indeed.

She became exhausted just thinking about it, and she fell into a dreamless slumber as her eyelashes drooped.

The days seamlessly flowed into each other, with each one mimicking the pattern set by the one before. After getting dressed and taking a stroll along the empty beach, they would come back to the covered terrace for a light breakfast before David retired to his study for an hour.

Even though he always had a phone in the car and a mobile cellular unit in his shorts, just once did either of them ring—it was his sole compromise for keeping an eye on business interests. On both occasions, his instructions had been terrifyingly brief.

Sometimes he'd get in his car, throw together a picnic, and head to a nearby park or beach. On sometimes, they choose to remain in and enjoy some television. They go for a stroll down the beach every afternoon in the late afternoon.

Anna saw progress every day as the swelling and pain in her hand diminished. Soon, she could put on and take off her clothing without assistance, which was a major accomplishment in her recovery.

Slowly but surely, she relaxed and looked at David with tentative fondness; he seemed to read her mind, made sure she didn't get tired and could make her laugh with little effort.

He began to touch her in subtle ways, his fingers would lightly glide over her flesh, and his hands would rest on her arm, her shoulder, her back, or even her waist. His lips gently brushing against hers was an unusual experience, and she had to fight back waves of pleasure on many occasions when he planted playful kisses on her lips. She stopped being apprehensive whenever he climbed into bed with her at night, and she stopped trying to pry his fingers out of hers when he did the same.

However, she was cognizant of his self-control and the suppressed desire that lay just underneath it the entire time. From time to time, she caught a glimpse of it in the way his eyes grew darker and felt it in his pulse when it suddenly quickened.

She felt uneasy, as if something concealed within her was being pulled by the revelation. A sense of impending doom washed over her, igniting a nervous energy that coursed through her veins, tensed her delicate body hair, and evilly twisted her femininity.

They stayed indoors during the weekend due to a series of sporadic showers. There was not a cloud in the sky when Monday morning rolled around.

David announced, "I thought we'd pack some food in the car and head north" as she finished clearing their breakfast dishes and watched him rinse and put them in the dishwasher.

"When would you like to depart?" His mouth curled into a soft, playful smile as Anna asked with such urgency.

Give me an hour I have business to attend to in my study, please. Roughly ten.

A gentle wind cooled the July heat as the sun soared high in an azure sky; the day was perfect. After stopping the vehicle, David turned off the engine. There was a sense of peace and quiet as one looked out over the park, which had a number of big trees along the grassy edge. In the early afternoon sun, the surface of the languid outgoing tide shimmered against the bleached white sand that edged the eastern boundary.

Is your stomach growling?

With a simple smile, Anna turned to face him. A ravenous beast.

With the park practically deserted, David climbed out from behind the wheel and made his way to the back of the truck, where he retrieved a rug, pillows, and a picnic basket. He then selected a level area of grass behind a nearby tree to set up his picnic.

When he started to divide the meal between two plates, Anna dropped to her knees and watched for a few minutes.

It was a real feast—cold chicken and salad, with crusty bread rolls and fresh fruit—and she eagerly bit into a chicken leg.

After David remarked, "Your appetite is improving," she gave him a sidelong look and wrinkled her nose in response.

His sun-kissed, muscular legs spread out in front of her as he sat.

By forgoing designer leisurewear in favor of a loose cotton shirt and cutoff jeans, he appeared to be the polar opposite of a wheeling and dealing international corporate boss. While admiring his chiseled jaw and firm sensual mouth, she slowly lifted her eyes to meet the dark intentness of his gaze, and she conceded that the effect was devastating. She allowed herself a cautious appraisal, all too aware of the effect he had on her mind.

A sexually motivated, studied vigilance pervaded the otherwise apparent laziness. Something inside her shook, pulsing through her veins and nerve endings until her entire body was ensnared in the thrall of bodily awareness; she could feel his powerful chemistry, like a magnetic force field.

"Would you like a little wine?" He said.

Chapter 54

She protested, "It will make me sleepy," as he held up the wine glass to her lips. Putting her lips to the edge where he had been only seconds before seemed very personal. She savored a small amount of the superb Chardonnay, allowing it wine to slide down her throat gently, before washing it down with multiple long sips of icy water.

Asking, "Would that be so terrible?"

Her eyes widened slightly as she detected a hint of humor in his voice. It would be incredibly satisfying to touch him, run my fingers down his square jaw, and feel the vertical line that cuts across his cheeks. She yearned to, intensely.

She wanted his touch nearly as much as she desired the sensation of his lips on hers and his hand molding her bust. An ardent prelude leading into an anthem. With the exception that she doubted her readiness for the series finale.

Such irrational ideas posed an enormous threat to her mental stability. She focused on the horizon, trying to block out their presence, while she watched his skillful movements as he plucked a peach and started to peel it.

In a romantic relationship, how was he? Animated, primal, and without shame. Is there any room for uncertainty, O Lord of heaven? "Who is Anna?"

As soon as she heard his voice, she spun around and gently plundered a piece of fruit from his extended hand, her fingers quivering ever so slightly. "Thank you."

It was juicy and refreshing, and she paired it with a glass of mineral water to cool down.

Perhaps if she relaxed and closed her eyes, her inner turmoil would subside. The gentle ocean wind, the bright sun, and their lunch break were all factors she had neglected to consider. The combination of the two had a soothing effect, and she was soon napping.

Aware that the little sense of lethargy had faded, Anna roused slowly, crossing over from sleep into a vague alertness. Whether it was due to her pregnancy or the healing process, it remained unclear.

Slowly letting her eyelashes swish upward, she pondered whether it might have been a mix of the two.

She blinked when David raised a hand and ran delicate fingers down the side of her jaw; he was splayed in a half-sitting position near her, his head propped in one palm as he faced her.

"Delightful fantasies?"

Not a single one could she recall. "How long did I sleep?" He said, "Nearly an hour," and she looked at him in shock. He observed the range of expressions on her face.

"Why didn't you wake me up?"

"Wake up at your own pace, It's much better that way"

Anna gazed at him, cognizant of the power of his physique and his capacity to render her feeling incredibly vulnerable. Warmth and a latent sensuality were palpable in those black eyes, and it was very unsettling.

As her emotions bounced erratically between cautious acceptance and denial, she felt increasingly fused with him, as if drawn to him by an invisible magnet.

She could have easily hired a nurse companion, and the man could have continued to focus on his vast economic empire, according to logic. However, he had refrained from delegating. Surely that was enough to show how much he cared.

"Are you prepared to walk a bit?"

Her expression softened into a smile as her eyes widened. You bet.

He got to his feet with grace and offered her a helping hand, he then placed the basket in the boot and added the rug and pillows.

They strolled in pleasant quietness, and Anna turned her face to the sun, relishing the gentle afternoon wind that had brushed off the water and carried with it the slightly acidic aroma of seawater.

A beautiful fat child sat on a rug under the shade of a large beach umbrella, and three other youngsters were playing who were less than five years old.

As the young mother skillfully changed the baby's diaper, Anna watched the child's big smile, swinging arms, and bright eyes.

As David slipped an arm around her waist and drew her near to his side, she remained silent as an overwhelming yearning, seemingly out of nowhere, drew her in.

Her fingers ran a delicate line across her waist without her knowledge, pausing in an instinctively protective gesture.

What would the offspring be? A baby with black hair who inherited his father's features, or an angel with light honey skin who won her father's heart? Their offspring would, without a doubt, enjoy a life of luxury.

David returned to the Beach in the late afternoon, while Anna frolicked about the home and David checked the emails and made some calls.

She made her way into the casual lounge, where she grabbed the remote control and began surfing the channels to find anything interesting to watch. She abandoned the unit in favor of a magazine since, by this point in the afternoon, most of the programs aimed at youngsters were either educational or entertaining.

Are you in the mood to dine out? Several dining options are conveniently located within a short drive.

David had entered the room silently, and she looked up in astonishment as he stepped across to stand at arm's length.

Out in the open? There was a clear allure to the concept. You bet.

She gulped violently as he seized her hand, brought it to his lips, kissed each finger, and then slid in to caress her palm, all while his gentle laughter carried an air of curious warmth. The feeling sent little shockwaves through her whole being, and the warmth in those dark eyes, which were so near to her own, made her shudder.

He let go of her and used both hands to slide under her shirt, unfastening her bra. His touch was delicate, and his fingers were warm; she couldn't help but feel a whirlwind of sensations.

Lifting a hand and bringing his head down to hers to start a lengthy, passionate kiss would have been far too easy. The only catch is that it would only get worse if she did.

David whispered, "If you keep staring at me like that for a while longer, I'll interpret it as a personal invitation to hop in the shower with you." He then pressed a finger to the delicate curve of her lower lip. 'Where and when we eat won't be a consideration after that,' he promised huskily.

She averted her gaze from him as she walked slowly to their suite, her cheekbones tinged with color. She went into the restroom after retrieving new underpants.

After a longer-than-necessary dip, she emerged to dry herself off with a towel and change into lace-edged underwear, all because the warm spray of the water eased her broken nerves.

Chapter 55

She entered the bedroom just as David was tucking a shirt into his pants, and she deliberately avoided looking at him as she made her way to the roomy wardrobe to find an appropriate outfit.

As she removed the garments from their racks, she made up her mind to wear black silk culottes, slim-heeled black sandals, and a lengthy white sleeveless button-through silk blouse. This set was perfect for any occasion because it was both practical and stylish.

After slipping into the culottes, Anna adjusted them to her waist and, with David by her side, reached for the top.

"Is there no bra to fasten?" He asked silkily.

"No, no need, the blouse is nicely fitted already." Her explanation was focused on the top being entirely lined, as she proceeded to close the buttons. His dark, unsettling stare met hers as she raised her head. Starting at her belly button, a whirlwind of sensations spread outward, enveloping her in an irresistible embrace of sensuality. Suppressing her excitement, she kept her voice steady.

"I will be right there."

"All I have to do is put some basic makeup on and brush my hair."

"You appear to be around sixteen years old." He teased.

A tentative grin escaped her lips. "That means I'm too young to be married and pregnant."

With a gentle laugh, he caressed her lips. "You are starting to feel better," he said with a hint of mockery.

"Behind every corner, you will soon find a way to test me."

Oh my goodness. It had taken courage for her to verbally duel with him, but was it also foolish?

"If you're ready, let's go and eat," he said easily.

Stepping into the bathroom, she styled her hair into a veil of light silk, delicately applied translucent gold shadow on her eyelids, and finished off her look with lipliner and gloss.

She was taken aback by the air of refinement that David exuded in his immaculately fitted reefer jacket as he stood waiting for her as she exited.

He took her to an Italian spot that was cozy and tiny, full of alluring scents that tantalized her sense of smell and taste. Additionally, there was a man and a small parquet floor square in their mid-thirties serenading a delicate love tune on a miniature electronic keyboard.

David had spaghetti with marinara sauce, and Anna sat back feeling full after ordering tortellini with mushrooms accompanied by garlic toast.

"What about dessert?"

Then she shook her head in disapproval. "Another spoonful would be too much for me."

His ease was palpable, and she couldn't help but notice that he piqued the curiosity of a few of the female customers.

If she were to hold them responsible, how could she? He was an exceptional male animal with plenty of sexual charisma. He was an irresistible temptation for many women due to his natural attractiveness and commanding presence.

She gave him a little nostalgic grin, captivated by the restaurant's flowing music and warm, welcoming ambiance.

"How about we give the dance floor a go?"

She cocked her head silently in agreement after staring helplessly at the little parquetry square that accommodated one couple.

She began to doubt the wisdom of the move after only a few minutes. Her left hand rested against his shoulder, while her right hand was propped up between her breasts. At this proximity, she could feel his body heat beneath the refined mantle of his clothing, and his hands were loosely clasped behind her hips, creating a protective cage.

He moved her with deft ease, his movements smooth and sure and his might a powerful entity. To her astonishment, the keyboard player played an achingly slow song while her steps remained unbroken, even if her breaths became faster in time with her heartbeat.

She felt a suffocating heat radiating from her veins, which brought her acute awareness of her body's many sensory pleasure spots as well as a yearning for his touch.

As the ballad ended and a new, more moving one began, she felt his hands move to curve around the little rise and fall of her butt. In the next few seconds, she sensed his lips gently caressing her hair as it cascaded down to her temple. Her tummy did a little somersault, and then a series of wild flips, all while his warm breath roused a few loose tendrils near her ear.

With a deliberate motion, she raised her head to examine his features, first taking in the wide bridge of his neck, then his jawline, nose, cheekbones, and finally, his deeply brown eyes.

She tried to put some space between them, but what she caught sight of there made the redness in her cheeks worse, and her jaw clenched a little.

He swiftly released her grip, guiding her from the floor with an arm that gently curled around her back.

"Can we have another drink?" David asked as they took their seats.

She politely declined.

While he placed his order, she sipped from her glass, puzzlingly desiring the evening to come to a close while absurdly being reluctant to depart from the restaurant.

'Why are you so worried?' As the Bentley glided effortlessly toward Manhattan Beach, she silently repeated the phrase to herself. It was absurd that she was so anxious, and there was no medical reason why they couldn't resume intimacy.

"Would you like to disclose?"

She was taken aback by his voice and silently turned to him confusedly.

David said, "Your thoughts," as he parked the big truck into the driveway and turned the key to open the garage door.

"It's nothing" Had he suspected? Oh my goodness! What would he say if she confessed that being his lover made her flinch? She dreadfully concluded that he would probably be moderately entertained.

She undid her seatbelt the second the car stopped and got to her feet. She waited for him to unlock the door and then he walked up to her side as they went inside.

She started running for the stairs the second she stepped inside, but she stopped dead in her tracks when he put his hand on her elbow and spun her around to face him. Her nerves were in shambles as he held her.

His voice had a subtle, almost husky drawl, and his eyes had a subtle hood. "You're acting clumsily, unsure whether to run away or stay put?"

"Maybe it's just my personal feelings."

Chapter 56

"You despise the way I touch you?"

Wow, way to go Anna. She whispered a denial. "I'm still not prepared to sleep with you."

"We already have a sleeping arrangement."

A chill ran down her spine as a result of how dangerously silent his voice was.

Her cheeks were stained with dull pink. He was completely cognizant of the chaos he was wreaking, and she despised him for his calculated attack on her conflicted feelings.

"You are aware that my intention was different."

He twisted her head so that she couldn't help but stare at him as he gripped her chin with his thumb and forefinger.

The knot that had suddenly formed in her throat made it impossible for her to swallow, and she was unable to utter a word. As she beheld his head stoop, her eyes widened uncontrollably. She froze as he leaned his mouth to meet hers in a kiss, claiming it as his own and relishing it with a mix of tenderness and controlled aggression.

Anna advised herself that she ought to be taken aback. On the contrary, she was swept away by an overwhelming primal urge.

He drew her close to him, one hand caressing her face and the other cupping her bottom drawing her closer. She felt his hard penis pulsating as evidence of his excitement. She moaned subtly in protest as his lips took on a lightly playful aspect before gradually withdrawing.

She could only gaze at him, oblivious to the profound sleepiness that was visible in her eyes. His intense, dark stare made her feel as though her lips were swelling and quivering.

It was as though time froze since all she could feel was the man—his eyes, his seductive mouth curve, his jaw's strong lines, his chin's power, and his skin's texture.

After what felt like an eternity of silence, he finally leaned forward, put an arm under her knees, and brought her up against his chest.

As he ascended the steps to the upper floor, a wave of sensation coursed through her body, starting from her stomach.

When he entered their suite, he gently helped her take off her shoes and placed her on her feet. He gently traced the curves of her mouth with his raised palm, probing its softness with such tenderness that she gasped for air.

"I hope we can make love."

Her pupils widened and her heart rate increased. The words refused to escape her lips, despite her need to express her nervousness.

While gazing into hers, he dropped his jacket and threw it upon a nearby chair. He then undid his shirt buttons, unfastened his tie, and abandoned it. His socks and shoes followed.

As his fingers undid his belt buckle, loosened the little metal clasp, and unzipped his pants, Anna watched helplessly while her heart pounded crazily.

His black silk briefs skimmed his hips, revealing just enough of his manhood to make her feel a shiver go down her spine as her awareness arrowed from her feminine center to him. He was concentrated and intense.

Moving closer, he reached out and gently grasped her left hand, guiding her towards the bed. As he sat on the edge of the mattress and pulled her close, his touch was powerful and warm, and she said nothing to resist.

As he raised a hand to delicately trace the lines of her face, she felt hypnotized by the dark, shimmering passion that was obvious they stared at each other intensely.

His fingers traced a route down the column of her throat and met hers at the edge of her top, the sensation was electric, and she swallowed violently.

She let out a little gasp as he caressed the full curve of her breast after he unbuttoned one button after another, till the edges dangled loose.

The idea of doing this has pushed David to the brink of insanity, he said. "All night long, your every action highlighted how free they were." Carefully, he detached the blouse and put it among his other abandoned garments.

Gently molding the creamy fullness, he said, "Beautiful." He tested the weight of the fullness as he delicately circled each sensitized peak.

She felt a sharp ache in her belly, and her throat tightened as he leaned in for a peak, rolling it on the roughened edge of his tongue till she could feel it grow and thicken under his touch.

As he showed the same level of care to its identical twin, she stifled a quiet moan. As he started to suckle deeply, she let out an audible moan and drew an exquisite pleasure from every sensitive peak, which she couldn't help but acknowledge.

At last, he lifted his head, and she looked up into his eyes through half-closed lids; she remained motionless as he gently pulled the silk fabric from her culotte waistband and began to let it fall over her hips and pool at her feet. As he gently assessed her, she felt heat sever her body as he proceeded to take off her satin and lace panty.

He raised a hand and ran delicate fingers up her ribcage, trailing them gently across her hip. He slid down to touch the slightly rounded bottom of her, then brushed a path to her thigh.

His fixation on her made Anna's pupils enlarge as he traced the gentle waves of her hair, caressed its upper edge, and rocked back and forth until her entire being swayed like an exquisitely tuned instrument.

He cautiously dropped his hand till he reached the point where her thighs met, she gasped aloud as he began an intimate investigation that she was not sure she wanted to participate in.

"Am I making you nervous, madam?"

The emotion she was experiencing wasn't exactly characterized by fear. To mention only a couple, joy and excitement. As in, "no." A gasp, barely audible, arose as the lone negative.

She trembled as an initial cramp gripped her and grew uncontrollably intense from his touch, which she described as an erotic torment.

"David." She moaned huskily as she spoke his name.

Oh my goodness, such lovely magic. It seemed as if I were whisked away to paradise and shown a myriad of wonderful things.

"Be careful, madam," he warned as she fumbled for his hand.

She was so engrossed in the incoherent sounds that she barely saw him helping her to the bed.

Before stretching out by her side, he delicately adjusted her damaged hand so it could rest in a comfortable posture.

His lips met hers in a long, languid, drugging kiss that alternated between tease and tantalize and she quavered in fear as he led her on a journey of sensual discovery.

She choked back a cry as he trailed kisses on the entrance to her very core. Her hands were on his hair as she savored the feeling of his tongue on her most sensitive center.

Chapter 57

As she reached stratospheric heights, she quietly confessed that it was brazen. Despicable as sin. Passionately, destructively, and hopelessly sensual. She wished it would go on forever, but the intense sensation spiral made her doubt her ability to control herself for much longer.

A deep, numbing oral reenactment of the sexual act, it was the most intimate kiss ever. A sensual present so beautiful and generous that it made her want to cry with happiness.

His bead slowly moved, and he started kissing her passionately all over her body, from her stomach to the delicate area under her breasts, and finally, he nailed one sensitized peak.

He then tilted his head back to stare down at her, observing her pale face, her parted lips, and the pinkish-blue hues that adorned her eyes.

As she cautiously reached out to touch his chest, Anna traced his shoulder, softly caressed his muscular rib cage, and then, unconsciously, lowered her palm to the taut, flat planes of his stomach.

A knot formed in her muscles, and she felt her tongue cautiously move along his lower lip, all without realizing it.

"If you don't stop immediately, I shall pass the limit of my control," David swore in a raspy disapproval.

With a close examination, she caught a glimpse of the dormant passion, the intense longing that was hardly concealed.

She felt an overwhelming surge of strength, culminating in a goddess-like sense of control over something so rare and valuable that she alone could provide him the freedom he craved.

Her fingers slowly traced the length of his enlarged shaft, as if on purpose. She felt it engorge further beneath her featherlight touch as she gently explored it, fascinated.

"Hmm, I might cum." The sound of fabric being torn from hair-roughened flesh was followed by his loud despairing groan, and her voice was a husky allure.

"I don't think you would approve of my lack of it," he said with a touch of religiosity.

He made sure she was ready to embrace him with great care, and she immediately arched to welcome his entrance. As his length was accommodated by moist tissues, she reveled in the complete enclosure, and the sensation was powerful.

She felt awe at his enthusiasm, as if they were meeting for the first time.

Ignoring the absurdity of the situation, she could feel her blood vessels swell as she embraced him, and her inner muscles were twitching in an attempt to stimulate and match his pulse rate.

She seemed to be experiencing an overwhelming urge to express her intense emotions in a way that her mind was hesitant to acknowledge, leading to an unexpected and somewhat startling outburst of passion. Tracing the length of his spine, she delicately kneaded his heavily muscled flank with her fingers.

Her fingers wandered almost freely to his hip, and then she started a long, sensual exploration of his most sensitive areas. She delighted in his labored breath as she delicately massaged his tailbone.

She wasn't satisfied until her lips explored a sensitive male nipple, which she suckled shamelessly, occasionally nibbling with her teeth, until she could feel his powerful body quiver in the beginning stages of delicious bliss.

She desired... Why on earth did she want that? Beyond this measured rhythm, he would plunge headfirst into her with a deluge of passionate strokes that would catapult them to new heights.

The gentle moan coming from her throat was almost imperceptible to Anna as her body moved in unison with him, effortlessly lifting and angling to match his every action.

With his hands resting on her shoulders, he supported her weight, and she eagerly met his mouth as it pressed against hers. She straddled him and matched his pace. Their passionate kiss reflected the depths of their intimacy, leading them on an exotic adventure to the center of her sensuous universe.

Even while her rational mind rejected the idea of her spirit, the sensual chords of her reawakened body were tuned to this one man—guided by his knowledge and captivated by a passion that knew no bounds.

That she was his was beyond any shadow of a doubt. Every delicate nerve ending bore the mark of betrayal, and the intense vivacity coursing through her veins turned her blood into an inferno of need that could only set her senses ablaze. Erosive, savage, and barbaric passion.

She was so emotionally exhausted by the time it was over that she questioned her very mobility.

As if his touch had intensely sensitized every nerve-ending, she felt tingly alive; yet exhausted and lethargic. She smiled as he ran his lips over the nape of her neck, then slid down to kiss her breasts open-mouthed, in that order.

She half-heartedly acknowledged his greatness. An attentive partner who is gentle and thoughtful toward her. Had he relished their time together to the same extent that she had? Did he feel fulfilled? Asking was just too much for her to handle.

He reached for the arm support and delicately fastened it into place, she turned her head to observe him.

His eyes were sleepy and black, while hers flitted to a spot beyond his left shoulder.

In a husky voice, David urged her not to try to conceal the profoundly wonderful experience that had been shared by the two of them. He felt her puffy lips with his thumb. A masterpiece.

He lowered himself to lie down at her side, bringing her close enough for her head to rest on his shoulder. Grasping the sheet and drawing it over them required almost no effort on his part. A gentle "Go to sleep, my love" was his parting word to her.

Still, she was unable to do so for quite some time. On the contrary, she remained motionless while she listened to his heartbeat.

Had this always been the case, from the start? On the other hand, did getting to this level of sexual fulfillment require effort and time?

Regrettably, she was unaware. A painful realization that her body remembered what her head had forgotten was all that remained.

Chapter 58

A gentle ocean wind brushed over Anna's skin and tangled her hair as she relaxed on the tranquil beach.

The sea was a rich blue color, and although it was flat out at a distance, it crested as it got closer to the coast, creating a foamy mess on the compacted beach.

She was enchanted by an eerie sense of uncertainty... with a hint of sadness. Here, she felt secure and safe.

The previous 10 days had been picture-perfect: spent leisurely in the sunshine with easy company, spent long evenings under the moonlight, and loved tenderly.

They were scheduled to go back to Los Angeles tomorrow. Her physiotherapy sessions were scheduled to start next week, and she also had appointments with the neurologist and obstetrician. Little time passed before David would hop in his car and head into the city, where he would spend the better part of each day in his office atop one of the many stunning inner-city modern structures in Los Angeles.

It reminded her that she was in the same building as well. It was the same building where she attended a board meeting with her father and other board members. She remembered an old man visiting her in the hospital and she had not recognized him at that time but now it is clear. He is her father.

"There is no need for you to feel unhappy, Anna." Her father spoke to her in a reassuring tone.

"David has something to say to you, and it may be the perfect solution." David was present at the moment.

Anna snarled at David, "Just a minute," while casting a venomous look in his direction.

"This is completely unrelated to you in any way. You have no right to be in this place at all."

"It's lucky for you I am," he drawled sarcastically, and Anna saw in the shadows of his dark brown eyes an awful sparkle that looked strangely like a triumph.

"Unless, of course, you want your father to end up in jail for fraud," he said sarcastically.

"'Jail!" She stared at her father in complete disbelief, fully anticipating that he would refute David's ridiculous remark. She pleaded with him to dispel the notion that it was even conceivable.

Her father mumbled an apology before rising to his feet and leaving the room. He was no longer the energetic guy with blue eyes that she adored; rather, he was a weary old man who looked every one of his sixty years plus ten more years than he was. His shoulders were sagged, his eyes were dim, and his face was pale and weathered. She was aware that David was being honest with her. Her father lowered his arm and placed a comforting hand on her shoulder, and she instinctively reached up to cover it with her own.

He was exhausted when he remarked to Anna, "I never meant for this to happen."

"If it's okay with you, I won't go to lunch with you," her father said weakly. Take David with you instead.

Anna felt a chill run down her spine as the picture vanished and refused to budge no matter how much she concentrated.

With his gaze focused, David paused alongside her, running his eyes over her bare cheeks.

"What is it?"

With a raised hand, she brushed a loose strand of hair behind her ear. Her dark, reflective eyes slowly shifted to meet his.

"We were in my father's study." After taking a long breath, she described it. Her forehead furrowed in perplexion as she met his gaze.

"You are talking about my father's business," she said with a hint of uncertainty.

"I was furious," she whispered gently.

A tangible being so real that it instilled terrible fear in her had been sensed and inhaled by her in those short minutes.

His look was incomprehensible. "What percentage of it did you recall?"

Had she married David for that reason? In order to rescue her father?

As her vision started to blur, she took a few deep breaths to try to control her vertigo.

"It was my father's birthday and I invited him to lunch but he said that I should take you instead," she whispered, her memory frantically searching for the ethereal picture that would not budge. Desperately, she remarked, "I can't remember anything after that." Sobbing, she continued. That, though, is it.

As he gently cupped her face in his hands, he locked his lips around hers for a subtle tasting that brought no reaction. It was as if the longing to relive the past had never left her thoughts, and she remained silent as they returned to the house.

Even throughout supper, Anna remained abnormally silent, and she struggled throughout the day to control her tendency toward reflection.

"Fear won't make your memory come back any faster," David said, brushing her dish aside.

Her gaze darkened as she caught a glimpse of the innate power that was plain to see.

"The sense of helplessness has always been there, and I can't shake it," she softly said, keeping his eyes.

There is absolutely no cause for you to be unsure. "Regarding anything," he added with purpose. She wasn't quite convinced, but she felt she had no choice but to take his word for it just now.

Getting to his feet, he started gathering silverware and piling plates.

"The dishes will be taken care of while you sort through Netflix."

Anna stumbled into the casual lounge, where she deliberated for a while before settling on an action flick that promised to overwhelm the audience with plenty of excitement.

Just as the previews ended, David entered the room and pulled her down to the two-seater next to him as she went to sit on one of the lone chairs.

He moved her around so she could lie back against his chest and rest between his thighs as easily as possible. He reached down and interlaced his fingers over her lower belly.

She redirected her attention to the television as the muscular male actor performed a risky choreographed karate dance alongside his adversary.

It was dawn when Anna woke up, so she must have slept off at some point.

Once David finished their leisurely breakfast, he threw their belongings into the trunk, secured the home, and returned to the city.

"You look so much better," Amy said with a real smile stretching over her face as she welcomed them upon their arrival. Returning a flush of color to your cheeks is a welcome sight.

With a touch of dry humor, Anna's mouth curled. "David has been providing me with food and transportation to stroll along the shore.

"I will have lunch ready early. Will you be available at two?"

"Yes, of course." Anna nodded.

· · ᨀ · ·

DESPITE ENJOYING A bowl of Amy's chicken soup, Anna couldn't shake an innate fear, so she fiddled with the salad, nibbled on the bread, and ended the meal with David getting back to the study.

There would soon be no excuse for her not to reintegrate into David's social circle when the daily physiotherapy sessions and professional visits had begun.

Jacob should drive her to the physiotherapist's office but it seems that her overprotective husband changes his mind.

Her spouse, though, slid in behind the wheel.

As soon as the Bentley pulled into a parking spot next to the main entrance, she acted as though she didn't need you to accompany her inside.

"I'll just stay in the waiting room," David said with a hint of humor, and she silently scolded him as he trailed behind her to the reception area.

Muscles get stiff, lose mobility over time, and hurt if they aren't used, which is why the physiotherapist gave her a detailed list of exercises to perform.

After Anna finished the easy exercises under David's watchful eye, the session ended and he drove her home.

The roadways were jammed, with drivers exhibiting varying degrees of impatience as the queues of vehicles ground to a crawl. Anger flared, sirens sounded, and vehicles screeched in disapproval. They recommenced their movement after a while.

Just as the Bentley started to gain speed, David slammed on the brakes. Several things were going through Anna's mind at once: the crunching of metal, the sudden jolt caused by the car's hit, and David's arm resting on her seat. David leaned over her, his features hard as he cupped her face, and she faintly registered a torrent of savagely spoken Korean phrases.

"Are you okay?"

At the wheel of a different vehicle, a BMW, she was navigating through an automated junction. In an attempt to evade the incoming car, she slammed on the brakes and twisted the wheel in an instant. Unfortunately, the minute had passed. A horrible crunch of metal was heard. Suddenly, her skull slammed against something, and the world went black.

"For God's sake."

Chapter 59

S he tried to refocus them and block out that terrifying vision, but Anna felt like her eyes were much too big for her face.

"Are you in pain?"

Then she heard David's voice—deep, dark, and throbbing—and saw his anxious face—every line etched with worry. His eyes nearly black as he tried to see through the mask she had worn.

"Anna."

She blinked once or twice before she was brought back to the present as his fingers delicately touched both cheeks.

"I'm—fine," she stammered, her voice barely audible due to her shaking lips. She looked directly into his intense eyes and forced herself to swallow the quick knot that appeared in her throat. With trembling hands, she reassured him, "Really," fending off the inquisitive gaze that seemed to attack her very being.

"You were aware of the incident." Instead of a question, it was a statement.

"Every cent?"

For some reason, her lips felt unusually parched, so she stuck out her tongue to dab them.

"All I can see is a whirlwind of blue speeding at me, and then the crash."

As he grabbed for his phone, he entered a string of numbers, requested the police, and provided a brief account of the collision and its location; his gaze never budged from hers, and her mouth quivered a little.

As David slid to his feet and pushed open the door, Anna could only look ahead; the combination of his hard, unyielding tones and those of the guy who had tempted providence with an error scarcely registered in her conscious mind.

Would her recollection be like this? Short, random occurrences every few days?

Just a few seconds after that, David got behind the wheel, and Anna calmly endured his intent inspection.

I'll be all right, she told him. "Has the vehicle sustained significant damage?"

"You are very important to me."

"Not the car," he said with a hint of sadness.

Sometime later, she perceived the faraway shriek of a police siren, and suddenly, with flashing red and blue lights, it approached. Hearing voices, doors banged.

When they got home, she noticed the significant scrapes and gouges as well as the damaged light and its surrounding area. She barely made it upstairs in time as the sight of them sent a wave of nausea rushing over her.

Despite her protests, David proceeded to call the doctor.

She said angrily, "Dammit, this is normal," and he appeared to tighten his face noticeably in response. A sign of seeming surrender, she raised her hands.

After an hour, she still couldn't help but repeat the doctor's words of comfort, and the only compromise she made in her pursuit of relaxation was to take a seat on the poolside sun lounger under the shade of the umbrella.

As Anna maintained her neurology appointment and went to the physiotherapy clinic, the following days became routine.

After an early morning workout in the downstairs gym and a few laps in the pool, David hid out in his study until Amy brought him lunch.

His presence in the city was required by an urgent phone call on Friday morning, and Anna was looking forward to spending the day by herself.

She had lunch and then settled down to peruse a stack of current glossy magazines in preparation for her mid-morning physiotherapy appointment.

As she leisurely perused the fashion pages, she noticed tall, attractive young women posing in stunning garments.

She couldn't help but notice a certain model—a long golden haired with classical features and cold blue eyes—and pondered the source of her innate attraction.

Suddenly, those identical features appeared to come to life; Anna felt as if she were watching a rerun of a scene from a film about a single episode in her life; she froze for a second as images flooded her mind. Stunningly clear, eerily vivid.

"Office of David Miller this is Amelia. May I be of service? Who do you claim to be? Ah, wife of David?" "Anna!" The receiver was ripped from Amelia's grasp by David.

"What happened?" David asked worriedly.

"Nothing—nothing at all" She said.

"Sorry for disturbing you, David."

"I'm merely calling to wish you a happy birthday, I can't reach you on your mobile phone that's why I called here".

"I didn't realize it was your birthday until Bryan rang this morning to speak to you, and I feel bad I didn't get you a present. But I'll have one ready for you when you return. I was thinking maybe a shiny new briefcase. Or anything you like. A choice is up to you."

"Would you rather I just take you by surprise? Look, I'll hang up now; you're clearly busy at the moment," she said in a hurry.

"You bet I'm not. A glass of champagne was just brought to me as a surprise by my assistant."

"She left, and at this point, I was going to leave." He explained.

"Just as well, I don't want to bother you," she said slowly.

"Never, ever hang up," he commanded. "I appreciate your calling to find out what I would like for my birthday," Anna gasped.

"Which was, of course, "you naked in bed." He said teasingly.

'Why has he lied to me?' Anna knows that female name and she wasn't the assistant.

"Anna?"

Anna brought her thoughts back to the present when she heard what sounded like Amy's voice from far away. She felt her heart racing and her skin moist from perspiration.

Tea has just been brewed. Do you want some? She came up with an appropriate answer somehow.

My goodness. For her, this stretch was the most direct she had ever encountered.

The more I try to forget, the worse it gets. Disagreement and wrath could flare up again if complete memory loss is involved.

It was as if the camaraderie and unique intimacy she and David had experienced at Manhattan Beach had been a faraway dream.

Something told her she was on the brink of reality, and she felt a shiver run down her spine, making her delicate body hair stand up in defense.

Squally wind-driven storms pounded the windows throughout the better part of the weekend, replenishing the city's depleted dams and easing the seasonal danger of bushfires.

After David taught Anna the fundamentals of chess and repeatedly checkmated her, Anna decided to stop letting him win and instead beat him at cards. That was a total bust as well; she came out on top twice, but she had a sneaking suspicion that it was all because he was trying to lose.

On Monday, the sky was clear and bright. David drove the Porsche into town while the Bentley was at the shop for repairs.

Jacob took Anna across town to her obstetrician appointment after she attended physiotherapy after lunch. She chose to check in instead of waiting in the car because they arrived early.

She was cordially received by the senior nurse. Mr. Miller is accompanying the doctor on a patient visit. I don't think he'll be late. Sitting down, Anna picked out a magazine and started perusing its pages. She perused the material with great interest.

She froze after glancing absently at another for a few minutes. On one page were two photographs of Amelia, and she let out a small cry of surprise as she realized what had happened; it was as if someone had pressed a shutter button and then released it, revealing a moving picture.

She watched it all happen with a terrified curiosity.

No way, holy cow. No. As she desperately tried to halt the succession of pictures that came flooding in like a reel of Technicolor film, the negation sounded like a thunderous inner monologue.

That was false. Nothing at all. Some awful mistake occurred. It was a cruel joke done by a wicked hand.

She could leave this place without losing her composure if she remained absolutely motionless.

Just in time, she reached the powder room, her stomach turning as the effects of the repeating flashback kicked in.

After that, for a few minutes, she rested her head on the cold tiles and stared aimlessly at the elegantly furnished restroom.

Fearing that a perceptive doctor would notice her pale complexion, and rapid heart rate, and ask her questions she didn't want to answer, she avoided addressing anyone, much less the medical expert.

What kind of response would she get if she just went out, hopped into the waiting car, and asked Jose to drive her home? Anna pondered.

Back at home. How on earth could she possibly travel to that place? She obviously could have. her decision was dully made. It would only take Jacob minutes to notify David if she asked him to take her somewhere else; after that, what would happen? An argument?

So much rage was building up inside her. Such intense fury within.

Tragically, her thoughts drifted back to the fateful lunch she had with David Miller

Chapter 60

She blinked to fight back the tears that were about to fall as she said, "I can sell my house, and in time the villa in Jeju Island, I suppose." It was inconceivable to her that her father would have implicated her in a criminal act as far back as 10 years ago.

He sat down on the bench next to her and cupped her chin in his palm before turning her face to look at him. "But I do have a solution; I'm prepared to invest all of the money necessary to get your father out of this mess and make the company viable again, but I want something in return," David said.

Anna said, "I have complete faith that my father will do whatever you ask him to do." "In general, he is a decent human being; however, there are..."

David concluded for her with a caustic comment, saying, "he had an expensive wife and lifestyle." "However, I am not interested in your father; rather, it is you, Anna," he said. I want to get married to you.

Her initial assumption was that the man had lost all semblance of sanity, but once she caught a glimpse of the steely resolve reflected in the depths of his eyes, she began to have second thoughts.

"We can announce our engagement at the birthday party for your father tonight."

Due to the ridiculous nature of his offer, Anna was jolted out of the cloud of sadness that had been threatening to devour her. She chuckled to herself internally as she pictured Annet's expression.

"Are you out of your mind?", she cried out in shock.

"For heaven's sake, you're my step-sister's boyfriend," Anna said, and all of a sudden, she had the bright idea that would solve the issue entirely.

"Instead of asking me, you ought to address your inquiry to her."

"I do not doubt that she will seize the opportunity."

His fingers became firmer on her chin as he continued to say, " Annet is nothing more than an old acquaintance."

"I swear I have never known her in the sexual sense—as I have you," he said, his heavy-lidded eyes staring into hers, the sensuous awareness in the shining depths causing heat to rush to her cheeks.

His long fingers slid from her chin to trace up her cheek and curve a thin tendril of hair behind her ear as he added, "So there's no problem there."

Internally, she shivered as he said, "Forget about Annet."

"If you want to save your father, marry me." His deep, dark voice grated across her raw nerves, and she darted out her tongue to moisten her suddenly too-dry lips. She noticed the knowing glitter in his eyes as she made a movement that betrayed him.

"You have a decision to make, and I need it as soon as possible."

The constant pounding at the door went unnoticed by Anna at first because her head was hurting so severely.

"Mrs. Miller? Do you feel okay?"

Oh my. How long has she been here? Could it be five, or ten minutes?

"I'm feeling fine." She timidly persuaded the nurse that it was just a bout of sickness. She would need to gather herself. Both physically and emotionally, she was lifeless.

"The doctor is ready to see you."

"Shall I procure a refreshing beverage for you? How about some tea?"

She used the disposable toothbrushes and toothpaste that had been generously provided before putting on lipstick and combing her hair.

"That sounds perfect, tea."

"Thank you"

She settled into a plush chair across from a little middle-aged man, who peered at her through half-moon spectacles that rested halfway on his nose bridge.

"Your pulse rate is elevated, and you appear pale," he whispered. Would you mind sharing what's troubling you?

"The baby is great."

"On the other hand, the mom is making me nervous."

He gave her a long appraisal before softly probing, "Your recollection. Have you had flashbacks that keep happening?"

She wished she could pretend they had never happened, since then she could convince herself that they were just a part of a terrible dream.

"'A few," she said gingerly, not wanting to reveal that her memory had fully returned.

"Your thoughts they were upsetting?"

"Truth in part was far better than truth in whole." This is, I suppose, an expected response.

"Not all of the details have been filled in by my hubby."

"It seems like I should give him a call."

She hesitated before responding rapidly, sensing his intense curiosity. "Excuse me?"

It was clear that he was giving it some serious thought. The fact that David Miller had demanded a comprehensive report following each of his wife's consultations was left out.

"I believe it would be most beneficial if we meet up again in two weeks."

Instantly upon her arrival, Jacob sprang out of the car to unlock the back door; after she had taken her seat, he got in behind the wheel.

"Do you have a preferred destination? What about going shopping?"

With her sufficient funds and credit card authority, she could buy anything she wanted at any store. She instantly considered splurging, knowing full well that her husband would roll his eyes when he saw the bill. However, her wardrobe was brimming with trendy garments, and she owned an assortment of shoes that would allow her to switch things up for weeks. Products for personal hygiene and cosmetics. Jewelry included. David had shown tremendous generosity considering the conditions of their marriage. She made the connection between the desire to seem to be the wife of a successful man and her incredibly kind nature.

"The Grove, Jacob," she ordered on an impulsive whim. "Here I am considering going shopping for a new outfit, and David is hosting a business associate tonight."

"Yes," Jacob said, smiling amiably.

Anna sank into the plush seat, shut her eyes to stave off the flood of pictures that were starting to flood her mind, and the car pushed ahead, out into the flow of traffic.

"Do you want me to come along with you?"

The sound of Jacob's voice caused Anna to squint, and she quickly gathered her wits before determining that the Bentley was parked outside one of several posh boutiques famous for their high-end designer labels and exorbitant prices.

"Jacob, I'm sorry, but no." She grinned at him warmly.

"Where could we meet for coffee?"

"Give me at least thirty minutes."

At least twice as long, and she needed extra time because she couldn't sign the necessary credit forms, which meant she needed special authorization.

Just minutes before David was due home, they made a beeline for their suite, and she hurried upstairs to get away from him, if only for a second. Maybe she could find a way to lock herself in the shower if she moved quickly.

She narrowly escaped, and as she came out of the bedroom, he was taking off his clothing.

His gaze met hers, but she quickly averted his as he undressed and made his way to her.

She had to put up an act for the next few hours, if not longer. She could let her pent-up fury out once their dinner guests had left.

She hurriedly began speaking because she felt an overwhelming urge to say something.

"I went to The Grove with Jacob."

"Shopping," she said, gesturing at the multicolored shopping bags lying at the foot of the bed.

"I wanted to try on a new outfit tonight." As they drew near enough to touch, she warmed her smile and he reached up to cup her face with both hands.

His kiss was hot, ravenous, and possessive as it pressed against hers. While he pulled her near to him, she could sense her own unanticipated reaction, the one that was unfolding from within.

She felt her lips quiver as he delicately ran his thumb over the kiss-swollen curves, and she could hardly meet the intense, menacing stare that met his rising head.

Parting her silk robe, one hand traced a path down her neck to caress the full curve of her breast. "What did the obstetrician say?"

Then how did she respond to that? A small voice cautioned with great care.

"The baby is fine, he told me."

The fullness and tension in her breasts hurt. It craves his touch.

How the dickens could her body respond in such a betraying way?

He seemed to know exactly what had transpired and was patiently waiting for her to tell him, his dark and analytical eyes piercing hers.

Chapter 61

The obstetrician called him already but why is he acting like he doesn't know?

She wouldn't be surprised by the prospect.

"A case of morning sickness struck me." After a brief gap, she tried to be humorous.

"At about three o'clock in the afternoon." David would not be fooled for long by her acting skills.

"Another flash of memory came to me." It was a continuation of the truth, and it gave her a little chill.

David reassured her as he caressed her temple with his kisses.

"I will call Rick and arrange for him to meet me at a restaurant if you are not in the mood for dinner this evening."

"Amy has gone to a lot of trouble," Anna said hastily, before saying, "No."

Even though she was fast asleep, she was startled when he climbed into bed and stretched out to her.

A showdown was what she desired. She wanted to go to battle with him, dammit. That was not the case, though, when a dinner guest was expected to show up in—how much time? In under thirty minutes?

"Shouldn't we prepare ourselves?"

Retracting his hand, David smiled ruefully at her. "I must get in the shower and get my beard cleaned."

She shopped for a form-fitting sheath dress with linen and a dazzling red viscose blend; the hemline fell just above the knee. Matching beaded shoes and a creative panel of red beaded embroidery took an otherwise understated design and gave it an air of glitz.

As she applied her final touches to her makeup, David walked into the room and helped her put on her dress after expertly adjusting the hook on her bra. She turned to face him slowly as the long zip fastener slid home.

His gaze swept over her delicate features, and he said the word "beautiful" with a lazy sense of admiration.

"How about your hair?"

"I was going to let it hang loose."

Carrying her hairbrush across the dressing table, she combed her long black locks till they glistened.

Tall and good-looking, Tim Jones was in his late forties and admired men and women of different genders. He was attractive and charismatic.

"I can't wait to finally meet the woman who got under David 's armor," he said.

"Raise your drink in salute," he said.

"You have my congratulations."

The meal was delicious since Amy had outdone herself in the kitchen, and the gentle teasing that each guy participated in revealed the depth of their friendship.

"We used to go on vacation together every year. The Swiss Alps. St. Moritz."

"I sent David to live with my family in Paris for a year." A mischievous glint was in his eye.

"It seems like we were a bit too daring for our own good; we were youthful, outgoing, and gregarious."

David drawled, "Tim, if you spend too much time telling stories, I might feel forced to tell Marianna some stories of my own the next time I see her."

"Marianna is fully aware of the kind of man I am," Tim said, returning to his Gallic shrug.

"Am I going to have my illusions shattered?" Anna asked a gentle question, which elicited a small smile from him. But his eyes were as mysterious as night.

"Which illusions are you referring to?" David smiled.

"Is it possible that you have not decided to take a mistress, making you different from other successful men?" Fearlessly meeting Tim's unwavering gaze, she was aware of the abrupt silence that had descended upon the room.

"Why would a man need to have a mistress if his wife provides for his needs and he values his family?" he asked softly.

Unconcerned, she ventured into a potentially perilous zone. "The difficulty it poses, maybe?"

"How about some excitement?" A clumsy shrug escaped her lips.

"In your opinion, is it reasonable for a wife to likewise have her needs expressed?"

Silk was the texture of David's voice. "My dear, you are expressing a nuanced grievance."

Her acting chops were on full display as she mustered up a slight laugh of disbelief.

"I don't even know where to start when it comes to criticism of you." She said with sarcasm while grinning.

She extended a comforting hand, remained motionless as he grasped it, and then brought her fingers up to his mouth.

His black eyes betrayed a vigilant watchfulness that sent warning flares licking down the taut edge of her nerves, and she caught a glimpse of it in his motion.

It was evident to him. He might not have known the exact moment her memory had returned, but he certainly knew she had gone through a complete recollection.

"How about we grab some coffee in the lounge?" David made a slick suggestion.

David survived the remainder of the night in some mysterious way. Tim gave no clue whether he thought her conversation was a touch too intense.

"You must excuse me," Tim finally stated. "My return to my hotel is imperative; it is late."

He came over to be by her side. "It was a pleasure spending the evening with you." Holding her hand for just a moment longer than was strictly necessary, he brought it to his lips.

"David needs to take you to Paris," he whispered softly. "Marianna would be quite pleased."

On their way to the front door, David nodded in agreement.

As soon as the car's taillights passed the gates, Anna averted her gaze from the door, keenly aware of David's movements as he reset the alarm.

On her way up the stairs, a chill ran down her spine. Her eyes became darker and her jaw tightened as the pent-up rage that had been latent since this afternoon finally surfaced.

As soon as she entered the bedroom, she removed her shoes and unzipped her dress.

She made no sound when David entered the room just as she started a third unsuccessful effort to slide the zipper down; he crossed to finish the task.

She removed the garment with great care and set it on top of a nearby chair while she peered over his shoulder as he took off his jacket and tie.

David asked, "When was it?"

She hesitated before gently turning to face him, afraid to give him away. His voice was low and menacing.

As she prepared to confront him, her chin tilted slightly, and her chocolate brown eyes gleamed with a terrifying intensity.

"Earlier in the day. In the waiting area of the obstetrician. Her eyes gleamed as she said, "A magazine photo of Amelia was the spark that set off a chain reaction that brought back every memory in slow motion."

His face turned somewhat darker as he reached out a hand, interlocking his thumb and forefinger to seize her chin. He clenched his grip even harder as she tried to free herself.

Anna's eyes met his with dark intensity. "Why?" she insisted. "Why did you trick me?"

His expression remained a mystery as he held her with ease. His lack of response infuriated her beyond measure.

"I demand an explanation, dammit!"

The penetrating darkness of his spirit was mirrored in his gloomy expression and husky voice.

"When were you expecting me to divulge information?"

As she patiently awaited his next move, she endured his relentless inspection with a furious sense of defiance.

"As you lay, wounded and terrified, in a hospital bed?" His pursuit was unrelenting.

"When did you initially return home?" His gaze begged her to deny him.

"Is it okay that I betrayed your faith? Refused to show you love and comfort?"

"You exploited me by manipulating my emotions," she sobbed, her agony evident in her tears.

He possessed an enchanting masculinity that shook her to her core with just a glance. Her profound self-awareness made her realize that no one could make her as defenseless as David Miller. She despised both him and herself for being so weak because of it. Above everything else, though, she despised the situation. It hung her in his grasp.

There was a part of her that wanted to reject, but she couldn't bring herself to say it. In a somber confession, she said, "You left me before the car accident, we are already separated."

"I was planning to consult a lawyer and initiate the divorce process." She said weakly.

His expression became noticeably more severe.

"You despise me to the point that you would want to conceal the fact that you're pregnant. Deny me my child's existence?" A creepy silkiness crept into his speech, sending little chills down her spine.

"Another possibility is that you intend to get an abortion."

She shrieked in amazement and denied it again, this time quietly. That idea had never crossed her mind.

Chapter 62

For what seemed like an eternity, he remained silent; when he finally did speak, it was with an unsettlingly harsh and depressing tone. "I will claim full ownership of the child you are carrying."

"Our child should be valued for more than just being a legal battle pawn in the custody battle."

"I wed you because I could not bear to watch my father suffer financially and emotionally. It was lethal for him to be bankrupt. He might not survive jail time because he is old."

She accused him angrily, saying, "You engineered a diabolical game."

He kept staring at her for what felt like an eternity. Reminding her, his eyes remained vigilant even though they were partially closed.

"You took the arrangement personally and tried to turn it into an advantage for yourself against me."

She had deceived herself into thinking she was doing well at first. The only difference was that she had developed romantic feelings for him during their journey.

"I never pretended that our relationship was perfect," David said, "in case you remember."

"You mentioned that we had minor disagreements," Anna threw herself at him, despising his deft use of language.

"Times," he clarified. He hesitated on purpose before continuing, "You'd have to agree that the resolution of such disputes was never satisfactory."

Frankly, that was a modest statement. When they were in bed, they were always completely in sync. At first, it caused her great distress, since she couldn't understand how she could become so emotionally invested in a man she claimed to despise.

"Our marriage defies all the norms," she said pitifully, her wrath visible in her stormy eyes as she shook her hand to brush her hair away from her face.

"The rationale behind its existence is unchanged, but I have already helped your father even after we broke up,"

"So, I have kept my end of the bargain." He stated with an air of seriousness.

She studied him intently, cognizant of his tremendous determination, the captivating primal aspect that instilled a sudden dread in her.

"You don't intend the marriage to go on, right?"

"Actually," David stated with unwavering certainty. He gave her a thorough, objective evaluation.

"I am adamant that you keep the three-year commitment we made in our prenuptial agreement."

"You have to keep your end of the bargain, to make it fair to me, wouldn't you agree?" David said with a grin.

Anger seeped out of her every inch. "That's absolutely savage!"

"Maybe." His eyes were intimidating and dark, and his smile was an imitation.

"But we have a signed agreement, and I have already fulfilled mine."

"Do you think I should play the part?" A fit of wrath wash ran through her. "Just act?"

He spoke with an endless amount of scorn in his voice and a determined look on his face.

"Your performance over the last seven months has been commendable."

"Six," she yelled out in a fit of rage, her frustration boiling over at his unwavering composure.

"My amnesia doesn't count!"

With a raised hand, he delicately ran his fingers along the jawline. "After a brief period of relief from your resentment," he added, "there is no need to harbor hatred toward your Korean husband."

Her eyes were closed for a moment before gently opening again. "I have already given you a child as part of the bargain, but I pity this child!" A heartfelt tear escaped.

As he took her chin in his hands and twirled it towards him, his voice softened. "However, the fact that it has shown up out of the blue is something I will not accept as anything less than a remarkable blessing."

His thumb delicately traced the contour of her lower lip. "We managed to avoid animosity for a few weeks." "Lovers and friends alike."

Her wrath sparkled in her chocolate brown eyes. "Being friends is hopeless for us!"

The corners of his mouth were drawn up in a sly, mocking grin. "Maybe right now you don't think so."

A sardonic humor shone from his dark eyes. "Get into bed already!"

Anger, not passion, she told herself, was to blame for her heart rate tripping and noticeably quickening.

"I would prefer not to go to bed at all, and I would be even less amenable to sharing a bed with you."

"We have shared from the beginning, Anna," he repeated with an alarmingly low voice.

He was serious about his warning, and she stared at him with a look of mute rebellion for a few long seconds. With a low-pitched vehemence, she vowed, "If you touch me, so help me, I'll hit you." She turned away from him, caught her nightgown, and stepped into the bathroom to remove her makeup.

The cream got into her eyes because her fingers shook so badly. She washed her face after feverishly dabbing at it.

She came to bed while David lay in bed, arms crossed over his head. Under the blankets, Anna closed her eyes and gave him a wary look. In the next few seconds, the room went black, and she could hear the bedside lamp snapping.

Her lashes slowly lifted, and she stared ahead in the dark for what seemed like an eternity, trying to make out shadows and a sliver of moonlight peeking through the curtains as her eyes adapted to the dreary nighttime light.

Her heightened awareness allowed her to perceive every sound—her breathing, David's, and the precise instant when his breathing became steady and rhythmic.

As her eyelids got heavy and fluttered down, she promised to wake up tomorrow. She was planning to attack him tomorrow over how involved he was with the beautiful Amelia Smith.

When Anna finally got up, it was too late to stop David from heading into town. Because her pent-up wrath yearns for the release that comes with a full-scale showdown, his absence served as an anticlimax.

While Anna ate her breakfast alone, Amy broke the news that they were both invited to a charity dinner that night. "David asked me to tell you."

David personally patronized a few groups, and Miller International was a famous philanthropist. The idea of mixing with David's cultured circle of friends made Anna's heart sink. She is a woman who doesn't like to socialize but she needs to change because of her status as the CEO's wife.

Guests would undoubtedly be wondering about the latest news involving the Miller heir, his wife, and the fashion designer/former glamorous model. She had been by his side for years until his unexpected marriage to a complete stranger with no social standing. Anna despised being at the center of speculation.

Anna had no doubt that everyone had noticed David's six-week social disappearance, commented on it, and made up or explained details of her injury.

The removal of the bandages from her hand today seemed to be a mere coincidence. Physiotherapy will no longer be provided every day but just once every week beginning this afternoon. A small scar on her palm would soon be the sole sign.

The idea of becoming free again was a powerful one. She will be allowed to drive again after today. She had to get in touch with a couple of friends, especially Sara. It immediately occurred to her that her best friend might be worried that she hadn't communicated with her in six weeks.

Unfortunately, she was unaware of whether Sara had been okay running their landscaping business by herself all this time.

Right after finishing her meal, Anna glanced at the clock and hurriedly called her friend.

After three rings, Sara finally answered, her voice filled with joy at finally knowing who was calling. Anna reluctantly ended the call, but she had to keep her appointment with the orthopedic surgeon. They spoke for about an hour.

She was adamant that they sit down for lunch soon.

"Remember that I'm a working girl?" With a playful eye, Sara teased.

"But I'll be away for the next two evenings." "Will tomorrow be soon enough?"

Anna let out a joyful laugh. "I will do it tomorrow."

"See you soon."

Just thirty minutes after Jacob dropped her off outside the consultant orthopedist's offices, she was free of her protective half-cast and bandages. The whole process took an hour. Driving on her own was approved by the specialist; however, he recommended careful hand movements and another examination in one month.

Finding a car, she could call her own, was the last step. Nothing had been said about what became of the BMW.

'Were you really expecting it to be completely broken?' She thought about it.

Chapter 63

Jacob was left with the Pajero wagon while David was driving the Porsche into the city while the Bentley was out of commission. She should talk to David about it tonight.

After lunch, she rummaged through her closet in search of an appropriate dinner gown. After much consideration, she settled on a deep yellow-fitting gown after narrowing her options down to two. The hue was a striking contrast to her black hair, complemented her dark eyes, and brought out her light honey skin's creamy smoothness.

Around four o'clock, Jacob brought her home from physical therapy. At five o'clock, she showered, cleaned her hair, and had Amy style her long hair with fat rollers. After that, she took care of her nails.

As she was putting on her makeup, David walked into the bedroom, and she calmly accepted his analytical assessment.

"How is your hand doing?" Anna was acutely aware of his nearness the moment he stepped towards her.

Showing off the pink scar, she remained silent.

"I assume the report from the expert has already been sent to you."

Her tone became more sardonic than she had intended.

He narrowed his gaze slightly. You bet.

"You also know that I am able to drive again," she added, observing as his head dipped to hers.

In an invasion that elicited a hushed pleading that he opted to disregard, she turned her head such that his kiss landed on her cheek. Suddenly, he seized her chin and held it firmly as he circled his finger on her mouth.

As he raised his head to look at her, she doomed him to hell in silence.

She took a deep breath and attacked him because she wanted to lash out at him so badly.

"I'd rather not pull Jacob away every time I want to go out."

"I'd rather become independent again."

After releasing the knot on his tie, David proceeded to unbutton his shirt.

"His work description includes that."

As her wrath flared up, her eyes took on a dazzling hue, and she had to work hard to keep her cool.

"Is he to be my jailer?" She asked sardonically.

"You're being overly imaginative."

"Am I?"

He appeared to be the epitome of a power broker—relentless, deadly, and unyielding.

"Are you planning to argue?"

She intended to hurl something at him in the hopes that it would inflict some minor injury.

"As far as I'm concerned, it's hard for me to justify nearly all of your actions." She added.

After removing his shirt, he threw it onto the bed. "Nearly everything is an issue?" A furrowed brow betrayed a subtle sneer. "Should I interpret that as a sign that things are looking up for me?"

She snapped at him, "Don't be so damn foolish," her anger boiling over as she caught a glimpse of his delight.

"We have to be on our way in thirty minutes. Can we postpone this conversation?" He said softly.

With complete ease, she held David's eyes and challenged, "Until when?"

"In a week or a month? A day from now."

She stared at him intently for a few long seconds as her wrath subsided; it was a better compromise than she had anticipated.

I was wondering, "Where is tonight's dinner?"

His skepticism was palpable as he arched an eyebrow. This is "The Peninsula." She wondered aloud if Amelia Smith would be present.

"I would think so. For the sake of seeing you, she enjoys going to the majority of the activities. It was completely accurate."

"Amelia has a lot of friends, and most of them are involved in the social scene," he said in a low, sarcastic voice that made her furious again.

"I don't understand why you didn't tie the knot with her." Anna tried her best to keep her tone innocent.

"She would have jumped at the opportunity!"

David confessed, "Perhaps," as he observed the range of expressions on her face.

"It never crossed my mind"

"I don't know why, either."

Her eyes took on a somewhat reflecting quality as their color intensified.

"She's got the perfect combination of good looks, composure, and social standing." The incredible tranquility of her voice was mind-boggling.

The cynical humor shone in his eyes. "That describes a lot of the women I know."

"Some of whom are very rich," she said, oblivious to the risk she was putting herself in.

"Poor David," She said softly.

"Were you worried that a financially beneficial merger was their primary goal?"

"Could it have been unappealing that they were only interested in your body if their own money had been enough to make that irrelevant?"

"Not to mention your—" she paused thoughtfully before finishing with a touch of subtlety, "— excellent skill in the bedroom."

"So, we only do it in the bedroom?" he said with a sly grin.

"I remember several enjoyable... meetings, shall we say?" he said, arching an eyebrow.

"When we bathed together." As a delicate shade of pink shaded her cheeks, his eyes sparkled. Asking, "Shall I proceed?"

"You've wasted no time getting ready, you dweeb!"

"Are you envious that I might have valued any of my ex-lovers more than you, dear? David teased.

Astonishment welled up in Anna's eyes. So open and honest, wasn't she? Is he aware of how much she despised the idea of his magnificently chiseled body making love to someone else?

"How could I possibly be envious?" she retorted with all the dignity she could manage, "when you laid out the rationale behind our marriage, set a price for it, and set a deadline?"

"Are you bothered by that?"

She was adamant about not admitting how much it bothered her.

"That you've decided to keep Amelia as your mistress is rather significant, too."

"A mistress is a woman who is kept by a husband while they live together as a married couple." His sulky, angry eyes betrayed his hidden fury.

"Do you really think I'd be so rude as to offend you like that?"

"It would be very appreciated if you could maintain the secrecy of the contact, but I'm not sure how to achieve that."

There was a noticeable gap, during which it appeared as though even the tiniest of drops would cause a riot of noise.

"Am I to take it that you're recommending such a relationship?"

Chapter 64

No. Inside her thoughts, the quiet denial roared. The slightest shrug required an enormous amount of energy. If I said anything, would it matter? She couldn't say a word.

It seemed as though he was using a force of extraordinary control to contain his anger.

With an icy tone, he reminded her, "We have a dinner engagement."

"I propose that you change."

The idea of attending a formal dinner with the city's social elite was too much for her to handle.

"I just can't bring myself to act this out tonight, David." She murmured with a bitter cynicism. Her eyes were dazzling deep chocolate hues.

"I have faith that you can rationalize my absence with an acceptable reason," She said adding, "Amelia would be happy." She said mischievously.

He stared at her for what felt like an eternity, his demeanor a captivating mask that she instinctively drew back from.

"You drive me to the edge of violence," he whispered with an ominously low voice that made her delicate hair stand on end in silent terror.

He undressed and marched briskly into the restroom without saying a word. For some reason, she found it far more unsettling that he refrained from physically expressing his fury by slamming the door.

She sprung to her feet in a flurry as he got dressed ten minutes later, a towel slung low over his hips.

"Have Amy make you dinner," he said.

"It's her night off," Anna said with a little chuckle.

"I would never dare to bother her." She made her way to the entrance.

"I can fix something on my own." Without waiting for David to reply, she slithered to the kitchen on the lowest floor.

There was plenty of food in the fridge and the cupboard. Deciding was the only thing that remained. Anything from a cheese and tomato omelet to a ham and mushroom one would do. She was not even remotely hungry. The very idea of eating sickened her.

With systematic indifference, she removed a skillet, placed the contents on the bench top, and began to chop, slice, and dice.

David walked into the kitchen just as she transferred the omelet to a plate. She prayed her hands wouldn't betray her as she reduced the gas heat.

She was more troubled by his scathing evaluation than by any words he could have said. Not only that, but she walked away from him while taking her plate to the expansive bench and came back to get the silverware.

Instead of hearing him move, she felt his hands gently resting on her shoulders as he drew her closer to him.

There was a long, painful moment when their eyes met, and then his head dipped as if in slow motion. She choked out a protest, and his jaw clamped down on hers in a brutal kiss that tore at her defenses and into her very being.

She stood there frozen in awe as he eventually lifted his head, signaling the end of the brutal assault that had verged on violation. Anna determined coldly that he had succeeded in punishing her, if that was his goal.

Her emotions were so raw that they seemed to be a tangible entity, engulfing her entire being. Tears welled up in her eyes, but she fought back the need to let them fall.

He walked out of the kitchen with a scowl and a stern expression on his face.

She waited a few minutes until she could make out the low rumble of an automobile engine starting up, and by the time it got to the end of the driveway, the sound had faded to quiet.

With her arms crossed, she fought mightily to keep her composure.

She remained there for what seemed like an eternity, trying to make sense of the madness of pitting her power against a guy whose mental and physical fortitude was light years ahead of her.

The simple necessity of eating redirected her thoughts, and she resolutely retrieved her silverware, methodically cut the cold omelet into bite-sized pieces and forked each one into her mouth.

After she was done, she wiped down the skillet, rinsed the plate and silverware, and put them in the dishwasher.

The home was dead quiet, and the living room was too big for her to sit there by herself. Discomforted beyond belief, she stumbled into the casual sala, plucked up a magazine, and collapsed into one of the plush seats. She tossed the magazine aside because it failed to pique her interest and instead turned on the TV using the remote control. Miserably, she continued to click on channels, thinking that surely there must be something she could become interested in.

She found some solace in two half-hour comedy shows, but her understanding of the humor was limited, so once they ended, she aimlessly browsed the channels in pursuit of a potentially engaging film.

She went to the cabinet and sorted through the video collection, removing all but one because there wasn't much to choose from.

Critically acclaimed for its gloomy Gothic style, she found it too intense and was relieved when the credits rolled.

Returning to the kitchen, Anna retrieved a glass from the freezer, filled it with ice, squeezed in some orange juice, and sipped gently.

When would David be back at his house? When he returned home, a small voice teased him. Oh, come on. It was inevitable. That was the wrong time to start staying out since he had never done it before.

Perhaps because you essentially granted him free reign to hang out with Amelia, that same little voice reminded her with a mischievous gleam.

She glanced at her watch and saw that it was after ten. With an abrupt sense of determination, she drank the juice and headed for the stairs. After she showered, she would retire for the night.

After twenty minutes, she drew the light switch, slipped under the cool linen sheets, and closed her eyes.

After half an hour of ineffective sleep, she opted to snuggle up in a recliner near the window, muttering a grumble as she got out of bed.

'Is there a way to make peace with the fact that you loved David Miller but also accept the fact that you could never make him love you?' Anna looked around the dimly lit room in contemplation.

She felt a strong magnetic pull, like a moth drawn to a flame, and was suddenly swept away by the lightning of intense sexual need.

During the day, she battled him, hating both him and herself for being so easily controlled by her desires and the desires of her body. As the sun went down, she gave up and reveled in his hypnotic touch.

Is there any possibility that it might change between them? With a heavy heart, she reminisced on the past. He fooled her into thinking he was a kind and loving husband for just six weeks. A man who had lavished her with his undivided attention and care.

'Did it really happen?' 'Or is it just an act?' She likely wouldn't find out.

Chapter 65

As her eyes welled up and tears started to fall down her cheeks, she swore. Tears were rare for her. Aside from that time, my mother, Allen, and Aunt Martha passed away.

Her hormones and her emotional heart must be at odds with each other, dammit. I was devastated. 'I couldn't believe it.' It seems like her pregnancy worsened her temperament.

Unending torment, she corrected. Her mind is full of pointless banter. A few minutes later, everyone was yelling in her head. She leaned back in her chair and nestled her head in the crook of her arm because she was exhausted from feeling so many emotions at once.

At that spot, David discovered her. He remained there for quite a while, staring at her delicate features—the way her hair clung to her neck, the beautiful arch of her slim neck highlighted by the bedside lamp, the slim curves beneath her plain white cotton nightgown. And the subtle sign of crying.

He undressed slowly, walked over to the chair, and gently took her into his arms.

Somewhere deep within Anna's subconscious, she sensed that something was off. She roused herself. Under her head, she felt the hard, muscular flesh, in contrast to the supple padding of the chair. Subtle rhythmic heartbeats were audible to her, and she felt an arm drawing her near to a lengthy man figure. As her hair was lightly brushed by fingers in a fleeting pattern, she sensed the gentle touch of lips on her temple.

Her lips parted in a gentle sigh, and her arm slipped out to wrap around his waist as if it were an automatic response.

She wants to feel the exquisite chiseled contours of his lips against her own. The mere thought of it aroused a longing that slithered treacherously through her entire being, lighting a fire in her essence.

Her head naturally cocked to one side, and a kiss that started very delicately found its way into her mouth. Tempting, alluring, and intriguing.

She reveled in his touch, the entrancing ecstasy that swept over her as he led her to a profound, life-altering release from her inhibitions and a complete and utter submission to the sensory pleasures of passion.

Anna gasped his name, "David," as his fingers gently stroked between her thighs, slowly, lightly. She felt electric shock-waves of sensation jolting through her body; she wanted him, and she wanted to cry out, but instead, she pressed her mouth to his throat and bit down in a fever of frustration.

David stifled a groan, and the swift kiss he pressed on her love-swollen lips turned into a savage duel of tongues. His long fingers parted the petals of her womanhood and found the hot, damp, velvet flesh throbbing, waiting for him...

He touched her gently, softly, fast, then slowly, until her hips arched towards him, her hands dug into his shoulders, and she was calling out his name.

Anna shook violently, a fierce tension she had experienced jerking her every nerve and muscle tight, driving every single thought from her head, and leaving only a fiery need that was almost pain.

"Please," she moaned, her head thrashing from side to side. His hands slipped under her hips and lifted her out of the bed. She felt the velvet tip of his hard male flesh stroke, and then, with one thrust, he was there, where she wanted him to be.

She moaned his name, and he moved deep and hard, filling her, stretching her, and taking her on a wild journey of almost mystical proportion. She felt the mighty strength of him thrusting, driving her on until she cried out as her slender body convulsed in an explosion of sensation, and he joined with her until she had lost all sense of self, and the two of them became one perfect whole.

They could only communicate on that level. No disagreement, no letdown. Stunning closeness. "Sex," she corrected, fully aware of the distinction.

Anna told Jacob to drop her off along Centinela Ave. It's a lovely day, and I'd like to go for a walk.

The Pajero cautiously crossed the intersection and parked in a space. "When can I pick you up, and where are you going?"

'I'll take a cab home,' she said, hesitant to impose a curfew for the day. Who could have predicted that lunch with Sara would take so long? Plus, she could be interested in perusing the stores for some time.

"Maybe you'll give me a call when you're ready?" On a nervous note, Jacob proposed. David would be adamant.

It was up to David to demand it! "I'll let you know," she admitted, her remorse at not calling Jacob being little at best. She greeted him with a friendly grin, unlocked the door, and descended to the sidewalk. She waited just a few seconds after he accelerated into the traffic before continuing to the next street.

They embraced as if it had been years, rather than a few weeks, since they had last seen each other, and Sara was waiting for her.

"You look stunning," Sara exclaimed as they made their way into the Coffee Shop.

The maître d' escorted them to a table, presented them with menus, and then stepped aside to let them decide.

"How is your hand doing?"

They tried to pick up where they left off the previous afternoon after ordering mineral water and discussing what to eat.

They walked out into the midday heat after three hours of sharing the bill.

"Those stores?" As Anna enthusiastically agreed, Sara couldn't help but crack out with an irrepressible grin.

After five, they said their goodbyes and agreed to call each other the next week to set up lunch again.

There was a long line at the closest taxi stand because of the increased demand for taxis. It seemed like there was no way to get a cab within thirty minutes.

Anna moaned under her breath as she realized she should have factored in rush hour. Perhaps she would have more luck if she waited in line for a rank on one of the nearby streets.

Not at all. It was probably longer than that. Calling Jacob was the only real option.

When she realized, she had forgotten to bring her purse with her, she sighed in frustration. Her phone is inside her purse.

She went back to one of the stores that they had visited and asked to use their phone.

The receiver was removed from the hook after the signal only sounded twice, finally allowing her to make a connection. But neither Jacob nor Amy responded, and her heart began to race. She had no other choice but to call David.

"David, it's me."

"Where are you?"

She almost snapped back at David because his voice was so icy and angry.

His fury radiated down the wire, and he seemed to be bringing himself under control. Anna, where exactly are you?

Chapter 66

"Let Jacob know that I'll be waiting at the Culver Blvd near Centinela Ave."

Thirty minutes later, though, the black Porsche, not the Pajero, was the one that rolled into the curb.

It just took one look at David's features to know that a fight was likely to break out.

Opening the passenger door, David leaned across. Then enter. Anna buckled her seatbelt and snuggled in next to him as his voice sounded raspy.

The sheer volume of vehicles leaving the city made it difficult for him to maneuver the Porsche ahead of the traffic, and it took until the following set of lights to do it.

"I was hoping to be home earlier than this."

The comment did not constitute an apology. A no-brainer.

She pivoted to face him, her anger bubbling to the surface.

"I refuse to be confined in a golden cage by you, David."

A glimmer appeared in the corner of his eye.

"The press has done a good job of covering my business stance." On the side of his jaw, a muscle tightened.

"A small number of extremists in today's culture like the opportunity to pick on prominent figures. Because of this, I am very cautious to make sure there are no hazards."

He gave her a sidelong look before turning back to the traffic.

"Therefore, safety precautions are required."

"That's why it's imperative that you have a cell phone on you at all times, and that every car has a phone."

"Someone needs to know where you are; that someone may be me, Amy, or Jacob."

"For goodness' sake, no excuses!"

She raised a hand in a highly agitated gesture.

"This would not have happened if I drove my own car."

He remained silent. Ten minutes after they arrived at Pasadena, the Porsche passed through the wide double gates that led to their home.

With the flick of a wrist, David's remote control raised the garage doors, and the vehicle glided into position between the Pajero and a breathtaking red premium Mercedes sedan.

David informed her, "Yours," as she looked at it with admiration.

She turned slowly to face him after her heart did a slow flip.

"You bought it for me?"

His look was incomprehensible. Jacob will give you a ride tomorrow so you can get a feel for it. He removed himself from behind the wheel after releasing his belt. Anna also did the same.

She paused just long enough to brush her cautious fingers over the crimson satin-smooth paint. In a low voice, she murmured, "It's beautiful."

Stepping closer to him, she gently kissed the tip of his chin. "I am grateful."

He smiled mischievously, and his eyes took on a depth of blackness that she couldn't understand.

"Your hand," David whispered.

"So, how does it feel without the plaster and bandages?"

It seems a bit unusual. She further explained, with a subtle shrug, how stiff it was.

"Physiotherapy is helpful."

"Should we head inside?"

"Dinner will be served shortly."

She felt the desire to go to the restroom and freshen up. "Just give me a little while."

Anna brushed her hair and then changed into silk pants and a matching blouse. Her lips were brought back to life with a swift swipe of pink.

With a little contemplative smile, she joined David in the dining room. She spooned her soup without much hunger, instead nibbling on the delicate beef and vegetables that came with it.

Am I not hungry?

Anna studied him intently, taking in his spectacular body, the combination of muscle and flesh that gave him his alluring good looks.

She would have started an argument with him without hesitation before the incident. On top of that, she would have relished the opportunity to engage in combat, celebrating with joy whenever she managed to incite his anger. She had no chance of winning against him, so it was completely insane.

She now seems determined to go along the same road. While they were at Manhattan Beach, his gentle affectionate style had broken her heart emotionally.

Even worse, it had eroded her animosity to its fundamental essence. Finally, she said, "No," setting her plate down.

"Enjoy a piece of fruit."

Anna shook her head in disapproval after seeing Amy's choice in the bowl. Water splattered across the table as she fumbled with her glass.

Her voice quivered as she fetched a napkin and started to soak up the spill.

"Oh, hell," she mumbled. Heaven forbids! What the heck was up with her?

"Just let it be."

She stood up straight. Planning to get more napkins.

"Leave it, Anna," David ordered with a smooth tone.

Her eyes welled up with foolish tears, and she blinked frantically to stop them from falling out. At this very moment, she would embarrass herself, and that would not be acceptable.

After getting up from the table and taking three steps, she felt a hand go up and grab her arm.

"Excuse me." She pleaded with him in dejected despair.

"Please," loathing the obvious display of vulnerability as he cocked her head.

"Once you inform me of the things that are troubling you."

To shield herself from seeing him, she drew her eyes tight and then gently opened them again.

"I didn't intend to stay in the city just to make you worried," I assure you.

"I didn't realize I suggested you had." He cradled her face between his palms and gently wiped away her tears.

Why on earth did she feel the need to be so sensitive around him? She never would have imagined a few days ago that she would feel compelled to explain or apologize to him. Both were now being done by her.

But no amount of introspection would help because the problem had no simple answer.

She mumbled something along the lines of "Thanks for the car," and he caught a glimpse of his subtle smile as he observed the roller coaster of emotions reflected on her face.

"My Love, you have such good manners," he said with a drawl. A more— dare I say it? passionate?—expression of your appreciation is something I'm looking forward to.

Her voice betrayed the anguish she was experiencing. She inquired, "Payment in sexual favors?" and saw a change in his expression.

While planting a punishing kiss on her lips, David said, "You little fool," his voice filled with lethal tenderness.

She continued to hold back a scream of passionate pleading for what felt like an eternity until he finally raised his head to listen.

His penetrating gaze ensnared hers, and she found herself fascinated beneath the surface of the obvious latent sensuality, a primal acknowledgment that was entirely sensory.

She let out a single negative cry as he skillfully embraced her, her mouth trembling slightly as its delicate contours were somewhat enlarged by his merciless power.

As he delicately cupped her face in the bedroom, she wanted to express her anger about his liberated seduction, which he allowed her to experience by sliding down to her feet.

As she was ensnared in hypnotic fascination, she felt her powerlessness rise in the face of the unbelievably sleepy eyes that held her hostage.

Did he realize how hard it was for her to embrace the betrayal she felt while holding him? Her breath caught in her throat as her angry yet incredibly vulnerable gaze locked onto his.

As his lips traced across her forehead, a hand slid beneath her hair, drawing her closer. He then gently proceeded down one cheek to rest at the corner of her mouth, a tantalizing, delicate, and exceedingly sensual tasting that left her yearning for more.

Chapter 67

She surrendered fully to the pleasures of unrestrained passion as, beneath his sensual dominion, a dormant fire burst into flaming life.

Anna did not object as he undressed her and himself; she voluntarily arched her back as his lips traced a path over her entire body. Her hands clasped his hair as he lingered in between her legs. A surge of pleasure rushed through her as he licked her sensitive clitoral area over and over until she trembled in ecstasy.

A series of hushed cries came from her lips as she pleaded with him, expressing her deep desire for his undivided attention. He slid on top of her and plunged deep into her. Anna savored his every thrust as her hands caressed his buttocks.

She let out a scream as she eagerly welcomed his mouth to hers, her intense sensations building to a joint climax that probed the depths of primal gratification. She unwillingly embraced the pinnacle of sexual bliss.

Anna took pride in her independence and decided to drive the Mercedes out every day.

Thinking about her life and her unborn child's future was an inevitable part of the experience. She desired... What was her desire? Adored by David? Had that been such a far-fetched fantasy?

A blaring horn cut through her train of thought, and she accelerated the Mercedes away from a street that had no relevance to her anymore.

Feeling unexpectedly hungry, she decided to have lunch before making her way to The Grove in Beverly Hills to visit the various boutiques. She may even go to a spa for a relaxing facial. Next, she may search for an appropriate evening gown to attend a significant end-of-year event at a downtown hotel the next night.

After a long search, she found the perfect item, paired it with matching evening shoes and a bag, and tapped her credit card.

As she felt his assessment of her looks just minutes before they were supposed to leave the house the following evening, David's admiration for her choice was visible.

"I will never be able to tear my eyes away from you," he drawled.

"Really?" she smiled playfully in response.

Something she was afraid to describe was in his gaze, but she could feel a hidden passion. A small fire burned inside her and coursed through her entire being.

"Should we leave?" David nodded.

As they made their way inside the hotel ballroom thirty minutes later, Anna whispered, "So many beautiful women."

"Spending a fortune on apparel and accessories in an individual effort to shine brighter than the rest," David replied.

As one of the multiple hostesses sprang forward to verify tickets and suggest table placement, David shot her a knowing look.

"Be careful, my dear," he said while grinning. "Your claws are visible."

She smiled at him. "Showing them is one thing, but using them is another entirely."

Eight hundred people may be seated in the ballroom at once at circular tables set up for tea. The city's social elite was mainly seen at this spectacular annual event. The primary objective of the gathering—to promote charity—was secondary.

Anna opted to take a seat a bit later and wondered if that wasn't being slightly harsh. Members of any charitable organization's committees deserve praise for the enormous amount of work that went into planning an event like this evening.

With two seats vacant at their table, Anna clenched her fists around the stem of her glass as she caught wind of who was about to join them.

"Amelia is always running late. She is one for the dramatic entrance," one of the ladies said.

It was inevitable that Amelia would be here tonight, but who could have thought to seat the stunning former model next to David and Anna without a sick sense of humor?

Anna could only infer that Amelia had personally engineered the seating arrangements because it seemed too staged to be coincidental.

The president of the organization lauded the sum raised and its mission as the lights went down and the spotlight shone on the platform. At the end of the supper, a distinguished dignitary would give a speech, and then there would be music for the guests to dance to.

As the lights went back on, the spotlight went out, and there was Amelia, breathtaking in her figure-hugging jade silk. As Amelia introduced the man by her side, Anna forced a grin onto her face, even though she had never met him before.

Was the fact that everyone was staring at their table her imagination? She admitted that it was possible that it wouldn't, but that Amelia's presence would certainly be noticed. It seems she has made Los Angeles her new territory.

"Yes, Anna. Hi, how's it going? You seem to be doing fine after your accident, right?" The slightly bored tone was balanced by a genuine smile that didn't quite reach her eyes.

"I'm doing great," Anna politely responded.

"David was really sad at last week's dinner without you." As she shifted her focus to David, the smile widened and had a more covert tone. "Darling, isn't it?"

"What a doting spouse. I seriously doubt he would have shown up if he weren't a distinguished guest speaker."

When the first dish arrived, Anna obediently spooned the delicious potato and leek soup until it was completed, and a waiter with a basket of bread rolls rescued her from having to answer.

When given the option between fish and chicken, she chose the former and ate it with meticulous attention. On occasion, she would take a moment to drink from her glass of ice water, well aware that Amelia was standing immediately across from her.

Absolutely stunning, with a flawless appearance that could turn heads wherever she went. Good fortune had assured that she was born into money, and nature had bestowed a plentiful hand. At such a young age, a modeling chance presented itself to her, and now she has become a prominent fashion designer.

Even though David Miller was the model's obvious goal, she was an enchanter of men in general. His marriage was brushed aside as insignificant, an annoyance that would be quickly forgotten.

"A glass of wine, would you?" Amelia asked.

With a shake of her head, Anna faced the man sitting to her left.

"I want to say no, but it's nice of you to offer."

"Are you managing with just water, my darling?" Amelia asked, her voice barely audible.

"Does that mean you're the one driving?"

David leaned forward in his chair just enough to grasp Anna's hand, which he then brought to his mouth. He contained her hand, his warm eyes betraying his affection as he delicately kissed her fingers one by one.

She wanted to break free of his grip, but the moment the idea crossed her mind, his hand tightened noticeably as a warning, leaving her with no choice but to smile. He was nothing more than a refined barbarian beneath that refined exterior, damn him. As she noticed Amelia's unwavering gaze, she couldn't help but feel a small chill.

"My darling, I hope you're not pregnant."

Chapter 68

A nna caught her breath as David locked eyes with the model, who appeared innocent, in a way that only Amelia could.

"Yes, to my great joy." Underneath the velvety smoothness of his voice, there was no mistaking the steely core.

As the guest speaker stepped up to the podium, Anna removed fruit segments from their meringue nest and set the plate aside, choosing tea as the dessert arrived, which was a letdown.

Then, a DJ played some tunes in the background and urged everyone to get down on the dance floor. With grace and elegance, Amelia and her partner were among the first to ascend the stairs.

She had an air of confidence and sophistication. Anna could tell the model was fully aware of the impact she was making on her partner from the subtle allure of her face.

She wanted to know if it was helping David out or not.

Meeting his shadowed stare unsettled Anna, who sneaked a peek at him. She blinked when he reached out and intertwined his fingers with hers, and she smiled tentatively because she was worried, he might have figured out her thoughts.

"So, how about a little dance?" She nodded.

She deeply needed the safety of his arms, and a part of her wished she could have them.

Her word of consent propelled her to her feet, and she gracefully stepped out onto the floor, falling into his embrace. David was aware of the risk she was taking by pressing her body against his tremendous, firm frame. She wanted to smell his scent.

With the mellow tunes playing in the background, they moved in perfect harmony. Mysterious, she thought to herself. Is it conceivable for one person to develop an addiction to another? Restrained as if his being was a potent drug?

He outshone every other guy in the room, with an innate savagery that had been sharpened by experience and amplified by his level of accomplishment.

It possessed an irresistible allure that both sexes could feel, but males could feel it more acutely than women could. Some saw it as an unseen force, set in motion by the curiosity of finding out whether the man, unfettered by corporate constraints, could make love as easily as he could amass millions in investments.

He was a guy of extraordinary intelligence, yet there was an air of wildness about him, as if some primal savagery was well under his control. Knowing that he would be incredibly cold-hearted as an adversary sent a slight chill down her spine.

"Are you cold?" As his voice delicately stroked her hair, she said a subtle "no."

As an effort at a dry joke, she said, "Someone just walked over my grave."

"Amelia huh?"

She stumbled and gasped so loudly that she couldn't be heard as he pulled her close to him. He had a unusual hold, and she cocked her head to look into his mysterious, dark brown eyes.

"You're too smart for your own good," she remarked with a voice that sounded muted.

"Do you see that as a weakness?" He asked humorously.

When the song changed, she stepped back and suggested they go back to their table, opting not to respond.

As she mumbled, "I need to use the powder room."

She was aware of the impact of her recent water intake. She snatched her evening bag in the hopes of fixing her make-up on the go.

"Could you use my services as an escort?"

A slow, amused smile was her expression as she turned to him.

"Listen, David, I'm fully grown up." He just grinned and let her go.

In the powder room, Anna was looking at herself in the mirror.

What on earth? Silently, she pondered for a few minutes before noticing Amelia analyzing her make-up against the backdrop of the lengthy mirror wall.

"Going for the win, my love?" Amelia asked in a low voice.

"Amelia, every time," she said evenly as she reached for her lipstick and applied the color evenly.

Snidely remarking, "You're very...small," Amelia offered her opinion.

"A little one in the eight?"

Anna recapped the lipstick and turned to face her adversary, thinking that there must have been a point to this conversation—figuring out her dress size was completely irrelevant.

Amelia gently argued that David is so...

"Enormously gifted?" Anna suggested while feigning an incredibly delighted grin.

"A clear benefit, don't you think?" Anna asked.

A tinkling of gentle laughter escaped the model's lips as her eyes sparkled with menacing poison.

"He's a passionate creature, my darling." Her eyes lingered on Anna's slim waist.

"The last stages of pregnancy are particularly unattractive. Regardless of how brief, I find it hard to believe that he will adhere to celibacy."

"And he can always rely on you?"

"Certainly, my dear." Amelia took a moment to collect herself before ratcheting up the verbal jab.

"In the same way that I always have been."

A faint smile required a lot of willpower on Anna's part because she felt queasy.

"I need to return to the table," she said. She averted her gaze, but her agonized gasp was met with Amelia's grasp of her wounded hand.

"You better not take me lightly."

"I never have," Anna said implacably.

"Would you kindly release your grip on my hand?"

"Even now, it hurts a lot."

Amelia clenched her fist for an instant, and a hard mask appeared on her face as her eyes sparkled with malice.

She threw Anna's hand aside with a cruel chuckle as she briefly worried Anna couldn't handle the agony.

"I would rather not cause you needless pain." She hurriedly retrieved her evening bag and exited the powder room.

Anna struggled to regain control of her trembling emotions and remained motionless for a few minutes. Her eyes were watery, and her cheeks paled as her fingers ached with such intensity.

"Are you okay?"

A gentle, feminine voice conveyed worry, and Anna forced a small grin.

"You seem noticeably paler than normal. It might be a good idea for you to take a seat for a while."

"Shall I go get your husband?" The woman asked.

"No," Anna replied with haste.

"My table is just next to yours, and I'll be OK in a little. How about we return together?" The woman nodded.

As Anna got back into her seat, she was acutely aware of David's intense stare. Amelia and her lover were nowhere to be seen, which was a relief for her.

"Are you in the mood for more tea?"

She wasn't sure she could handle the liquid. "No, thank you, I have enough," she whispered.

"Would you like to return home?" Even though he kept to himself, his critical assessment was impossible to ignore.

"Not yet," she said with admirable composure. There was no way she was going to give Amelia satisfaction if she left now; doing so would be admitting defeat.

Chapter 69

When another couple joined them, Anna let out a breath of relief because most of the people were aimlessly wandering from table to table. While the woman had a light talk with Anna, the man—a business associate of David's—began an intense debate with him.

Anna glanced at David with a look of surprise as he rested his arm across the back of her chair twenty minutes before they departed.

"It is getting close to eleven o'clock."

"Our mission has been accomplished."

"Are you ready to go?" Anna nodded in agreement.

Without saying a word more, he had them leave the ballroom and start to lead the way. A number of his friends wanted to talk to him, and while he waited a second to say a few expressions of courteous reply, he did not remain.

Anna sank into the leather-cushioned seat and relaxed as David lowered the Bentley to street level, joining the steady flow of traffic leaving the city.

It was pleasurable just to relax in the car. The pulsing in her hand had diminished in intensity, and the agony had transformed into a dull ache. Passable, she admitted, though only somewhat so.

As the automobile cruised leisurely towards Pasadena, music blared from the audio speakers, and she closed her eyes to listen.

As soon as she stepped foot inside, she hurried to the stairs to change into her bedroom attire. David showed up while she was in her bra and underwear.

"Would you like me to ask you what's wrong?"

"I don't think so." A tinge of defiance was visible in her eyes.

"When you entered the powder room, Amelia followed you and came out a few minutes before you did."

"You are quite perceptive to have noticed."

He stepped across to stand at arm's length. As he murmured, "I notice everything about you," he cupped her nape and ran his fingers through her hair.

"How you react while we are intimate."

"The little things that bring a grin to your face."

"The pain is so great that you squint your eyes," he whispered.

"Amelia and I had a brief conversation." She tried to shrug, but she stared directly into his eyes.

"Is there a rationale for not doing it?"

"Absolutely none." He drew slightly to the shadows. As he moved closer, his thumb traced the delicate contour of her mouth.

As he reached to release her breasts from the sliver of silk and lace that was her bra, she battled an internal struggle to resist his tender brand of foreplay. His touch was a powerful sensual zone.

A small sound of pleasure leaked out of her as he caressed the velvety fullness, then turned his focus to each dark peak; the swelling peaks yearned for his touch.

He undressed himself. He was tracing his fingers down her ribcage, over her waist, and under her briefs.

As he bowed his head, he extended both hands to her, encircling her face.

She eagerly embraced his kiss, reveling in the intense pleasure that coursed through her body, as his mouth tantalized her senses. Because she needed the physical touch, she leaned in close to him, as if her entire body were tingling with intense sensation. Amelia and her nasty comments would be thrown to the fringe of rational thought if she could only be swept away by primal need and become so engrossed in his lovemaking.

He seemed to know exactly where to take her, and she let out a low moan of pleasure as he lowered her to the bed and started to tenderly explore all of her delicious pleasure spots.

She reveled in the level of sexiness he expertly imparted and the intensity of feeling she felt under his touch; as a result, she could hardly contain her elation when he finally took her.

Subsequently, she lay snuggled up in his embrace, blissfully replete and about to fall asleep.

Upon waking up later, Anna discovered that David had already departed for the city. She proceeded to stretch luxuriously before getting out of bed. Thankfully, she had not yet suffered morning sickness, even if she did occasionally feel a little queasy upon awakening.

She changed into shorts and a shirt after a refreshing shower and jogged lightly to the kitchen.

"Hello, Amy."

The elderly woman smiled and said, "Hello, it is a beautiful day." "Allow me to fetch your breakfast." She was cleaning the house when Anna came.

"No Thank you; I can manage." The ingredients—cereal, fruit, toast, orange juice, and tea—were easy to put together. On the other hand, she had been self-sufficient for a long time and appreciated that freedom.

Before going outside for a stroll around the gardens, Anna had a leisurely breakfast, perusing the morning newspaper.

Carefully pruned bushes framed the flower beds, which were a sight to behold due to the blooms' color coordination with the borders: pale pinks and whites, vivid reds and yellows. The steps down from the terrace were decorated with several urns, and in the middle of a square of the well-kept lawn stood a magnificent concrete-tiered birdbath.

The pool and cabana, complete with a bar and change rooms, were located beyond that.

The property was very breathtaking, with the architecture and grounds harmonizing flawlessly. She was cautious to put a price on it because of its prime position and picturesque views.

Had Amelia's desire for the man who possessed it not been piqued? His place in the city's elite was undeniable, and women were naturally drawn to men in positions of power and wealth. In their pursuit of stardom and wealth, some even sold themselves. For the same reason that she had.

While not seeking recognition or financial gain. Her dad... Oh my goodness, that kind of self-reflection was risky. Nothing came of it, and all it did was bring her insecurities into sharp focus.

For love, there was a touch of hell and heaven. It was especially difficult when you felt unloved. The act of making love was present, but the emotional investment was missing.

Would things change at some point? May it be so? She was pessimistic. It was indeed a misfortune that she was one of those women who sold themselves for money. No matter how much she reasoned with herself, it was inevitable because she was her father's daughter. Her own company cannot save her or her father, and David Miller is the only option. Speaking of which, how was her landscaping company?

'I need to call Sara.'

'It's been more than a month that I was not working, and I missed it.'

Unfortunately, she wasn't able to work because of her hand.

'I need to keep myself busy.'

'Being pessimistic is not good for my mental health.'

It's just so ironic that she now owns the majority of the stocks in Posh Naturals and is a part owner of Anna and Sara Designs, but she is fully dependent on David.

'From now on, I must read everything before signing anything.'

'Being naive is not an excuse for the mess that I put myself into.' All this thinking has put everything in perspective. When the time comes, David will no longer see her as a novelty and will soon tire of her.

'What will she do then?'

It is because of her stupidity that she is in this predicament, and this feeling of helplessness is eating away at her self-esteem. Then a thought came to her, she must learn how to do well in business, so she decided to enroll in an online business course. When the third year of their marriage comes, she will be prepared.

Heartbreak is inevitable if David leaves her at the end of their contract, but at least she will be wealthy and a lot wiser. After all, she had already gotten what she wanted. This child is mine, and to ensure that, I must make myself wealthy.

Chapter 70

'Would it ever be any different?'

'*Could* it be? Sadly, she didn't think so...'

Even if she prepares herself for what is to come, she knows that David will also fight for this child to be his. 'It will be a long battle.'

Anna wandered down to the swimming pool and sat in one of the chairs positioned beneath a wide sun umbrella. The sun felt warm against her bare skin, and she leaned her head back and closed her eyes.

"Anna? It is eleven-fifteen."

She came sharply awake at the sound of Amy's voice, amazed that she could have lapsed into a light doze. Her hand had swollen slightly and was beginning to show signs of bruising. There was also a degree of pain when the physiotherapist supervised her exercises, a fact which he noted, adding an admonition to be more careful. There didn't seem to be much point in assuring him that it was not self-inflicted.

At home, she ate the chicken salad Amy had prepared for lunch, and then she changed into a bikini,

selected a book, and wandered out to sit beneath a shade-umbrella by the pool.

It was almost six when David arrived home, and Anna cast him a warm smile as he entered the

lounge.

"How was your day?" she asked lightly, unprepared for his brief, hard kiss.

"A series of meetings, appointments." His tone was dry, his eyes dark and inscrutable.

"I'll change."

"Then we'll have a drink before dinner."

"I'll go and check with Amy," she said.

The table was already set, and there was a delicious aroma emanating from the kitchen.

"Vegetable soup," Amy informed her as she stirred the contents of a saucepan.

"Paella, with fresh fruit to finish."

"Sounds wonderful. Can I help with anything?"

"It is all under control," the older woman said companionably.

"I will serve in fifteen minutes."

Anna wandered towards the lounge and was busy watching the televised news when David entered the room.

He looked vaguely satanic in casual dark trousers and a polo shirt, which highlighted his light tan skin and emphasized his length and breadth.

"A cool drink?"

She glanced toward him and her breath caught in her throat as she glimpsed his hard demeanor

just beneath the surface of his control.

"Please," she managed to say evenly, returning her attention to the television.

She turned as he reached her side, and instead of handing her a glass, he placed both down on a

nearby pedestal.

"Let me see your hand."

He knew. *How!* The physiotherapist? There was no one else who could have told him, she reasoned silently.

"It's a bit stiff," she admitted with a helpless shrug, unwilling to extend it for his inspection.

"Some bruising, pain, and reduced mobility," David stated with dangerous softness. He reached forward and carefully caught hold of her arm.

His intent examination filled her with a peculiar sense of dread, and she almost died at the savagery apparent as he seared her features. "Amelia?"

She swallowed nervously. "What if I accidentally knocked on my hand?"

His expression became inscrutable, and his voice contained dangerous indolence.

"Did you?"

"No." Evasion of the truth was hardly wise, for there was already visible evidence of bruising.

He said something vicious beneath his breath in Korean, then lifted a hand to cup her jaw. His

finger traced a gentle pattern over her lower lip, probing slightly before moving to caress her

cheek. His eyes became dark, their depths unfathomable as he searched her features.

"My relationship with Amelia was..." He paused fractionally, then said deliberately, "Mutually

convenient."

Mutual need, Anna qualified, sickened at the picture that conjured up.

"Marriage was not something I had considered until I saw you again at your stepsister's birthday party." His smile held wry cynicism.

"That same evening, I decided, I wanted your loyalty, your fierce pride, and your honesty."

He had deliberately tested her, and it rankled unbearably.

He brushed her mouth lightly with his own. "Eventually—your love," he added quietly.

He had placed the chess pieces on a board and played the game with infinite patience and skill. She hurt too much to let him know that he had won.

"Along with good health, love is something that money can't buy," Anna declared carefully, and

glimpsed a flicker of pain in the depths of his eyes, so fleeting that she wondered if she had

imagined it.

"The time between being informed of your accident and discovering the extent of your injuries

were the worst minutes I have ever spent," he assured her ruminatively as he took possession of her mouth in a kiss so incredibly gentle that she simply closed her eyes and gave herself up to the

sensual eroticism of his touch.

It seemed minutes passed before he broke contact and slowly lifted his head.

It took enormous will-power to step away from him, and her voice was not quite steady as she offered,

"Amy will be ready to serve dinner."

"Then let us go in and eat."

IT WAS a week later that Anna entered the elegant Beverly Hills salon and checked with Reception.

"Michael will be five minutes, Anna," the stunning blonde said with a bright smile.

"He's running a little late. Perhaps you'd care to take a seat? Would you like some tea or coffee? Orange juice, mineral water?"

Anna nodded in silent negation, adding a polite, "Thanks," before selecting a chair.

A year ago—make that nine months ago, she corrected mentally—she wouldn't have been able to afford to walk into this exclusive hairdressing salon. To have had Michael himself apply his artistic cutting expertise to her hair would have been unthinkable.

The name Miller opened doors, commanded respect, and produced a desire to pander to any whim

with such flattering effusiveness that it was almost obscene.

Anna reached for one of several thick glossy magazines and began flipping through the pages,

Noting the elegant models, the beautiful clothes, designer make-up, articles written in stylish prose, a feature profile on one of America's social influencers, and another profile on a top designer. The usual society pages have a run-down of recent events with accompanying photographs.

She skimmed over them without interest, only to be riveted by a frame depicting David with

Amelia at his side.

Her stomach gave a painful lurch, and she took a deep breath as she willed herself to check the

magazine's issue date. The event highlighted was a dinner organized specifically to raise money

for a well-known charity.

Oh, hell. Why did she have to pick *that* particular magazine? She could have remained in ignorance.

Besides, she silently attempted to reassure herself, that the photograph was probably the result

of coincidence, taken when Amelia just happened to be standing by his side.

There was nothing innocent in any one of Amelia's actions.

The way Amelia was gazing at him in open adoration was positively sickening.

Chapter 71

"Anna. How are you, darling? Sorry to keep you waiting."

She closed the magazine and rose to her feet with a ready smile. "Michael."

"Your hand? It is still giving you pain?' He drew her towards the far end of the salon and seated her at a basin.

"It aches a little."

Michael's personal attention was rare, and Anna, by virtue of being David's wife, appeared to
be one of the favoured few.

She wrinkled her nose as he sluiced water over her hair and applied shampoo, rinsed and repeated the process with conditioner, then towelled it dry before leading her to a mirrored cubicle.

"Are you able to drive again?"

'The specialist says I can. David would prefer Jacob to continue in the role of chauffeur. Although he has compromised and bought me another car.'

"He is being protective, hmm?"

"You could say that," she agreed with suitable dryness.

Michael picked up his scissors and comb and went to work. "Don't knock it, darling," he cautioned wryly.

"Men are not usually protective unless they care."

David's brand of caring was linked to their unborn child. *She* was merely a secondary
consideration.

Or was she? From the beginning, his lovemaking had generated a desire for her pleasure as much as his own, and there had never been an occasion when she had felt—*used*.

When had she fallen in love with him? Sadly, Anna couldn't pinpoint a single moment when the revelation had hit. She was aware only of its stealthy possession, and the agonizing knowledge that her life would never be the same without him.

"Tonight is the exhibition of fine art held in one of the Beverly Hills Galleries," Michael informed her.

"You are attending, of course."

David was a known patron of the arts, and he had a reputation for adding one or two paintings each year to his collection of works of Asian Americans.

The evening's event included cocktails and hors-d'oeuvres, and attendance was strictly by invitation.

"Yes."

"A notable occasion," Raphael proffered as his scissors moved with crafted expertise.

Without a doubt, she agreed mentally. The social glitterati would be present, together with members of the Press, and several photographers, each attempting to outdo the other.

She had even bought a new black gown. Sleeveless, its simple slim-fitting style was enhanced with intricate silver embroidery on the bodice. A high scooped neckline precluded jewelry, and there were matching shoes and an evening bag.

Raphael reached for several fat rollers and positioned them in place, collected a magazine for her to read, and then moved toward Reception to greet the next client.

It was almost four when Anna emerged, another half-hour before she brought the car to a halt beside the main entrance of David's Pasadena home.

She could hear the shower running as she entered their suite, and she stripped down to panty and

bra, collected a silk robe and slipped it on, then she crossed to the dressing-table to attend to her

make-up.

David entered the bedroom, with a towel hitched low on his hips, as she applied the finishing

touches, and she watched in mesmerized fascination as he moved to her side and bestowed a lingering kiss on the soft curve of her neck.

His touch sent warmth tingling through her veins, and her expression held a faint wistfulness as he stood behind her and viewed their mirrored reflections.

"What time do you want to leave?" she queried, unable to tear her gaze away.

"Fifteen minutes. The traffic will be heavy." His hands rested on her shoulders, then slowly slid down the front edges of her robe to slip beneath the silk and gently tease the softness of her breasts. With tantalizing care, he began to brush the pad of his thumb over each sensitive peak.

Anna felt them swell and harden, and she gave a soundless gasp as his fingers slid to unfasten her bra.

" David—-"

"Humour me," he said huskily. His eyes held hers captive, their depths alive with leashed passion.

"I thought of doing this all day."

"The intoxicating texture of your skin, its delicate perfume, the way your beautiful eyes soften when I touch you."

Sensation spiraled from her feminine core as intense sexual awareness swept through her body. All he had to do was pull her into his arms and she would be lost.

"Shouldn't we get ready?" she asked in a strangled voice and glimpsed the edge of his mouth twist in a gesture of wry self-mockery.

"Indeed." His hands lingered, then slowly withdrew to settle briefly on her shoulders.

"If I kiss you, we'll never leave this room."

"In that case, perhaps you'd better get changed and let me finish my make-up," she suggested

shakily, and he laughed, a deep, soft, husky sound that sent goose-bumps over the surface of her

skin.

"Eventually we will return home, *my love,* and then we shall resume where we have left off."

"If I'm not too tired." It was a tame attempt at denial and didn't fool him.

"I promise to do all the work, darling." His lips brushed her temple, then slid down to nibble an

earlobe.

Not all, she promised silently as he moved away and selected underwear, a dress shirt, and black

trousers that formed parts of a sophisticated shield for the primitive strength of his body. Socks

and shoes came next, and when he reached for the immaculate bow tie she hurriedly transferred her attention and picked up a shiny gold tube to stroke pastel color onto her lips.

. . ᥫᩭ . .

FIVE MINUTES LATER she slipped into the gown, and she stood perfectly still as David slid the zip fastener into place.

"You look beautiful," he complimented as she stepped into the elegant evening shoes.

Collecting her evening bag, she turned towards him and proffered a faint smile.

"The women will vie with each other for your attention," she anticipated lightly.

"I have no control over inherited genes," he responded in an amused drawl.

"And the only woman I am interested in is you."

For now, Anna added silently, wishing she could believe him. It would be incredible to feel truly

secure in a man's love, to know without any element of doubt that you were adored, and that even if he displayed visual appreciation for another no other Woman had a chance of capturing his heart.

Such a hope belonged in the realms of fantasy, she decided ruefully, as the car became part of the flow of traffic entering the inner-city perimeter.

The reality was a combination of harsh facts and formidable statistics that existed as irrefutable

proof that love did not always last forever. The first heady bloom often flared brilliantly, only to

diminish all too frequently to a state of prosaic affection.

The car slid to a halt, and Anna's eyes widened with the realization that they were stationary. The car park was brightly lit, and there were sounds and movements as guests vacated their cars.

David caught her elbow in a light clasp and led her towards the main entrance. Inside, several

guests mingled in small groups, and there were several smartly uniformed waiters and waitresses

proffering drinks and bite-sized food.

Immediately, David was greeted by the gallery owner, Elena. They engaged in conversation, and,

Anna found herself drawn into a civilized debate on the advantages of free artistic expression over the confines of conformity.

"Do you enjoy David's artistic taste?"

Oh, hell, she wasn't even sure which artists he favored. The paintings hanging on the walls at Pasadena and Manhattan Beach were visually pleasing, although a few were a little too abstract for her enjoyment.

"Mostly," she agreed.

"Although he has a hint, of which I'm not particularly fond."

"My wife is a traditionalist," David relayed smoothly.

"Her taste runs to Zhang Hongtu."

"Oh, my dear. Zhang Hongtu is quite brilliant."

"So are many other noted Asian American artists," she offered firmly.

"It's very much a personal choice, don't you think?"

"I like paintings that have more lively colors and depict nature's beauty and landscapes Hongtu's work is like that."

"And, of course, I love plants and gardens, and landscaping design is my business and interest."

"Well, that explains everything!" and they all laughed.

Chapter 72

"There's an excellent piece you really must see. Expensive, but worthy of investment." He riffled

through the catalog pages and brought the item to David's notice, then made his excuses as

someone else demanded his attention.

"I happen to like Zhang Hongtu," Anna protested as David's amused gaze rested on her expressive features.

"So do I," he assured her, and, placing an arm around her waist, he directed her towards a display.

"Shall we begin viewing?"

Some paintings verged on the bizarre, others resembled caricatures of design over brilliant slashes of color. One, in particular, looked as if a very young child had indulged in a wild battle with numerous pots of multicolored paint.

"What do you think?"

Anna turned towards David and tried to present a considered viewpoint. After several

seconds she voiced with restraint, "I'd prefer not to answer on the grounds that anything I say

could be overheard, taken into account, and held against me."

"A remarkable nonconformist piece," David drawled knowledgeably, and her eyes danced as

she nodded in silent agreement.

"Shall we move on?"

"Please."

There were several guests present whom she had met before, and for the next hour she exchanged pleasantries, accepted an invitation for an upcoming fashion parade, and deferred to

David had no less than three dinner invitations, and she was just beginning to find the evening

a relaxing venture when she glimpsed a familiar head several feet distant.

Amelia. As if by design, the guests shifted position so that the model's body profile was in clear

view: a stunning figure, attired in a flamboyant gown that on anyone else would have looked

outrageous.

Anna forced herself to meet Amelia's intent gaze, and for one brief second, she witnessed unadulterated venom before it was masked. A slight smile appeared in acknowledgment before Amelia turned towards her partner, and Anna could not prevent a slight shiver.

Did David know Amelia was here? It was a distinct probability.

"More mineral water?"

"Thank you."

"We should be able to get away in less than an hour. We'll go on to dinner afterward," David

said quietly.

"Have you already booked?"

He named a well-known restaurant famed for its fine cuisine.

"You would prefer somewhere else?"

"Quiet, out of the way, with little chance of meeting anyone we know?" she suggested, hopefully.

"I can recollect a few."

Suitable for clandestine meetings? Damn, she had to stop resorting to destructive thinking!

"Of course, we could buy a take-away meal on the way home."

"Anything in particular?"

"Chinese."

His eyes gleamed with humor.

"I'll cancel the restaurant from the car."

"Thank you."

He lifted a hand and brushed his fingers lightly across her cheek.

"Just where precisely do you intend, we eat?"

She looked at him with undue solemnity. "Dressed like this?" she inquired innocently.

"At the dining room table. Where else?"

"We could always change first."

"And eat out on the terrace?" She offered a singularly sweet smile.

"What a wonderful idea."

The depths of his eyes took on a dark brilliance. "Saucy little minx. You know you have to pay me later for this change of plan."

"You wouldn't dare."

A slow, wicked smile tugged the edges of his mouth, and his voice held infinite indolence.

"Just watch me."

Every bone in her body began to feel liquefied at the thought of precisely how he would exact

atonement.

"I think," she said unsteadily, "we should attempt to continue our viewing, don't you?"

"An excellent suggestion."

It was after eight when they left, and almost nine before David garaged the car. The plastic carrier bag with its various containers emitted a mouthwatering aroma, and Anna slid off her shoes the moment they entered the house.

"You intend to change before we eat?"

She cast him a studied glance. "This gown cost a small fortune."

"So did my suit," drawled David.

"Perhaps you should exchange it for something less formal."

"And save on the dry-cleaning bill?"

"Naturally."

"I gather eating in bed would be considered the height of decadence?"

She failed miserably to suppress an impish smile.

"It would be such a shame to waste the food."

"The terrace?"

Her eyes twinkled with devilish humor. "Think of the moonlight."

He shrugged out of his jacket and placed it over a nearby chair. "Plates, cutlery, glasses?"

She pretended to give due consideration. "I guess we could opt for informality," she decided as she picked up her shoes and made for the staircase. "Two forks, two glasses."

She began mounting the stairs, then paused to look down at him. "Do you think you can manage that?"

He removed the bow tie and loosened the top buttons on his shirt. "Don't be too long, *darling*,"

he warned gently, and her mouth curled into a guileless smile.

"Patience, David." She turned and slowly traversed the remaining stairs. In the bedroom, she

slipped out of the gown, then dressed in silk culottes and a loose top.

Minutes later, she walked out onto the terrace to find David seated at one of the outdoor tables,

a portable lamp providing essential light, the food displayed in its various containers, and a slim

flute of wine within easy reach. His shirt was undone almost to the waist, and the cuffs rolled

halfway up his forearms.

Anna sank into a chair opposite, dipped a fork into chop suey, and savored a mouthful with

suitable enthusiasm, then repeated the process.

"Isn't this better than eating in a restaurant?"

He forked a prawn into his mouth, then shot her a musing look.

"This is quite good."

"Don't sound so surprised." She met his gaze and wrinkled her nose at him in admonition.

"The trouble is you've been thoroughly spoiled, with a personal cook and professional chefs to pander to your gourmand taste."

"Planning to re-educate me, Anna?"

"In some areas, it mightn't be a bad idea."

"And what areas are those, my darling wife?" He sounded distinctly amused, and dangerously

indolent.

"You could do with a lesson in humility," she said with mock severity.

"Where you are concerned, I am remarkably humble," David claimed solemnly. His eyes held

hers, and she couldn't look away as he lifted his glass in a silent salute before placing the rim to

his mouth.

He sounded sincere. It was almost as if he cared very much. The breath caught in her throat, and she

found it difficult to swallow.

Her fork was suspended in midair, and she slowly replaced it on the table, her appetite gone.

He leaned back in the chair, his large frame displaying an indolent grace that was deceptive, for

there was a watchfulness apparent, a leashed air she found infinitely disturbing.

"Lost for words, Anna?"

She looked at him for what seemed an age, wanting more than anything to move into his arms, to

lift her mouth for his kiss. But she seemed locked into immobility, and there was a strange ache in the region of her heart.

There was so much she wanted to say, yet she felt hesitant, afraid that if she revealed too much,

it would render her vulnerable.

"Shall I make coffee?" Even her voice sounded breathy and uncertain, and she cursed her own

insecurity.

"No coffee," David said gently. "I'll dispose of these containers, then we'll go to bed."

Bed. That was her downfall. It was where she sold her soul and lost control.

"I'm not tired," she offered quietly and glimpsed his faint smile.

"Neither am I. Sleeping wasn't exactly what I had in mind."

Chapter 73

S he rose to her feet and gathered the cutlery and glasses, then carried them through to the
kitchen.

David followed, and she heard him locking the outer doors and setting the security alarm.

It was a simple task to load the dishwasher, and she had just finished when he entered the room.

He looked over all the powerful masculine: dark trousers, light tan skin, dark hair, in stark contrast to the white shirt. Tall, he almost seemed overpowering, and, while she craved his touch, there was a part of her that cried out against any sexual defeat.

She watched as he dispatched food down the waste disposal unit, then dropped empty
containers into the pedal bin before washing and drying his hands. In silence, he turned and
caught hold of her hand, leading her through to the lounge, and then he selected a slow song.

Soft music emanated from the speakers and Anna looked at him speechlessly as he drew her into
his arms.

Crazy, she thought, as he pulled her close against him and began to drift slowly around the room.

She felt his lips brush her hair, followed by the warmth of his breath against her temple. His
heartbeat was strong beneath her cheek, and her hands crept to link together at the back of his

waist. His embrace gave her a sense of fulfillment. She felt as if everything she needed was here, and she felt content; nothing was lacking in her life. To have him and their baby makes her feel complete, and she wants to take it all in and preserve this moment in her mind.

The music was so slow and dreamy that after several minutes, they hardly bothered to move at

all, and simply stood still in the dim light reflected from the foyer.

His kiss was so incredibly gentle that it almost made her cry, and she offered him her mouth, exulting in an erotic taste that excited her without demand.

When the music finished, he raised his head and subjected her to a long, searching gaze, then he

placed an arm beneath her knees and carried her up the stairs.

Anna wanted to cry, and when he lowered her to her feet in the bedroom, tears shimmered like crystal droplets in each corner of her eyes. It has been a year since they got married, and today was their first wedding anniversary. She is now more than four months pregnant with their child.

Without a word, he led her to the bed, and he sat down on its edge, then he drew her to stand between his thighs.

Her mouth began to tremble, and there was nothing she could do to prevent the slow downward

path of a single tear as it overflowed.

David lifted a hand and halted its passage with the pad of his thumb before moving to trace

the outline of her mouth.

"I was almost hesitant to question the cause," he drawled gently.

"Do you want to blame it on uncertain emotions?"

"I guess that's as good a reason as any," she said shakily, and almost died at the wealth of passion evident in those dark eyes so close to her own.

"Happy Anniversary, Darling," he said softly.

"I thought you had forgotten,"

"How could I forget the day that I claimed you to be mine."

"I need you," he said gently.

"Every day of my life. All night long in my bed."

Need. Need had to be better than *want,* didn't it? And 'every day in my life' sounded permanent.

As in forever? Forever, I wish it to be true, Anna thought.

She wanted to say, 'I love you.' But the words wouldn't emerge. What if he wouldn't reply with the same words? It would crush her.

He pulled her onto his lap and kissed her, then carefully eased her onto the bed.

Her arms lifted to curve around his neck as she gave herself up to the magic only, he was able to

create. Soon she was filled with an agonizing sweetness as her body began to respond to the exquisite tenderness of his touch. She throbbed with intense awareness when he entered her, glorying in the mutual joy of complete possession as they journeyed towards a mutual fulfillment of the senses.

It was a wild, sweet pleasure tempered by raw desire. Erotic, primitive, yet so incredibly sensual

she was held captive in its thrall ...*his* without any equivocation.

On the edge of sleep, she was conscious of his arms enfolding her close, and she gave a tiny sigh

of contentment before drifting into a dreamless state that lasted until morning.

"Anna. there is a telephone call for you."

Very few calls for her came through the house phone. David rang directly on her mobile phone, likewise, the few of her friends to whom she had given the number. Perhaps it was the

obstetrician's receptionist rescheduling her appointment

"Who is it, Amy?"

"Sara Walker."

If Sara was calling at this time, it meant it was an emergency, but what happened to her mobile phone? Perhaps they could meet for lunch, Anna mused as she crossed to the nearest handset.

"Sara. How are you?"

There was a brief silence. *"It's Amelia,* darling," What! Did Amy get it wrong?

A chill feeling settled in the pit of her stomach. Even allowing for misunderstanding, Amelia's

surname was vastly dissimilar to that of Walker. Which meant Amelia had deliberately set out

to deceive. There could be little doubt as to why.

"Is it essential we have this conversation?" Anna managed steadily and heard a faint intake of

breath down the line.

"I suppose you think you're clever," Amelia opined viciously.

It was a game that had to be played out to its conclusion, Anna decided, saddened, that it should

have even begun.

"Perhaps you'd care to elaborate."

"You poisonous little bitch. You had to tell him, didn't you?"

Anna closed her eyes, then slowly opened them again.

"If you're referring to my hand... blame the physiotherapist," she managed carefully, "and David, for insisting on a first-hand report every time I visit any member of the medical profession."

There was a long pause.

"Watch your back, darling."

"I always do." Without hesitation, she replaced the receiver then sat on the sofa.

'Who do you think you are, Amelia?' Anna was furious.

Chapter 74

A nna dialed a memorized number on her phone.

A sleepy voice answered her call, and Anna felt a surge of relief. "Sara? How about lunch?"

"I didn't get to bed until three, you impossible person. Must it be today?"

"We could make it a late lunch," Anna persisted and heard Sara's laughing approval.

"Name the time and place, and I'll meet you there."

"One-thirty. At the Grove," she returned without hesitation.

They met within minutes of the appointed time and managed, by good fortune to be shown to a

table overlooking the fountain. After the serious business of ordering was completed, they settled

down to exchanging news, something which lasted through the starter, and well into the main

course.

"You're positively blooming," Sara complimented quietly.

"Your hair, your skin. everything about you. I couldn't be more pleased everything is working out."

Anna managed a bright smile that didn't fool her friend in the slightest.

"Not quite, huh? What's the problem?"

"I didn't ask you to meet me to discuss any problems."

"Hell, no. You love my wit, my charm." She leaned forward, her expression pensive.

"I refuse to believe it has anything to do with David. Is it Amelia?" she hazarded.

"Why not David?"

Sara shot her an old-fashioned look. "My God, you really can't see it, can you?" she

queried, shaking her head in silent disbelief.

"Did you never wonder why I didn't visit you in hospital?" Her expression sobered.

"David *requested &* insisted that I stay away until you regain your memory."

Her eyes took on an earnest fervor. "He called me every day to let me know how you were."

Anna could only look at her in shocked silence. Why would he do something like that if he didn't

want to make the most of an opportunity to repair her perception of him? It was crazy. Yet only

last night...

"Go figure, Anna," Sara advised gently.

"I still haven't heard him say he loved me, Sara"

"Even if he does genuinely care, He still hasn't said the word." To this, Sara only nodded in silence.

It was almost four when they left the restaurant, and a short while later Anna garaged the car, then moved lightly indoors.

Amy was busy peeling vegetables as she entered the kitchen, and she uttered an appreciative sound as the delicious aroma of roast chicken assailed her nostrils.

"Anything I can do to help?"

Amy's smile, like the woman herself, was warm and friendly. "David rang. He will be home

early. If you must do something, you could set the table."

Afterward, she took a long, leisurely shower, then dressed in a white silk blouse and tailored straight skirt. She was putting the finishing touches to her make-up when David entered the

bedroom.

Anna offered him a tentative smile, then concentrated on coloring the lower curve of her mouth.

Her eyes widened as she saw his reflected image in the mirror, and she stood perfectly still as he

turned her round to face him.

"I had a call from the physiotherapist. It appears you forgot your appointment this afternoon."

Surprise flitted across her features. Damn, it had completely slipped her mind.

"I'll call tomorrow and offer my apologies. I met Sara for lunch."

His eyes pierced hers. "Amy said Sara phoned. Strange," he continued thoughtfully, "when the only number she knows is your mobile phone."

Anna lifted her hands, then let them fall to her sides in a helpless gesture.

"Amelia rang, and tricked Amy into thinking she was Sara, then attempted to have me believe Amy had made a mistake over the name."

"Do you want to tell me about it?"

"Not particularly."

"Anna—"

"Don't, David. Please." She felt so incredibly vulnerable that if he touched her she would shatter

and fall in an embarrassing heap at his feet.

Even now, the pain was still there, yet she managed to hold his gaze with dignity. Will she dare to risk it all and reveal how she feels? Expunge the anguish, and pray that Sara was right.

Drawing a deep breath, she took courage in both hands and began.

There was no doubt he desired her, but desire alone had little to do with need and love.

"After the accident," she began shakily, "you were always there, the image of a devoted husband."

Her eyes searched his, seeing the darkness apparent, the faint tenseness as he waited for her to continue.

"When my memory returned, I felt betrayed. I had trusted you," she cried in anguish.

He was quiet for a long time. "There was no reason for you to distrust me."

"You perceived it as a game," Anna went on with incredible sadness.

"With me as the pawn."

"From the beginning," he corrected quietly, "you were the prize."

"Prey," she countered. "Ruthlessly hunted, and relentlessly lured into a trap."

His gaze was unwavering, intense, and impossible to read.

"You acted a part," she accused and saw his eyes darken.

"Never," he assured her after a long silence, and her features paled.

"I don't believe you."

"No? You perceived our lovemaking as a calculated coupling without any depth of emotional
involvement?"

"*Love* isn't a prerequisite for satisfactory sex."

She felt as if she were breaking up inside, her body slowly shattering with each successive word
he uttered.

He was silent for what seemed an age, and his voice when he spoke sounded like silk being sliced by the finest tempered steel. "You can describe what we share as merely clinical satisfaction?"

She looked at him carefully, seeing the strength apparent, the hint of passion in the depths of those chocolate eyes. "No," she owned at last.

Then suddenly she touched her belly, and she felt a little pain. She was already seven months pregnant at this time.

"What is it, Anna?" David was worried about her reaction.

"I felt a little pain,"

David looked at her pale face and asked, "Do you want me to get you to the hospital?"

"I don't think it's necessary." Anna tried to stand from the vanity chair, and David helped her.

Then Anna looked at his terrified expression, He was looking at the vanity mirror, which reflected her backside.

"What is wrong?" She asked.

"There is blood on your skirt." David was terrified.

"We need to go to the hospital." He swiftly carried her downstairs.

Anna felt alarmed, but she tried to relax in David's arms. She kept thinking, 'Dear God, please take good care of my baby.'

She tried to control her expression because, right now, the pain is starting to feel intense.

Chapter 75

A nna woke up in the hospital the next day. Last night, she had a c-section because of the preterm labor. David was sitting near her.

"Is the baby, okay?" She asked weakly.

"The baby is in intensive care," David said calmly.

"Oh my God, is she going to be, okay?" concern was evident on her face.

"All her vital signs are okay; however, she is in the incubator." David cupped her face gently.

"No need to worry, Anna, her pediatric doctor is a known specialist." David reached for Anna and hugged her.

At this very moment, she wanted to feel his warmth because she couldn't control her anxiety. Then the Doctor came to visit.

"Good morning, Mrs. Miller." She was an older woman with kind eyes.

"I'm Doctor Avery Samuel, nice to meet you," she said.

"Nice to meet you too Doctor," Anna replied. "Can I see my baby?"

"Yes, but We had to wait for your OB-GYN, Doctor Ethan's recommendation."

"When it's safe to move you, then you can visit your baby, but you have to understand that you cannot carry her."

"You mean, I cannot touch her?" Anna asked softly.

"Yes, because she is a premature baby at only 28 weeks, extremely delicate, and still needs to be incubated," Doctor Avery explained.

"When can we be able to hold her?" David asked.

"She needs to be inside the incubator for around 3 to 7 days until high levels of humidity are no longer needed."

"She is extremely fragile, so I hope both of you understand."

"Thank you, doctor," Anna said.

An hour later, Doctor Ethan came to check on Anna.

"Hello, Anna, how are you?"

"I'm okay, doc."

"When can we go home, doc?" David asked.

Doctor Ethan was looking at Anna's medical charts. "You can go home tomorrow; the test came out okay."

"But I don't want to leave my baby here." Anna sighed.

"It's okay, Anna, there is a penthouse next to this hospital, we can live there for the time being," David explained. "And visit her every day," he continued.

"Thank you, David."

The next day, they went to see their baby in the intensive care unit. Anna felt a sense of awe as she stared at her child through the incubator. She wanted to blame herself for what happened to this baby. Her married life is a roller coaster ride. First the accident, then the amnesia, and now this. Her pregnancy was preterm, and she had put a risk on this child. 'Have I not taken such good care of myself to allow this to happen?'

'No,' she refused to believe she was irresponsible.

'I take my vitamins every day, and go to medical check-ups regularly, so why is this still happening.'

'I think, it's my mental health, I get stressed all the time with these intrusive thoughts.' She did not notice David studying her.

"What's wrong, Anna?"

"Nothing, David, I'm just overwhelmed," She replied.

"Have you thought of a name?" He asked.

"Yes, I want to call her Selene, like the Goddess of the moon." She smiled.

"Yes, it fits her because she is so beautiful like you." David looked at her.

"We will visit again tomorrow," He assured her.

They went to the penthouse and Amy was there, arranging her things in the bedroom.

"Hello, Amy." She smiles.

"Nice to see you, Anna."

"Thank you."

"I will be here for the time being until you are fully healed."

David's mobile phone rang, and he picked it up and talked to the person on the other line.

"Anna, I have to go to the office, I'll be back later," he said to her

"Okay," He kissed her and turned to Amy, "Please take care of her." Amy nodded.

As soon as David left, Anna came to the bathroom.

In the quiet of the penthouse, Anna found herself grappling with a tumult of emotions. Amidst the chaos of their new reality, she sought solace in the sanctuary of her thoughts.

Tears streamed down her cheeks, a silent testament to the magnitude of her fears.

David's departure only amplified her sense of isolation, leaving her to confront her fears in the silence of her thoughts.

"Is everything alright, Anna?" Amy was concerned.

"I'm okay, Amy, I just need time for myself."

"Okay, just let me know if you need me, I will be in the living room."

Her phone rang, and she saw that it was Sara.

"Hello Sara"

"Hello, hon, how are you?"

"I'm worried about my baby."

"It's normal to feel that way, and it's okay to cry. Just don't be too stressed because you are still recovering."

"Thank you, Sara" Anna sighed, "I know I have to be strong for her."

"I will see you tomorrow, okay," Sara said. Then she hangs up.

Sara's pregnancy in the past was smooth, she had to carry her baby at full term. She was also an excellent mother to her son.

'It seems I'm the unlucky one'

'I will be the best mother to my daughter as well'

Anna came to the bedroom and lay down. She was exhausted, and soon after, she dozed off.

When she opened her eyes in the morning, David stared at her while sitting on the bed.

"David, when did you come?" She rises to a sitting position.

"I slept in bed last night, you were sleeping deeply, how are you feeling?" There was concern in those chocolate eyes.

"I'm doing well, except my body felt sore all over,"

"Where does it hurt?"

"My breast and my backside in particular."

"How about your wound, Can I see it?"

Anna opened her blouse and David looked at the wound on her lower belly. David inspected it and said, "Come, I will help you take a shower, you need to change your clothes."

She wanted to protest, but she felt weak and also uneasy as her sanitary napkin was full of blood.

"I don't think so," Her cheeks burned. She felt ashamed that David could see it.

"I know you think, this is an embarrassing situation, but I am your husband."

"It is my responsibility to take care of you."

"You might feel queasy with the bloody discharge," Anna said, lowering her eyes while her cheeks burned with embarrassment.

Chapter 76

David cupped her face and said, "There is nothing that can make me queasy when it comes from you."

"Your body is where my child grows, and your blood is her blood also."

"Don't ever think that it is something to be embarrassed about."

Anna smiled weakly at the man before her. 'How could she not love this man?'

David led her to the shower while helping her out of her clothes.

He reached out to take the soap, but she said, "Please let me do it on my own, my breast is so sore, and it hurts too much."

"Okay, but let me do your back." he insisted as he watched her.

"We can visit the baby after breakfast." he said.

At this point, Anna was excited to see Selene. She swiftly finished her bath and changed into a wrap-around pink floral dress.

They ate their breakfast and went to the hospital after.

They were looking at their child through the incubator, she was so beautiful yet so fragile. 'I can't wait to hold her in my arms,' Anna thought. She felt so mesmerized by her. David wrapped his arms around Anna.

She looked at her husband, and she could see the awe in his eyes as he stared at their daughter. He grew up without a father and told her before that he would never be an absentee father to their child.

'I'm pretty sure he will be a great father.'

Weeks turn into months and finally, it's time for them to take little Selene home.

Jacob garaged the car in their Pasadena home.

Anna was carrying Selena while David was beside her.

"She has grown," Anna said, laughing.

"Yes, and she looks like you more and more every day," He smiled

"Anna!" She heard a familiar voice when they got inside the house.

"Bryan!" When did you come back from Seoul?

"I arrived 2 days ago and stayed here waiting for my grandchild." The old man was smiling from ear to ear as he looked adoringly at Selene. He was talking to her in Korean.

They settled in the living Area. Then a tall, young blond lady with blue eyes came. Anna looked at her, confused.

"Anna, this is Leah, she will be Selene's nanny," David said.

"Nanny? You didn't seem to mention her." Anna asked.

"I've asked my secretary to look for a nanny, and she was highly recommended," David explained.

"Welcome, Leah," Anna smiled.

"Thank you, mam," Leah replied.

"I think it's time for dinner," Bryan said. They could smell the aroma of roasted baby back ribs from the kitchen.

"Dinner is served," Amy called out from the dining area.

Leah came to take Selene from Anna. She still wouldn't want to give her the baby but Bryan and David were waiting for her.

"Okay, here she is,"

"Don't worry mam,"

It was a pleasant evening. Bryan and David were talking to each other in Korean. Anna just looked at the two. 'They seem to miss each other,' She thought.

"Anna, when will you and David visit your Villa on Jeju Island?"

"When Selene is a year old, we will visit you, Bryan," She smiled.

"It seems, you like it there more than in Seoul?" Anna teased.

"Yes, of course, that place holds a lot of memories for me."

"I know, It's why our paths crossed." Anna smiled teasingly.

"Yes, and exactly the reason, why I have a beautiful great-granddaughter." Bryan laughed while David smiled at him.

"How do you spend your life on the Island?" She asked.

"Well, thanks to my grandson, every day was a vacation," Bryan said as he looked at David.

"I always sail in his yacht with my dear friend Kim," Bryan winked at David.

Anna and David laughed at the old man's expression.

Anna's phone rang, it was her father calling.

"Dad"

"Anna, we will come to visit you tomorrow, Jeanne will be coming with me."

"Expect us at lunch, okay?" Her father said at the other line.

"Okay," Anna replied.

"I suppose everyone wants to see our little Selene," Anna smiled

"A child does that, it makes the family closer," Bryan said.

"Of course," David agreed.

Selene was sleeping. Anna insisted that their baby would sleep in the crib inside their room.

"I want her near us when she is sleeping."

"I hired a nanny for you to sleep well at night," David was concerned.

"I am a mother; it's just fair that I will experience that as well," Anna insisted.

"Yes, but see to it that you catch up on sleep whenever you can," David raised his hand to touch her face.

Anna held his hand on her face. There is a sense of tenderness in his touch and his gaze. He held her closer with his other hand and kissed her mouth softly. His right hand caressed her shoulder, and it travelled teasingly towards her breast.

She stared at his face, his hunger for her was evident. It's been months since he touched her passionately.

"I miss you," David said softly.

"I'm always here,"

"Yes, I know, but I am concerned about your well-being."

"I know, you are such a good husband, even if you don't love me."

"Who says I don't love you?"

"You didn't say you loved me, either."

"But I love you."

At that word, Anna was surprised. "You do?"

"Of course, I love you! I have loved you ever since I saw you on Jeju Island and I haven't forgotten our first night together on my yacht."

"But, why didn't you tell me?" Anna was shocked, she couldn't believe it.

"Because you were so in love with your deceased husband, it hurts my ego," David admitted.

"But it didn't stop you from blackmailing me into marrying you?" Anna smiled.

"I always get what I want, but I don't know if I have your heart too..." David was hesitant to continue, but Anna looked at him. She saw how vulnerable he was. She took his hand and put it on top of her left breast.

"I love you, David," Anna smiled while tears fell from her eyes.

"I have loved you for a long time that we are together," At that, David smiled and hugged her.

It was a moment when their hearts were one, and the lovemaking that followed took their breath away.

About the Author

Welcome to the world of Ann, an author who weaves tales of strong heroines on a journey to discover their destiny and love.

Ann is not only a talented author but also a licensed teacher with a specialization in English and literature. Her understanding of language and storytelling is reflected in the eloquence and depth of her writing. https://www.facebook.com/A.M.Zanoria

Read more at https://www.facebook.com/A.M.Zanoria.